Science Fiction, Imperialism
and the Third World

Science Fiction, Imperialism and the Third World

Essays on Postcolonial Literature and Film

Edited by Ericka Hoagland and Reema Sarwal

Foreword by Andy Sawyer

McFarland & Company, Inc., Publishers
Jefferson, North Carolina, and London

LIBRARY OF CONGRESS CATALOGUING-IN-PUBLICATION DATA

Science fiction, imperialism and the third world : essays on
  postcolonial literature and film / edited by Ericka Hoagland and
  Reema Sarwal ; foreword by Andy Sawyer.
        p.   cm.
  Includes bibliographical references and index.

  ISBN 978-0-7864-4789-3
  softcover : 50# alkaline paper ∞

  1. Science fiction, American — History and criticism.
  2. Science fiction, Indic (English) — History and criticism.
  3. Science fiction, Mexican — History and criticism.   4. Science
  fiction films — History and criticism.   5. Imperialism in literature.
  6. Postcolonialism in literature.   7. Literature and globalization.
  8. Utopias in literature.   9. Dystopias in literature.
  I. Hoagland, Ericka, 1975–   II. Sarwal, Reema.
  PS374.S35S335   2010
  809.3'8762 — dc22   2010023305

British Library cataloguing data are available

©2010 Ericka Hoagland and Reema Sarwal. All rights reserved

*No part of this book may be reproduced or transmitted in any form
or by any means, electronic or mechanical, including photocopying
or recording, or by any information storage and retrieval system,
without permission in writing from the publisher.*

Cover image ©2010 Brand X Pictures

Manufactured in the United States of America

McFarland & Company, Inc., Publishers
  Box 611, Jefferson, North Carolina 28640
  www.mcfarlandpub.com

Acknowledgments

We would first like to thank all our contributors, not only for their articles, but also for their patience and co-operation.

Thanks also to Stephen F. Austin State University for the research minigrant to Ericka Hoagland in the early stages of the project.

Whole-hearted thanks to Prof. Andy Sawyer for his enthusiastic response to the manuscript and for writing the Foreword.

Personally, a big thank you to Amit Sarwal for all his help and unconditional support.

Some of the essays in the collection have been published previously. They have been re-edited and revised here to make them more up-to-date and relevant. Permission given by the following copyright holders (authors, editors, and publishers) is gratefully acknowledged.

Gerald Gaylard, "Postcolonialism and the Transhistorical in *Dune*," *Foundation* 104 (Summer 2009): 84–101.

Diana Pharaoh Francis, "The Colonial Feminine in Pat Murphy's 'His Vegetable Wife,'" *Phoebe: Journal of Gender and Cultural Critiques* 17.2 (2005): 35–43.

Shital Pravinchandra, "The Third-World Body Commodified: Manjula Padmanabhan's Harvest," *Un/Worldly Bodies,* Special. issue of *eSharp* 8 (Autumn 2006): http://www.gla.ac.uk/esharp.

Debjani Sengupta, "Sadhanbabu's Friends: Science Fiction in Bengal from 1882 to 1974," *Shaping Technologies*, Spl. issue of *Sarai Reader 03* (2003): 76–82.

Herbert Klein, "Loonies and Others in Robert Heinlein's *The Moon Is a Harsh Mistress*," *Revista Litteralis* 3 (2004): 39–60. Permission granted by EdiUri, Santo Angelo, Brazil.

Dominic Alessio and Jessica Langer, "Hindu Nationalism and Postcolonialism in Indian Science Fiction: *Koi... Mil Gaya* (2003)" *New Cinemas: Journal of Contemporary Film* 5.3 (2007): 217–229 (Intellect Books).

Table of Contents

Acknowledgments — v

Foreword
Andy Sawyer — 1

Introduction: Imperialism, the Third World, and Postcolonial Science Fiction
Ericka Hoagland and Reema Sarwal — 5

Part One: Re-inventing/Alternate History

1. Postcolonial Science Fiction: The Desert Planet
   Gerald Gaylard — 21

2. History Deconstructed: Alternative Worlds in Steven Barnes's *Lion's Blood* and *Zulu Heart*
   Juan F. Elices — 37

3. *The Calcutta Chromosome*: A Novel of Silence, Slippage and Subversion
   Suparno Banerjee — 50

4. Organization and the Continuum: History in Vandana Singh's "Delhi"
   Grant Hamilton — 65

Part Two: Forms of Protest

5. The Colonial Feminine in Pat Murphy's "His Vegetable Wife"
   Diana Pharaoh Francis — 77

6. Body Markets: The Technologies of Global Capitalism and Manjula Padmanabhan's *Harvest*
   Shital Pravinchandra — 87

7. "Smudged, Distorted and Hidden": Apocalypse as
   Protest in Indigenous Speculative Fiction
   Roslyn Weaver 99

Part Three: Fresh Representations

8. Sadhanbabu's Friends: Science Fiction in Bengal from
   1882 to 1974
   Debjani Sengupta 115

9. Critiquing Economic and Environmental Colonization:
   Globalization and Science Fiction in *The Moons of
   Palmares*
   Judith Leggatt 127

10. Loonies and Others in Robert A. Heinlein's *The Moon
    Is a Harsh Mistress*
    Herbert G. Klein 141

11. Science Fiction, Hindu Nationalism and Modernity:
    Bollywood's *Koi... Mil Gaya*
    Dominic Alessio and Jessica Langer 156

Part Four: Utopia/Dystopia

12. The Shapes of Dystopia: Boundaries, Hybridity and
    the Politics of Power
    Jessica Langer 171

13. Narrative and Dystopian Forms of Life in Mexican
    Cyberpunk Novel *La Primera Calle de la Soledad*
    Juan Ignacio Muñoz Zapata 188

14. Octavia Butler's *Parable of the Sower*: The Third
    World as *Topos* for a U.S. Utopia
    Gavin Miller 202

About the Contributors 213
Index 217

Foreword

Andy Sawyer

"Sf," writes Uppinder Mehan in an essay on Indian science fiction published in *Foundation* in 1998, "is as Western as Coca-Cola, big cars and computers" (54). He then, however, points out that science fiction in several of the languages of the Indian sub-continent has been published since the early years of the twentieth century. Some years later, Mehan, with Canadian-Caribbean writer Nalo Hopkinson, edited *So Long Been Dreaming*, an anthology of explicitly "postcolonial" science fiction and fantasy. In her introduction (as at least one essay in this book reminds us) Hopkinson noted that while heading off into the galaxy to colonize new worlds is often a theme of science fiction "for many of us that's not a thrilling adventure story; it's non fiction" (7). However (as again we are reminded), the *tools* of sf, its speculative drive and its ability to subvert language and situation, are among the most powerful weapons available to those who want to "[make] it possible to think about new ways of doing things" (9).

Far too many arguments about what sf is and does center upon describing an origin for the form in sources such as Shelley's *Frankenstein*, Wells's "scientific romances," More's *Utopia* or simply the identification in Hugo Gernsback's first issue of *Amazing Stories* in April 1926 of the "Jules Verne, H.G. Wells and Edgar Allan Poe type of story — a charming romance intermingled with scientific fact and prophetic vision" as *scientifiction* (3). A more creative approach, perhaps, is to consider whether *all* cultures, at all times, have reacted to the idea that change is fueled by both actual science and technology and the very speculation that sciences and technologies do change the world. Such an approach, perhaps, allows more voices to be heard and a more open (and critical) examination of the nature of such change, and of what we mean by such slippery concepts as "change," "difference," and "otherness."

An explicitly postcolonial science fiction not only has to be *written* from outside the traditional strands of Western science fiction (claiming them as progenitors, perhaps, while recognizing that the future nowadays is a very different world to that which it once was) but explained and criticized from outside them too. Writers such as Octavia Butler, Nalo Hopkinson, or Vandana Singh; and anthologies such as Sheree Thomas's *Dark Matter* (2000), Andrea Bell's *Cosmos Latinos* (2003) or the aforementioned *So Long Been Dreaming* have brought new and exciting fictions to sf. Equally, however, the recent issues of *Science Fiction Studies* on Afrofuturism (July 2007), or Latin-American sf (Nov 2007), and books such as Marlene Barr's *Afro-Future Females* and John Rieder's *Colonialism and the Emergence of Science Fiction* (both 2008) present new and fruitful approaches to how writers and critics make it possible to utilize the toolkit given to us by sf in this process of thinking about new ways of doing things. This collection continues the debate. By examining such examples as sf in Bengal, Mexican cyberpunk, the portrayal of the Native American in science fiction, sf written by Indigenous Australians and texts such as the Arthur C. Clarke Award–winning *The Calcutta Chromosome*, as well as the undercurrents of colonialism and Empire in such traditional examples of twentieth-century sf as Robert A. Heinlein's *The Moon Is a Harsh Mistress* or Frank Herbert's "Dune" sequence, this book adds to the conversation. It explores the nature of sf's critical stance as well as its sometimes uncritical acceptance. It emphasizes, as the editors stress in the introduction, the fact that both "postcolonial literature" and "science fiction" are in fact processes characterized by contradictions and qualifications; *dynamics* rather than "things." As such, and as approaches which focus upon change and difference, they have much in common, especially their resistance to easy definition.

A *postcolonial* science fiction allows space for the different "voices" of science fiction in Europe, Latin America and the Asian and African Disaporas, and explores the nature of Otherness and Futurity, and what happens when these ideas are expressed by those who were the *subjects* of earlier versions.

It arises from the sense, articulated by Farah Mendlesohn in the introduction to *Foundation 100: The Anthology*, that the default future of what John Clute calls the "First SF" of the Hugo Gernsback/John W. Campbell model is neither possible nor desirable from where we stand now. (Mendlesohn goes on to note that the futures of the science fiction which echoes the model of the sf many of us grew up with are "so clearly *not* the futures of the places that so many of us live in" [3].) It asks what happens now that Gernsbackian "First SF" is, if not dead, a very different animal from what readers of the early American pulp magazines were encouraged to grow up to create, or what happened to that future which H. G. Wells, whose scientific romances firmly engaged with exposing the anxieties of Empire, proclaimed would be brought about by "the honest application of the Obvious" (322). Neither the wonderful inventions of a Ralph 124C41+, nor a Wellsian "Modern Utopia" offers solutions we are comfortable with today. We may justifiably ask Wells: what *is* "honest"? What *is* "the Obvious"?

Similarly, the conquest of space hymned in the 1950s and 60s by Arthur C. Clarke (much of whose fiction betrays the anxiety aroused by that significant word "conquest"), or the cyberfuture hailed (and partly created) by the young readers of *Neuromancer* in the 1980s, or the post-human future of the Singularity which appears so much in contemporary sf, are all features which demand the critical treatment William Gibson himself gave "First SF" in his short story "The Gernsback Continuum" (1981).

A postcolonial sf criticism will also consider whether traditional concepts of genre are even worth holding on to in the light of the revisioning of these ideas from writers whose connections with the traditional generic histories and structures of science fiction are second- or third-hand. This collection, reminds us that science fiction, like the world, is not owned by those who named and claimed it. I welcome the opportunity to learn from it.

Works Cited

Gernsback, Hugo. "A New Sort of Magazine." *Amazing Stories: The Magazine of Scientifiction* 1.1 (April 1926): 3.
Hopkinson, Nalo, and Uppinder Mehan. *So Long Been Dreaming*. Vancouver, BC: Arsenal Pulp Press, 2004.
Mehan, Uppinder. "The Domestication of Technology in Indian Science Fiction Short Stories." *Foundation* 74 (Autumn 1998): 54–66.
Mendelsohn, Farah. "Introduction." *Foundation: The International Review of Science Fiction* 3.4 (2007): 3.
Wells, H.G. *The Shape of Things to Come*. London: Hutchinson, 1935.

Andy Sawyer is the Science Fiction Foundation Collection Librarian at the University of Liverpool. He is a reviewer and contributor to reference books in the sf/fantasy field and has been a judge for the Arthur C. Clarke Award.

Introduction

Imperialism, the Third World, and Postcolonial Science Fiction

ERICKA HOAGLAND AND REEMA SARWAL

As some would have it, genre — any genre — even one that has existed on the outskirts of "Literature" for most of its existence like science fiction, is a fixed category, and some critics have spent entire careers defending the borders of various genres from definitional onslaughts that would render the genre too broad, and thus meaningless. Other critics have fought another battle: preventing the borders from closing in, and the genre collapsing in on itself, starved for new voices, new meanings. As many who study science fiction know, the "definition war" within the genre is ongoing, as attempts to both purify the genre and blast its cargo doors open occur alongside each other. On the other hand, postcolonial literature is not a generic category in the same sense as science fiction or even fantasy. It does not have any standard settings (spaceships, imagined planets, pseudo-medieval fantasy lands), motifs (time-travel, quests, war) and characters (scientists, aliens, knights, dragons, wizards) of science fiction and fantasy. The mode of postcolonial literature may vary from the realist to the magic realist and everything in between. In fact, postcolonialism is a theoretical lens through which any literature may be read — from the epics, the Bible and Shakespeare through to spy thrillers, westerns and pulp romance.

This introduction, then, seeks to establish a middle ground through which to articulate some thoughts regarding the emerging genre of postcolonial science fiction, a hybrid genre that reflects intriguing affinities between two genres whose own parameters continue to be vigorously contested. Indeed, postcolonial literature and science fiction share much in common: both have been perceived at some point in their histories as literary outcasts; both have borrowed liberally from other genres, and in so doing have refashioned those genres in their image; both have been used in explicitly political ways; both have attempted to make sense of a world that is startling in its complexity and brutality; and both have undergone serious, and sometimes damaging assaults questioning the integrity of the genres themselves, how they are used, and by whom. Both genres are inherently moralistic and ethics-driven; each genre may force upon its readers difficult questions regarding complicity, loyalty, responsibility, and obligation. Despite these many similarities, how each genre is perceived in popular culture reveals a striking difference: science fiction has for some time been the repository of special effects-laden blockbusters, iconic television shows, and sweeping sagas tailor-made for miniseries. By comparison, postcolonial literature is a stranger to popular culture, specifically, Western popular culture. If science fiction is plebian, then postcolonial literature is patrician, an elitist literary genre, and by extension, postcolonial cinema is the province of the independent art house, not the suburban megaplex. While this is certainly an exaggeration, it is clear that even in the current political and cultural climate, postcolonial literature is, for lack of a better word, foreign to many Western readers. Yet the blending of one "familiar" genre with a "foreign" one represents rich creative and critical possibilities, as the pieces collected in this volume show. One of these possibilities, as the title of this collection indicates, is a closer examination of the relationship between science fiction and the Third World. Science fiction has long been viewed as a genre "produced and consumed by young white males" (Roberts 29), and as such has been "regularly condemned as the quintessentially masculine genre ... filled with muscle-bound macho heroes swaggering and bullying their way through the galaxy" (Westphal qtd. in Roberts 29). Hardly a genre where one would expect to find a sensitive, thoughtful portrayal of difference, or a critical exploration of how the Third World is imagined and represented. And yet, as Adam Roberts points out, the genre "has always had sympathies with the marginal and the different" (29). It is no surprise, then, that the genre has found a natural home amongst Third World writers, who are using the genre to reimagine themselves and their world, to "set the record straight" by dismantling the stereotypes that science fiction in part has helped to support, and in essence "strike back" at the empire. Thus this study offers a new way to think about what the "Third World"—both the ideological construct and the geographical space/s represented by the term—means by presenting diverse pieces that reflect the complex nature of the conversation about the Third World as presented in the pages of science fiction. The introduction presented here is intended to provide both a grounding of the terms central to this study, namely "postcolonial," "science fiction," and "third world," as well to explore the overlaps between science fiction and postcolonial literature in order to articulate a working theory of postcolonial science fiction.

First, it is worthwhile to consider science fiction's relationship to imperialism, a relationship that has never been simple. While on the one hand science fiction "either ignore[s] the problems that exist between different human cultural groups or perpetuates the prejudices of the dominant culture," presenting alien races in such a way as to assuage imperialist guilt or affirm imperialist desire, on the other hand science fiction has long been critical of the far-reaching arm of empire (Leggatt 109). Within one of the most famous sf franchises, *Star Trek*, one can perceive a third strain, what can be termed "ambivalent imperialism" etched within the genre through the prime directive, the highest principle by which the Federation of Planets, and its militaristic-scientific arm, Starfleet, operates. The directive enjoins its representatives to refrain from intervening with the natural evolution of a species, even if that intervention could save that species from annihilation. Acting like an intergalactic disclaimer, the directive is less about protecting the aliens Starfleet encounters than it is about protecting Federation interests and its reputation, a reputation perceived in idealistic ways — cooperative, tolerant, humane, noble — in a future likewise presented idealistically, where humanity has overcome the problems and prejudices Leggat alludes to above. In this sense the prime directive serves as a counternarrative to the violent imperialist encounters of the past, but is no less marked by imperialist desire than the African land grab of the nineteenth century. Imperialist desire in the prime directive is coded through terms like "aid" and "protect," the larger goal being to encourage planets to willingly join the Federation, and thus be drawn into the empire by choice, rather than force. Furthermore, by imposing strict guidelines as to how Starfleet technology may be shared, Federation superiority is maintained. Episodes exploring the tension between the principle of the directive and the reality of interstellar relations abound in the franchise, and one of the most successful *Star Trek* films, *First Contact,* draws heavily from this tension. In one particular episode of *Star Trek: The Next Generation*, for example, a technologically inferior planet in danger of destruction from violent volcanic activity is saved through the Enterprise's intervention, and the only alien, a child, that knows of the *Enterprise* is returned to her appropriate "state" of ignorance when her memories of the ship and Commander Data are removed. The status quo the directive reflects is preserved, and the *Enterprise* can revel in its role of intergalactic protector without any residual guilt for interfering with natural processes because the aliens *do not know*. In that regard, then, the prime directive operates like any purportedly benign imperialist principle:

expressed in the language of disinterest (we do/do not do this for you, not for us), rather than desire (we do/do not do this for our gain, whatever the cost to you), such principles, whether they are called prime directives or the White Man's Burden, have infamously supported imperialist practice in both the real world and the world of science fiction.

"In a sense," Adam Roberts writes, science fiction serves as the "dark subconscious to the thinking mind of Imperialism" (66). That "dark subconscious" is present even when a science fiction text refrains from "questioning, critiquing, or moving beyond the colonizing impulse" (Grewell 26). Indeed, Patricia Kerslake argues that "empire" is integral to any discussion of the genre itself, a viewpoint this collection shares. "As a positive tool for social awareness," the theme of empire allows science fiction to "seek out and identify [the] most problematic issues" that attend the actual practices of empire (191). The days of empire are not over, which is readily acknowledged within science fiction and postcolonial studies (and beyond). This fact of course troubles the very idea of "postcolonial" literature, theory, and studies, and while it is not the purpose of this introduction to offer a detailed discussion of the controversy surrounding the actual term "postcolonial," it is useful to highlight some of the central observations of that debate. First, "postcolonial" is a deceptively neutral term, suggesting an apolitical nature to the discipline and assuming that colonialism has come to an end. As such, more appropriate terms, particularly "neocolonialism," which recognize colonialism's continued presence, albeit in different forms, have been proffered as a replacement for "postcolonial." Second, "postcolonial" implies that the "post" can be firmly situated at a specific date; that is, just as the term appears to be politically neutral, so too does it present itself as temporally general, and this occludes the fact that colonies did not become "post" at the same time. Likewise, any broad categorical marker tends to favor the generally applicable, and as such, the specific differences between India's experience as the jewel in Britain's imperial crown and the Caribbean's history of displacement and slavery can be easily subordinated to basic similarities. Ania Loomba points out that the term "is not only inadequate to the task of defining contemporary realities in [...] once-colonised countries, and vague in terms of indicating a specific period of history, but may also cloud the internal social and racial differences of many societies" (8). Indeed, the experience of colonialism within a society can vary at least according to gender and class. At best, the term should be considered as loosely binding, acknowledging similarity, but not ignoring the "contradictions and qualifications" which "riddle" the term (Loomba 12). In this collection, then, "postcolonial," is understood more "flexibly as the contestation of colonial domination and the legacies of colonialism" (Loomba 12). As

Robert J.C. Young notes, "postcolonialism seeks to intervene, to force its alternative knowledges into the power structures of the west as well as the non-west. It seeks to change the way people think, the way they behave, to produce a more just and equitable relation between the different peoples of the world" (7).

Like "postcolonial," science fiction "resists easy definition," and thus, numerous definitions of the term abound (Roberts 1). This leads Paul K. Alkon to note that "the polysemy of the term *science fiction*, reflected in the inability of critics to arrive at agreement on any one definition, is a measure of science fiction's complex significance for our times" (9). A literature of the imagination, yet often grounded in the logic of science; an ethical enterprise packaged as entertainment; and a forward looking project that is frequently rooted in anxieties about the present (as well as the past): science fiction is a genre that feeds off of conflicting impulses — of exploration and xenophobia, conquest and exchange, and technophilia and technophobia, to name a few. Rather than attempt to summarize the genre's many definitions, which range from the incredibly specific to the laughably broad, four particular aspects of the genre will be considered, all in relation to one of sf's most dominant definitional markers, imperialism. These are the genre's relationship to history; the centrality of the other in the majority of sf narratives; what Greg Grewell, borrowing from Fredric Jameson, calls the "master narratives" of sf film — the explorative, the domesticative, and the combative (28); and "the contemplation of the human condition," or in other words, the genre's emphasis on social and ethical issues (Alkon 5). Taken together, these elements serve as a framework for articulating a definition of postcolonial science fiction.

Science fiction is often perceived as being prophetic, but as Roberts notes, "the truth is that most SF texts are more interested in the way things *have been*" (33). At best, he argues, science fiction has a "surface attachment to 'the future'"; instead, the genre is driven by nostalgia (Roberts cites several examples, including *Dune's* Arabic Middle Ages socio-political setting). In essence, the nostalgic drive of sf can be understood as the future made familiar. Thus, the future is relegated to mere stage dressing, as the past is obsessively revisited and reconsidered. This is particularly evident in the pages of alternative histories, like Philip K. Dick's *The Man in the High Castle* or Harry Turtledove's Worldwar series, in which the possibilities of the "what if" are vigorously pursued. By exploring an alternative timeline, such "histories" actually "make [their] readers feel better about their own timeline, however troubled it may be" (Duncan 216). In this way, then, nostalgia for the *now*, as well as for the past that created that now, is encouraged. *Star Trek* hurtles that nostalgia for the now into an imagined, yet familiar future; in this instance, one strikingly

American in its celebration of galactic democracy and equality. As texts like *War of the Worlds* and *The Martian Chronicles* show, however, sf does not view the past, or the present, only through the lens of nostalgia. These three texts — *Star Trek*, *War of the Worlds*, and *The Martian Chronicles* — highlight science fiction's supposedly divided relationship with / to history. On the one hand, history is a record of the inevitable, both good and bad, and is itself immutable; on the other, history is perceived both more critically and fluidly. Yet both positions lead to the same end: a revaluation of the past, where it has brought us, and where it might take us. The history of imperialism, as it is presented in both science fiction and postcolonial texts, reflects that dynamic tension between inevitability and stasis, and productive change. Authors like Wells and Bradbury reject imperialism's inevitability and instead highlight the damage — physical, psychological, and ethical — of a project that is still viewed by some nostalgically. Science fiction texts that draw such explicit and critical attention to how imperialist history is constructed and maintained is in part how postcolonial science fiction may be defined. Embedded in Eurocentric values and frames of reference, the historical record is seen as suspect, in desperate need of, at the very least, revising, if not outright rejection. The rewriting/revising of history and the recovery of the subaltern subject, integral components to postcolonial studies, are mirrors of science fiction's complex relationship with history and the haunting presence of aliens and others like Bradbury's Martians.

The "Other" is one of the most well-known markers that science fiction and postcolonial literature share in common. As Adam Roberts has noted, "...the key symbolic function of the SF novum is precisely the representation of the encounter with difference, Otherness, alterity" (25). In postcolonial studies, the "Other" is not only situated as the aberrant of the imperialist norm (a norm that is the same as that which marks difference in sf), but significantly by the denial of the "individuation" that is the right of the norm only (Loomba 52). The function of the "Other" is intriguingly similar in both genres: the "Other" consolidates difference as well as solidifies the norm; as both a theoretical concept and a tangible object, the "Other" is used to justify the exploitation and annihilation of peoples, whether red, black, or green; it is used to explain how repulsion and desire can exist concurrently; and it signifies an ever-looming threat of contamination (by sex or disease) as well as violence. Perhaps the most significant function the "Other" serves in both genres is that "...encountering the Other forces us to encounter ourselves," Roberts writes, and "the way it can reveal things about ourselves which are intensely uncomfortable" (27). It is for this reason that Damien Broderick "wonders if SF does 'above all else, write the narrative of the other/s?,'" but

Broderick "goes on to say that even if we take that 'in the spirit of description (though hardly of definition)' we still have to accept that 'SF writes, rather, the definition of the *same, as* other'" (Broderick 1995: 51 qtd. in Roberts 28). The same/other relationship is similarly complex in postcolonial literature, where identification of the norm with the other can lead to disgust, just as identification with the same can create intense feelings of betrayal and self-hatred in those marked "Other." Bradbury's sympathetic portrayal of the other, the doomed Martians in *The Martian Chronicles* is a solid example of how science fiction is frequently used as a space to challenge longstanding attitudes. "In other words," Roberts writes, "in societies such as ours where Otherness is often demonised, SF can pierce the constraints of this ideology by circumventing the conventions of traditional fiction," an end that postcolonial literature shares, even if its methods do not always entail writing against the stylistic grain of "traditional fiction" (30).

The encounter with the Other in the pages and on the screens of science fiction texts and films, reveals yet another way to understand the genre's relationship with imperialism. In "Science Fictions Then, Now, and in the (Imagined) Future," Greg Grewell argues that the "whole of the science fiction [film] industry's productions" are driven by a "fear of colonization" (26). This fear has been shaped by "the literature of earthly colonization," which has provided the industry with the raw material — the "plots, scenes, and tropes" found in the pages of Puritan narratives of the New World or the accounts of British explorers — to craft their cinematic tales. Focusing specifically on one type of "alien contact science fiction" film, in which the "earthly desires and anxieties" about alien discovery, interaction, and threat are projected "outward" into the universe, Grewell identifies three central master-plots (27; 28). The first is concerned primarily with the effect of discovery of alien worlds and beings on the "galactic colonist," while the second, what Grewell calls the "domesticative," focuses on the establishment of a home, "whether in the singular or plural as a small settlement, trading post, or larger colony somewhere out there" (28). The third master-plot is the "combative," which Grewell notes is the most dominant of the three plots in science fiction film. In this plotline, interstellar war predominates; the conflict is rooted either in the desire for survival or territory (29). Grewell darkly, but rightly, concludes by noting that "Earthlings are still very much acting out colonial impulses, designs, and fantasies," something which the "continued proliferation of colonial narratives" in science fiction reflects (39; 40). This shows how far science fiction has yet to go, but should not undermine how far it has already come in critiquing imperialism and its relationship to it, or for that matter, the general ethical "work" it has engaged in throughout its history.

One need only look to *Frankenstein*, considered by many to be the genre's ur-text, to note science fiction's deep ethical underpinnings. Indeed, a cursory inspection of some famous sf texts—*Brave New World* and *Ender's Game*, to name a very few—reflect the genre's longstanding exploration of the impact of technology on humanity's soul—while other sf texts, such as *Dune* and *The Female Man*, showcase sf's engagement in environmental and gender issues. Characterized by an overwhelming desire to understand who, and what, we are, science fiction engages in serious work that some argue relies heavily on a mutual partnership between writer and reader. In *Science Fiction After 1900*, Brooks Landon argues that "what sets SF apart from other popular genres and from mainstream literature is that its readers and writers share a sense of participation in an agenda" (33). This agenda "has to do with the very broad assumption that science fiction is not just a literature of ideas or of 'thought-experiments' but also somehow points to or promotes better thinking" (33). This leads Landon to conclude that SF's "agenda" is more epistemological, rather than ideological, in nature; as such, SF serves as a "vehicle for gaining new perspectives," often involving "the challenging and then overthrowing of an established paradigm," what Landon calls, borrowing from Peter Nicholls, a "conceptual breakthrough" (33). The SF writer and SF reader are viewed as partners in this act, engaged in "a dialogue, a dialectic" that encourages the reader to reexamine both the world and herself (Schafer qtd. in Landon 38). Viewed dialectically, then, one reads science fiction and is also read by the genre.

Landon's comments about how science fiction "somehow points to or promotes better thinking" and its epistemological and dialectical nature are also clearly evident in postcolonial literature, a genre which itself can be defined as a kind of "conceptual breakthrough." As Ania Loomba's and Robert J.C. Young's observations about postcolonial literature above indicate, the genre challenges the imperialist paradigm and offers alternatives to that paradigm, both positioned within an ethical framework in which responsibility, equality, and justice are central. Furthermore, the reader of postcolonial literature is situated to the text in much the same way as the reader of science fiction. Take, for example, Manjula Padmanabhan's play *Harvest*: in its thinly veiled portrayal of the organ trade between rich and poor nations, Padmanabhan's play implicates its privileged (read: First World) readership's participation in the ongoing exploitation of Third World bodies by bringing into sharp relief how First World comfort and health is quite literally realized at the expense of the Third World. While Padmanabhan is sympathetic to the Prakash family, in particular "the ways in which poverty can limit moral options and degrade human lives," she reserves some criticism for the family, and by extension, readers positioned outside of the First World (Gilbert 215).

Padmanbhan's play about Third World exploitation brings us, then, to a closer consideration of the controversial term within the context of this project. The history of the term "third world" reaches back to the French Revolution; modeled after the Third Estate, which was comprised of the laborers, peasants, and bourgeois members of French society, this class was further divided by the bourgeois, who resented being grouped with the peasants and laborers. Within this division can be discerned an association of "third" with manual labor, illiteracy, and limited social and political power, associations that would only consolidate in the twentieth century as the world at large was divided along three lines: the First World (or capitalist countries), the Second World (the socialist countries), and the Third World (the non-aligned nations predominantly comprised of the newly independent former colonies of the imperial powers) (Young 16). The Third World was imagined along very specific axes of economic, political, and militaristic power, not to mention cultural development, and thus was cast within very Darwinian terms. For Aijaz Ahmad, the division of the world into three parts is an ideological classification involving "those who make history, and those who are mere objects of it" (100). The Bandung Conference in 1955, at which various non-aligned nations, mostly from Africa and Asia participated, sought to address that problem by forwarding an alternative, or "third world" perspective "on political, economic, and cultural global priorities" (Young 17). While the Bandung Conference, and the Tricontinental Conference held in Havana in 1966, focused on challenging the racism, inequality, and exploitation upon which the "Three Worlds" was based, reflecting the radical, even subversive potential of the third world, by the end of the twentieth century, the association of the term with powerlessness, underdevelopment, and violence was far more common. As such, the "power" of the term is rooted in the negative, the pejorative, an "atrocious nuisance" (Said 28). Thus the term itself is something to be avoided, a maneuver that does little to actually challenge the precepts and suppositions that make the term so controversial. However, E. San Juan, Jr. argues that "juxtaposing movements of disenfranchisement and of empowerment, of ruptures and convergences" are reflected in the term (259). Projects such as this one seek to reflect an awareness of both the perverse and subversive significations of the term, its problems and its promise, and in so doing recover in some small measure the empowering alternatives the third world represents, rather than perpetuate its negative connotation.

To do so, certain clarifications are in order. First, "third world" as a category presupposes a shared experience and common history with those countries that fall under the term's dominion. As Ahmad is quick to point out, "not even the singular 'experience of colonialism and imperialism' has been in specific ways the same or similar, say, in India and Namibia" (104). Eliding difference and assuming similarity, much like "postcolonial," "third world" becomes a too easy and comfortable maneuver of geographical, historical, and cultural slippage. Yet complete rejection of the term on this basis is to overlook those shared experiences that link countries like India and Namibia, or for that matter, that link First World countries like America and Germany (and to ignore, furthermore, what differentiates those First World nations). Note, then, that Ahmad states "*specific* ways," a qualification that allows for the space of shared, albeit broader experiences. However, and to offer a second point of clarification, "third world" too often encourages defining countries primarily and only in relation to colonialism and capitalism; in this instance, having been shaped only by the experience of the former, and the lack of the latter, which stands as a significant marker of cultural development. Third, the countries designated as part of the "third world" are positioned "as a residue and as a 'periphery' that must eternally palpitate the center" (Sangari 146). As Kumkum Sangari further points out, the "center-periphery perspective" reflected in the First and Third Worlds "cannot but relegate the 'Third World' to the false position of a permanent yet desired challenge to (and subversion of) a suffocating Western sovereignty. From there it continues to nourish the self-defining critiques of the West, conducted in the interest of ongoing disruptions and reformulations of the self-ironizing bourgeois subject" (146). Both of these clarifications point to another clear problem with the term "third world;" that is, just as it perpetuates the marginalized status of the countries it "represents," so too does it reinforce the sovereignty of its opposite, the "first world." This alone is a powerful reason for rejecting the term and its use. To dismiss the term outright on these grounds, however, denies the term's power as a disturbing reminder of the very exclusions and divisions it represents. In other words, "third world" *should* be an uncomfortable term; it does, and must, reflect the inequality of current cultural global dynamics. Fourth, designating a writer as a "third world writer" can lock such individuals into narrow functions, and specific expectations, in much the same way that those nations mapped as "third world" are fettered by limited perceptions of their histories and cultures. Seen in this way, the "third world writer" is viewed as little more than a writer of protest or revolution (whether that protest be against the imperialist or chronicling post-independence revolution and violence), and even when her work is understood beyond those parameters, it is still perceived nonetheless within the context of imperialism and the West (i.e., recovering traditions "lost" during the Age of Empire). Circumscribing such writers in this fashion, then, occludes not only their respective cultural and ethnic specificity, they are stripped of their creative agency and subjectivity as well. Fifth, alternatives to this term, namely, "postcolonial," or even "Commonwealth," do not obliterate the problems associated with "third world." Indeed, as noted above, "postcolonial' merely neutralizes those problems in ways that "third world" does not, while "Commonwealth" does not include all of the "third world" and simply functions to confuse as Britain, a first world country, remains a very part of that Commonwealth.

All of this does not change certain (not so simple) facts. The term "third world" is recognizable; inasmuch as it conjures negative images of the cultures and peoples it purportedly represents, it also creates a direct means of identification. Put another way, when uttered or read, many people have a sense of what (and where) the third world is, even if they are unaware of the nuances, and to be forthright, the racism, attending the term. Arguing for using the term because people recognize it is a poor reason, indeed, but as this portion of the introduction has endeavored to show, mere recognition or for that matter, linguistic laziness, are not the reasons for using the term. In this regard, then, the collection is in clear agreement with Ella Shohat, who writes: "The invocation of the "Third World" implies a belief that the shared history of neo/colonialism and internal racism form a sufficient common ground for alliances among such diverse peoples. If one does not believe or envision such commonalities, then indeed the term "Third World" should be discarded. My assertion of the political relevance of such categories as [...] the [...] problematic Third [World], is not meant to suggest a submission to intellectual inertia, but to point to a need to deploy all the concepts in differential and contingent manners" (111). The pieces collected here are intended to show that the ways in which the third world as imagined in science fiction, and how the third world "writes back" through science fiction, is a reflection of the subversive and unsettling potential of the term.

A brief introduction to the papers included in this volume might better illustrate the above assertions at this juncture. In "Postcolonial Science Fiction: The Desert Planet," Gerald Gaylard begins his essay by positioning sf and postcolonialism at two opposite poles with sf as the literature that celebrates progress and modernity, and postcolonialism as suspicious of modernity, which is seen as a tool of subjugation. But he immediately goes on to demolish this simplistic dichotomy to point out how the two are intrinsically related, with reference to Frank Herbert's *Dune* series written at a time when most of the erstwhile colonies had newly gained independence or were fighting for it. According to Gaylard, Herbert "was not merely critiquing an abstract, mythological imperialism, but wanted to show via the allegory with contemporary American imperialism in the Middle East that imperialism is alive and well [...]." He reads *Dune* as "a fascinating science fiction version of nationalistic postcolonialism," which is in turn critiqued in favor of a postnationalist form of postcolonialism. In his study of Steven Barnes's alternate histories *Lion's Blood* and *Zulu Heart*, Juan F. Elices examines the speculative construction of an alternate history of black supremacy. Elices shows how this imaginative genre is used effectively to lay bare the Empire's discourse that legitimized racism, through "Darwin's evolutionary theories and Ruskin's polemical writings." Yet, according to Elices, the two novels do not simply present a reverse colonialism but arrive at reconciliation of the two races, at the same time demolishing the validity of official recorded history. Amitav Ghosh's *The Calcutta Chromosome* is also discussed in a similar context by Suparno Banerjee, who focuses on the use of subaltern silence to challenge the Western history of science and rupture the comfortable binaries of colonial discourse. In the last piece of this group, Grant Hamilton analyzes Vandana Singh's speculative short story, "Delhi" where the protagonist Aseem, whose name itself means "limitless" in Hindi, is not bound by the limitations of historical time and can see the past, present and future of his city simultaneously. According to Hamilton, this story "reconfigures the European organization of time" and rewrites history by giving more importance to the mundane everyday life of the anonymous Delhiites across different temporalities than to the famous Shah Jahan, so that "history is no longer about explaining the causes of national conflicts or economic trends." As the essays in the first section, "Reinventing/Alternate History" make clear, the construction of history was and remains a very powerful tool in the imperial project and an exploration of science fiction texts with regard to their imagination and extrapolation of third world history is undoubtedly one of the most rewarding aspects of studying postcolonial science fiction.

The essays in the second section, "Forms of Protest," explore various forms of resistance, beginning with Diana Pharaoh Francis's analysis of Pat Murphy's short story, "His Vegetable Wife," which explores the gendered third world that also defies geographical boundaries in both its very existence and its power for silent resistance. While the "Vegetable Wife" of Murphy's tale enacts her resistance through violence against her oppressor, Jaya, the heroine of Manjula Padmanabhan's play *Harvest* asserts her resistance by claiming her own body, including the right to harm herself. In "Body Markets: The Technologies of Global Capitalism and Manjula Padmanabhan's *Harvest*," Shital Pravinchandra clearly demonstrates the fact that colonialism is not restricted by either historical temporality or political domination over another nation. Pravinchandra analyzes the dynamics of the organ trade in the context of global capitalism and argues that it is the particularly tempting lure of "making" money rather than earning it that traps the hapless unemployed impoverished third world individual and "effectively reduce[s] Om and his family to little more than sites of *investment* for first-world capital." Further, the only form of protest available is that of suicide to deny the first world male buyer access to the purchased third world female body and in that sense, Pravinchandra argues, the trap is really inescapable. Further, Roslyn Weaver's analysis of Aboriginal speculative fiction unearths another powerful metaphor of colonial discourse often used to justify the persecution of the colonized by imagining a future devoid of minorities and colored peoples — the metaphor of apocalypse — which is in turn being appropriated in this emerging speculative fiction as a form of protest, and to "educate" the white Australian readership about Aboriginal history and struggles.

It is made apparent again and again in the essays of this volume that protest alone is not sufficient to counter the first world colonial discourse unless important lacunae in representations are also filled in order to move towards a new order by changing absence into presence. Debjani Sengupta's seminal article charting out the development of Bengali sf from 1882 to 1974 is a step in this direction as it investigates how this new genre helped to "accommodate[ed] Western science into an Indian world-view" so that science was not something to be simply discarded due to its Western origins, but was instilled with Indian ethics and life-style concerns in order to be embraced in the popular imagination. And thus was created, as Sengupta points out, a world of sf stories full of friendly, Indianized (or Bengali to be precise) robots and machines for the consumption of children and young adults. Another important site of representation for postcolonial science fiction involves indigenous peoples, who, even in the far flung reaches of space, continue to struggle with the threat of Empire. In her essay, Judith Leggatt calls attention to the popular sf trope of Native Americans on alien planets, focusing specifically on forms of neo-colonialism. The "thin veneer of the Palmarans' political independence," Leggatt points out, cannot prevent their environment from becoming a site for colonialism and in fact underlines the "cost-effectiveness of indirect control." Herbert G. Klein explores the representation of the struggle for independence by a subjugated people in Robert A. Heinlein's novel *The Moon Is a Harsh Mistress*. This struggle, of course, does not take place anywhere on Earth, but on the new colony of the Moon, allowing for a comfortable reading, as in nearly all other first world works of sf that deal with the Empire, including Asimov's contemporary *Foundation* series. Klein observes that it is the framework of the settler colonies that is being replicated in this novel and postulates that "the relationship between man and machine can also be regarded as that between Self and Other, that the two are intricately linked and mirror each other, and that the SF elements thus introduce a new angle into the concept of alterity." He also examines the gendered Other in a matriarchal society (born out of the scarcity of women) that still reinforces all the stereotypes. In the final piece in the "Fresh Representations" part, Dominic Alessio and Jessica Langer analyze the 2003 blockbuster Bollywood SF film *Koi... Mil Goya*, which poses a particular challenge to viewer and critic alike. One the one hand, Alessio and Langer celebrate the film as a post-colonial response to Western cultural hegemony, but also fear that the film is a reflection of the recent rise of "Hindu nationalism" in India that seeks to obliterate, according to them, other minority communities in the country.

This leads us to the consideration of dystopic and utopic sf vis-à-vis the third world. Jessica Langer offers a postcolonial perspective of dystopia with reference to three texts — George Alec Effinger's *When Gravity Fails*, Nalo Hopkinson's *Brown Girl in the Ring*, and China Mieville's *Perdido Street Station*. Langer rejects the "center-periphery model" for understanding colonialism because for her, the "center-periphery construction is at best a simplification and at worst a misrepresentation of the historical dynamics of colonialism" so that the city-center shows the potential to subvert colonialism. Such an argument again demolishes the geographical and political boundaries of the third world, taking it and its protest to the very heart of the colonial centers, which offer a space for what Langer calls "radical hybridity." The literary device of dystopia is also explored at length in Juan Ignacio Muñoz Zapata's analysis of a third world cyberpunk novel *La Primera Calle de la Soledad* by Mexican author Gerardo Horacio Porcayo. According to Zapata, Porcayo's use of this literary device contrasts with its use in first world cyberpunk, so that it effectively offers "resistance to globalization and new cultural colonization" in a way that first world cyberpunk does not. On the other hand, Gavin Miller critiques Octavia Butler's novel *Parable of the Sower*, which "transposes U.S. geography and culture into the contemporary Third World" for its "exploitation of the Third World as a literary *topos*" so that the third world is reduced to merely a backdrop from which emerges a U.S. utopia.

It is evident that the essays in this volume deal with a wide range of primary science fiction texts — the sf novel series, the stand alone novel, short story, a science-fiction play, a Bollywood science fiction film, and a cyberpunk novel. The papers explore postcolonial science fiction from the perspective of revisiting or re-inventing the empire's history both by going back and/or forward in time, the manifestation of colonialism in its various different forms from the gendered and the bodily to the environmental that permeate the past and the present of the world, the relationship between reactionary nationalisms and postcolonialism, and finally, the relentless search for moving forward and beyond the warp of colonialism into a truly post-postcolonial future.

Works Cited

Ahmad, Aijaz. *In Theory: Class, Nations, Literatures.* London: Verso, 2008.
Bradbury, Ray. *The Martian Chronicles.* New York: Bantam, 1979.
Gilbert, Helen. "Manjula Padmanabhan." *Postcolonial Plays: An Anthology.* London: Routledge, 2001. 214–216.
Landon, Brooks. *Science Fiction After 1900: From the Steam Man to the Stars.* New York: Twayne, 1997.
Leggatt, Judith. "Other Worlds, Other Selves: Science Fiction in Salman Rushdie's *The Ground Beneath Her Feet.*" *Ariel* 33.1 (2002): 105–125.
Loomba, Ania. *Colonialism/Postcolonialism.* London: Routledge, 1998.
Padmanabhan, Manjula. "Harvest." *Postcolonial Plays: An Anthology.* Ed. Helen Gilbert. London: Routledge, 2001. 217–49.
Roberts, Adam. *Science Fiction.* London: Routledge, 2000.
Said, Edward. *Culture and Imperialism.* New York: Vintage, 1993.
San Juan, E., Jr. *Beyond Postcolonial Theory.* New York: St. Martin's Press, 1998.
Sangari, Kumkum. "The Politics of the Possible." *Cultural Critique* 7 (1987).
Schafer, William J. "On Being Read by Science Fiction." *New England Review & Bread Loaf Quarterly* 12.4 (Summer 1990): 387–94.
Shohat, Ella. "Notes on the 'Post-Colonial.'" *Social Text* 31.32 (1992): 99–113.
Young, Robert J. C. *Postcolonialism: A Very Short Introduction.* Oxford: Oxford University Press, 2003.

"result." Consequently, the term postcolonialism, like postmodernism, suggests the demise of colonialism and the period subsequent to that demise, but it also suggests the ongoing survival and heritage of colonialism, that the past is never entirely erased. So postcolonialism has two main aspects: in its first guise it has historically appeared as nationalist rebellion against colonialism, the liberation struggles based upon the writings of Marx, Amilcar Cabral, Frantz Fanon and many others that convulsed the so-called "Third World" in the second half of the twentieth century. This initial type of postcolonialism, what I refer to as the postcolonialism of nationalist resistance, usually sought an immediate respite from colonial oppression and hence was critical of the colonial power, often violently so; typically there was social organization around resistance, usually in the form of guerrilla uprisings. Moreover, it was also critical of the empiricist rationality, belief in progress and über-science typically accompanying Western imperialism; this postcolonialism showed that culture was not confined to the West, that science did not hail from just one culture. As a result of this nationalist resistance, postcolonialism of the first sort was often aggressive, assertive, binaristic, and apocalyptic.

However, since the achievement of independence in "Third World" nations, an independence that often failed to deliver on its promises, postcolonialism has become concerned with a longer term utopian possibility of living without colonialism, a concern with the transhistorical aspects of power. Too often nationalist rebellions led not to the upliftment of the indigenous people in colonized nations, but to dictatorship and massive social suffering. A new, more analytical type of postcolonialism arose out of this spectacle of failed revolutions and examined the transhistorical realities of power and control in an effort to understand why anti-colonial rebellion frequently established neo-colonial regimes. Theorists in this school included Gayatri Spivak, Homi K. Bhabha, Bill Ashcroft, Robert J.C. Young and Edward Said. This transhistorical postcolonialism tended to be skeptical, even cynical, as one might imagine for an intellectual movement filled with post-revolutionary fatigue, yet it also sought a long term or permanent escape from colonialism and imperialism and to this extent was idealistic, even utopian. Unlike its parent rebellion it tended to be non-reactive and unwarlike, instead embracing satyagraha in the belief that there are no goodies and baddies, no imperial center to react against. Even if there was an evil empire, its individual agents were not all evil, but often just mislead, so moral ambiguity characterized this theory and fiction. Likewise, there was an emphasis upon the hybrid and the creole rather than pure, organic, rooted singularity. This hybridity has become increasingly popular in sf and fantasy: the ambiguity of the protagonist Deckard in *Blade Runner* is echoed by the amorphous androgynous protagonist in Samuel Delany's

Stars in My Pocket Like Grains of Sand, for instance. Further, transhistorical postcolonialism has been concerned with avoiding anthropocentric projection by respecting the incommensurability of aliens and alterity with the self. However, to suggest that postcolonialism has moved completely away from its nationalist political roots would be wrong; it was incubated in the pressure cooker of the independence struggle and liberationist rhetoric, historical materialism, psychedelic libertarianism, postmodernism and other radical critiques of modernity, and it has been unable and unwilling to eschew these even whilst it tackles the uneven political terrain of the present. We might describe postcolonialism today as a kind of geo-politically charged postmodernism.

Dune appears to be a classic example of the first school of nationalist postcolonialism in sf. As Macleod has it, "the great glaring exception to sf's broadly liberal consensus can be found in Frank Herbert's *Dune* (1965) and its sequels" (236). The novels are highly skeptical of the notion of progress, and one of the protagonist's sayings is, "*The concept of progress acts as a protective mechanism to shield us from the terrors of the future*" (271). Moreover, there is a binaristic adversariality between the imperial hegemony that wants the spice required for interstellar travel, the houses Atreides and Harkonnen that are set warring in this polarity in their attempts to control Arrakis, home of the spice, and, on the other hand, the planet itself and its inhabitants and interests. The human desire to colonize the other, the alien, is something that clearly inspired Herbert in the sense that he chose an alterity that would be particularly inhospitable and difficult to colonize (a desert planet), but yet which was appealing because it had a single highly desirable resource: the spice. The colonization of inhospitable alien planets with a vital resource was a common theme for sf between the 1960s and 1980s, unsurprisingly given the sociohistorical context on earth. Indeed, *Dune*'s prescient alertness to the relationship between power and resources was a prototype for this theme. The highly desirable life-prolonging drug, "the water of life," only available from the sentient mer creatures that live in Tiamat's ocean in Joan Vinge's classic *The Snow Queen* may well have been borrowed from Herbert's novel. Just like *Dune*'s spice, "the water of life" is the most valuable substance in the galaxy and the mer creatures are hunted to extinction for it. Moreover, the ocean on Tiamat is equivalent to Arrakis' desert; both ecoscapes, along with a similarly impenetrable jungle, recur in postcolonial sf as signifier of incommensurable alterity that can only be subjugated, not integrated, by an imperial mission. That Herbert was fascinated by the colonization of inhospitable environs is apparent in the comment by a journalist colleague at Herbert's one-time newspaper, *The San Francisco Examiner*:

> The bearded Herbert used to come prowling into our book department asking for "anything you have on dry climate ecology." Most visitors want Burdick or O'Hara;

Herbert lusted after the desert. T. E. Lawrence, the Koran, Mojave botanicals, all were grist for his arid mill [*The Road to Dune* 292].

Moreover, given that both *The Snow Queen* and *Dune* posit a tribal society that utilizes a mind-expanding and life-altering organic drug, both novels perhaps are imbued in a version of ethnopsychopharmacological consciousness origins that is found most prominently in the work of Terence McKenna (in *The Food of the Gods*, for instance). This not only reflects the politics of the zeitgeist, but also suggests that both works were at the cutting edge, if not over it, of their eras.

Further, Herbert not only chose a desert landscape as a dramatic backdrop for his analysis of imperialism, but also a human culture of coexistence, scarcity and thrift in this landscape as an apocalyptic end-point against which to contrast the excesses (often ecological) of imperialism. His model for this culture was Arabic and Islamic; the imperialism of the West in relation to the oil of the Middle East can be seen as an analogy for the desire for the spice in the text. This imperialism precipitates an apocalyptic nationalist movement, perhaps most visible in Herbert's use of the word "Fedaykin" which echoes the Palestinian "Feda'yin" or guerrilla fighters (Baheyeldin), though other instances abound. So Herbert was not merely critiquing an abstract, mythological imperialism, but wanted to show via the allegory with contemporary American imperialism in the Middle East that imperialism is alive and well, and hence establish a contextual relevance for his critique. However, in this postmodern allegorizing that transposes an historical Terran culture and language into a far future culture there is a worrying imperialism that relies on audience ignorance to disguise its sf orientalism.

I find it particularly significant that T. E. Lawrence, presumably of *The Seven Pillars of Wisdom* (1922), is quoted as an influence on Herbert. Edward Said's *Orientalism*, a seminal text in postcolonialism, mounted a powerful yet affectionate critique of Lawrence's novel:

> The great drama of Lawrence's work is that it symbolizes the struggle, first, to stimulate the Orient (lifeless, timeless, forceless) into movement; second, to impose upon that movement an essentially Western shape; third, to contain the new and aroused Orient in a personal vision, whose retrospective mode includes a powerful sense of failure and betrayal [241].

Said's analysis of Lawrence reads like a critique of Herbert's novel. Firstly, Herbert, unlike Lawrence who loved the Arabic culture in which he had been physically immersed, uses the Arabic language for the Fremen uncritically. Moreover, in its messianic prophecy and individualist heroism *Dune* is apocalyptic, cultivating a deliberately eschatological tone in its evocation of an esoteric prophecy via which an outsider will lead the local indigenous people to freedom. This apocalyptic tone is developed through the novel as Paul grows in stature, fulfilling the Bene Gesserit legend that his mother knows has been planted: "Jessica thought about the prophecy—the Shari-a and all the panoplia propheticus, a Bene Gesserit of the Missionaria Protectiva dropped here long centuries ago—long dead, no doubt, but her purpose accomplished: the protective legends implanted in these people against the day of a Bene Gesserit's need" (53). So although the prophecy is held by the secret Bene Gesserit order of female witch initiates, it is a male who is the messiah, the only man who can take the water of life and have the vision that they cannot. This apocalyptic, and perhaps sexist, element links to the postcolonial binarism noted above, for any stark polarities tend to carry a danger of major conflict and disaster with them. Paul is able to become the prophesied "Kwisatz Haderach," successfully taking the water of life and leading the Fremen to a glorious expulsion of the Imperium and the Harkonnens, regaining their independence in the process. In this often violent apocalypticism and messianic opposition to imperialism, *Dune* is a fascinating science fiction version of the first form of nationalist postcolonialism and a novel of its time. Indeed, the novel contributes to this nationalist form of postcolonialism by showing that imperialism is truly universal and perennial in the form of greed for resources and ruthless self-interest.

So it would seem that with *Dune* Frank Herbert created another archetypal anti-colonial text along the lines of those produced by Ngugi wa Thiong'o, Chinua Achebe, Nadine Gordimer, Gabriel García Márquez, Mario Vargas Llosa, Salman Rushdie and so on. Certainly the novel is characteristic of the nationalist postcolonial sf of the time, and echoes texts like *The Snow Queen*, *Lord of Light*, *Kirinyaga* and *Stand on Zanzibar*. To the extent that this is true, Said's critique of Lawrence would seem to apply to the novel. For Said, the problem with Lawrence's work is that he does not foreground his position as an outsider seeking to free the indigenous people from imperialism. Gayatri Spivak in her famous "Can the Subaltern Speak?" supported Said's perspective: for Spivak the representing intellectual must foreground their position, heritage and interests in order to avoid eliding the voice of the other, the subaltern, the indigenous, the oppressed. According to Said, Lawrence failed to foreground his positionality in this way, and thus presented himself as a transparent conduit for the oppressed, indeed even *becoming* the oppressed. So Lawrence transformed metaphor into metonymy, he *was* the Orient until it no longer suited him:

> Like Conrad's Kurtz, Lawrence has cut himself loose from the earth so as to become identified with a new reality in order—he says later—that he might be responsible for "hustling into form ... the new Asia which time was inexorably bringing upon us."

The Arab revolt acquires meaning only as Lawrence designs meaning for it; his meaning imparted thus to Asia was a triumph, "a mood of enlargement ... in that we felt that we had assumed another's pain or experience, his personality." The Orientalist has become now the representative Oriental, unlike earlier participant observers.... And when, for whatever reason, the movement fails (it is taken over by others, its aims are betrayed, its dream of independence invalidated), it is Lawrence's disappointment that counts ... Lawrence *becomes* both the mourning continent and a subjective consciousness expressing an almost cosmic disenchantment.... Indeed what Lawrence presents to the reader is an unmediated expert power — the power to be, for a brief time, the Orient. All the events putatively ascribed to the historical Arab Revolt are reduced finally to Lawrence's experiences on its behalf [*Orientalism* 242–3].

For Said, then, Lawrence's uncritical metonymic substitution of himself for the indigenous oppressed ironically replicated imperialism, despite Lawrence's championing of the cause of freedom, for it silenced the voice of those oppressed people. Some have applied the same critique to *Dune* (see Zaki and Balfe) which similarly has an outsider metonymically replace the voice of the Fremen and lead them to freedom. Metonymic substitution is archetypical for colonial discourse as Bhabha pointed out in his seminal postcolonial essay "Of Mimicry and Man." The white man may replace the black at any stage, but the reverse does not obtain because the colonial subject is *"almost the same, but not quite.... Almost the same, but not white"* (Bhabha 235–8). The metonymic promise of enlightenment — "you can be one of us," is actually the merely metaphorical — "you can be like one of us." Moreover, as noted previously, Herbert's utilization of mostly unaltered Arabic as the Fremen language and European languages for the Galactic empire might replicate the othering of exotic cultures of imperialism. My sense is that this could be a valid critique of the *Dune* novels, for they were partially a product of their era and context, but it seems to me that Herbert was aware of this problem and preempted it in the texts, and it is in this way that he moved beyond the simpler nationalist resistance version of postcolonialism and into a more complex and skeptical postcolonialism.

That Herbert cannot be accused of quite the same type of Orientalist imperialism as Lawrence can be seen in the subtle portrayal of apocalyptic nationalist prophesy in *Dune*. From the start it is clear that messianic prophecy has been purposefully created by the Bene Gesserit as part of their program of long term selective breeding in order to create the perfect human, a superhuman being who can ingest deadly psychoactive poison and survive to prophesy. In the quotes from the "Manual of Maud'Dib" by the Princess Irulan in which Paul's life and activities are recorded and ruminated upon, Herbert suggests the process via which events are codified into myths and doxa, heroes made, prophecies confirmed, holy books created. This is a process of conspiratorial control and the seeding of blood lines by a secret society, the creation and dissemination of "sacred" texts by these secret societies or others that preys on the hopes of downtrodden peoples, the wish-fulfilling recognition of the prophecies of these sacred texts in a particular person or happenstance (Paul Atreidies in this instance), the consequent elevation of that person to messiah status. The creation of heroic myths and stories is thus not only a process of conspiratorial manipulation and misinterpretation, but also one of hyperbole ramified via retelling: after destroying the Sardaukar spies that accompany Gurney Halleck, Paul "thought bitterly that here was another chapter in the legend of Paul Muad'dib. *I didn't even draw my knife, but it'll be said of this day I slew twenty Sardaukar by my own hand*" (357).

Myth is a vital part of Herbert's "genetic theory of history" according to O'Reilly (49), for it is the structure of myths and stories that at least partially determines human thought and action. Herbert shows that myth in the *Dune* universe is a totalizing discourse of final, singular explanation and control because it is imbricated with power, and this has manifold political ramifications: in this case the need to overcome imperial invasion and exploitation and the unwitting subsequent spawning of a dictatorship and an intergalactic jihad. The Fremen need the myth of a messiah leader to maintain their culture in the face of the withering Harkonnen onslaught and provide them with hope that they will free themselves of its imperial yoke. However, whilst Paul does fulfill the project of postcolonial nationalism to eject the Harkonnens and the Imperium from Arrakis, he also does much more, which brings into play the issue of what happens after the revolution and the second mode of transhistorical postcolonialism, explored in more detail in *Dune Messiah*.

In the first instance, Paul institutes Liet-Kynes' project to terraform Arrakis which affects not only the ecology of the planet (worms, for instance, find water poisonous and are driven away from the new project — which echoes the Israeli attempts to make the desert bloom), but also the culture of the Fremen, so that they appear to lose some of their "desert" strength and become increasingly absorbed into imperial culture and bureaucracy. This is a dramatization of Hobson's choice of short term consumption versus long term sustainability that haunts human civilisation and progress. The terraforming project leads to debate among the Fremen about Paul's indigeneity and status:

> "The desert takes him — and deifies him," Idaho said. "Yet he was an interloper here. He brought an alien chemistry to this planet — water."
> "The desert imposes its own rhythms," Stilgar said. "We welcomed him, called him our Mahdi, our Muad'dib, and gave him his secret name, Base of the Pillar: Usul."
> "Still, he was not born a Fremen."

"And that does not change the fact that we claimed him ... and have claimed him finally." Stilgar put a hand on Idaho's shoulder. "All men are interlopers, old friend" [*Dune Messiah* 219].

This debate appears to settle questions of Paul's origins, and does so in the mold of transhistorical postcolonialism which emphasizes transience, impurity and hybridity. Indeed, this mode of analysis contradicts the earlier form of postcolonialism to the extent that it suggests that the Fremen myth of unified, singular, pure, organic tribal origins was actually an expedience that resulted from the necessity to oppose a single imperial enemy. Secondary postcolonialism is less politically sure because it does not have a singular enemy to oppose; resistance must be conducted on multiple fronts.

Secondly, Paul's jihad does not remain confined to Arrakis and is described thus in *Children of Dune*: "Muad'Dib had ignited an explosion of humanity; Fremen had spread from this planet in a jihad, carrying their fervor across the human universe in a way of religious government whose scope and ubiquitous authority had left its mark on every planet" (6). Paul himself laments the facts: "'Statistics: at a conservative estimate, I've killed sixty-one billion, sterilised ninety planets, completely demoralised five hundred others. I've wiped out the followers of forty religions'" (*Dune Messiah* 92). Here Herbert enters a full postcolonial sensibility which is painfully aware of the dangers of nationalist reaction: violent reaction all too often ironically enthrones precisely what it is reacting against, even if what it enthrones initially appears different. This postcolonialism moves beyond the first stage of nationalist resistance because it is aware that this first stage is often reactionary, violent, orthodox and conformist in its ideals. As Stilgar asks in *Children of Dune*: "*How simple things were when our Messiah was only a dream*, he thought. *By finding our Mahdi we loosed upon the universe countless messianic dreams. Every people subjugated by the jihad now dreams of a leader to come.... If my knife liberated all of those people,* [by killing Paul's children] *would they make a messiah of me?*" (7). The myth of national liberation leads towards a new religion of righteousness that cannot tolerate dissent of any kind from its orthodoxies. So, as Feyd-Rautha realises, "*That which makes a man superhuman is terrifying*" (*Dune* 283); the power of myth is terrifying, especially if it is realized. Paul is "*less than a god, more than a man ... who ordered battle drums made from his enemies' skins, the Muad'dib who denied the conventions of his ducal past with a wave of the hand, saying merely: 'I am the Kwisatz Haderach'*" (391). Yet despite the novel's postcolonial critique of messianic imperialism via the Fremen jihad unloosed upon the galaxy, the novel shows that this was not intentional: Paul finds himself caught up within something he helped to start, but once it has begun it is not within his control (*Dune Messiah* 53). Paul is a victim of the force of history that he helped to galvanize, to catalyze, but there are clearly other components to this force than genetics: postcolonial inevitability, the power of myth and the "primitive" warrior strength of the Fremen. This warrior naivety is revealed in *Dune Messiah*:

> Alia continued to look at the old Fremen Naib. Something about him now made her intensely aware that he was one of the primitives. Stilgar believed in a supernatural world very near him. It spoke to him in a simple pagan tongue dispelling all doubts. The natural universe in which he stood was fierce, unstoppable, and it lacked the common morality of the Imperium [80].

Paul uses this organic warrior tribalism to rid Arrakis of imperial exploitation, but once that violent rebellion spreads to the rest of the humanoid universe via the messianic myth of Muad'dib and by his crowning of himself as emperor, then Paul lives to regret seeing "*a friend become a worshiper*" (394) and "in a rush of loneliness ... noting how proper and on-review his guards had become in his presence. He sensed the subtle, prideful competition among them" (394). Like Cortez and Mistah Kurtz from Conrad's *Heart of Darkness*, Paul is now a prisoner of his own ideals and must live out their darker aspects. This is emphasized repeatedly in *Dune Messiah*:

> Frustration tangled him. He felt the pressure of mass-unconscious, that burgeoning sweep of humankind across his universe. They rushed upon him with a force like a gigantic tidal bore. He sensed the vast migrations at work in human affairs: eddies, currents, gene flows. No dams of abstinence, no seizures of impotence nor maledictions could stop it [110].

This image of a gigantic tidal wave of unconscious human will sweeping, rushing, flowing through the universe conveys a transhistorical sensibility. Paul, from being the catalyst of this wave, is now its victim: "From the moment the Jihad had chosen him, he'd felt himself hemmed in by the forces of a multitude. Their fixed purposes demanded and controlled his course. Any delusions of Free Will he harbored now must be merely the prisoner rattling his cage" (155–6). So some of his family and confidants recognize that "'He didn't use the Jihad.... The Jihad used him. I think he would've stopped it if he could'" (127); according to Alia, "'Paul's entire life was a struggle to escape his Jihad and its deification'" (220).

Dune, and more so, *Dune Messiah*, are therefore novels along the lines of "Third World" novels of dictatorship and autocracy: classic examples include García Márquez's *The Autumn of the Patriarch* and *The General in His Labyrinth*, Roa Bastos' *I, the Supreme*, Vargas Llosa's *The Feast of the Goat*, Ngugi's *Matigari*, Laing's *Major Gentl and the Achimota Wars*, and so on. In most of these novels the dictator finds himself, and he is always a he, trapped within a labyrinth of deceit of his own devising because he had to engage in subterfuge and violence in order to come to power, both of which demand obeisance and money in order to remain hidden. Once isolated within this labyrinth, the autocrat inevitably loses touch with the reality of the people on the ground, a contact that was often what swept him to power in the first place. Looking for contact with the everyday within that labyrinth, the dictator does not know who or which informant to trust, and often finds himself enmeshed within intrigues in which he plays one informant off against another, spawning unmanageable complexity and contradictions. This complexity and its contradictions lead to the inevitable downfall of the tyrant: "'Power tends to isolate those who hold too much of it. Eventually, they lose touch with reality ... and fall.'" (*Dune Messiah* 88). As the series progresses, this transhistorical sense of historical inevitability increases, so that by *Children of Dune* there are repeated references to time as "self-perpetuating" (98), the discovery of "'the future in the past, and both are part of a whole'" (81).

However, this postcolonial analysis of prophecy, conspiracy, control and tyranny also shows that historical inevitability is just one side of the coin; the other side involves chaos, choice and free will. If Paul had chosen differently, then he would not have become Maud'Dib, the prophesied guerrilla leader. Both Jessica and Paul play a complex guessing game with the Fremen, feeding into the messianic prophecies sewn by the Bene Gesserit generations before in much the same way as Cortez and his imperial mission did to Montezuma and Aztec mythology (although, of course, the outcome is quite different to that in Mexico as Paul does lead the Fremen towards freedom). Herbert neither lauds nor condemns Paul and the forces that enthrone him. Rather, his project is a truly postcolonial one in that it shows the mutual imbrication of the individual with history, and the limited potential for liberation within both. This postcolonial project is contemplated thus by the Princess Irulan:

> Greatness is a transitory experience. It is never consistent. It depends in part upon the myth-making imagination of humankind. The person who experiences greatness must have a feeling for the myth he is in. He must reflect what is projected upon him. And he must have a strong sense of the sardonic. This is what uncouples him from belief in his own pretensions. The sardonic is all that permits him to move within himself. Without this quality, even occasional greatness will destroy a man [Dune 111].

The point here is that Herbert created a critique of apocalyptic nationalism within the generally nationalistic framework of his narrative, and thus the novels provide an interestingly finessed version of postcolonialism in which archaic belief systems and ecology are as important as space ships with firepower, in which personal choice and freedom are as important as opposition to injustice. This nuanced postcolonial sensibility allowed Herbert to go on to create a series of novels critical of messianism. Indeed, John W. Campbell, legendary editor of *Analog*, which initially serialized *Dune*, refused to publish its follow-up, *Dune Messiah*, because "Paul winds up as a God That Failed" (*The Road to Dune* 293). As Brian Herbert pointed out in *Dreamer of Dune* (191–92):

> *Dune*, the first novel in what would ultimately become a series, contained hints of the direction (Frank Herbert) intended to take with his superhero, Paul Maud'Dib, clues that many readers overlooked. It was a dark direction. When planetologist Liet-Kynes lay dying in the desert, he remembered those words of his father, spoken years before and relegated to the back reaches of memory: "No more terrible disaster could befall your people than for them to fall into the hands of a Hero." And at the end of an appendix it was written that the planet had been "afflicted by a Hero." ... The author felt that heroes made mistakes ... mistakes that were amplified by the numbers of people who followed those heroes slavishly....
> Among the dangerous leaders of human history, my father sometimes mentioned General George S. Patton, because of his charismatic qualities — but more often his example was President John F. Kennedy. Around Kennedy a myth of kingship formed, and of Camelot. His followers did not question him, and would have gone with him virtually anywhere. This danger seems obvious to us now in the case of such men as Adolf Hitler, who led his nation to ruination. It is less obvious, however, with men who are not deranged or evil in and of themselves. Such a man was Paul Muad'Dib, whose danger lay in the myth structure around him [*The Road to Dune* 295].

Herbert's genius in *Dune* and the subsequent novels is to create a work of messianic and apocalyptic anti-imperialism, with all of the potential for drama that that entails, that is self-reflexively critical of our desire and need for messianic apocalypticism. This desire and need for strong leaders seems partly to be a "hangover" from the mythologization of our tribal and mediaeval pasts, and it is surely no mistake that much of the imagery and iconography of the novel is strongly mediaeval, perhaps derived from the Ottoman empire. To the extent that these novels are self-reflexive and metacritical they are postmodern texts and exemplify the second type of postcolonialism that has a long term view of anti-imperialism. As Jessica, Paul's mother, writes:

> Government cannot be religious and self-assertive at the same time. Religious experience needs a spontaneity which laws inevitably suppress. And you cannot govern without laws. Your laws eventually must replace morality, replace conscience, replace even the religion by which you think to govern. Sacred ritual must spring from praise and holy yearnings which hammer out a significant morality. Government, on the other hand, is a cultural organism particularly attractive to doubts, questions and contentions. I see the day coming when ceremony must take the place of faith and symbolism replaces morality [*Dune Messiah* 171].

So, in a sense, Said's critique of Lawrence's Orientalism was a critique that Herbert was aware of and integrated into *Dune* and its successors. Like

Lawrence, Herbert's agent of colonization, Duke Leto Atreides, is a benign ruler, somebody who is only too aware of the dangers of ruling and colonization: "'To hold Arrakis,' the Duke said, 'one is faced with decisions that may cost one his self-respect.' He pointed out the window to the Atreides green and black banner hanging limply from a staff at the edge of the landing field. 'That honorable banner could come to mean many evil things'" (*Dune* 93). Determined not to replicate the cruel colonialism of the Harkonnens, Arrakis's previous overlords, and to find support on the planet in the face of the threat of imperial conspiracies with the Harkonnens, Atreides attempts to rule benignly and win the support of the indigenous Fremen. Like Lawrence, Atreides has the ability to switch perspectives, to see beyond his own interests and those of his people, to take the side of the natives. For me, this perspective-switching is one of the masterful formal aspects of *Dune* as it adds a great deal to dramatic tension; the constant toing-and-froing between the Imperium, the Harkonnens, the Atreides and Fremen on Arrakis, and so on, provides the drama of historical urgency, the gravitas of high stakes and the excitement of conspiracy and escape. The oscillation resulting from the "pressure environment" of colonialism not only creates drama, but also foments hesitation and undecideability that are hallmarks of postcolonialism (*The Road to Dune* 282). This is the novel of an author who is only too aware of the dangers of imperialism, whether resource-based, psychological, power-driven, ecological or otherwise, and who sought to find a way to avert those dangers and provide an alternative in his fiction.

This aversion of dangers and search for an alternative is embodied in the development of Paul Maud'Dib, whose meaning and valency are difficult to decide, an undecideability that permeates the series as a whole. Such undecideability is because Paul teeters in an occult zone between competing forces, a zone characteristic of postcolonialism once nationalist revolutions have achieved their initial goals.

> On one side he could see the Imperium, a Harkonnen called Feyd-Rautha who flashed toward him like a deadly blade, the Sardaukar raging off their planet to spread pogrom on Arrakis, the Guild conniving and plotting, the Bene Gesserit with their scheme of selective breeding. They lay massed like a thunderhead on his horizon, held back by no more than the Fremen and their Muad'dib, the sleeping giant Fremen poised for their wild crusade across the universe.
>
> Paul felt himself at the center, at the pivot where the whole structure turned, walking a thin wire of peace with a measure of happiness ... [305].

All around Paul is imperial scheming, powerplay. So Herbert's critique of imperialism shows that it invariably involves Machiavellian scheming, plotting and maneuvering. The Baron, for his part, has survived for so long because he is a master of perfidy.

Imperialism, both Harkonnen and otherwise, involves the ambition for total singular control which requires the subjugation of others through "fear over ambition" (420), a subjugation requiring cunning, deceit and maneuvering. Herbert, taking the long, transhistorical view characteristic of secondary postcolonialism, shows that this imperialism is doomed to failure because it is based on fear, which is an insecure footing, and deceit, which cannot remain hidden forever. Transhistorical postcolonialism sees that imperialism, indeed perhaps Western modernity in general, is a thought process dependent upon individualist isolation and alienation from others, from nature; its totalitarian singularity is based upon fear and power and is thus inherently violent.

Herbert's vision in the *Dune* novels is what one might call eco-postcolonial: it is a vision of nature as "multiple, cross-linked events" which is not amenable to the totalizing singular analysis and scheming of imperialism. It is a vision of multiple others in constant motion, a vision not amenable to unifying totalization. Herbert seems to have arrived at this vision from his interest in ecology and his consequent transhistorical realization that the dictum of man having dominion over the flocks of the earth is the first step down an imperial path that can only lead to isolation, alienation, conflict and disaster. This vision is perhaps best summed up in a passage from *Children of Dune*:

> *A sophisticated human can become primitive. What this really means is that the human's way of life changes. Old values change, become linked to the landscape with its plants and animals. This new existence requires a working knowledge of those multiples and cross-linked events usually referred to as nature. It requires a measure of respect for the inertial power within such natural systems* [*Children of Dune* 66].

So whilst it is clear that the vast majority of sf fails to depict alterity, the other, constantly appropriating alterity into the same, and whilst Herbert replicates some of this appropriation in his novel, this by no means entirely contains the postcolonial thrust of his text which contains a powerful critique of both imperialism and nationalist opposition.

The argument that I am advancing is that postcolonialism and sf are highly relevant to each other, both in terms of postcolonialism providing a valuable historical and theoretical lens through which to see sf, and in terms of sf providing a futurological extrapolation that expands postcolonialism's purview. Postcolonialism adds a nuanced political concern to the issues of travel, migration and imperialism because these issues inevitably involve confronting alien cultures and their resistance. The postcolonialism of alterity within the long term and the consequent issues of respect and non-anthropocentrism that arise is relevant to sf because sf is a genre that tends to relativize the present via its habitual mode of extrapolation and interplanetary cosmic event; it is also concerned with the issue of the representation of the alien other and whether there is a mode of representation that will allow the alien to speak for itself. On the other hand, the transhistorical mode has become central to postcolonialism because it has witnessed the betrayal of so many of the promises of history. Sf similarly deals in the realm of the transhistorical, though this is more often for the reason of futurological interest than present political disenchantment. Extrapolation has been highly developed within sf, a development that can only add to postcolonialism's desire for clues about how history will evaluate the present, how we might change our actions and inactions in the present and future. Frank Herbert's *Dune* series seems to me to be a good example of postcolonialism, both in its nationalist form, but more importantly in its postnationalist form, in that it displays a keen interest in the light that is shed upon the present by the transhistorical. This light shows that complexity is characteristic of both nature and cultural politics, and that only a complex ideology and aesthetics that is prepared to reflect upon itself and possibly change its course via extrapolation can hope to convey this in fiction whilst not falling into the traps of ignorance, projection, reaction and mythologization.

Notes

1. Originally published in *Foundation* 104 (2009): 84–101.

Works Cited

Baheyeldin, Khalid. "Arabic and Islamic themes in Frank Herbert's *Dune*." http://baheyeldin.com/literature/arabic-and-islamic-themes-in-frank-herberts-dune/html. 2004.
Balfe, Myles. "Incredible Geographies? Orientalism and Genre Fantasy." *Social & Cultural Geography* 5.1 (March 2004): 75–90.
Bhabha, Homi K. "Of Mimicry and Man: The Ambivalence of Colonial Discourse." *Modern Literary Theory: A Reader*. Eds. Philip Rice & Patricia Waugh. London: Arnold, 1992. 234–241.
Herbert, Frank. *Children of Dune*. London: NEL, 1982.
_____. *Dune*. London: Gollancz, 2001.
_____. *Dune Messiah*. London: NEL, 1986.
Herbert, Frank, Brian Herbert & Kevin J. Anderson. *The Road to Dune*. London: Hodder & Stoughton, 2005.
Macleod, Ken. "Politics and Science Fiction." *The Cambridge Companion to Science Fiction*. Eds. Edward James & Farah Mendlesohn. Cambridge: CUP, 2003. 230–240.
McKenna, Terence. *Food of the Gods: A Radical History of Plants, Drugs and Human Evolution*. London: Rider, 1992.
O'Reilly, Timothy. *Frank Herbert*. New York: Ungar, 1981.
Said, Edward. *Orientalism*. London: Penguin, 1995.

Spivak, Gayatri. "Can the Subaltern Speak?" *Colonial Discourse and Post-Colonial Theory: A Reader.* Eds. Patrick Williams & Laura Chrisman. Harvester: London, 1994. 66–111.
Vinge, Joan. *The Snow Queen.* London: Orbit, 1981.
_____. *Tangled Up in Blue.* New York: Tor, 2000.
Zaki, Hoda M. *Phoenix Renewed: The Survival and Mutation of Utopian Thought in North American Science Fiction, 1965–1982.* Mercer Island, WA: Starmont House, 1988.

2

History Deconstructed
Alternate Worlds in Steven Barnes's Lion's Blood *and* Zulu Heart

Juan F. Elices

Dealing with two disciplines as close and at the same time divergent as history and fiction has originated an intense theoretical debate, especially among poststructuralist scholars. The proliferation of the historical novel, now considered a commercial and editorial stronghold, the emergence of the so-called historiographic metafiction, under the auspices of postmodernist critical theorists, and the re-flourishing of history in intellectual and academic circles has reactivated the already significant presence of historical references in the works of most contemporary authors. Nonetheless, with the *entrée* of post-modernism, the approaches towards history have been dominated by the deconstruction of the epistemological pillars that sustain it, mainly, the empirical basis of fact or the linearity and causality of historical development. History, in this sense, has been shielded behind the façade of being an immutable entity and, more importantly, of being the only project capable of studying the past from impartial and objective standpoints. In a period of apparent skepticism and rupture, these premises, often associated to a more realist framework, have been unable to maintain the fixedness of history to give way to a more unstable and challenging vision of the past. To this change of perspective have contributed not only the abovementioned genres, but also other—some might say "minor"—literary modes such as science fiction and fantasy, whose coming to terms with history has widened the once limited scope of the discipline.

Furthermore, the growing presence of ethnic authors within this field has opened up the path for new and revealing readings of history, producing a corpus of literary works that rescue and celebrate events so far overtly ostracized. African-American novelist and script writer Steven Barnes is a brilliant exponent of how black history can be re-invented by means of defying the idea that only winners can construct the past and, thus, control the present and future. *Lion's Blood* (2002) and *Zulu Heart* (2003) are probably his most ambitious projects, where he speculates about the advent of an era of black supremacy, in which the white population is enslaved and marginalized. This reversal of roles is embedded within the frame of the so-called "alternate history narratives" and this is precisely the starting point of my discussion. This study seeks, therefore, to analyze how Barnes, from the vantage point of alternate history, problematizes issues such as slavery, language or religion that postcolonial criticism has recurrently revolved around. It goes without saying that Barnes's main aim is to dismantle all those clichés and stereotypes that have stigmatized and objectified black people, which explains why he recurs to a kind of narrative that enables him to do so.

Alternate history appears as a remarkable advance in the revision of historical factuality, for it proposes a completely innovative method of handling with events that form part of more "standardized" cultural paradigms. This sub-genre, as Darko Suvin has labelled it (150), has, on most occasions, passed unnoticed due to its frequent inclusion under the general category of science fiction, in spite of the scarce similarities that exist between them. Among the many scholars that have dealt with this sub-genre, Paul Alkon provides a definition that accurately encompasses the main features of this kind of works: "Essays or narratives exploring the consequences of an imagined divergence from specific historical events, thus distinguishing it from parallel history, which may be defined as accounts that present a different past or present not caused by a divergence from real history at some key moment such as a French victory at Waterloo" (68). Alkon points at concepts, such as "parallel" or "real" history, that have been deeply scrutinized by critics in the line of Linda Hutcheon, who highly questions the assumption that history is made up of real facts proposing, instead, the idea that, like fiction, it is open to the interpretation of the writer/historian.[1] This trend, generally known as historiographic metafiction, allowed many authors to withdraw from the tight impositions of historical discourse to deepen into questions that had been either overshadowed or ignored. Alternate history, in this sense, gravitates around the "What if...?" or "What might have been/happened if...?" formulae that echoes what Alkon suggests in his previous definition. What these narratives purport, thus, is to fictionalize an event that departs from history as we have received it or as it is recollected in annals in order to hypothesize about the possible consequences that this deviation might have caused.

Although the very spirit of these narratives has been, as William H.

Hadesty suggests (81), to cast doubts upon the way we have unquestioningly taken for granted most historical preconceptions, the fact is that most of them focus on the events that constitute the pillars of Western, "mainstream," civilization. In this like vein, critics and writers have theorized about questions such as the defeat of the Allies in the Second World War and the subsequent permanence of the Third Reich in power (as seen in Robert Harris' *Fatherland* [1992]), the victory of the South in the American Civil War (the main subject in most Harry Turtledove's best-sellers), the invasion and posterior subjugation of the United States under the German-Japanese Axis (proposed by Philip K. Dick in *The Man in the High Castle* [1962]), or the German occupation of the United Kingdom after the Luftwaffe's destruction of the Royal Air Force in the Battle of Britain (depicted by Len Deighton in his worldwide famous *SS-GB* [1980]). As can be concluded, although these conform to some major moments in the course of modern and contemporary history, none of them seems to have deepened too extensively into non-Western, non-mainstream *histories*, usually considered secondary or irrelevant. However, an increasing number of postcolonial authors have realized the possibilities that both science fiction and alternate history can offer as mechanisms to rewrite and disclose the most polemical aspects of these "sub-histories," creating, thus, a most suitable arena for envisioning more positive worlds or contexts. Walter Mosley or Nalo Hopkinson, not to mention the canonical Samuel R. Delaney or Octavia E. Butler, have lately attempted to vindicate black science fiction and dystopia in their collections and novels as a means to lay bare all the injustices that have accompanied the black population throughout history.[2] In this sense, rewriting for these authors is not only conceived as a playful or formal trick but as a way to protest against the harsh oppression, racism, slavery and rejection undergone by black people. As Linda Hutcheon rightly explains: "Postmodern fiction suggests that to re-write and to re-present the past in fiction and in history is, in both cases, to open it up to the present, to prevent it from being conclusive and teleological" (110).[3]

Steven Barnes's attempt in *Lion's Blood* and *Zulu Heart* falls accurately within Hutcheon's reflection in that he proposes to reopen the long-standing debate on the black question and how its own alteration provokes the delegitimizatation of the atrocities perpetrated by white colonialists. Both novels present an alternate world in which most occidental lands are under the yoke of Bilalistan, formerly North America, now dominated by black emperors and empresses.[4] Barnes makes explicit the overthrow of white authority already from the novels' opening pages, where he inserts a couple of maps in which the new territorial topography is delineated. Similarly to the despicable "Scramble for Africa" that shared out the continent in portions that were arbitrarily assigned to the most powerful European countries, Barnes also suggests that Europe as a whole had become a colonized territory, and thus subject to the commands of the metropolis. It is clear, from the very beginning, that "conventional history"—that which is convincingly marketed as a truthful and objective account of the past—is overturned and the long-suffering period of humiliation and exclusion among the black population has reached its end. From this moment onwards, Barnes's alternate histories focus primarily on the dismantling of the clichés that have downgraded black people and, generally speaking, all minority races, by means of applying them to the former exploiter. For the first time, the traditional power-relations that were established *perforce* between the white master and the black slave are definitely undone, and erstwhile slaveholders now become "others," brute labor force at the disposal of the imperial power. For "Otherness," as Said brilliantly explained in his *Orientalism*, is the first and most pernicious stage in the deconfiguration of the native self, exposed to the gradual "whitening" of his/her language, religious, beliefs, cultural background and value system.

In *Lion's Blood*, however, Barnes places white characters down in the social scale, relegated, as mere others, to a position of utter dereliction: "With casual brutality, the guard slammed a leather truncheon against Aidan's fingers. Then with a roar he slammed the club against anyone in reach, sending them reeling back with bloodied hand and gashed scalps" (56). Black people are no longer the victims of torture as James Baldwin, Richard Wright or Langston Hughes manifested in their works, but the ones who inflict severe physical punishment against white Europeans. In most classical antebellum slave narratives, these images of violence were epitomized by both the ships that transported them from their African settlements through Liverpool and finally to the United States, and the plantations, evidence of the most deplorable side of slavery. These two interconnected phases in the constitution of the master-servant relation are dramatically turned upside down in Barnes's novel, for it portrays how entire white communities are driven away from their hometowns and pushed to plantations without their consent. The author depicts the transatlantic voyage from Europe to the United States with sheer accuracy thanks to the inclusion of images that remind us of the overrun, malodorous cargos that somehow anticipated the living conditions that awaited black slaves in North American territory. It turns out to be paradoxical to see white people going through hardships that, history tells us, seemed to be reserved for black people. As the following passage demonstrates, Barnes turns this paradox into a very plausible alternative:

> Rows of horizontal wooden shelves were mounted on each side of the hold, with a narrow aisle running between. Without another word they were shoved onto the

planks. Their chains were shackled to metal claws that were mounted in the thick wood at their feet. Someone's feet were in Aidan's hair, and his own rested almost upon some women's shoulders [26].[5]

Images of Steven Spielberg's film *Amistad* come rapidly to mind, but they are soon dissipated when we assume that the protagonists of these Dantesque scenes are white characters. Equally shocking are Barnes's descriptions of the plantations in which slaves are employed as animal labor force. The function of the plantation was twofold: from a more practical point of view, it was designed to provide high profits to the metropolis; more subliminally, as Bill Ashcroft asserts, the plantation marked the huge differences that separated these two unreconciled worlds and strengthened the essential role of slavery in the empowerment of these differences (70). North American and Caribbean cotton and sugar plantations emerged as symbols of metropolitan prosperity gained through the suffering and death of thousands of black people working on them day and night. Through the eyes of Irishman Aidan O'Dere, Barnes presents a diametrically different vision, since only white people are forced to labor the lands under the whip of black masters: "The intervening territory was mostly sandy soil and scrub brush. From time to time they passed rows of white slaves laboring in the sun, under the watchful eye of white and black overseers. Aidan did not recognize the crops being worked: strange plants in neat rows that extended almost to the horizon" (*Lion's* 64). As postcolonial theory argues, the plantation proved to be a realm where slaves lost any trace of humanity to become passive objects whose only goal was to make the land productive. However, African-American history demonstrates that in the plantation, and even more significantly during the construction of the railway network in the United States, the bonds and comradeship among black slaves were reinforced even to the extent of creating secret codes of communication that were transmitted through the so-called "railroad songs." With these tunes, they managed to exchange valuable information mostly related to the best ways of running away from the camps. With time, these songs turned out to be the precursors of the "blues," perhaps the most distinguishable icon of African-American culture. Barnes also borrows this typical aspect of black culture in order to describe a group of white slaves working on the fields and singing ancestral Celtic melodies: "To Aidan's ear it was a mournful song, a song of loss and pain, and it was hard to believe that his proud, educated masters could not hear the fury behind the sweetly twining melody" (*Lion's* 232).

The effects of slavery caused not only physical scars, but a progressive loss of identity and self-esteem. As Wakil Abu Ali states in *Lion's Blood*, the institution of slavery sustains the state and keeps the social order under strict surveillance, providing those who are in power with all privileges and pleasures imaginable (346). On the contrary, the pressures exerted upon slaves result in their, voluntary or involuntary, withdrawal from their racial, linguistic or cultural roots in favor of the colonizer's, whose only aim is to re-educate the native population according to the dictates of the metropolis. This eventually brought about that the only way out for many colonized individuals was assimilation, which means rejection of their own identity. In this line, Albert Memmi suggestively points out that: "The major impossibility is not negating one's existence, for he soon discovers that, even if he agrees to everything, he would not be saved. In order to be assimilated, it is not enough to leave one's group, but one must enter another; now he meets the colonizer's rejection" (124). In *Lion's Blood* and *Zulu Heart*, Barnes explores the same contradiction Memmi refers to above and arrives at the same conclusions. The novels present typologies of characters that differ in their approach to their state as enslaved and dislocated subjects. Some, like Aidan or Brian, seek to recuperate freedom as a means to regain their lost self; others like Aidan's mother understand that the only way to come to terms with this new reality is to unconditionally surrender to the impositions of the colonizer. It is important to note that the formal mechanisms of alternate history again enable Barnes to, somehow, normalize the paradoxical situations that are posed in the novels.

One clear instance of this unreserved desire of assimilation is examined in *Zulu Heart*, where the writer depicts the efforts of white men and women to look "blacker": "Women shaded and braided their light hair to make it seem more African. Men worked in the fields until the sun had broiled them, seeking to add a few precious shades of bronze. Sometimes they tinted or painted their skin to achieve the desired effect" (48). The author again frolics with traditional clichés associated particularly with the African-American idiosyncrasy and transposes them to the former object of imitation. In this vein, African-American writers such as Toni Morrison or Zora Neale Hurston have largely explored the standards of beauty shared by black women, concluding that most of them pursued to achieve a "whiter," more Europeanized look. According to Bertram D. Ashe:

> African-Americans, with their traditionally African features, have always had an uneasy coexistence with the European (white) ideal of beauty.... For black women, the most easily controlled feature is hair. While contemporary black women sometimes opt for cosmetic surgery or colored contact lenses, hair alteration (i.e., hair-straightening "permanents," hair weaves, braid extensions, Jheri curls, etc.) remains the most popular way to approximate a white female standard of beauty [579].

Furthermore, it is interesting to note that the very idea of hybridization is put at stake in the novel, for most white women's wish was to marry a black man so that her offspring would attain freedom automatically. If, in most cases, it was black women who aspired to enjoy the privileges of "whiteness" through these marriages of convenience, Barnes demystifies this notion by suggesting quite the opposite view: "Mixing of blood was inevitable when people of different races lived in proximity.... More than one former slave woman had coupled with a native or black townsman, so that her children might enjoy the advantage of mixed blood" (48). Hybridity, therefore, is not contemplated as an end in itself but as means to gain access to the advantages of a new social status, although, as John MacLeod appropriately asserts, hybrid identities always "remain in perpetual motion pursuing errant and unpredictable routes, open to change and reinscription" (219).

In this discussion on the dangers of assimilation, language and religion become decisive parameters to measure the degree of integration of the colonized subject within First World socio-cultural structures. Language has been an issue largely addressed in postcolonial theory, but it still generates numerous debates in relation to the effects that imperialism had over native linguistic use. For critics like Ngugi Wa Thiong'o, language is not and cannot be only a mechanism of communication for it is the verbal realization of the cultural legacy of a country. The appropriation and systematic annihilation of native linguistic expressions and the imposition of the colonial language is the first step towards a complete de-familiarization of the colonized individuals with respect to their own values. Once this is accomplished, the language and literature of the colonizer take over in order to perpetuate the foundations of the imperial rule and also to erase any remaining trait of native consciousness.[6] As Ania Loomba says, "Language and literature are together implicated in constructing the binary of a European self and a non–European other, which, as Said's *Orientalism* suggested, is a part of the creation of colonial authority" (73). Language also becomes a moral dilemma since, although most colonized people are forced to speak in an alien tongue, some others struggle to preserve their own. Wa Thiong'o remembers how, in his childhood, English was established as Nigeria's official language, thus marginalizing any other dialectal or autochthonous varieties. Once he decided to follow a career as full-time writer, he was always set before the crossroads of using English — then safeguarding the circulation of his works and his economic stability — or writing in his own mother tongue, which he considered a better option to express his feelings and emotions (438).

The influence of language in postcolonial terms is exemplified in Barnes's *Lion's Blood* when, coinciding with the arrival and settlement of European slaves in Bilalistanian territories, Aidan is faced with the reality of having to speak in a language that is completely alien to him. His first reaction is to stand up against this coercion by speaking Gaelic and not Arabic as it is sanctioned by the authorities: "Luckily, most slaves in the village were from Eire, and spoke the same tongue. He had heard that this was unusual, that on most farms and land holdings they were mixed from over the Isle and the Far Lands as well, forced out of their languages and customs and made to accept those of their new masters. He would not." (114). Only in such an alternate scenario can major languages be rejected and even prosecuted. Aidan's initial bravado is soon chastened by his more experienced and tempered mother, who forces her son to learn the master tongue for his own good: "'We are in this land now,' she said, then lapsing into Irish, continued.... *It is vital to learn and practice these new customs.* 'The words don't fit in my mouth,' he protested.... *As you make mistakes, you will learn.* Then as though angry with herself for lapsing into his native tongue, she stumbled through her Arabic sentences. 'Aidan, *la tayyib*. Not good. Learn to speak. Practice to speak" (117). The overt sense of dislocation and displacement manifested by Aidan in these passages is the direct consequence of forced immigration and the cultural clash that ensues it, which places him in a frustrating "no-man's land" of uncertainties and doubts. In *Zulu Heart*, Aidan's wife Sophia also reminds him of the place where they are living and of their need to adjust to the conventions of the country, including language.[7]

As a response to this blatant exclusion, Barnes aims to parody some of the icons in European, mainstream culture, in the same way as African or Asian referents were ignored. For a white reader, this results in a jocular undertone for nobody has ever dared to question the pre-eminence of such crucial personalities as Wolfang Amadeus Mozart or Leonardo da Vinci: "'Our composer Al-Hadiz wrote a recent piece building upon a white composer named ...' Abu Ali squinted. 'Amadeus. Mozart, I think. Wrote some perfectly respectable songs eighty years ago or so. Found patronage in Alexandria, I believe'" (*Lion's* 232). The fact of not even remembering the name and the reference to the supposed patronage Mozart found in Alexandria are Barnes's playful literary vengeance articulated within the framework of alternate history, a realm in which he manages to mock the prestige of these figures and the way this has been internalized in the white, European conscience. Even more comic is this allusion to Leonardo da Vinci in *Lion's Blood*:

> And this diagram was, unquestionably, a painstaking copy of the original, designed by a mad Frank named Da Vinci in about 700. Da Vinci possessed a genius unknown to others of his kind and found patronage with the royal house of Abyssinia. Even in the darkness of Europe, Allah had birthed a spark of light. Although genius or no, the idiot had killed himself testing some manner of flying machine off the top of Khufu's pyramid. Pigbellies [272].

In this passage, da Vinci is addressed as a pigbelly, the pejorative way of referring to the white people populating Bilalistan. The quasi-anonymous identity of such a symbol in universal culture as da Vinci is sent into oblivion and considered an "idiot" for his attempts to invent those eccentric flying machines.

If language plays out a determinant role in the consolidation of an imperial power, religion also formed part of the colonial agenda as an indispensable tool for the domination of native populations. The religious question is recurrent in both *Lion's Blood* and *Zulu Heart*, becoming an element that reveals the in-betweenness many characters experiment. The clash between Christian and Muslim doctrines is latent throughout Barnes's narrations and emerges as one of the origins of the epistemological confrontation between members of the two groups. In fact, colonization was initially seen as part of a religious enterprise undertaken to civilize the indigenous savages and to do away with their primitive beliefs. It was precisely the assumption that native religions were nothing but mischievous voodoo and hoodoo practices and sorcery that had to be urgently extirpated that impelled many European explorers and colonialist advocates to adopt a quasi-missionary guise. The need to erase local religious expressions sought to preserve the ideological supremacy of the colonizer so that it could not be contested through these divergent creeds or faiths. This explains why the conversion of "pagan" slaves into "good Christians" was so important for the Empire, a fact that Barnes brilliantly reverses in his novels. In this case, blacks are no longer seen as witches or shamans, since it is white slaves that deviate from the accepted norm: "Those who worshipped trees or the sky or the spirits of their ancestors were forced to renounce their pagan beliefs at the edge of a sword" (*Lion's* 153). Religious freedom was severely penalized in colonized territories and the practice of the native's doctrine was considered heretical.

The suppression of language, literature and religion as potential causes of insurrection among the colonized population resulted, as stated before, in the disappearance of its identity. The negation of these socio-cultural distinctive traits led to a progressive objectification of the individual, who became a mere good that could be purchased, traded or sold according to the desire of the master/owner. In the novels, this objectification is achieved by means of animalizing slaves, who are placed at the level of horses or cows, and also by turning them into sexual objects, always at the disposal of the master's uncontrollable appetites. Ania Loomba, paraphrasing the words of Aime Césaire, points out that colonialism not only exploits but also buries the very essence of the human condition, turning the colonized into a mere puppet (22). Black slaves were assigned the most humiliating tasks under the assumption that work was edifying and beneficial for them. It was believed that the native was a lazy and worthless brute who needed punishment to be reformed and reinserted in society as a docile and brainwashed individual. As Wakil Abu Ali asserts, this idea was legitimized by the very institution of slavery: "Ali seemed doubtful. 'But you allow our slaves to be beaten,' he said. 'Only to correct them, that they might serve us better, and in serving us, serve Allah as well'" (*Lion's* 237). The use of religion to justify the necessity of indoctrinating free people was a crucial foundation for imperialism, which, in a sense, hid its atrocities behind a veil of apparent sanctity.

Even more painful than this dehumanization of slaves was the deprecating treatment that native women received from the exploratory squads that were sent out to Africa. Under the influence exerted by Darwin's evolutionary theories and Ruskin's polemical writings, colonial administrators took for granted that black or oriental women were sexually insatiable creatures and that this entitled them to rape those women in the same way as they plundered lands. Related to this question, Kadiatu Kanneh believes that this false and manipulative preconception derived from "a network of European knowledge systems, which Fanon identifies as: 'written accounts, photographic records, motions pictures'; and the gaze of 'the tourist and foreigner'" (346). The metaphor of the overseas lands being "penetrated" was also significantly associated with the massive rapes that were committed and which reinforced the violent treatment of women. The land and the female body, thus, were seen as open to possession, exhaustion and abandonment, reinforcing this objectifying approach.

Zulu Heart presents an ironic debasement of this derogatory image of native women since Barnes decides to present Aidan, a white man, as the sexual goal of Nefriti, the Caliph's whimsical wife. It is important to remark on the idea that Aidan is a white man because Barnes seeks to debunk the image of native women as objects. At this moment, it is Aidan who becomes objectified and treated as a voiceless slave who must yield to the commands of the master: "'You seemed so courageous in the arena,' said the Calipha. 'Even in defeat. Do not tell me that your courage fails now, when I need it most'.... The Calipha opened the sheet the rest of the way. She was extraordinary, and utterly alien to him. She was taller, leaner than Sophia, but her breasts were full and heavy, the nipples a deep and luscious cocoa" (363). Nefriti assumes the rights to gain Aidan's sexual favors because she contemplates him and, generally the entire slave class, as primeval creatures simply guided by their primary instincts: "'They say that you whites are closer to nature, closer to the beast. That you privy to secrets that civilized man forgot when he began to build cities. What say you to this'" (367). If in traditional colonialist accounts, native people were often regarded as "natural," "bestial" and mysterious creatures, Barnes's alternate narrative allows him to revoke this long-standing stereotype repeatedly included in canonical historical registers to associate it with a white man.

To finish with, although *Lion's Blood* and *Zulu Heart* explore all those questions that motivated the outburst of slavery and the barriers that separated races due to ideological, religious or linguistic misconceptions, these two novels also celebrate interracial friendship, as the almost fraternal relationship between Aidan and Kai demonstrates. The spirit of the two novels, in spite of the huge gaps Barnes describes, ends up being conciliatory and claims for a mutual respect and comprehension between races. The friendship between Kai, Wakil of Dar Kush, and Aidan, a slave who becomes his closest confidant and comrade-in-arms in the battlefield, go through periods of mutual devotion with moments of disloyalty and distrust, although they are always under the suspicion of members of both groups. Aidan's proximity and involvement with the symbol of tyranny is recriminated by some of his fellow-mates, who believe that he is a traitor: "'So, Aidan. Been oot a' night with the young master, have ye?' He blocked Aidan's path. Aidan locked eyes with him, a challenge. 'And if I have?' ... 'Nothing, nothing. Except despoilin' our womanfolk. Do ye sleep easy, Aidan'" (*Lion's* 208–209). Crossing the borders and being caught in this liminal in-betweeness drags Aidan into the very complex position of helping Kai out and at the same time perpetuating the constraints exerted upon his own community.

Aidan's faithfulness to Kai even leads him to voluntarily renounce the freedom granted by the Wakil after participating in the battle against the Aztecs to embark in a secret mission of espionage. On the other side, Kai challenges and duels his mighty uncle Malik for the unconditional release of Aidan's wife Sophia, even to the extent of sacrificing his honorable position as Wakil: "'By right of arms, by all that is holy, I say that this man [Aidan] and his family are under my protection'.... 'This is my house,' Malik said. 'I will not release her'.... 'Then I must proclaim myself Aidan's champion,' he heard himself say" (*Lion's* 568). Malik's defeat at the hands of his nephew marks a turning point in the relationship between Aidan and Kai, whose desire to liberate his friend and his family stands firmly against all the ideological pillars of his world. Kai's last words to Aidan in *Zulu Heart* reflect the optimistic tone with which Barnes puts an end to these epic stories: "'Farewell, my brother,' Kai said. 'Thank you so much, for everything. For every day you have been in my life, even before I knew who you were. 'I won't say it's always been a pleasure,' Aidan said. 'But it's always been ... extraordinary'" (459).

The success of alternate history resides in the author's intention to explore a world as it would/should have been, something Barnes seems to be pointing at through Kai's all-embracing words. *Lion's Blood* and *Zulu Heart* must not only be taken as key examples within the genre of postcolonial alternate history, but also as powerful indictments upon the excesses committed by colonialism. Throughout these pages, my attempt has been to dissect the way Barnes manages to reconstruct an alternative scenario in which he lays bare the incongruities underlying slavery, racism and exclusion due to racial differences, while proposing a context in which these gaps are eventually bridged and dissolved. These two novels prove the extent to which alternate history can re-examine some of the truths long accepted and question the veracity of the historical discipline itself.

Notes

1. In this respect, Hutcheon argues, "Knowing the past becomes a question of representing, that is, of constructing and interpreting, not of objective recording" (1989: 74).
2. In this respect, Gavriel D. Rosenfeld argues that "the postmodern movement's general valorization of 'the other' and its attempt to resurrect suppressed or alternate voices dovetails with alternate history's promotion of unconventional views of the past" (2005: 7).
3. Karen Hellekson reinforces this idea: "Alternate histories question the nature of history and of causality; they question accepted notions of time and space; they rupture linear movements; and they make readers rethink their world and how it has become what it has" (2000: 255).
4. These stories take place in the 19th century, when colonialism reached its heyday, especially during Queen Victoria's reign in Great Britain.
5. Transatlantic slavery has been a recurrent object of study among postcolonial scholars, since it symbolically becomes a "point of no return" for all those African people that were dragged into the slave market. For further references, see Barnor Hesse's interesting study "Forgotten Like a Bad Dream: Atlantic Slavery and the Ethics of Postcolonial Memory" (2002).
6. Related to this idea, Braj B. Kachru suggests that "the English language is a tool of power, domination and elitist identity, and of communication across continents.... English has become an integral part of this new complex sociolinguistic setting. The colonial Englishes were essentially acquired and used as non-native second languages, and after more than two centuries, they continue to have the same status" (1995: 291).
7. Sophia eloquently explains her position in relation to the linguistic complexities referred to above: "'Yes,' Sophia said. 'To hell with them. But with us, too. I didn't want this world, but it's the one I live in. And my children, or my children's children, are going to have their chance to benefit by my sweat and blood. If you can't speak Arabic, if you don't understand the men who rule this land, you'll never get your piece of it" (2003: 60).

Works Cited

Alkon, Paul. "Alternate History and Postmodern Temporality." *Time, Literature and the Arts: Essays in Honor of Samuel L. Macy.* Victoria: University of Victoria Press, 1994. 65–85.

Ashcroft, Bill. *On Postcolonial Futures: Transformations of Colonial Culture*. London and New York: Continuum, 2001.
Ashe, Bertram D. "'Why don't he Like My Hair?': Constructing African-American Standards of Beauty in Toni Morrison's *Song of Solomon* and Zora Neale Hurston's *Their Eyes were Watching God*." *African American Review* 29.4 (1995): 579–92.
Barnes, Steven. *Lion's Blood*. New York: Aspect/Warner, 2002.
_____. *Zulu Heart*. New York: Aspect/Warner, 2003.
Hadesty, William H. "Towards a Theory of Alternate History: Some Versions of Alternate Nazis." *Classic and Iconoclastic Alternate History Science Fiction*. Lewiston, NY: Lampeter: Mellen Press, 2003. 71–92.
Hellekson, Karen. "Toward a Taxonomy of the Alternate History Genre." *Extrapolation* 41.3 (2000): 248–56.
Hesse, Barnor. "Forgotten Like a Bad Dream: Atlantic Slavery and the Ethics of Postcolonial Memory." *Relocating Postcolonialism*. Eds David Theo Goldberg and Ato Quayson. Oxford: Blackwell, 2002. 143–73.
Hutcheon, Linda. *A Poetics of Postmodernism: History, Theory, Fiction*. London and New York: Routledge, 1988.
_____. *The Politics of Postmodernism*. London and New York: Routledge, 1989.
Kachru, Braj B. "The Alchemy of English." *The Post-colonial Studies Reader*. Eds. Bill Ashcroft, Gareth Griffiths, and Helen Tiffin. London and New York: Routledge, 1995. 291–95.
Kanneh, Kadiatu. "The Difficult Politics of Wigs and Veils: Feminism and the Colonial Body." *The Post-colonial Studies Reader*. Eds. Bill Ashcroft, Gareth Griffiths, and Helen Tiffin. London and New York: Routledge, 1995. 346–48.
Loomba, Ania. *Colonialism/Postcolonialism*. London: Routledge, 1998.
MacLeod, John. *Beginning Postcolonialism*. Manchester and New York:Manchester University Press, 2000.
Memmi, Albert. *The Colonizer and the Colonized*. New York: The Orion Press, 1965.
Rosenfeld, Gavriel D. *The World Hitler Never Made*. Cambridge: Cambridge University Press, 2005.
Suvin, Darko. "Victorian Science Fiction, 1871–85: The Rise of the Alternative History Sub-Genre." *Science Fiction Studies* 10.2 (1983): 148–69.
Thiongo, Ngugi wa. "The Language of African Literature." *Colonial Discourse and Post-Colonial Theory: A Reader*. Eds. Patrick Williams and Laura Chrisman. New York: Columbia University Press, 1994. 435–55.

3

The Calcutta Chromosome
A Novel of Silence, Slippage and Subversion

Suparno Banerjee

Amitav Ghosh's *The Calcutta Chromosome* (1996) challenges the notion of Western science, tries to foreground the silent subaltern "stories" of the marginalized people and in the process sets the conventions of science fiction into play. Ghosh rewrites the history of Ronald Ross's discovery of the malaria vector by exploiting its "slippages," reorients the reader's epistemological reference by placing silence and secrecy as vehicles of knowledge and power, and distorts the genre of science fiction by bringing in the elements of the supernatural. This postcolonial science fiction challenges the hegemony of the West by questioning the basic assumptions of Western knowledge, and thus making a very strong statement of nonconformity. Yet, the importance and the success of indigenous knowledge and tradition in this book are intertwined with foreign interventions, and vice versa. The alternative epistemology that this book presents is subaltern knowledge — knowledge possessed by the social outcasts and practiced in secret, knowledge that is never acknowledged as such — not the great ancient Vedic tradition. Thus *The Calcutta Chromosome* not only subverts Western normativity by empowering a native secret cult with their practice of counter science, but it also subverts the established Brahminical knowledge represented by the indigenous elite class. In doing so the novel also ends up endorsing hybridity in all forms — epistemological, philosophical, and physical.

Amitav Ghosh exploits the science fiction genre in order to foreground the binaries that mark colonial discourse and in subtle ways reorients the manner in which these binaries are conceived. However, unlike using the genre in the manner of feminist science fiction authors, who undermine the male-capitalist world order,[1] Ghosh exploits the silence ascribed to the subaltern in the colonial discourse to hold out an alternative order of things; an order that exists despite the deletion, or, in fact, as the book shows, because of the deletion. Thus, he addresses the question of the subaltern's access to power raised by the postcolonial scholar Gayatri Chakravorty Spivak. His central thesis of the book becomes: power of the subaltern rests in silence and secrecy.

Ghosh employs a Derridean approach to expose the binaries of power, where the first term is dominant in the "normative" colonial discourse — white/black, European/Indian, West/East, reason/faith, science/counter-science, male/female, utterance/silence, evidence/belief. These binaries work as devices of domination of the Others for the white, European, colonial, male order. Donna Haraway uses a similar approach in "A Manifesto for Cyborgs" to claim that in the fragmentary postmodern existence the myth of an organic wholeness, to which these dualisms lead to, is inapplicable. She explains that such myths are social constructs, as are the social identities of human beings. She deconstructs such myths by marking them as devices of domination used by the patriarchal, Christian and by extension capitalist society. She points out that marginalized entities should operate on the principle of affinity rather than on some essential identity.[2]

This center/margin dichotomy informs the central focus of *The Calcutta Chromosome*. The novel deals with a host of peripheral groups — refugees, immigrants, natives of colonial India, people from lower caste, spiritualists, and women. But rather than positing them as Harawyan cyborg entities, Amitav Ghosh presents them as subaltern entities that exist in a parallel world alternate to the dominant colonial and imperial principles of the West. He deliberately sets these peripheries up against the dominant center to demonstrate their apparent vulnerability. But, in *The Calcutta Chromosome* these marginalities thrive by the very exclusiveness of their existence. Their lack of presence in the colonial discourse is essential to their existence. In this context Gayatri Chakravorty Spivak's question, "Can the subaltern speak?" becomes pertinent.

In her 1988 essay "Can the Subaltern Speak?" Gayatri Chakravorty Spivak raised the issue of the subaltern's access to voice in the colonialist/imperialist power structure. And her answer to the problem was negative. Though in the later revisions of the essay that stance changes into something more optimistic, her main concern that even the best of the intentions can end up having an adverse effect in articulating the unheard voices remains true. She cites the example of "the white man's burden": the well intentioned colonizer with a mission to "civilize" the darkest corners of the world ends up as the oppressor. Spivak brings in Foucault's concept of "epistemic violence" to support her doubts about the feasibility of a discourse that would allow the subaltern to speak. She quotes Foucault in arguing that this "epistemic violence" ends up privileging the imperial narrative as the "normative one":

> Perhaps it is no more than to ask that the subtext of the palimpsestic narrative of imperialism be recognized as "subjugated knowledge," "a whole set of knowledges that have been disqualified as inadequate to their task or insufficiently elaborated: naïve knowledges, located low down on the hierarchy, beneath the required level of cognition or scientificity" [2197].

This colonial/imperial discourse is constantly being challenged by postcolonial scholars, especially by the Subaltern Studies Group led by Ranajit Guha. According to Spivak they are working not to give the subaltern a voice, but to clear out a space from where the subaltern can speak. But, Spivak is also more bent on exploring the possibilities of uttering the heterogeneity of the colonized subject than the Gramscian interpretation of the term would normally allow. She, however, recognizes the ambiguous relationship in which the subaltern stands to power: at once subordinate and dissenting, outside the ideational act of the colonial discourse as well as outside the scope of colonial language. In other words, silence and invisibility are the two preconditions for the existence of the subaltern; thus the subaltern cannot speak, or can do so only in an indirect manner.

In *The Calcutta Chromosome* Ghosh uses silence and invisibility as the weapons/instruments through which he deconstructs the colonial "normative" narrative of the "enlightened" Europeans. The colonial narrative that *The Calcutta Chromosome* follows is Ronald Ross's discovery of the malaria parasite.[3] Ross's discovery is one of the pillars of colonial scientific discourse. It is a discourse that at once asserts the supremacy of science as well as the supremacy of the white man against the unyielding colonial space. The epigraph of the book, which is a poem written by Ross on his finding the malaria parasite, foregrounds this supremacy:

> This day relenting God
> Hath placed within my hand
> A wondrous thing; and God
> Be Praised. At His Command,
>
> Seeking His Secret deeds
> With tears and toiling breath,
> I find thy cunning seeds,
> O million-murdering Death.

Ross attributes the discovery to *his* "toil" and God's "command" and grace. This draws a clear battle line between the white man and the "million-murdering death" which the white man must fight with the aid of *his* God in order to carry out his "burden" of "civilizing" the ignorant natives, to bring to them the light of science and reason. Any reference to the colonized space, where this battle takes place, has been written out, or at least any positive agency has been taken away from it. Ross's obsession with the sole authority over his discovery can also be seen in his *Memoirs* (1923) published twenty years after he received the Nobel Prize for medicine in 1902. The only history that we have of his research is written by Ross himself. Claire Chambers in her essay "Postcolonial Science Fiction: Amitav Ghosh's *The Calcutta Chromosome*" mentions that Ross's *Memoirs* is highly selective and he tries to exercise full control over the "history" of his experiment. As Murugan claims, Ross "wants everyone to know the story like he's going to tell it" (52). Chambers also cites Ross' biographers Edwin R. Nye and Mary E. Gibson to support her claim of the dubiousness of the *Memoirs*.[4]

In *The Calcutta Chromosome* Ghosh draws liberally from Ross' *Memoirs*, but he uses it to find slippages that lend themselves to the re-inscription of the history that Ross tried so hard to control. The process of deconstruction starts off with identifying Ross's native assistant, Lutchman, as the subaltern who has been silenced totally in Ross's account of the malaria discovery. Chambers points out that in his memoir Ross talks about Lutchman only in passing; he is never shown as having any influence in the outcome of Ross's research; at least there is no "evidence" of that. However, Murugan claims in the novel that the very lack of evidence is the kind of proof that can discredit the history written down by Ross: "secrecy is what this is all about: it figures there wouldn't be any evidence or proof" (104). As we trace down Lutchman's story we find Mangala, the native woman, working as a sweeper at Cunningham's laboratory in Calcutta. She also turns out to be the leader of the subaltern group that is searching for immortality by using the malaria parasite as a medium of conveying human personality traits. The progress from authority to subalternity is clearly marked, and what lies in the margins of or excluded from the colonial history reclaims the center in the postcolonial fiction. This reclamation is subtle and silent; visible only to the discerning eye. Ghosh plays on the binaries of the text and flips them over. Control gives way to chaos; written history gives way to rumor; and at the heart of the story a British colonial scientist's research leads to the syphilitic native woman's search for immortality. But this flipping over is not a sudden empowerment of the subjugated half within the same structure of knowledge; in *The Calcutta Chromosome* the reader is epistemologically reoriented. Murugan explains to Antar the mode of operation of the secret sect behind Ross's discovery:

> You all know matter and antimatter, right? And rooms and anterooms and Christ and Antichrist and so on? Now, let's say there was something like science and

counter-science. Thinking of it in the abstract, wouldn't you say that the first principle of a functioning counter-science would have to be secrecy? [...] It would have to use secrecy as a technique or procedure. It would in principle have to refuse all direct communication, straight off the bat, because to communicate, to put ideas into language, would be to establish a claim to *know*— which is the first thing that a counter-science would dispute [105].

This claim against knowledge is not exactly a claim to ignorance. Rather it is a refusal to communicate the knowledge in the conventional manner. Spivak mentions in her essay that speaking is an act involving two components — verbal and auditory. Absence of a listener forecloses the possibility of the act of speaking. The subaltern's location outside the capitalist colonial/imperial discourse prevents its speaking, hence preventing it from any direct act of communication. In *The Calcutta Chromosome* the subaltern disclaims knowledge in the sense that this knowledge is not "knowledge" in the conventional normative discourse. The colonizer by definition is excluded from this knowledge, because the subaltern is a subject position that the colonizer can never assume.

In the novel Ross works on the malaria project without any suspicion of the existence of a secret observer. However, Murugan is certain that a secret group of natives have guided Ross in his efforts at every step, without him ever knowing. In fact, Ross is embedded too much in the colonial ideology to be able to listen to the whispering voices around him. Grigson, the linguist who comes to visit Ross's first laboratory in Secunderabad, pays attention to the language of the natives, despite belonging to the same ideological position as Ross. He immediately discerns an air of mystery surrounding Ross's laboratory. But Grigson is scared away from his investigations by Lutchman: he takes Grigson for a ghostly chase along the railway tracks at night, in which Grigson almost gets killed. Cunningham, the doctor in whose Calcutta laboratory Ross ultimately comes to work, is also blind to the subversive activities that take place around him. However, as his presence becomes an impediment to the furthering of the subaltern "knowledge," he is made to flee Calcutta by methods inexplicable to the rational mind. Elijah Farley is the only white man who sees the procedure through which Mangala (the leader of the cult of silence and a figure much like a demigoddess, who lives an immortal life through different incarnations) performs her rituals and discovers the extent of the subaltern "knowledge." However, his threat to violate the cult's silence and secret knowledge leads to his disappearance and possible death at Renupur. Countess Pongracz, the Hungarian psychic who later becomes an archaeologist, recorded the supernatural occurrences with C. C. Dunn (probably Cunningham in disguise), which revealed the power of the cult of silence. She too disappears while looking for the shrine of silence in Egypt.

Even Murugan, who tries to grasp this non–Western mode of counter-scientific knowledge through a Western scientific methodology of gathering of evidences (or non-evidences), ends up in the asylum — lost for all practical purposes to the corporate house that employed him. Phulboni, the famous Bengali writer who had a brush with this cult of silence in his youth, also plays a similar role trying to "know" the secret that eludes him throughout his life. He begs to the Mistress of Silence (most likely Mangala) to accept him in her folds (much like Murugan does towards the end of the story): "I beg you, I beg you, if you exist at all, and I have never for a moment doubted it — give me a sign of your presence, do not forget me, take me with you [...]" (125). It seems that not only are the colonizers excluded from this silence but also any voice that can utter the secret into words.

However, it is also important to note that for this counter-science group, to know something is to initiate change about that very thing.[5] As Murugan puts it: "[...] just suppose you believed that to know something is to change it, it would follow, wouldn't it, that to make something known would be one way of effecting a change? Or creating a mutation, if you like" (217). But this act of knowing must be performed not in the manner of direct communication but through real acts of discovery by the completely unaware subject — like Ross, like Urmila, like Antar. The inscrutability of the lack of knowledge must be present all the time for the person who must perform the act of knowing for the change or mutation to take place. Murugan first explains to Urmila, the young woman who along with her mentor Sonali helps Murugan in his investigation about the cult of silence and who at the end of the book becomes Mangala's latest incarnation:

> Fact is we're dealing with a crowd for whom silence is a religion. We don't even know what we don't know. We don't know who's in this and who's not [...]. We don't know how many of the threads they want us to pull together and how many they want to keep hanging for whoever comes next [218].

Later talking about the Mistress of Silence he further reveals:

> She wants to be the mind that sets things in motion. The way she sees it, we can't ever know her, or her motives, or anything else about her: the experiment won't work unless the reasons for it are utterly inscrutable to us, as unknowable as a disease. But at the same time she's got to try and tell us about her own history: that's part of the experiment too [253].

However, this experiment of "telling her own history" is unlike Ross's version of the history. Her history can only be told through patches, through scraps of stories, through folklores, through subtle hints left for the attentive observer to pick up, through rumors, and through the unrecorded memory of the subaltern.

Ghosh pits the two very unlikely parallel stories against each other. On the one hand there is Ross's version of the history of the malaria experiment asserting its authenticity through recorded evidence, silencing any competing voice. On the other hand is Mangala's story; constantly mystifying even its own reality; silencing any voice that exposes or threatens to expose its existence. One protagonist is a colonial British military officer and a renowned scientist. The other is not only a native but also a woman belonging to the lowest social stratum. What they have in common is Lutchman or Laakhan. He acts as assistant to both of them: first to Mangala and then to Ross. In fact whatever trace is left of this "other experiment" in Ross's narrative is the mention of Lutchman. We don't have any mention of Mangala anywhere in the factual history except in Farley's uncataloged letter to Manson, which mysteriously disappears from the library when Murugan tries to photocopy it. The vestiges of Mangala's presence, or rather Mangala-Bibi's (that's how she's known to her initiates) presence, can be found only in the rituals and secret practices of the people who don't have any voice in the world of power—neither in colonial India, nor in the free country. Her history is communicated indirectly, as Phulboni puts it: "I see signs of her presence everywhere I go, in images, words, glances, but only signs, nothing more [...]." (124). In fact the hybrid Murugan and Phulboni acts as the mediums through which the Mistress of Silence "speaks" her history. But her purpose remains beyond the ken of both the mediums. This inscrutability presents its final face at the end of the novel, when Antar, the Egyptian immigrant in New York, who is also probably the only survivor of a malaria epidemic in the small Egyptian hamlet that Countess Pongracz was searching for at the time of her disappearance, discovers the existence of the cult and simultaneously he is also "discovered" by the cult as the new subject for reincarnation. However, it remains a mystery if he is the person chosen for "interpersonal transference" or if he is the receiver for someone else's "Calcutta Chromosome."

It can be argued, though, that Phulboni, Murugan, and Antar, even Farley, are in a certain sense subaltern—subaltern cannot be heard even if it speaks. Nobody can really hear what these characters have to say. The transplantation of the whole cult to New York, the metropolitan space, from the post-colonial space, India, also suggests an interrogation of subaltern identity formation. The new subaltern does not belong only to a colonizer/colonized relationship, but to the invisible power of the new corporate empires, where Antar loses his job and is monitored by a computer. The transference of the location of the metropolis from England to America too hints at a new world order and new power relations in imperial politics and, in a way, re-inscribes the notion of the normative power structure. Murugan's metamorphoses from the employee of an multinational organization, sending papers to scientific journals, to an inmate of an asylum, telling delirious stories is also a transformation into subalternity. The Western world is deaf to his voice. Only Antar can hear him, because his transformation is soon to be completed. Conversely, one can argue that Mangala and Lutchman in a certain sense transcend subalternity by having access to power over others, which the Spivakian subaltern cannot posses. But here Ghosh moves away from Spivak by positing that the very conditions that apparently make the subaltern vulnerable hide its source of power. This is a completely different notion of power that debunks the conventional model and begs the reader to ask where power really lies.

Similar questions are asked in other postcolonial science fictions like Nishi Shawl's "Deep End," Andrea Hairston's "Griots of the Galaxy," and especially in Ven Begamudré's "Out of Sync" (all anthologized in *So Long Been Dreaming: An Anthology of Postcolonial Science Fiction and Fantasy* by Nalo Hopkinson and Uppinder Mehan in 2004). "Out of Sync" like *The Calcutta Chromosome* creates a discourse of subalternity and silence in a off-world human settlement, where the colonizing humans are constantly threatened by the inscrutability of the subjugated natives of the planets, the "Khonds," or their ancestors, the "Ah-Devasis" ("ahdivasi" means native in Sanskrit and Hindi). Though the text ultimately suggests a contact between the two races through the hybrid race "Demi" (half human half Khond), the constant presence of some unutterable power, which resides outside the discourse of colonialism, permeates the story till the end.

Furthermore, *The Calcutta Chromosome* also questions the conventional power structure in the aspect that it shows power relations as fluid. Subalternity is ascribed to the historically marginalized groups as well as to Europeans and people from educated classes. This not only destabilizes the conventional binaries of power, but also points towards an endorsement of hybridity— hybrid identities sharing different subject positions as well as physical characteristics. This hybridity is something that also corresponds to the generic hybridity of the novel.

The inscrutability of purpose and the inexplicability of the processes that pushes the novel towards its climax are central to its resistance to any effort to categorize it under any simple genre heading. Commentators like Claire Chambers, Diane Nelson, and Suchitra Mathur put it under the heading of "postcolonial science fiction." But all of them seem to agree that Ghosh twists the convention of science fiction. Mathur, in her excellent essay "Caught between the Goddess and the Cyborg," focuses on Ghosh's treatment of women as subaltern subjects. She goes on to show that what Ghosh presents here is a combination of the science fiction and supernatural — and the subaltern subject here becomes a hybrid of the Harawayan cyborg and the goddess, which she describes as:

> a mode of being that combines the artificial with the natural *and* the supernatural, that thus posits a "third" identity for third-world (women) natives which combines the past with the future, the innocence of the organic with the knowledge of the technological. Symbolically, this is represented by combining, in Mangala's experiments, blood imagery with technology. The shedding of blood, an image that is associated not just with ritual sacrifice, but also with women and fertility, is as necessary as the "scientific" knowledge of malaria in its myriad manifestations to enable the project of overcoming death [135].

This very apt summation of Mangala's methodology points towards a scientific discourse; this is a major factor of considering the novel as a work of science fiction. On the other hand, Bishnupriya Ghosh in her essay "On Grafting the Vernacular: The Consequences of Postcolonial Spectrology," brings up the issue of the ghost stories that may put the novel in line with the native tradition of supernatural tales.

However, combining the scientific with the supernatural has been a characteristic of Indian postcolonial science fiction. Most notable in this regard is Satyajit Ray's Professor Shanku stories (1965-1992). Shanku, the world famous Bengali scientist and inventor, regularly delves into myths, legends, and folklores in the process of his scientific discoveries and adventures and more than often attributes his major inventions to native traditional resources. Shanku often takes the supernatural and tries to analyze that from a scientific point of view. Ray's fusion of Western scientific methodology with the supernatural and alternative traditions of East in these short stories presents the postcolonial hybridity that is to become the trademark of postcolonial literature in general. But this is not the only instance of the coming together of the apparent opposites — the scientific and the supernatural. In Narayan Sanyal's 1976 novel *Nakshatryaloker Devatma* (The Gods of the Starry Heaven), and in the works of Shieshendu Mukhopadhyay.

Nonetheless, the most important point in *The Calcutta Chromosome* is that in the bringing together of the scientific and the supernatural elements, and also in subverting Western epistemology, it does not employ classical Hindu mythology or invoke traditional Vedic knowledge. Rather, the book also subverts established Indian epistemology. This is apparent not only in the fact that the techniques that the cult of silence uses is not associated with the Vedic traditions in any way, specifically in the matter that a woman performs the rituals, not a Brahmic priest. The rituals are more similar to the subjugated tribal cultures (or some may argue to Tantric practices). Furthermore, Phulboni's supernatural encounter at Renupur points towards a clash between indigenous caste structures. We are informed that the haunting at the railway station originates from a Brahmin station master's death on the railway tracks, in his effort to kill a lower caste boy. The hint that this boy becomes the semi-immortal Laakhan (or Lutchman) through the method of interpersonal transference, while the higher caste Brahmin perishes clearly indicates the book's rejection of the Brahminical tradition. The clay idol of Mangalabibi holding a scalpel and a microscope also tells of a non-traditional goddess. It is an entity that rises from the peripheral folk culture rather than from the main body of Hinduism. This not only hints towards an undermining of traditional Hinduism but also at an advocacy of hybridity in every form.

What Amitav Ghosh does in *The Calcutta Chromosome* is not only a bringing together of the scientific and the supernatural, but exploiting the supernatural, or the counter–scientific, to challenge the very notion of scientificity itself. He posits a totally alternative methodology of "knowing" or for that matter not knowing; he presents an alternative method of "explaining" nature of things, which is just the opposite of explanation — secrecy. However, the novel's defiance to the West is not limited to the challenging of the tenets of science and endowing the silent subaltern with power; neither is it limited to shifting the focus of the discourse to the margins and questioning the authenticity of the colonial "normative" narrative. In *The Calcutta Chromosome* Ghosh sets some of the basic tenets of the genre of science fiction itself into play. On the one hand the use of the genre of science fiction allows him to explore the postcolonial subjectification from a removed point of view. But, on the other hand the use of science fiction puts the novel firmly into the tradition of Western literature, because science fiction is a genre that developed specifically in the industrialized nations of Europe — it is primarily the literature of the developed countries.[6] The novel's transaction and vacillations between the country and the city, the metropolitan center and the third world periphery, however, subtly displaces the city centered notion of science fiction. And when we see science giving place to secret rituals this displacement becomes more glaring, especially if we look at science fiction as a literature of cognitive estrangement following Darko Suvin.

In *Metamorphoses of Science Fiction* Darko Suvin tries to define the genre in very definite terms:

> It [science fiction] should be defined as a fictional tale determined by the hegemonic literary device of a *locus* and/or *dramatis personae* that (1) are *radically or at least significantly different from empirical times, places, and characters* of "mimetic" or "naturalist" fiction, but (2) are nonetheless — to the extent that SF differs from other "fantastic" genres, that is, ensembles of fictional tales without empirical val-

idation — simultaneously perceived as *not impossible* within the cognitive (cosmological and anthropological) norms of the author's epoch [viii].

He goes on to say in Chapter One:

> SF is, then, a literary genre whose necessary and sufficient conditions are the presence and interaction of estrangement and cognition, and whose main formal device is an imaginative framework alternative to the author's empirical environment [7].

Applied to *The Calcutta Chromosome* some of these premises start to create slippages that open up alternative scopes of interpretation. The framing narrative time of the novel is situated in the near future New York, with Antar at its focus. All the futuristic gadgets and globalized economy that the novel presents were very much feasible during the author's own time frame yet are different from his empirical environment. Again the supernatural occurrences: Phulboni's story, the incident of the séance, as well as the rituals of interpersonal transference would be considered by a large section of the subaltern mass to be "not impossible"; yet these are alternatives to the daily reality of the author's time. But, again all those are narrated through a lens where fact and fiction lose their distinctions; in both Phulboni's and Murugan's stories there is no way that one can extricate reality from fiction. Moreover, there is no doubt that through its imaginative framework the novel forcibly creates an interaction between the estranging devices of the narrative and the reader's cognitive abilities. The novel's ability to reorient the reader's cognitive capacity lends the strange occurrences a peculiar logic of their own.

For Suvin, science in itself is not the most important thing in a science fiction. According to him the "hypothesis" from where science fiction takes off is not a scientific but a fictional one; it is the estranging device, much like the Russian Formalist Shklovsky's concept — to defamiliarize an object in order to draw attention to it. And from that point onwards the story is developed with a totalizing rigor, which is the "scientific" element. This estrangement acting as a formal framework allows the detached eye to focus on the tale's cognitive aspect — where the critical gaze is always fixed on the fundamental realities lying underneath the estranged surface. Thus, as Suvin says, science fiction "shares with the dominant literature of our civilization a mature approach analogous to that of modern science and philosophy, as well as the omnitemporal horizons of such an approach" (20–21). He also points out that unlike the other forms of "estranged" fictions (fantasy, folk tales, myths etc.) science fiction does not exist outside time.

It is needless to say that *The Calcutta Chromosome* defamiliarizes the whole situation to attract the reader's attention to the subaltern voice. The novel conforms to many of the components of Suvin's definition. The time line in *The Calcutta Chromosome* jumps forward and backwards — from 1995, when most of the action in Calcutta takes place, to the near future, when Antar investigates Murugan's disappearance, and then again to the colonial past of Ross's experiment. But nothing in the novel exists outside time. The trans-temporal existence of Mangala and Laakhan, which appears as the supernatural element, is also not really outside time. Rather it is very much located in specific temporal realities; hence the evolution of the subaltern — from the colonial subject, through the postcolonial periphery, to the secluded immigrant existence in the metropolis.

However, according to Suvin's definition the novel's association with ghost stories and folk elements may put it in the category of "other estranged fictions." This is the point where the author twists the convention of science fiction. He uses the "totalizing rigor" of science fiction to develop the themes of the supernatural and irrationality. His logical analysis of strange inexplicable occurrences and methodical research of an inscrutable purpose distort the genre from within. Although the novel delves into occult practices and counter-scientific activities, it follows their development through a theoretical point of view. It proposes certain postulates and then follows them through, which creates the "cognition effect." Murugan proposes:

> Not making sense is what it's about — conventional sense, that is. May be this other team started with the idea that knowledge is self contradictory; maybe they believed that to know something is to change it, therefore in knowing something, you've already changed what you think you know so you don't really know it at all: you only know its history. Maybe they thought that knowledge couldn't begin without acknowledging the impossibility of knowledge [105].

The book follows this through with its inscrutable logic and subtle hints at the events that take place off stage. The reader is always left out of the main actions. Never is the reader actually shown how Laakhan and Mangala achieve immortality, or how the act of interpersonal transference takes place. Even when Sonali (who is also the promoter Romen Halder's mistress and Phulboni's secret daughter, and at the end of the story is identified by Antar as Maria, a probable host to someone else's personality) sees the ritual it is shrouded in the holy smoke of the burning fire. The novel spares the reader the tyranny of knowledge, and behind the hectic action of the book a silent line of logic brings the narrative towards its ambiguous end. This internal consistency of the plot logic is very science fictional, and, according to Campbell, sets this genre apart from fantasies.[7]

This generic hybridity again reinforces the novel's tendency towards nonconformity. Breaking down of rigid generic boundaries has been a mark of postmodern fiction in the West as well as postcolonial science fiction. In the works of China Mieville, Joanna Russ, Michael Moorcock, as well as Ursula K. Le Guin, the boundaries between fantasy and science fiction constantly collapse. The same can be said of postcolonial science fiction writers like Shirshendu Mukherjee, Vandana Singh, Eden Robinson, Sheree R. Thomas, and Nnedi Okrafor-Mbachu. In fact by anthologizing works by some of these postcolonial writers in *So Long Been Dreaming: An Anthology of Postcolonial Science Fiction and Fantasy* Nalo Hopkinson and Uppinder Mehan posit that generic hybridity is a mode of resistance regularly employed by postcolonial writers. By hybridizing its form *The Calcutta Chromosome* at once allies itself with Western as well as postcolonial modes of resistance. The hybridity that the bringing together of the opposite qualities of supernatural and science, logicality and irrationality, and silence and utterance engenders becomes the stylistic parallel of the thematic questioning of the normativity of Western logic and Western form of literature at the same time. This hybridity also works against privileged Indian traditions, thus placing the novel at the center of two sets of dialectics: Indian/Western and traditional/hybrid. As the subaltern cult preserves its unique identity through its silence and through the refusal to join the normative colonial discourse, the novel preserves its uniqueness by uttering the story preserved by that silence in a subversive form.

Notes

1. Marge Piercy's *Woman at the Edge of Time* and *He, She and It* are brilliant examples of this kind of resistance literature.
2. Donna Haraway in her "A Manifesto for Cyborgs: Science, Technology, and Socialist Feminism in the 1980s" uses a deconstructive approach to explain that certain dualisms have been intrinsic to Western civilization, which have been its logic and instrument of domination of the "Others"—self/other, mind/body, culture/nature, male/female, God/man, maker/made, reality/illusion, whole/part etc.—the first term always being the dominant one. She argues that modern high-tech culture puts these binaries into play:

> It is not clear who makes and who is made in relation between human and machine. It is not clear what is mind and what body in machines that resolve into coding practices. Insofar as we know ourselves in both formal discourse [...] and in daily practice [...] we find ourselves cyborgs, hybrids, mosaics, chimeras. Biological organisms have become biotic systems, communications devices like others. There is no fundamental, ontological separation in our formal knowledge of machine and organism, of technical and organic [2296].

3. Sir Ronald Ross (1857–1932), an Anglo-Indian physician, received the Nobel Prize for medicine in 1902 for discovering the life cycle of the malaria parasite Plasmodium. During the final phase of his work he was in Kolkata (Calcutta).
4. On the matter of this controlling methodology of history Chambers says: "Ross tried to steer the course of his own posthumous reputation as a lone genius by keeping a tight control over those documents that would be preserved for posterity" (7). This is indicated in the following statement of his biographers, Edwin R. Nye and Mary E. Gibson:

One thing that stands out in assessing Ross's view of his own self worth was the fact that he kept everything. He kept letters sent to him, apart from family ones, and whenever he could he got back his own letters from people. He kept cuttings, telegrams, copies of articles and so on. The Ross Archives, distributed between London and Glasgow, comprise about 30,000 catalogued items, all of which he carefully saved for posterity [7].

Chambers further indicates that

> Ross's obsessive collection of documentary evidence about himself, and his choice of what would be retained and what omitted for posterity bears an uncanny resemblance to the novel's portrayal of the International Water Council, which keeps an astonishing amount of its own documentation and trivia in order to direct the way in which its history is interpreted, or as Ghosh puts it, "to load the dirt with their own meanings" [7].

5. In *In an Antique Land* (1992) Ghosh constructs a similar situation where the presence of the subaltern slave is traced through the narrative of his master. Interestingly this book too deals with the theme of an unexplored link between Egypt and India, the two ancient civilizations of the East, like *The Calcutta Chromosome*.

6. In the "Introduction" to *The Oxford Book of Science Fiction* Shippey writes:

> A revealing way of describing science fiction is to say that it is part of a literary mode which one may call 'fabril.' 'Fabril' is the opposite of 'pastoral.' But while 'the pastoral' is an established and much-discussed literary mode, recognized as such since early antiquity, its dark opposite has not yet been accepted, or even named, by the law-givers of literature. Yet the opposition is a clear one. Pastoral literature is rural, nostalgic, conservative. It idealizes the past and tends to convert complexities into simplicity; its central image is the shepherd. Fabril literature (of which science fiction is now by far the most prominent genre) is overwhelmingly urban, disruptive, future-oriented, eager for novelty; its central image is the 'faber,' the smith or blacksmith in older usage, but now extended in science fiction to mean the creator of artifacts in general — metallic, crystalline, genetic, or even social [ix].

7. Campbell writes in his "Introduction" to *Analog 6* (1966):

> The major distinction between fantasy and science fiction is, simply, that science fiction uses one, or a very, very few new postulates, and develops the rigidly consistent logical consequences of these limited postulates. Fantasy makes its rules as it goes along ... The basic nature of fantasy is "The only rule is, make up a new rule any time you need one!" The basic rule of science fiction is "Set up a basic proposition — then develop its consistent, logical consequences" [xv].

Works Cited

Campbell Jr., John W. "Introduction." *Analog 6*. New York: Garden City, 1966.
Chambers, Claire. "Postcolonial Science Fiction: Amitav Ghosh's *The Calcutta Chromosome*." *Journal of Commonwealth Literature* 38.1 (2003): 57–72.
Ghosh, Amitav. *Calcutta Chromosome: A Novel of Fevers, Delirium & Discovery*. 1995. New York: HarperCollins, 2001.
Ghosh, Bishnupriya. "On Grafting the Vernacular: The Consequences of Postcolonial Spectrology." *Boundary 2: An International Journal of Literature and Culture* 31.2 (2004): 197–218.
Haraway, Donna. "A Manifesto for Cyborgs: Science, Technology, and Socialist Feminism

in the 1980s." *The Norton Anthology of Theory and Criticism.* Ed. Vincent B. Leitch. New York: Norton, 2001. 2269–2299.

Mathur, Suchitra. "Caught between the Goddess and the Cyborg: Third-World Women and the Politics of Science in Three Works of Indian Science Fiction." *Journal of Commonwealth Literature* 39.3 (2004): 119–138.

Nelson, Diane M. "A Social Science Fiction of Fevers, Delirium and Discovery: The Calcutta Chromosome, the Colonial Laboratory, and the Postcolonial New Human." *Science Fiction Studies* 30.2 [90] (2003): 246–266.

Ray, Satyajit. *Shanku Samagra.* Kolkata: Ananda Publishers, 2003.

Sanyal, Narayan. *Nakshatraloker Devatma.* Kolkata: Mitra & Ghosh Publishers, 1976.

Shippey, T. A. "Introduction." *The Oxford Book of Science Fiction Stories.* Ed. T. A. Shippey. Oxford: Oxford University Press, 1993.

Spivak, Gayatri Chakravorty. "A Critique of Post Colonial Reason [Can the Subaltern Speak?]." 1988. *The Norton Anthology of Theory and Criticism.* Ed. Vincent B. Leitch. New York: Norton, 2001. 2197–2208.

Suvin, Darko. *Metamorphoses of Science Fiction: On the Poetics and History of a Literary Genre.* New Haven: Yale University Press, 1979.

4

Organization and the Continuum

History in Vandana Singh's "Delhi"

GRANT HAMILTON

The influential science fiction critic and theorist Darko Suvin once described science fiction as "a literary genre whose necessary and sufficient conditions are the presence and interaction of estrangement and cognition" (Suvin 8). It is a graceful formulation, the elegance of which lies in the nuances made possible by a literature understood purely in terms of its affective resonance of "estrangement" and "cognition." Indeed, it was the operation of this economy that framed H.G. Wells's own speculation about the nascent literary genre of science fiction. "The fantastic, the strange property or strange world," Wells writes in the preface to an anthology of his own works in 1933, "is only used to throw up and intensify our natural reactions of wonder, fear or perplexity" (cited in Kerslake 2). What both Wells and Suvin identify, then, is that estrangement and cognition are twinned in a process of noesis, a perception-thought that demands a certain kind of distance from its object of contemplation (the noema). In this arrangement, the thinking self, which experiences Wells's percepts of awe, fright and bewilderment, works to create a distance from that which is "other" to the self— the object of awe, the object of fear, or the object of bewilderment.

Of course, we have seen this conceptual formulation before — the distance forged between self and other. It is the abstract conceptual rendition begun in Hegel's master/slave dialectic, taken up in the existential philosophy of Sartre in *Being and Nothingness*, and returned to its condition of "mastery" by Jacques Lacan in his discussion of the development of the ego. However, it is also the uneasy political terrain upon which the imperium of European colonial discourse attempted to construe the differences it encountered as a simple negative image of itself. This, then, is the critical territory shared by both science fiction and postcolonial studies: the examination of the relationship between the distances of matters of expression that ultimately mark territories. For, it is the distance between the self and this "awful, frightful, and bewildering" world of the other that allows the self to organize itself as a site of opposition to that which it simply cannot incorporate into a dominant style of thought.

But what makes science fiction and postcolonial studies valuable to each other — what unites them — is the way in which both claim such critical territory in order to contest the imposed and perceived ontological and epistemological limits and boundaries brought about by these dominant styles of thought. For the genre of science fiction, this contestation takes place in its very form. As Patricia Kerslake writes, "Science fiction has historically been perceived as a genre of the fabulous, a form of writing far outside the canon of 'literature,' one that lacks boundaries, connections with reality or formal precedent" (Kerslake 1). Free from the obligation to recognize its literary genealogy and released from the fealty to render perceived reality, the science fiction novel wilfully transgresses the limitations and organization of boundaries that work to partition, and thereby, describe other literary genres.

Now, this radicalism or dynamism of science fiction — evidenced in its willful disrespect for any kind of state of limitation — is interesting in the context of its relationship to postcolonial studies, since it is the very legitimation of such genealogies that postcolonial studies takes as one of its major concerns. While Gayatri Chakravorty Spivak has spoken at length of the very specific kind of violence that was induced in indigenous communities through the European colonial project of cultural over-coding, key postcolonial theorists such as Ngugi wa Thiong'o, Dipesh Chakrabarty, and Stephen Muecke have written in various ways of the need to re-establish some sort of link with pre-colonial indigenous ontologies and epistemologies in order to legitimize contemporary local ways of thinking about, and existing as part of, the world — however problematic it may seem to be to do so. So, Ngugi has written of the need to re-establish the use of the Gikuyu language in certain areas of Kenya (*Decolonising the Mind*); Dipesh Chakrabarty has written of the need to re-establish links with local Indian narratives that do not necessarily fit in with the rationalist and modernising project of the Western discipline of history ("The Artifice of History"); and, Stephen Muecke has demonstrated the importance of Australian Aborigines re-connecting with Aboriginal place-specific philosophy (*Ancient & Modern*). In each account resistance to the version of reality constructed and imposed by European colonial discourse is found in recognizing and legitimizing indigenous — or local — ontologies and epistemologies through tracking the genealogy of such ideas into the past. As such, the representation of the past and, specifically, the way in which the representation of the past has been dominated by the Western practice of history, has become a key issue in Postcolonial Studies.

Of course, history has always been ripe for mutation and contestation in the literature of science fiction. In addition to the fairly well-known territory of alternate histories seen in novels such as Philip K Dick's *The Man in the High Castle* (1962), which postulates a contemporary world in which Nazi Germany emerged victorious from World War II, science fiction's reconsideration and reconfiguration of history also includes juxtaposed or parallel histories, such as Jorge Luis Borges's "El jardín de senderos que se bifurcan" ("Garden of Forking Paths," 1941) and the narration of future histories such as those penned by Robert A. Heinlein in his aptly named series, *Future History*. But, the importance of history to postcolonial studies is rooted in the way in which it acts as a means of legitimizing a Western *Weltanschauung*. So it is that history is seen as an important site of strategic cultural resistance for postcolonial writers. As Australian postcolonial critic and theorist Bill Ashcroft writes:

> when we investigate history itself we find that, particularly in its nineteenth-century imperial forms, it stands less for investigation than for perpetuation.... At base, the myth of a value-free, "scientific" view of the past, the myth of the beauty of order, the myth of the story of history as a simple representation of the continuity of events, authorized nothing less than the construction of a world reality [Ashcroft, 2001: 82–83].

In short, postcolonial studies recognizes that the discipline of history is less about recording the events of the past than it is about promoting a specifically Western way of thinking.

Now, it is important to recognize that this particular way of thinking about the strange worlds Europe contacted during the years of its imperial and colonial expansion rested on the privileging of order and continuity. These two operators conditioned history as an ordered and continuous narrative — an objective chronology of events — that ultimately had the effect of over-coding any other competing histories, such as those mythic and oral histories of indigenous cultures that simply could not be incorporated into the scientific enterprise of Western history. So, as Foucault recognized, what this kind of history revealed was not the "truth" of an historical situation, but rather the fact that this practice of history went hand-in-hand with a sense of self-legitimation. How can we think of this fabricated teleology in any other way, Foucault asks, than as a process that merely legitimizes what we know ("us") and thereby leaves aside what we don't ("others") (Foucault, 219–220)? Given this powerful re-reading of historiography, history can no longer be considered as simply the objective record of past events; it must be reconsidered as nothing less than a Eurocentric interested reinvention of the past.

As such, it is clear that these moments of "interest" that are witnessed in history are explained by the act of organization that is required in the production of history itself—evidenced in the need to abrogate, appropriate and arrange certain significant events in order to facilitate a sense of the continuity of history. What this means is that Western history is composed through a continuous process of division: that which is "necessary" against that which is "unnecessary"; that which must be included against that which must be excluded—the historian writes English history not Australian history, social history not economic history. Now, talking specifically of this aspect of organization that rests on the twinned process of exclusion and inclusion in colonial discourse, celebrated postcolonial theorist Edward Said asked in his seminal work *Orientalism*: "Can one divide human reality, as indeed human reality seems to be genuinely divided, into clearly different cultures, histories, traditions, societies, even races, and survive the consequences humanely (45)?" That is to say, can one ethically engage in this interested activity of division that must finally position people in terms of either "subject" (us) or "object" (them)? For Said, this seemingly simple question placed in the context of his concern that a Western history left unchecked exhibits the potential to colonize reality itself, reminds us of what is lost if we allow the political agendas of those who write history to be naturalized within it. He continues: "By surviving the consequences humanely, I mean to ask whether there is any way of avoiding the hostility expressed by the division, say, of men into 'us' (Westerners) and 'they' (Orientals)" (45).

It is a call to reinvest a sense of ethical responsibility back into a system that had discarded it in the name of scientific enquiry. And, in order to begin doing so, Said writes of the need to collapse such vulgar essentialisms as "us" and "them" and thereby embark on a project to disrupt the comfortable and conveniently polarized view of reality prescribed through European colonial discourse.

Here, then, is the way in which we should look at the work of those writers who are compelled to track the genealogies of local ontologies and epistemologies back into the past—as a means of contesting the validity of European colonial discourse. For, implicit to the claims of writers such as Ngugi, Chakrabarty, and Muecke is the idea that to build sustainable *contemporary* local ontologies and epistemologies, which have the potential to truly contest the over-coding impetus of a dominant European colonial discourse, we must situate our contemporary-self in relation to our past-self. This is not to say that we engage somehow in the impossible task of retrieving an authentic past, but merely that we overcome the distance between contemporary and historical subjectivities by regarding ourselves as "other"—the embodiment of both noesis and noema. And, as fellow French philosopher Gilles Deleuze writes here, Michel Foucault's reconceptualization of history facilitates precisely this kind of arrangement:

> History, according to Foucault, circumscribes us and sets limits, it doesn't determine what we are, but what we're in the process of differing from; it doesn't fix our identity, but disperses it into our essential otherness.... History, in short, is what separates us from ourselves and what we have to go through and beyond in order to think what we are [Deleuze 1995: 95].

Deleuze identifies two important elements in Foucault's reconceptualization of history in this passage that help us to understand the manner of the relationship between the contemporary-self and the past-self. First is the observation that history does not determine what we are, "but what we're in the process of differing from." For Deleuze, this process is best thought of in terms of a "becoming." As a present participle, becoming refuses to hierarchize, privilege, or determine specific discrete points in time. As such, it not only insists that the world is a dynamic environment characterized entirely by the fact that it is in a condition of constant change, but also that the subject is in a perpetual state of movement. That is to say, the subject no longer exists as a static entity but rather as a trajectory—an event, if you like—that folds both the temporality of the past and the present together and renders them immanent to its very constitution.

It is, then, this dramatic revision of the subject that leads into Deleuze's second observation: "our essential otherness." The radical reconceptualization of the self as an event that holds in its very constitution the past and the present means that the "other" self—that is to say, the "past" self—is always already included in the formation of the self-as-subject. So, in this dramatic reconfiguration of the subject the self must be regarded simultaneously as both the self-as-subject *and* the self-as-other. Of course, this is why both Foucault and Deleuze realize that history must fail in its bid to fix our identity. In such an environment of perpetual movement, history's simple act of showing us what we *were* in order to show us what we are *now*—by contrasting our present-self with our past-self—loses any kind of critical value. If the contemporary subject is understood as an event that always already inhabits the space of both the past and the present then, as Foucault and Deleuze argue, all history can do is "separate us from ourselves."

Now, this conceptually difficult position — of a subject that holds the seemingly divergent temporalities of the past and present immanent to its very constitution because of the simultaneity of a becoming that posits the subject as both subject and other — brings us to the very heart of Vandana Singh's short story "Delhi." Singh's short story appears in a recent anthology of writing in the nascent field of postcolonial science fiction and fantasy, *So Long Been Dreaming* (2004). It charts a passage in the curious life of the story's main protagonist, Aseem — a man who resides in today's Delhi and seems to be a particularly unremarkable figure, save for his ability to apprehend visions of people and landscapes of days-gone-by and days-yet-to-come. Now, it is Aseem's ability to see and, in a limited manner, interact with these other temporalities that allows Singh to reconfigure the European organization of time in a way that ultimately questions the validity of the British imperial historical project. In so doing, Singh also responds to Said's call to reinvest a sense of ethical responsibility into the production of history by demonstrating the way in which a series of personal testimonies become a collective enunciation that combat the reductionist drive of essentialism.

Aseem is undoubtedly a curious character. It seems he has the ability to see the everyday occurrences of people living in both the past and (somewhat unexpectedly to Aseem himself) the future of Delhi. So it is that the reader is told in the opening few paragraphs how Aseem once saw: "a milkman going past him on Shahjahan road, complete with humped white cow and tinkling bell. Under the Stately, ancient trees that partly shaded the street lamps, the milkman stopped to speak to his cow and faded into the dimness of twilight" (80). These kind of passive visions that Aseem seems to have experienced fairly commonly finally develop into more personal encounters, where Aseem has the opportunity to talk with people from other temporalities. He recalls quite clearly the sense of the conversation he held in the first of these intimate encounters — a woman from around the year 1100 AD: "She named Prithviraj Chauhan as her king. Aseem told her he lived some 900 years after Chauhan. They exchanged stories of other visions — she had seen armies, spears flashing, and pale men with yellow beards ..." (81).

Now, it is because of both his passive visions and these intimate exchanges with people from other temporalities that the history of Delhi takes on a personal character for Aseem. That is to say, such intimate access to the history of Delhi encourages Aseem to stop thinking about those people represented in "well-thumbed history text books" (80) as simply anonymous players in the rampant teleology of a European history. For Aseem, history no longer "separates us from ourselves" because these anonymous people of European history take shape, are literally made manifest, and in so doing reclaim their individuality. Under such conditions, history is no longer about explaining the causes of national conflicts or economic trends; it is about everyday people who are engaged in the largely mundane activities of everyday life. And, as such, it is also about recovering the eminently sensual moments of everyday life, moments that an academic history could never even attempt to capture. Consider, for example, the way in which Aseem narrates the sensual qualities of the moment before he meets the "mad emperor," Muhammad Shah:

> There was a smoky tang in the air.... As the sun set, the red sandstone fort walls glowed, then darkened. Night came, blanketing the tall ramparts, the lawns through which he strolled, the shimmering beauty of the Pearl Mosque, the languorous curves of the now distant Yamuna that had once flowed under this marble terrace [81].

It is clear that such "historical" moments possess the phenomenal characteristics of the contemporary world for Aseem and because of this they highlight the fact that Western history's appreciation of historical reality is ultimately impoverished. In a world where the past and the present is shown to inhere and subsist in the reality of the other, the European idea of history as something that explains an earlier time is no longer either conceptually viable or valuable. In this formulation, history understood as a practice of marking time ceases to be important. Rather, it enters into a process of becoming that refuses to privilege one temporality — say, the present — over any other. This is why it is important to recognize that Aseem similarly appears as an apparition to the other people who share his ability to look across into other temporalities. Significantly, Aseem's temporality is not terminal (he witnesses, for example, the future of his contemporary world) and as such his is not determined as the conditioning temporality from which other times are made possible (such is the implicit case of writing history). His is just another temporality taking place on the landscape of Delhi, and therefore Aseem, the writer of this personal history of histories (82), is recognized to be just another person living out their daily life.

Since the need for the Western project of history has collapsed into what can be considered as a continuum of multiple temporalities, the figure of the other — that conceptual figure which allows European history to forge a critical distance from the contemporary-self in order to arrange a strong teleology of events — necessarily disappears. Or rather, it is relocated. Standing within this continuum of multiple temporalities, Aseem comes to embody this conceptual figure. That is to say, Aseem becomes both subject and other. As someone who both sees and is seen as either a historical person or somebody from the future, Aseem acts in terms of both subject and other. Clearly, he is the subject of his own observations and experiences, observations and experiences that drove him to "endless rounds of medications and appointments with doctors and psychologists" (85) and then on towards the very edge of sanity; but he is also the object of other people's observations — the other who, as Deleuze writes, ensures an anticipated coherency to the world (Deleuze, 1990: 305). That is to say, he is also used as a conceptual foil against which both historical and future "others" build a reality of the world. He becomes the structure by which others are assured of not only the solidity of the world but the passage of it through time.

This situation is made explicit when Aseem encounters his future self— an other/future-self who stops him from committing suicide by jumping to his death from a bridge across the Yamuna River. At this moment, the conceptual aura of his self-as-other, something which he has begun to recognize more clearly in himself through recent encounters with other people, ceases to be simply an interesting empathetic phenomenon and becomes tangible — that is to say, *realized*. Thus, Aseem "becomes" the people he is going to save, becomes the other through understanding and responding to their deepest sensibilities: "After all these years in the city he's learned to recognize a certain preoccupation in the eyes of some of his fellow citizens: the desire for the final anonymity that death brings. Sometimes, as in this case, he knows it before they do" (83). Of course, it is the same ability to see "the desire for the final anonymity that death brings" which his future-self sees in him, and a process of infinite return is instigated: the contemporary self-as-subject becoming other (in this case, the self-as-other), and the self-as-other becoming the contemporary self-as-subject. In this way, Aseem opens himself up to inhere in the continuum of time.

Now, this curious arrangement of the self which inheres in the continuum of time rather than inhabits a strict temporality in history necessarily instructs a reconsideration of the way in which the past is understood. Undoubtedly, Aseem at times still holds on to a particularly European way of understanding the past. For example, Aseem still recognizes the significance of the relationship between object and memory that European history holds dear: a relationship that is evidenced by the incontestable, tangible products of history acknowledged in such things as memorials or colonial architectures that were imprinted on the landscape of Delhi. But, such objects of memory are found to be in various states of material decay, reflecting the fact that the psychological link between object and memory is beginning to falter — Aseem sits and eats ice-cream on the India Gate lawns (81); he walks past the "faded white colonnades of some building in Connaught Place" (80); and, he rests in the shade of "one of the many nameless remains of Delhi's medieval era" (88). Here, the profound link between object and memory is shown to be failing and with it, consequently, the very ground upon which British Imperial history is built.

Yet, like the seedling of the pipal tree that Aseem sees flourishing in a crack in the concrete of a bridge across the Yamuna River, something else develops in this growing fault-line of history. As Milan Kundera notes, "beyond the slender margin of the incontestable" aspects of history: "stretches an infinite realm: the realm of the approximate, the invented, the deformed, the simplistic, the exaggerated, the misconstrued, an infinite realm of non-truths that copulate, multiply like rats, and become immortal" (148–149). This is the realm of history that Vandana Singh champions and Aseem lives: the realm of the temporal continuum or, more precisely, the realm of infinite variation. It is the recognition of both the infinite mutability of the past as it is perceived, conceived, and rendered, and the legitimation of heterogeneous narratives that such mutability (or variation) instructs. So it is that in distinction to the striation or organization of time, which characterizes the formalizing impetus of Western history, Singh represents history as a process of infinite variation that can accommodate the multiplicity of narratives that constitute it.

The reader is introduced to this revolutionary idea in a fairly gentle manner, as Singh reconsiders the history of Delhi and re-writes it as a palimpsest. Under such conditions, *the history* of Delhi becomes *the histories* of Delhi — its composition based on four intertwined movements of time:

- *Material artifacts*: such as buildings;
- *Written histories*: such as the histories of imperialism that Aseem relates — the Persian massacre of citizens of Delhi in the early eighteenth century (81); the "India Gate" memorial to the soldiers of World War I (81); and references to "the British Invaders" (81);
- *Cultural memories*: such as those Aseem relates of the development of Delhi — from myth (the fable city Indraprastha of 3000 years ago); through medieval times (the seven cities of Delhi); then the British Raj (the eighth city of Delhi); to the present day (the ninth city); and
- *Personal memories*: his grandmother's nostalgic recollection of "Old Delhi" (83) and his own reflections of the contradictory nature of the contemporary city (88).

The palimpsest, though, goes only a certain way to conceiving of time in terms of its infinite variation. The narrator tells us, "only for Aseem are the old cities of Delhi still alive, glimpsed like mysterious islands from a passing ship, but real nevertheless" (80). In conjunction with a palimpsest that only begins to hint at the complexity of Delhi's history, the reader is returned to the significance of Aseem standing across temporalities and opening himself up to inhere in the continuum of time. In the sporadic moments of the fantastic when temporalities coincide, Aseem compromises the integrity of the teleological grasp of history and so renders causality, founded on a belief in the linear flow of time, meaningless. Struggling to reconcile this strange trans-temporal arrangement of time, Aseem begins to consider where causality might situate itself. And so it is that he begins to question whether his ability to communicate across different times in Delhi's history has actually *caused* some moments of history to happen. However, the narrator tells us that Aseem calmed himself by thinking, "apart from the Emperor [Muhammad Shah], nobody he has communicated with is of any real importance in the course of history" (82). But, of course, this is exactly the significance of his trans-temporal visions: such people are the important agents of history; these "apparitions of the past," which he communes with, are the ones who affect "history." He is given access to the lives and the stories of "ordinary" people, individuals who have been erased from the meta-narrative of history; and taken together their stories form an important unwritten history of Delhi. That is not to say that these are "the people" written of in a vulgar type of Marxism — "the masses" who institute social change — but rather simple individuals who produce an apolitical, amoral collective enunciation: the milkman who drives his cow through the streets in the early hours of the day (80), and the woman walking the lanes of an ancient Delhi as she goes about her daily life (80). They are the unpredictable, unwritten, unknown individuals of history — virtual elements of the real world.

It is important, then, that these visions appear unexpectedly to Aseem, for such unpredictability not only reinforces the character of the unwritten individuals of history but also describes the movement of the infinite variation of time conceived as a continuum. As an always already existent force, time erupts infinitely, even through itself. Aseem attempts to theorise this complex quality of time by arguing that "the visions are tricks of time, tangles produced when one part of the time-stream rubs up against another and the two cross for a moment" (80). This is an admirable understanding of the complexity of the continuum of time, but the significance of its infinite variation and movement is elided somewhat. When time is out of joint, time itself is unhinged. In the words of Gilles Deleuze, this marks the great Kantian reversal: the moment when movement becomes subordinated to time. Under such conditions, Deleuze writes, time "ceases to be cardinal and becomes ordinal, the order of an empty time. In time, there is no longer anything either originary or derived that depends on movement" (1998: 28). Of particular critical interest here is the collapse of the originary, which allows for a conceptualization of the point and therefore the specificity demanded by "the date." It is the originary point — the date — that stands as the illusory (yet always determined as authentic) beginning from which any teleology is developed. Both Western history and colonial discourse know this mythical point well; but as Aseem reveals, the originary point (the date) is rather a vector: a line which represents the originary point in motion. "The date" becomes "the event" and Western history slowly loses its foundational coordinates upon which it orientates its genetic process of organisation. As such, Aseem's speculation that his visions are "tangles produced when one part of the time-stream rubs up against another" is perhaps better understood in terms of Friedrich Hölderlin's notion of a labyrinth made of a single straight line which is "indivisible, incessant" (108).

In this complex world where it is no longer a question of defining time by a principle of succession but rather immanence, the self can no longer be defined by its center. Rather, it can only be hinted at by charting the limits and borders of its relationship with others. As such, under these curious conditions of a fantastic world, Singh demonstrates that the self necessarily holds an essential ethical quality. Understood as a dramatic conflation of both subject and other, the self works to connect disparate elements of the world and in doing so enlivens the heterogeneous and marginalized narratives of the unwritten and unknown individuals of history. There is no program of organization here, just the operation of a continuum — a continuum that marks the very moment in which this short story disturbs the reality, morality, and the economy of the "real" world. Singh's disturbance of the ordered world is a product of a reconceptualization of history that frees the ghostly world of the unpredictable, unwritten, and unknown individuals of history from the actual. The unwritten world of such people no longer only announces the world of the margins or the world of possibility, but becomes an integral element of the entire field of history.

Works Cited

Ashcroft, Bill. *Post-Colonial Transformation*. London: Routledge, 2001.
Deleuze, Gilles. *Essays Critical and Clinical*. Trans. Daniel W. Smith and Michael A. Greco. London: Verso, 1998.
_____. *The Logic of Sense*. Trans. Mark Lester with Charles Stivale. New York: Columbia University Press, 1990.
_____. *Negotiations: 1972–1990*. Trans. Martin Joughin. New York: Columbia University Press, 1995.
Foucault, Michel. *The Order of Things*. London: Tavistock, 1970.
Hölderlin, Friedrich. "Remarks on 'Oedipus.'" *Essays and Letters on Theory*. Ed. and trans. Thomas Pfau. Albany: State University of New York Press, 1988. 101–108.

Hopkinson, Nalo, and Uppinder Mehan, eds. *So Long Been Dreaming*, Vancouver: Arsenal Pulp Press, 2004.
Kerslake, Patricia. *Science Fiction and Empire*. Liverpool: Liverpool University Press, 2007.
Kundera, Milan. *The Curtain: An Essay in Seven Parts*. Trans. Linda Asher. London: Faber and Faber, 2007.
Said, Edward W. *Orientalism*, London: Penguin, 1978.
Singh, Vandana. "Delhi." *So Long Been Dreaming*. Eds. Nalo Hopkinson and Uppinder Mehan. Vancouver: Arsenal Pulp Press, 2004. 79–94.
Suvin, Darko. *Metamorphoses of Science Fiction*. New Haven: Yale University Press, 1979.

PART TWO: FORMS OF PROTEST

5

The Colonial Feminine in Pat Murphy's "His Vegetable Wife"[1]

DIANA PHARAOH FRANCIS

In Pat Murphy's "His Vegetable Wife" (1990), the farmer Fynn plants a Vegetable Wife. In time, the seedling grows into a feminized plant, complete with a curvaceous body, breasts, pubic hair and nipples. But though the plant is called a wife, and identified as *she*, she has no more power over her own body than Fynn's cimmeg crops — cash crops. Yet unlike cimmeg, her value to Fynn resides not in her exchange value, but in her use value as a sexual object: a disposable, inexpensive, home-grown concubine.

But as Fynn's Vegetable Wife ripens and he begins to use her, his expectations change. He wants an emotional response from her, though he is titillated by her passivity and lack of expression. He grows lustful and then violent as his Vegetable Wife resists his sexual advances. Soon he binds her to the frame of his dome dwelling and begins to keep her under constant surveillance. Her struggles for freedom inflame him sexually and he sexually assaults her, later remonstrating her for crying. After all, he says, "you are my wife. It can't be that bad" (630). Later, he discovers that "she seemed to react only to violence, to immediate threats" (631). He beats her bloody, repeatedly assaulting her, finally attempting to kill her in a fit of rage and jealousy.

Fynn perceives the Vegetable Wife as inferior — both as a female and as a colonial subject. Woman is nothing more than a flawed man: emotional, unreasonable, irrational. She is ruled entirely by erratic passions. The colonized subject is atavistic — primitive and superstitious — and like a woman, is ruled by emotions and characterized by animalistic drives and an incapacity for logical thought. Both are in need of a firm hand to "husband" them — in the same way a farmer husbands his land and livestock. A farmer takes firm possession of his property, manipulating and altering it, torturing and wooing it, to suit his economic needs. Farmers take what is wild and unproductive and civilize it. Their reward is personal wealth and power, as well as an accumulation of cultural capital and a stronger position on the hegemonic power pyramid.

Gayatri Chakravorty Spivak has written of the experience of the female subaltern in her seminal essay, "Can the Subaltern Speak?" (1988). In the essay, Spivak argues that "if, in the context of colonial production, the subaltern has no history and cannot speak, the subaltern as female is even more deeply in shadow" (83). The female subaltern is objectified both as a female and as a colonial subject — an inextricable doubling of oppression that is far more acute in its domination than the experience of the subaltern male. In fact in this story, the Vegetable Husband does not exist — it is an oxymoron. A husband — a force of domination, ownership and imperialism — cannot be Vegetable, unlike a woman or a wife. Murphy's "His Vegetable Wife" emphasizes the duology of the Vegetable Wife's oppression. In the capacity of a colonial subject, the Vegetable Wife is commodified. Fynn views her as a conquered subject of his farm "empire," and she becomes an asset to the business, like a tractor or fertilizer, to be used or disposed of as he sees fit. From the first, the language Murphy uses in describing the Vegetable Wife is the same as that applied to colonial subjects. She is merely a plant, lacking emotion, lacking civilized qualities. She is an object to be used and profited from, an infant to be fed and watered, a "wild thing" to be kept from harming itself (631). In the capacity of wife, she is objectified. By definition, she is nothing more than a pliant, sexual receptacle for her husband's desires. This is the purpose for which she is grown. When she eventually ceases to be capable of that role — as when fruit trees no longer produce adequately and must be torn out and planted with new trees — when the Vegetable Wife no longer fulfills her ontological role, she must be discarded, in the same way men have traditionally discarded older/uglier wives in favor of newer, sexier models.

In either capacity — indigenous subject or wife — she has no legal or moral standing or recourse. Such a concept would be as inconceivable and ludicrous to Fynn as granting such rights to his pillow, toothbrush, or toaster, or perhaps a better comparison would be his celery, broccoli or cabbage. This then, is the position of the colonized woman: she is the subaltern who cannot speak; she is raped, but unraped. Yet even as "His Vegetable Wife" dramatizes the doubled oppression of the colonized woman, it also demonstrates that the Vegetable Wife is not powerless. She is Other, with a power that is unnoticed and unacknowledged and tremendously subversive. Mimicry is a double-edged sword, and the Vegetable Wife, as the colonized woman, responds with the strength of her dual heritage.

Cultivating the Empire

A vegetable is, by definition, a consumable. It is the edible product of a plant; in some cases, it is the plant itself. It is to be cultivated until ripe, and then eventually eaten, whether by the farmer or the consumer. A vegetable is a passive thing, lacking consciousness, incapable of thought or feeling. The term is often used pejoratively to refer to a human in a comatose state: she's a vegetable. Medically, when someone has slipped into a coma and lost cognitive brain function, she will be diagnosed as being in a persistent vegetative state. A simplified explanation is that the person loses higher cerebral brain powers, but the brain stem continues to function — breathing and circulation continue without aid. However, despite the seeming of consciousness — sleep cycles, grinding teeth, blinking, and so forth — the patient is generally believed to be "brain dead," though there is argument in the medical community about whether the patient is truly "brain dead" or whether the condition is reversible. The dispute becomes particularly thorny when the question arises as to whether the patient is beyond recovery, and should therefore be taken off lifesupport. The hidden issue driving the question is whether there is any value to a life lived, in the slang term, as a "vegetable." The overriding presumption is not. For a vegetable is unthinking, unreasoning, and in fact, many believe that the inhabiting soul is likely departed from the husk of the body. The point I am getting to here, is that a body decreed "vegetable" is in fact an object that has been reduced to a subhuman category.

This is Fynn's perception. He believes his Vegetable Wife to be "only a plant, she felt no pain" (629). He knows this, not because of observation, which would have challenged that perception, but because "the instructions had said so" (631). These instructions represent the articulation of colonial hegemony that insists on positioning the indigenous Other as a commodity whose value lies solely in its use to the Empire. The instructions on the package not only describe how to manage that use, but their insistence that the Vegetable Wife feels no pain, suggests an ambivalence in situating the indigenous Other as inhuman, resulting in an effort to discount empirical evidence to the contrary.

This ambivalence is dramatized by Fynn. He does not entirely believe that his Vegetable Wife lacks all consciousness, for indeed, he feels guilt when he fondles her and breaks leaves and must convince himself that the guilt is unfounded (629). As she grows and develops feminine qualities — waist, breasts, pubic hair — he begins to think of her as a person, referring to her as a "she," rather than as an inhuman thing: "the seedling" or "the wife" (629). He recognizes her discomfort with his touch as an urge to escape, and responds by tying her up and devising a system of surveillance. When he sexually assaults her the first time, she cries, a reactive response to a horrifying stimulus, and one that would be expected from a woman and not from an unconscious plant. Her tears "woke compassion in him" and he attempts to reason with her: "come now [...] you are my wife. It can't be that bad" (630).

In her well-known essay "The Unspeakable Limits of Rape: Colonial Violence and Counter-Insurgency" (1994), Jenny Sharpe argues that in the 1984 film version of E. M. Forster's *A Passage to India*, "a masculinist reading of the mystery of the cave [Adele's presumed rape] [...] is based on the 'common knowledge' that frigid women suffer from sexual hysteria and that unattractive women desire to be raped" (223). It is this "common knowledge" combined with the legal right of ownership inherent in the designation of "wife" that allows Fynn to presume that he can use his Vegetable Wife's body as he desires, with or without her consent. Fynn's behavior reflects the misogynistic belief that a wife belongs totally to her husband without any rights of her own. According to Anne McClintock in her seminal work *Imperial Leather* (1995), "Women are the earth that is to be discovered, entered, named, inseminated, and above all, owned" (31). Thus it is impossible for a husband to rape his wife, since she is reduced to property and therefore has no right of refusal, nothing that might be deemed human rights whatsoever. While it is true that a woman can be raped (but only in the context of the damage done and loss of value to another man's property), a husband cannot rape his wife (for a useful discussion of the exchange of women within a patriarchal culture, see Irigaray 170).

Fynn's selection of the Vegetable Wife rather than the Maiden or Bride indicate that his intent is not only to satisfy himself sexually, but to establish himself *a priori* as the absolute authority in this relationship, as well as the property owner. A maiden or bride might be expected to resist copulation. Neither of the two has been subject to a man's touch. Both might expect kindness and consideration — a kind of wooing. A wife, on the other hand, is expected to have been indoctrinated into her role and to accept her husband's dominance and power over her body. Which is to say, she has already been made docile; she is domesticated and trained. In selecting a wife, Fynn is not selecting a companion, but a creature — not even a pet — who will succumb to the uses he intends for her body, no matter how violent or distasteful to her.

Simone de Beauvoir (1952) writes that in the act of sex, particularly the first time, the woman is "overpowered, forced to compliance, conquered [...]. [She] lies in the posture of defeat; worse, the man rides her as he would an animal subject to bit and reins" (385). And in fact, by hobbling his Vegetable

Wife around the ankle, Fynn equates her with a horse or cow. When he rapes her, the description is eerily akin to Beauvoir's: "When he tried to embrace her, she did not respond except to push at his shoulders [...]. Excitement washed over him, and he pushed her back on the hard ground, his mouth seeking her breast [...] his hand parting her legs" (630). When he is through, he rolls off her and she is left "in the dust" (630).

The conjunction of wife and animal begins to get at the real position of the colonized woman represented by the Vegetable Wife. Not merely is she feminized and therefore robbed of the rights to her body, but she is also colonized. McClintock argues "colonized women had to negotiate not only the imbalances of their relations with their own men but also the baroque and violent array of hierarchical rules and restrictions that structured their new relations with imperial men and women" (6).

Typically, the colonizer feminizes the colonial project — both the land and indigenous peoples. McClintock notes that "the world is feminized and spatially spread for male exploration, then reassembled and deployed in the interests of massive imperial power" (23), and that "the feminizing of terra incognita was, from the outset, a strategy of violent containment" (24). With the colonizer serving the paternal role of father and disciplinarian, the indigenous peoples were hierarchized according to imperialistic notions of gender value. According to imperial hegemony, the "natives" were inevitably barbaric, degenerate, irrational — uncivilized. These qualities were the same qualities associated with women. McClintock, discussing the British Empire, states that "racial scientists and, later, eugenicists, saw women as the inherently atavistic, living archive of the primitive archaic" (41). The colonizers then set a hierarchy of "native" value, with men at the top, followed by mothers (Spivak 82). This does not make economic sense, since childless women contribute heavily to the labor force of colonized territories. However it does reflect the hegemony that perceives women as flawed men, whose value resides in their services as wives and mothers, and who, even in a colonial context where all indigenous peoples are positioned as degenerate, are perceived as more corrupt, more primitive and debased, than the men of their race.

Given this hierarchy, the Vegetable Wife resides in the substrata — the least of the subaltern ranks. She is neither male nor mother. Nor does she work. The "crop" she has to offer is her sexuality. She has no other economic contribution to make. Nor is she unique — she comes from a packet of seeds. Any man who wanted her could simply grow another. Her only worth as a female, or as a colonized subject, exists in her use value as a concubine to Fynn.

To return to Sharpe's argument, she contends that the official discourse of colonization "erases colonial women's agency" (238). She argues that this discourse removes the colonized subject from the category of rapeable. A colonial subject is no more rapeable than a wife by her husband. She, or even he, is not entitled to any protections of law, culture or morality. The discourse does not permit a concept of rape in association with "natives." Because they are defined as feminine and subhuman, their assigned role in the hierarchy is essentially tools, livestock, or vermin, depending on the needs of the empire at any given moment.

In the colonization of Australia, the British declared the continent uninhabited — terra nullius — allowing the aborigine peoples to be categorized as nonhuman, or subhuman — vermin. In aligning the discourse to suit the imperial agenda, colonizers were encouraged by bounties to eradicate the vermin, without endangering their moral superiority, simply by reducing the inhabitants to the equivalent of filthy cockroaches. Destroying pests is a cleansing act, necessary for the god-authorized spread of civilization.

Sharpe contends that the signifying function of the colonial native cannot be permitted to undermine the imperial discourse. By inscribing the genocide of the aborigine peoples of Australia as an act of heroism, essential to serving God (as in cleanliness is next to godliness), the British affirm the imperial hegemony as patriotic, moral, and inevitable. Similarly, the brutal, nonconsensual act of sex with a colonial subject is not rape, but instead it is the symbolic representation of the colonizer overcoming the violent barbarity of the "native" and inserting into "her" the seed of civilization. That she resists is only to be expected — civilization comes at a price. If she proves a fertile ground, then those seeds will grow, cultivated by the colonizer — the farmer. Thus rape is not rape, but a moral battle against degeneracy and barbarism. The colonizer is not only justified, but he is venerated, for the performance of this dangerous and difficult duty. The justifying ideological foundation of imperialistic hegemony remains intact.

Mimicry and the Power of the Other

Fynn's fields are surrounded by the tall native grasses. They besiege his self-described farm empire, "a vast expanse of swaying stalks" (628). The image hints at a threat, recalling the sense of malice Marlow feels as he travels into the African interior in *The Heart of Darkness* (1902), and reminding the reader that Fynn is essentially alone amongst a horde of unfriendly "natives" who have ample reason to hate him: "[Fynn] had enjoyed hacking down the grass that had surrounded the living dome, churning its roots beneath the mechanical tiller, planting the straight rows of cimmeg" (628). His power of authority and rule resides in his machinery — the weaponry of creating a farm empire, of carving civilization out of the wilds. Fynn is confident in his superiority and control.

Yet despite his pride in his empire, despite his feeling of mechanical and moral strength and ownership, he finds the surrounding grasses unsettling. They make him nervous and annoyed: "The soft sound of the wind in the grasses irritated Fynn; he thought it sounded like people whispering secrets" (628). It is the same sound the wind makes in his Vegetable Wife's hair the first time he attacks her. And later, when he attempts to strangle her, his goal is to "stop the whispers that he heard, the secrets that were everywhere" (632).

As the story progresses, Fynn loses sight of the fact that the Vegetable Wife is Other:

> She was not quite what he expected in a wife. She did not understand language. She did not speak language. She paid little attention to him unless he forced her to look at him, to see him. He tried being pleasant to her — bringing her flowers from the fields and refilling her basing with cool clean water. She took no notice [...]. She seemed to react only to violence, to immediate threats. When he made love to her, she struggled to escape, and sometimes she cried [...]. After a time, her crying came to excite him — any response was better than no response [631].

In this passage, it becomes clear that Fynn's expectations have moved beyond the merely sexual to the emotional. He wants her to interact on a level beyond the physical exploitation of her body. He wants her to like him, to care about him, to appreciate him. When she does not respond appropriately, he begins a program of violence beyond that which he's already set in motion with his repeated sexual attacks. He beats her with a belt until she's bloody with sap. He begins to brood on her recalcitrance, positing her with "all the women who had ever left him" (631).

Homi Bhabha (1994) argues that "colonial mimicry is the desire for a reformed, recognizable Other, *as a subject of a difference that is almost the same, but not quite*" (86). The colonial subject is encouraged to believe he can attain equality with the colonizer, if only he becomes sufficiently civilized. But in fact, the colonial subject can never achieve equality because he will never be "the same." Specifically, he will always be physically identifiable as Other, either by skin color, facial features, or in the case of the Vegetable Wife, she is a plant. There is a deeply fracturing anxiety in the colonial hegemony revolving around the concern that a colonized subject could ever "pass" as equal, and thereby "infect" the imperial culture through what Stephen Arata (1990) has called reverse colonization. In examining Bram Stoker's *Dracula*, Arata says that Dracula is particular frightening because he infects his victims with his atavism, marked by passion, lewdness, blood-hunger and violence. He "imperils not simply his victims' personal identities, but also their cultural, political, and racial selves. Horror arises not because Dracula destroys bodies, but because he appropriates and transforms them. Having yielded to his assault, one literally 'goes native' [...]" (Arata 630).

And this is the danger of mimicry. It is a powerful technique of colonization. The colonial subject is indoctrinated into hegemony, becoming complicit in his own domination. He seeks to belong, to conform, to earn his way to equality. In doing so, he defuses his own threat. But mimicry can also be a powerful form of resistance when the colonized subject *pretends* to conform. Fynn conducts surveillance of his Vegetable Wife, situating her by a window or near the door where he can watch her often during the day, and checking her bindings to be sure they are secure. But when he begins to consider her a woman, a wife — albeit a recalcitrant one — he loses sight of the fact that she is still Other. He becomes infected with the notion that she has humanity. He is blinded to what she is. Ironically enough, this grants her little power, as she is still subject to the ideological conception that a woman is the property of her husband. Thus he continues to beat and sexually attack her with impunity.

Fynn has convinced himself that his Vegetable Wife is what the seed package claims she is: a "native" whose menace has been eliminated. He is fooled into believing that because she appears to be domesticated and powerless, she must therefore be so. But in fact, the Vegetable Wife is symbolic of the danger of mimicry to the colonial power — that she is only wearing the seeming of subjection. And she may not be the only one. Recall that Fynn's farm empire is surrounded by the tall native grasses that whisper secrets. What secrets? Plots of rebellion? Truths that defy imperial hegemony?

In the end, Fynn attempts to strangle his Vegetable Wife, forgetting that she is a plant, and not a woman. Her body, while appearing human, almost the "same but not quite," is still a plant. She is no more strangleable than she is rapeable. In an ironic manifestation of the deadly power of "native" mimicry, the Vegetable Wife copies Fynn's actions: "she lifted her hands and put them to his throat, applying slow steady pressure. He struggled drunkenly, but she clung to him until his struggles stopped" (632).

She kills him, not out of any hatred for his abuse, or even because she desires to escape. She kills him because his behavior has demonstrated that he is sick, barbaric, and uncivilized. In another ironic mimicry of imperial hegemony, just as Fynn performed a symbolic seeding of the barbaric lands with civilization through sexual violence against his Vegetable Wife, so she plans to "plant the man, as she had seen him plant seeds. She would stand with her ankles in the mud and the wind in her hair and she would see what grew" (632). And in fact, we can predict that Fynn will not grow, but will decay, the victim of his own misogynistic and imperialistic arrogant blindness. His rotting flesh will be the evidence that he did not provide fertile ground for civilization — he was too corrupt. But eventually his body — imperialist hegemony — will break down to unrecognizable elements, and those elements will provide the fertilizer for more "native" plants to grow, and eventually retake the farm empire.

Carrots, Radishes and Murder

In this story, what we see is the inherent corruption and weakness of imperialism. It is inconceivable to Fynn that his Vegetable Wife might be anything more than what the seed package says she is, what the colonialist hegemony says "native" women are. The fact that she is a colonial subject and a woman ontologically defines her as weak and helpless. Fynn cannot imagine that she could be dangerous because he believes her very nature is powerlessness and vulnerability. He is stronger physically and by virtue of his superior mechanical technology, and by his white masculinity. He is confident in his abuse of her, bolstered by the imperial hegemony that justifies his behavior and existence, as well as her general lack of resistance.

In the end, however, she kills him easily. But the final question remains: Can a plant commit murder? When the government agent returns to investigate why Fynn has failed to harvest his cimmeg fields, he will find Fynn's decaying carcass planted knee-deep in the ground, maggots burrowing into his flesh and the stink unbearable. The government agent will be horrified and will call for investigators to uncover who committed such a brutal act. He will once again admire the Vegetable Wife, her "naked skin glistening in the sun, smooth and clear and inviting" (631). Once again he will think she is beautiful, and perhaps even think — what a waste, that she be left here when the farmer is dead. He will pack her in his copter and sign off on the investigation, notifying the local authorities to be on the lookout for a murderer, a strong man who could strangle the farmer and bury him upright. Then he will take the Vegetable Wife home. And there the wind will blow through her hair and there will be whispers and secrets and a sharing of information and the quiet resistance will spread.

And so the government agent, the representative of the larger hegemony, will make the same mistake as Fynn. He will be fooled by the Vegetable Wife's seeming. Because to even entertain the notion that she might have murdered

Fynn would be ludicrous. The idea confers too much power on a being that is by her very nature, incompetent and powerless. Everyone knows this. It is the Truth.

The Vegetable Wife is unrapeable because she exists outside the category. Similarly, she exists outside the category of murderer, because she is too weak to make such an act possible. And thus she makes mimicry work for her, disguising her menace, and subverting the imperialist hegemony that is incapable of recognizing the threat she embodies.

Notes

1. Originally published in *Phoebe: Journal of Gender and Cultural Critique* 17.2 (2005): 35–43.

Works Cited

Arata, Stephen. "The Occidental Tourist: Dracula and the Anxiety of Reverse Colonization." *Victorian Studies* 33.4 (1990): 621–645.
Bhabha, Homi K. *The Location of Culture*. London: Routledge, 1994.
De Beauvoir, Simone. *The Second Sex*. 1952. Trans. and Ed. H. M. Parshley. New York: Vintage Books, 1989.
Irigaray, Luce. "Women on the Market." *This Sex Which is Not One*. 1977. Trans. Catherine Porter and Carolyn Burke. New York: Cornell UP, 1985.
McClintock, Anne. *Imperial Leather: Race, Gender and Sexuality in the Colonial Contest*. New York: Routledge, 1995.
Murphy, Pat. "His Vegetable Wife." *The Norton Book of Science Fiction*. Ed. Ursula K. Le Guin and Brian Atterbery. New York: Norton, 1993. 628.
A Passage to India. Dir. David Lean. Columbia Pictures, 1984.
Sharpe, Jenny. "The Unspeakable Limits of Rape: Colonial Violence and Counter-Insurgency." *Colonial Discourse and Post-Colonial Theory: A Reader*. Eds. Patrick Williams and Laura Chrisman. New York: Columbia University Press, 1994. 221–43.
Spivak, Gayatri Chakravorty. "Can the Subaltern Speak?" 1988. *Colonial Discourse and Post-Colonial Theory: A Reader*. Eds. Patrick Williams and Laura Chrisman. New York: Columbia University Press, 1994. 66–111.

6

Body Markets
The Technologies of Global Capitalism and Manjula Padmanabhan's Harvest*

SHITAL PRAVINCHANDRA

In June of 1995, Indian writer Manjula Padmanabhan decided to write a play in response to an announcement advertising the Alexander S. Onassis Public Benefit Foundation International Competition. The evaluating committee was looking for "a new, original, unproduced, unpublished play" dealing with "the problems facing Man on the threshold of the 21st century" (Padmanabhan 105). The ensuing play, a futuristic dystopia set in Bombay (now Mumbai), was completed and submitted one year later. Entitled *Harvest*, the piece offers a trenchant postcolonial critique of the harsh socio-economic inequalities created by globalization and exposes the dangerous and predatory effects of the biomedical and digital technologies that accompany the rise of global capitalism. *Harvest* went on to win first prize and subsequently premiered, in Greek, at the Karolous Koun Theatre, Athens in 1999. What is significant about the story of *Harvest* is not only that a play focussing staunchly on the third world should win this transnational competition, but that Padmanabhan should choose to explore what she sees as the most pressing problems confronting mankind today through a genre rarely employed in drama: science-fiction. This article examines the ways in which Padmanabhan deploys science-fiction to stage the way in which wealthy first world populations with greater access to biomedical and digital technologies increasingly commodify, cannibalize and exploit the third world populations who remain excluded from the endless wealth promised by global capitalism.

*Originally published in a different form in *eSharp*, Issue 8, *http://www.gla.ac.uk/* esharp.

Bombay, 2010. Om, an unemployed Indian man comes back home to his wife Jaya, and his mother, Ma. Om announces to them that he has been selected for a "job" with Interplanta Services, a multinational corporation which buys the rights to third-world citizens' body parts in exchange for a radical improvement in the seller's living conditions. Om's family soon learns that the purchaser of the rights to Om's body parts is Ginni, an American woman who repeatedly appears in their house thanks to what Padmanabhan calls a "Contact-Module," a high-tech gadget placed in Om's house ostensibly to enable communication between the third-world organ donor and the first-world organ recipient. The Contact-Module, however, serves simultaneously as a screen, communication device and monitoring system that allows Ginni to police Om and his family without requiring her physical presence in their home. Her frequent, unannounced "visits" to Om's house allow her to observe his family's diet and toilet habits, and she wastes no time in policing their daily routine to ensure it conforms to her personal standards of hygiene. When the fateful day of Om's transplant operation(s) finally arrives, he cowers in fright, and allows Interplanta's employees to take away his brother Jeetu — secretly Jaya's lover — instead. This supposed accident, however, is actually part of a larger scheme. Ginni, in fact, was never a real person, but a computer-generated image created by Virgil, the real, *male* receiver who uses Jeetu's body parts in order to rebuild his own deteriorated body. All along, it transpires, Virgil's plan has been to use Jeetu's body to seduce Jaya and impregnate her through artificial insemination to then keep the baby as his own.

Padmanabhan's decision to use science-fiction in order to dramatize the trade in human organs — a phenomenon that is by no means a fabrication of her imagination — is a wily one.[1] Firstly, thanks to the high-tech gadgets that the genre allows her to place on stage, Padmanabhan is able to explore the curious brand of seduction and coercion according to which the digital and biomedical technologies of late capitalism operate. Secondly, *Harvest's* futuristic setting allows for a plot that centers around a *legal* contractual agreement between a first and a third world citizen. By asking us to imagine a world in which all judicial, moral and bioethical debates about organ sales and transplants have supposedly been overcome, Padmanabhan is able to focus on the vulnerable populations of the third world and interrogate the ethics behind the utilitarian and neo-liberal principles espoused by those who advocate a free market in human body parts by claiming that the body, like any other form of property, can be freely disposed of as its free and autonomous owner sees fit.[2] *Harvest* repeatedly exposes the profound Eurocentrism underpinning such arguments.[3] When Jaya accuses her husband of making the wrong decision, Om is adamant that, though voluntary, his decision was not made of his own free will:

> OM: I went because I lost my job at the company. And why did I lose it? Because I am a clerk and nobody needs clerks anymore! There are no new jobs now — there's nothing *left* for people like us! Don't you know that?
> JAYA: You're wrong, there are choices — there must be choices —
> OM: Huh! I didn't choose. I stood in queue and was chosen! And if not this queue, there would have been other queues — [...] [238].

Harvest conjures up a world in which the organ trade, like any other service industry, is now fully institutionalized, smoothly operating under the control of an entity embodying all the rapacious forces of global capitalism: the transnational corporation. Interplanta Services, Padmanabhan's make-believe multinational, is only a small leap of the imagination away from the International Kidney Exchange, an organization set up, anthropologist Nancy Scheper-Hughes informs us, by U.S. physician H. Barry Jacobs with the aim of procuring living donors in the third world, most of whom hailed from India.[4] Scheper-Hughes has written extensively about the global, if clandestine, trade in human body parts, describing the phenomenon as a case of "neo-cannibalism" (14–17). It is tempting, at first glance, to read this illicit global economy as merely a further consequence of the unequal economic conditions that global capitalism gives rise to. Scheper-Hughes herself suggests that the trade in human organs is best understood in the context of global capitalism when she points out that the global circuit of organs mirrors the circuit of capital flows in the era of globalization: "from South to North, from Third to First world, from poor to rich, from black and brown to white" (197). And yet, as I shall argue here, *Harvest* shows us that the human organ cannot be assimilated to goods and services produced in the third world for first-world consumption because the organ is not a product of the third-world body's wage-labor. Om, we recall, is *unemployed*. Padmanabhan's play thus reveals how third-world inhabitants with no land or property to their name, and no buyer for their labor-power, are lured into bargaining with the sole remaining possessions they can count on to generate any income: their body parts.

I propose, however, that we first situate the organ trade within the dynamics of the late capitalism that Padmanabhan is at such pains to critique. Many theorists writing about global capitalism today have pointed out that first-world economies are increasingly reliant not on production but consumption (see Bauman 1998; Harvey 2000; Hardt and Negri 2004). The workforce of the first world is ever more disengaged from industrial labor and manufacture either because, in the wake of technological advances, such labor is carried out by non-human means, or alternatively, because human labor is obtained elsewhere. In their drive to multiply profits, first-world economies rely on production sites where labor is "cheaper, less assertive, less taxed, more feminised [and] less protected by states and unions" (Comaroff and Comaroff 295). Typically located in the third world, such production sites displace human labor to remote geographical locations, allowing for industrial production to become increasingly less visible in the first world. The first world, on the other hand, sees a proliferation of service-economies, economies which rely on consumers to purchase increasingly non-material commodities.

Yet organ trade does not strictly correspond to this global economic pattern. The organ is indeed a material good originating in the third world, but it is *not* the end product of the labor process. It is, rather, a non-manufactured product that promises to generate "wealth without production, value without effort" (Comaroff and Comaroff 313). Undreamt of amounts of money with little to no labor: this is the particular promise that organ sale extends to the impoverished and disenfranchised populations of the third-world. In order to understand the often irresistible lure of this promise, we must explore not the transformation in the conditions of capitalist production, but rather the transformation in the *social imaginaries* of the laboring poor.

Jean and John Comaroff theorize just this transformation. According to the Comaroffs, capitalism today presents itself to the laboring poor in a millennial, messianic form, advertising itself as "a gospel of salvation; [as] a capitalism that, if rightly harnessed, is invested with the capacity wholly to transform the universe of the marginalised and the disempowered" (292). Thus, the key to understanding millennial capitalism lies in the particular brand of seduction upon which it operates. This seductiveness, they argue, is most visibly manifested in the unprecedented proliferation of "occult economies" in the third world (312). The Comaroffs cite not just organ trade as an example of these occult economies, but also the sale of services such as fortune-telling, or the development of tourist industries based on the sighting of monsters. Occult economies are characterized by the fact that they respond to the allure of "accruing wealth from nothing" (313). In other words, occult economies are animated by the same tendency that motivates wealth-accruing actions like gambling or speculation on the stock market.

It is within this millennial context, I want to argue, that we need to understand Om's decision to embark on the sale of his body parts. Organ trade is no longer a criminalized activity in the futuristic Bombay he inhabits, but this only makes the promises of millennial capitalism seem all the more alluring. "We'll have more money than you and I have names for! Who'd believe there's so much money in the world?" he says to his mother ecstatically

(219). Om's decision is brought on by that set of contradictory emotions, hope and despair, that millennial capitalism and its predatory economies unleash upon its targets. His defensive retort to Jaya when she expresses her reservations for what he has done is plagued by these conflicting emotions:

> You think I did it lightly. But [...] we'll be *rich*! Very rich! Insanely rich! But you'd rather live in this one small room, I suppose! Think it's such a fine thing — living day in, day out, like monkeys in a hot-case — lulled to sleep by our neighbours' rhythmic farting! [...] And starving [223].

Immiserated, poor and hopelessly excluded from capitalism's promise of global prosperity, why, Om reasons, should he not cash in on his healthy body? Herein lies the hope extended by this new economy: a quick fix to his condition by presenting a new, quasi-magical means of making undreamt of amounts of money.

Making money. This is the promise that the occult economy of organ trade extends to its objects: sell your organ and you will *make* more money than you will ever *earn* through years of toil and labor. The promise of millennial capitalism works because it allows the third-world individuals like Om to see their body as that which contains a natural 'spare' part, a naturally occurring surplus — a kidney, a cornea — that is not the end product of labor yet is still in high demand. Padmanabhan depicts the extent to which the organs economy presents itself as a miraculous option through Ma's reactions to Om's contract. Unlike Jaya, Ma is puzzled by her son's promises of unimaginable riches: "What kind of job pays a man to sit at home?" she asks (220). As she begins to understand what Om's new "job" entails, she resumes her queries as though she cannot believe their good fortune: "Tell me again: all you have to do is sit at home and stay healthy? [...] And they'll pay you? [...] Even if you do nothing but sit at home and pick your nose all day?" (222).

By Act II of the play, Ma has become completely captivated by their new life of opulence. When the curtain rises for the second act, Padmanabhan's stage directions tell us, the main room of the family household is littered with an array of high-tech gadgets that Ginni has provided them with in order to entertain them and keep them comfortable: "TV set, computer terminal, mini-gym, an air-conditioner, the works," (227). Designed to pamper the body, and provide it with entertainment and comfort, these devices lure Ma into recklessly enjoying a lifestyle that was hitherto unavailable to them: the life of unrestrained consumption that late capitalism advertises. Addicted to the endless soap operas and commercials now available to her via cable television, Ma is the perfect recipient of Ginni's gifts, indulging in undreamt-of luxuries without realizing that they are designed to numb her against interrogating the price that her son has had to pay in exchange for their newfound comfort. By the end of the play, Ma has locked herself away in what Padmanabhan terms a VideoCouch, a capsule into which Ma can plug herself, watch one of 150 television channels and not worry about food or digestion because the unit is entirely self-sufficient. Surrendering to the joys of technologically-induced bliss, Ma is thrilled that, for literally performing no labor at all, "they will be rich forever and ever" (235).

Not all the high-tech devices that Ginni delivers to the donors are designed to pamper the body, however. In the very first scene of the play, shortly after Om's return with a new "job," representatives of Interplanta Services barge into the donors' home to install a series of gadgets. As Om, Jaya and Ma watch, they dismantle the family's rudimentary kitchen and replace it with their own cooking device and jars containing multi-colored food pellets. They then install the Contact Module, a device that hangs from the ceiling and which looks, Padmanabhan tells us, like a "white, faceted globe" (221). Each time the Contact Module springs to life, Ginni repeatedly invades the privacy of Om's family. I wish to dwell at length on the sci-fi gadget that is the Contact Module. What interactions between the third-world donors and the first-world receiver does the Contact Module permit? And what does this device allow Padmanabhan to achieve on stage?

Let us begin with this latter question. Ginni communicates with the donor family only through the Contact Module. She is thus never physically present on the stage, a fact that is highly significant because Padmanabhan's chosen genre — theatre — is explicitly concerned with a tangible, embodied and physical presence on stage. Yet throughout the play, Ginni is only ever visible in two-dimensions, on the screen of the Contact Module. The only embodied performers on the stage are the racially and visually distinct bodies of the third-world donors. Thus, the audience has no choice but to gaze on a body whose sheer presence on stage challenges the supposed remoteness of the laboring and now cannibalized body, the very body that capitalist production in the era of globalization has displaced into the remote third-world. Furthermore, the Contact Module allows Padmanabhan to establish a structure of gazing and surveillance that mirrors the role of the audience. For, like the receiver, the audience too, gazes at the only physical bodies on stage: the donors.' The audience is thus impelled into an uncomfortable identification with the receiver, the very entity who is responsible for the objectification of third-world bodies that the play so overtly criticizes.[5]

Keeping the first-world receiver's body remote serves a second purpose. It allows Padmanabhan to signal to the profound tensions underlying the predatory relationship between third-world donors and first-world receivers.

The donor's hitherto healthy body harbors, on the one hand, the possibility of prolonging the ailing receiver's life. Yet, on the other hand, the third-world body produces in its new owner, the first-world receiver, a profound anxiety. For like the receiver's own body, the donor's body too is vulnerable to the encroachment of disease and degeneration that must be kept at bay at all costs. The biotechnologies of global capitalism may indeed fuel fantasies of "a regenerative body, whose every loss can be repaired" (Waldby and Mitchell 30), but, as Zygmunt Bauman notes: "the search for the 'truly fit' body is plagued by anxieties which are unlikely ever to be quelled or dispelled. [...] [N]o amount of care or drilling of the body is likely ever to put paid to the gnawing suspicion of malfunctioning" (227). Padmanabhan's Contact Module thus emerges as an ironic set of signifiers, for its actual purpose is to guarantee that no physical contact whatsoever occurs between first and third world environments. The Contact Module effectively enables Ginni to intervene in the donor world without having to set foot in the geographical location that the donors inhabit. Nor would she want it any other way. She has purchased the rights to Om's organs in order to fend off disease and death and has no intention of risking a visit to their unhygienic dwellings. Safely ensconced in her sanitized first-world home, Ginni is able to use the Contact Module to police the daily habits of Om's family in order to ensure that the organs that will one day be hers remain healthy too. Thus, realizing, after her first "visit," that Om's family shares a toilet with forty other families, Ginni reacts with horror, not because of the precarious economic predicament this state of affairs testifies to, but because it is distinctly unhygienic. "It's wrong," she exclaims. "It's disgusting! And I — well, I'm going to change that. I can't accept that. I mean, it's unsanitary!" (225). Accordingly, Interplanta is commissioned to install a toilet in their home that very same day.

The regular monitoring that the Contact Module permits is rendered even more effective given that only Ginni is able to operate it at will. Om's family never knows when Ginni will "visit" them next. By the opening of Act II of the play, we see how well her strategy is working. Two months have elapsed, and Om is panicking because they are late for lunch. (Lunch, of course, consists of the multi-colored nutritional pellets provided for them by Interplanta Services.) "You know how [Ginni] hates it when we're late to eat" Om says, worriedly (228). The Contact Module thus allows the receiver to establish a permanent structure of surveillance in Om's home. Fearing Ginni's rebuke, or worse, a revoking of his contract, Om urges his entire family to police their own behavior. The Contact Module inculcates self-discipline, rendering the third-world bodies into perfect sites of "docility-utility," optimal sites, in other words, from which to extract the healthiest possible organ (Foucault 135–169).

Irrespective of whether they are designed to monitor or pamper, the digital technologies that Ginni has access to effectively reduce Om and his family to little more than sites of *investment* for first-world capital. As Ginni says to the family, warping the pronunciation of Om's name:

> The Most Important Thing is to keep Auwm smiling. Coz if Auwm's smiling, it means his body is smiling and if his body is smiling it means his organs are smiling. And that's the kind of organs that'll survive a transplant best, smiling organs ... [229].

Reading Ginni's actions as an investment signals to the parallels between the human body and land that the play's title, *Harvest*, alludes to. The play, of course, takes its title from the term "organ harvesting," steeped in connotations that need unpacking. If the term "harvest" refers to the process of gathering crops, then "organ harvesting" effectively assimilates the whole human body, from which a part is extracted, to a crop-producing piece of land, and thus, by extension, to the possibility that land harbors of *generating life*. The extractable human body part is accordingly assimilated to the yield or crop; this is the commodity with genuine use-value, the part that it is profitable to detach from the whole. In order to obtain the best possible harvest, as Ginni is well aware, one must not only select the best possible site in which to invest: one must maintain a continued investment in this site. Quality input will produce quality output: namely, a healthy harvest.

But the analogy between the human body and land is hardly exhausted yet. We recall that *Harvest* concludes with an unexpected plot twist. Inter-planta Services has taken away both Jeetu and Om, and Ma, locked away in her Video Couch, is oblivious to the world. Jaya, now alone in the house, watches as the Contact Module springs to life and listens as the real purchaser of Om's body parts, a "red-blooded all-American man" (247) named Virgil, reveals to her that Ginni is literally "a nobody. A computer-generated wet dream" (246). Aware of the illicit relationship between Jaya and Jeetu, Virgil has appropriated himself of Jeetu's body which he intends to use to impregnate Jaya. His intentions when securing a contract with Om were simple: "We look for young men's bodies to live in and young women's bodies in which to *sow* their children" (246; my emphasis). Padmanabhan's carefully chosen words reveal that the association of the body to the life-generating earth lends itself to a fruitful reading of the maternal body in relation to the dynamics of production. As Helen Gilbert (2006) points out, "with this bizarre final twist to the story, Padmanabhan puts organ transplantation and reproductive science [...] on a continuum that suggests ways in which interested capital penetrates the very corpus of its multiple and diverse subjects" (125).

In his part of the world, Virgil explains, they have begun to live longer and longer at the cost of no longer being able to reproduce. The solution to this problem lies in a program which allows first-world citizens to purchase third-world bodies, thus profiting from their lack of economic resources: "We support poorer sections of the world, while gaining fresh bodies for ourselves" (246). Thanks to its futuristic setting, *Harvest* is able to make literal the ideas theorized by critics of the postmodern, late-capitalist world order. Padmanabhan portrays a world in which first-world citizens are so alienated from the dynamics of production, and so dependent on the third-world laboring body that they even rely on this body to obtain the products-infants with which to perpetuate the existence of their own people.

Given the nature of Padmanabhan's critique of global capitalism, it is hardly surprising that the ultimate aim of first-world body buyers is to acquire control over the third-world woman. As Gayatri Spivak points out, "the possession of a tangible place of production, the womb, situates women as agents in any theory of production" (57). Virgil, it would seem, acknowledges this. And yet, as he also knows, the female body is not only the site from which *new* laboring, producing and consuming bodies are made but simultaneously the site responsible for the insertion of the body into materiality and hence the very *mortality* that Virgil is compulsively trying to delay (Braidotti 65).

Virgil's fear of death, the arrival of which he has invested so much in delaying, colors the strategy he uses to seduce Jaya. Typically, impregnation requires that two bodies, one male, one female, engage in *physical* contact and have *unprotected* sexual intercourse. But Virgil is paranoid about the threat of disease that this act entails; even the environment that Jaya lives in is "too polluted" for him to travel there and physically be with her (247). Once more, he resorts to biotechnology to avoid any exposure to germs, viruses and disease that material bodily practices might entail:

> VIRGIL: The guards will make the child possible Zhaya. It's just a formality, a device —
> JAYA: Device?
> VIRGIL: You know, an implant. Something I sent, which they're ready to deliver. And you can take your time. About three days are still within your fertile cycle.
> JAYA: What are you talking about?
> VIRGIL: Zhaya, I'd love to travel to be with you, but I can't —
> JAYA: Then do it! You who are so powerful — you who can travel from body to body — [247].

Jaya refuses Virgil's proposal outright. She does not want simulated sex or a baby that has been artificially inseminated inside her; she wants "real hands" to touch her, a "real weight" upon her body (247). Rejecting the utilitarian framework that Virgil proposes to her, where the maternal-productive aspect of her body is extrapolated and privileged over her physical desire, Jaya responds to Virgil's advances with an ultimatum: "If you want me, you must risk your skin for me" (248).

Bragging that she cannot win against him, Virgil sends his Interplanta employees to break down Jaya's door. But Jaya has discovered "a new definition for winning. *Winning by losing*" (248; my emphasis). She announces to Virgil that she plans to reclaim the "only thing [she] ha[s] which is still [her] own: [her] death" (248). Thus, Jaya resists Virgil's advances and retains her bodily integrity in one swift stroke: she embraces the very mortality that Virgil and his fellow receivers seek to eradicate from their own bodies. "I'm holding a piece of glass against my throat," she warns an increasingly frustrated Virgil (248). The play concludes on this unresolved note. While Virgil weighs his options, Jaya threatens (promises?) to reclaim her own body through suicide. If Jaya refuses to be reduced to a body-part and embraces the material limitations of the corporeality that digital and biomedical technologies seek to override, her act of resistance is undercut by the fact that it requires her to die.

Ending her play in this paradoxical vein allows Padmanabhan to merge dystopia and utopia in a gesture that signals to both the promises and threats unleashed by new technologies under late capitalism. The play thus takes deliberate care not to make biotechnological innovations into a convenient backdrop against which to unravel a thriller plot that might act as an allegory for neocolonialism in which third-world citizens figure as mere victims of first-world exploitation. Rather, *Harvest* deliberately transposes the genre of science fiction onto a third-world context, posing a potent critique of a global capitalism that has harnessed biotechnology in order to prey on third-world bodies that appear to their first-world counterparts as repositories of biological resources with which to increase their own life-spans rather than as purveyors of cheap wage-labor. Crucially, however, *Harvest* is alert to the complex array of circumstances that make the likes of Om, Jeetu and Ma participants, at once unwitting and complicit, in this process. The conventions of science fiction thus allow Padmanabhan to situate biotechnological developments in transplantation and new reproductive technologies at the forefront of this text as it enjoins us to examine, critically and globally, the human relationships, economic conditions and social dynamics that biotechnological developments both generate and rely upon.

Notes

1. Padmanabhan herself conceived of the idea for *Harvest* when she was confronted with the brutally real phenomenon of the trade in human organs, during a visit to her sister in Madras in early 1995. On a morning walk around the town, Padmanabhan tells us in her essay "The Story of *Harvest*" (1998), she saw several men "wearing pajamas, dressing gowns and sterile gauze mouth-masks." Upon making enquiries, she was told that they were "clients of the flourishing trade [in human organs] whose source was the poor villagers of Tamil Nadu" recovering from kidney-transplant surgery (106).
 2. Several scholars and biomedical ethicists have recently advocated a legal market in human organs. See, for instance, Mark Cherry (2005) and John Harris and Charles A. Erin (2003).
 3. Nancy Scheper-Hughes makes a similar point about the idea of free choice in third-world contexts: "Bioethical arguments about the right to sell [one's organs] are based on Euro-American notions of contract and individual 'choice.' But social and economic contexts make the 'choice' to sell a kidney in an urban slum anything but a 'free' and 'autonomous' one" (2001 n.p.).
 4. "By the early 1990s," Scheper-Hughes reports, "some 2000 kidney transplants with living donors were being performed each year in India." A large number of ill, wealthy purchasers were patients in renal units in the UAE or Oman, who paid living donors, most shantytown dwellers of India's largest cities — Bombay, Madras and Calcutta — between $2000 and $3000 (195).
 5. Admittedly, this situation would be considerably different if the play were performed in a third-world country. The third-world bodies on stage would be more familiar to the audience, whereas the first-world American character would be visible in the same way as the majority of third-world audiences are already accustomed to from television, cinema and magazines: in two dimensions. However, Padmanabhan has herself admitted that her frustration with the lack of opportunities for English-language playwrights in India led her to enter the Onassis competition and write *Harvest* specifically for production in the first-world (Gilbert, 2001: 214).

Works Cited

Bauman, Zygmunt. "Postmodern Adventures of Life and Death." *Modernity, Medicine and Health: Medical Sociology Towards 2000.* Ed. Graham Scrambler and Paul Higgs. London/New York: Routledge, 1998. 216–233.
Braidotti, Rosi. "Mothers, Monsters and Machines." *Writing on the Body: Female Embodiment and Feminist Theory.* Ed. Katie Conboy, Nadia Medina and Sarah Stanbury. New York: Coumbia University Press, 1997. 59–80.
Cherry, Mark. *Kidney for Sale by Owner.* Washington D.C.: Georgetown University Press, 2005.
Comaroff, Jean, and John L. Comaroff. "Millennial Capitalism: First Thoughts on a Second Coming." *Public Culture* 12:2 (2000): 291–343.
Foucault, Michel. *Discipline and Punish: The Birth of the Prison.* New York: Vintage, 1995.
Gilbert, Helen. "Introduction to *Harvest*." *Postcolonial Plays: An Anthology.* Ed. Helen Gilbert. London/New York: Routledge, 2001. 214–216.
_____. "Manjula Padmanabhan's *Harvest*: Global Technoscapes and the International Trade in Human Organs." *Contemporary Theatre Review* 16:1 (2006): 123–130.
Hardt, Michael, and Antonio Negri. *Multitude.* New York: Penguin, 2004.
Harris, John, and Charles A. Erin. "An Ethical Market in Human Organs." *The Journal of Medical Ethics.* 29:3 (2003): 137–138.
Harvey, David. "The Work of Postmodernity: The Laboring Body in Global Space." *Iden-

tity and Social Change. Ed. Joseph E. Davis. New Brunswick: Transaction Publishers, 2000. 27–51.

Padmanabhan, Manjula. "Harvest." *Postcolonial Plays: An Anthology*. Ed. Helen Gilbert. London/New York: Routledge, 2001. 217–250.

_____. "The Story of Harvest." *Harvest*. New Delhi: Kali for Women, 1998. 105–109.

Scheper-Hughes, Nancy. "The Global Traffic in Human Organs." *Current Anthropology* 41.2 (2000): 191–224.

_____. "The Global Traffic in Human Organs: A Report Presented to the House Subcommittee on International Operations and Human Rights, United States Congress on June 27 2001." 2 December 2008 <http://www.publicanthropology.org/Times Past/Scheper-Hughes.htm>.

_____. "The New Cannibalism: A Shocking Report in the International Traffic in Human Organs." *New Internationalist* 300 (1998): 14–17.

Spivak, Gayatri. "Feminism and Critical Theory." *The Spivak Reader*. Ed. Donna Landry and Gerald Maclean. New York: Routledge, 1996. 53–75.

Waldby, Catherine, and Robert Mitchell. *Tissue Economies*. Durham: Duke University Press, 2006.

7

"Smudged, Distorted and Hidden"

Apocalypse as Protest in Indigenous Speculative Fiction

ROSLYN WEAVER

> I do not like the way we are being treated by successive governments, or the way our histories have been smudged, distorted and hidden, or written for us. I want our people to have books, their own books, in their own communities, and written by our own people. I want the truth to be told, our truths, so, first and foremost, I hold my pen for the suffering in our communities.
>
> Wright, "Breaking Taboos"

In many representations of the future in science fiction and fantasy texts, white characters often feature at the expense of other ethnic groups, while Indigenous people are missing entirely or their presence is superficial. In his discussion of Australian science fiction, Brian Attebery suggests that "such absences are the fictional equivalent of the longstanding legal principle of *terra nullius*, by which the Australian continent was treated as if it had no ownership before white settlement" (387). He argues that exclusions of races in speculative fictions imply that "the days of that group are numbered," for "silence, too, can be a form of control" (385).

Yet some Australian Indigenous authors, or those who sympathize with Indigenous people, have presented their own speculative fictions that place non-white characters firmly at the center. They use apocalyptic themes and language to protest the silencing of their voices. The following discussion surveys the ways in which apocalypse and Indigenous issues can intersect, and then examines the works of three writers — Sam Watson, Alexis Wright, and Archie Weller — who use the metaphor of apocalypse in their speculative fictions to discuss the impact of colonization on Indigenous peoples. Critics have argued that apocalypse provides a discourse through which dominant members of society can legitimate their persecution of minority groups. Yet the narrators of Revelation and Isaiah and other apocalyptic texts were themselves from persecuted groups in society, and their use of apocalypse was arguably subversive. Apocalyptic literature can thus function as a protest, as a critical voice for minorities to speak against dominant powers and prophesy their overthrow. The genre has particular appeal for colonized groups such as Australian Aborigines, because the apocalyptic paradigm of revelation and disaster can work effectively to interrogate the history of colonization and relations between white and Indigenous Australians, and propose spaces of hope for the future.

Apocalypse and Indigenous Writing

Critics have described apocalyptic writing as a genre that can legitimize or even encourage the persecution of minority groups. Ken Cooper, for instance, claims that apocalypse panders to ethnic superiorities, calling it a "curiously liberating genre" which displays "repressed racial fantasies" (83):

> Postholocaust novels — fables, really — propagated flagrant, blood-will-tell stereotypes that were inflammatory [...] blacks reverting to cannibalism after nuclear war, while others envision Caucasian holocaust survivors joining noble bands of Native Americans and adopting their ways, frequently with sexual undertones [...] a nuclear attack would actually regenerate a Midwestern city by enabling a suburban "world brand-new" to rise from the ashes, but only after the bomb exploded — not coincidentally — above the Negro district [83–84].

Cooper argues that after a catastrophe such as a bomb, white people reign supreme while ethnic populations die, because the nuclear bomb was, after all, built by white people to protect themselves (81).

Speculative texts not only regularly focus on a white future, but also often privilege that scenario over a non-white or multicultural past, in a practice that echoes colonial processes. There is a strong tendency in speculative texts towards linear accounts of time that dismiss history and emphasize the present. Apocalyptic fantasies can therefore conveniently reject the past as irrelevant, a strategy that suppresses other (Indigenous) versions of history. This contrasts with some Indigenous fictions that conflate past, present and future to give equal weight and value to all times, such as Watson's *The Kadaitcha Sung* and Wright's *Plains of Promise*, which reject traditional white constructions of "history" and propose new approaches to time.

Apocalyptic tales of the future, then, can be susceptible to racist attitudes to minority groups and dismissive of non-white history, yet other critics suggest that apocalypse offers hope for a future that will rectify the present world's injustices. Lois Parkinson Zamora argues that:

> Novelists who employ the images and narrative perspectives of apocalypse are likely, therefore, to focus less on the psychological interaction of their characters than on the complex historical and/or cosmic forces in whose cross-currents those characters are caught. Their awareness of the historical forces conditioning and constraining individual existence suggests a dissenting perspective [3].

James Berger has claimed that apocalypse has the potential to be radical, and that readings of apocalypse as conservative ignore "how profoundly hostile most apocalyptic imagination is to the versions of hierarchy, truth, and morality currently in power" (223). Similarly, Christopher Rowland suggests that while apocalypse may appear "unsavoury" and "unhealthy," it has nonetheless "expressed a critical response to the injustices of the world, frequently on behalf of the powerless, and opened eyes closed to realities which have become accepted as the norm" (56).

There are several reasons why apocalyptic literature is an appropriate choice to interrogate the effects of colonization on Indigenous people. Firstly, apocalypse functions as revelation, uncovering the truth and disclosing hidden things. Writers can use apocalyptic fiction to critique Eurocentric political and historical systems and reveal an alternative history, ideally with the consequence of challenging reader perceptions of history and society. Secondly, apocalypse has strong associations with the end of the world and new beginnings, utilizing the imagery of life, death, disaster, and renewal. In this context, postcolonial literature is apocalyptic because it resonates with themes of the end of the world and annihilation of tribes and cultures, and also because the colonial search for "new worlds" inevitably involves the ending of one (Indigenous) world and the imposition of another (white) one. Such writing challenges the commonly held colonial belief that the Indigenous populations of colonized countries were inevitably dying out, instead unveiling a transforming perspective that the end was not part of the natural order, but was in fact caused by white people. Finally, writers can use the apocalyptic paradigm of renewal following disaster to suggest new ways forward.

Apocalyptic fiction can thus be a powerful medium for minorities. Lydia Wevers argues that novels by Indigenous writers can challenge a white audience because readers are given "new and different knowledge" (127):

> [White readers] have to participate, to cede agency, accept concepts, landscapes and actions that challenge not just power relations but also their apprehension of what history is and how it is understood, that challenge also their epistemologies,

taxonomies and contingencies. Part of the attraction of indigenous texts [...] may be the revisioning they force, and the hope they offer of imagining the world locally, specifically, but also radically redrawn [127].

When Indigenous writers use apocalyptic themes, this potential is magnified. Apocalypse can be an empowering tool for Indigenous authors because the revelation and disclosure of new perspectives and hidden truths show the writers to be in possession of a greater knowledge than their readers. The writer is revealing, the reader is discovering. Apocalypse offers an opportunity for Indigenous writers to reinscribe the unwritten future with themselves as a significant part of the landscape. The authors position Aboriginal characters as central and vital to the future, and they narrate catastrophes that have actually occurred rather than fictional disasters.

To explore this potential, the following discussion will focus on three speculative fictions: Watson's *The Kadaitcha Sung*, Wright's *Plains of Promise*, and Weller's *Land of the Golden Clouds*.[1] Both Watson's and Wright's novels approach magic realism with their mix of ordinary life and the spiritual world, while Weller's tale is a fantasy, set in a post-nuclear future Australia. These writers set their particular works in diverse times from pre-colonial days to several thousand years in the future, and in urban and rural areas around Australia. Each of the novels utilizes apocalyptic motifs and language to revisit and retell colonial history, and to interrogate the legitimacy of white rule by exposing the damaging consequences of Australia's European settlement and revealing it as a terrible apocalypse, the ending of the world. Yet the authors also propose spaces of restoration and hope for the future that reconciliation and Indigenous power offer.

SAM WATSON: THE KADAITCHA SUNG

> My land! My land! What have the migloo [white people] done to you? They have bound you in chains of concrete and steel. They have raped you. How can you live with such terrible shame? [*Kadaitcha* 132].

Sam Watson sets his novel, *The Kadaitcha Sung*, in both colonial and contemporary times, and tells the story of the central character Tommy to take revenge on a traitorous black Kadaitcha (sorcerer), Booka, who betrayed his people and joined with white people in their oppression of Aborigines. Booka steals the "heart of the Rainbow Serpent from the fountain of life" (33) from its place in Uluru, and Tommy's task is to find and return the sacred heart to its rightful place, an act that will restore the land to its former glory. While Tommy is successful in saving the land, the novel ends with his execution after a jury convicts him of the murder of a white policeman, a crime that he did not commit. This final act positions Tommy as the messianic figure of salvation for the future.

Watson has said in an interview that he wrote *Kadaitcha* for didactic purposes, as a protest message against the colonization of Australia. "I think you've got to slam people between the eyes with a hard-hitting message and that's the way I write. I don't apologize for it" ("I Say This to You" 595). The message of the novel is specifically for white people:

> I wanted to make a statement and I wanted to get into the hearts and minds of the great unwashed, white Australian masses. Those are the people I wrote for. I wrote in the language of the conqueror, but the dialogue between the Aboriginal people is in nonstandard English. I wanted to be as honest as I could [...]. But I wanted to do it in a way that still gave people the opportunity to draw back without feeling too confronted ["I Say This to You" 589–590].

If Watson's strategy is to educate white readers about their inherited guilt without alienating them, the graphic sex and violence in his novel make these aims problematic, because they are likely to confront and alienate some readers. Furthermore, Eva Rask Knudsen has suggested that Watson has designed his message to "mobilize his fellow Aboriginals" rather than inform white readers, because the novel assumes that white people are guilty instead of establishing this fact (308). In a review, Marion Halligan noted that one can read the novel as a "distillation of hate;" it is "a vast construct of revenge and dwells horribly on all its dark pleasures. Its prose is an equally terrible construct, of [...] clichés and tired phrases and secondhand syntax [used to] describe murder, torture, rape of men and women" (11). Yet Halligan writes that this "awful prose [...] is the right vehicle for his message" (11).

Watson uses the tropes of apocalypse — revelation, destruction, judgment, and hope — to offer new perspectives on colonization, the devastation that white people caused, and their coming judgment. The novel describes an Australia before colonization that is idyllic, a sanctuary: "One god, a greater being, made his camp on the rich veldts and in the lush valleys of the South Land" (1). The god, Biamee, had "chosen" the land for his own camp, and it was not desolate but "rich and brown [...] bountiful in life" (32). A "veil of mists" covered the land to protect it from the "savage" world (1), paralleling the protection of the Garden of Eden by powerful angels. This south land is a garden (3), the "wealthiest land on the earth," even "the promised land" (203). Yet the coming of white people produces a wasteland: "The evil one caused the mists to lift from the land and other mortals saw its wealth and abundance [...]. The fair-skinned ones laid waste to the garden and the chosen people" (3).

In language echoing biblical apocalypse, the white people in *Kadaitcha* are "the evil ones" (204); they are "a terrible plague that had come upon them with an evil suddenness" (62). Watson writes that colonization was a violent battle, not a relatively benign event: "The mass murderers of the NMP reminded the rest of Australia that colonisation in the north had been a vicious and bloody process [...] the great native wars" (41). White people are brutal: they are "driven by a blood lust that was never far from the surface" (61) and have a "mindless savagery" (62). Tommy's enemy, Booka, an excessively violent and evil Aboriginal Kadaitcha, adopts a white body in order to "walk more easily in the camp of the migloo" (41). The superficial meaning of this act is merely to facilitate his work and existence in a largely white society, but the implication is clearly that one can easily overlook Booka's aggression and savagery among whites because he blends in. The violence of whites is alien to most Indigenous people. The "camps of the innocent" belong to the Indigenous population, while the white people have a "love for blood" (204). Watson posits that this aggression and violence is antithetical to Indigenous life: "The migloo ways — their language and their violence — were foreign to the land of Uluru" (62). As Ken Gelder and Jane M. Jacobs point out, the novel also narrates violence between Aboriginal groups, between Indigenous people who adhere to tribal laws and those who do not (111). Yet Booka and other violent Indigenous characters are exceptions. White people are foreign, alien, and outsiders, a distinction that Watson reinforces with his use of "migloo" to designate whites.

As apocalypse reveals, its disclosures can be warnings of judgment, as in Revelation, and Watson's novel warns that the time is coming when whites will suffer punishment for their crimes against the Indigenous people and land. The return of the sacred heart does not satisfy Tommy, who demands that the god Biamee accede to his request that "for every one hundred migloo, there had to be one that would know depthless tragedy and sorrow. That chosen one would be ridden by a hunger that could never be satisfied, that single life would be a lasting sacrifice to the land of the people" (310). The violence of colonization is a sin that can "never be expiated" (241), and the punishment motif reflects the judgment warnings in Revelation if the guilty do not seek forgiveness. Tommy's final words before his death makes this clear: "You will be doomed to the end of time to wear the blood of my people [...]. The blood is upon the land until the end of time, and it is upon you until the end of time" (311). Watson has said that Australia is a "bastard nation with a history of bloodshed" ("Aboriginal"); elsewhere he argues that a treaty between white and Aboriginal groups is a way for white people to "right the wrongs" ("Treaty or Ghost Dance" 15). If there is no treaty, a "racial holocaust" will occur and the nation will begin "a time of terrible darkness" ("Treaty or Ghost Dance" 15). These apocalyptic ideas of evil and judgment recur in his novel. Tommy says that: "No migloo who walks on this land is innocent. They are all guilty! And they shall all be punished for what they have done" (131).

In spite of the negative depictions of white people and the long-lasting disastrous effects of colonization on Indigenous people, the novel nonetheless expresses some optimism for a better future. Tommy's quest to restore the land is successful, and there is evidence of some reconciliation between Indigenous and white groups. For instance, Tommy has both white and black heritage; he has not only his father's Kadaitcha blood but also his white mother's blood. He wonders if this combination places him in "two camps" (182), although at times both groups deny him any advantages. Yet it is he, not a full-blood Kadaitcha, who is destined to exact revenge on Booka. Moreover, Tommy's job as a court interpreter, a mediator between white and Indigenous groups, reinforces the connection. For Attebery, the figure of Tommy in both modern and ancient contexts "asserts the continuity of Aboriginal tradition within modern urban Australia" (400). Gelder and Jacobs also point out that Tommy's name, Gubba, is an Aboriginal abbreviation of government meaning a white person (110). Tommy's racial identity, then, means that he is able to represent both groups at different times. Indeed, Watson singles out Tommy's white mother in particular as a key reason for his ability to defeat his enemy: "But Koobara's son had been born of a white woman, and Biamee promised his people that the Kadaitcha child would deliver them" (4). The particularly unusual aspect of this is that even while Tommy's hatred for white people has punctuated virtually every page of the novel, his mother has been chosen because her "blood reaches back to sorcerers from the northern lands. They worshipped stones, great standing stones, and their powers are equal to those of the Kadaitcha" (228). It is this English blood that the novel credits with unlocking the sacred heart (229), and the final association of English sorcerers with the Kadaitcha suggests that the two groups are, in fact, equal.

In the context of Tommy's mixed heritage, this equivalence of black and white groups is a striking choice in a text that is otherwise hostile to white people, seeming as it does to suggest that there may be hope for a new world in which reconciliation and racial equality is possible. Watson has spoken of his own tolerance towards white people and recognition of common ground:

> I have an open mind about all the different cultures and all the lands. Also I was trying to provide white readers with a link back to their own past because I have always argued that white Australians, every single white Australian does have a history dating back to a land-based culture ["I Say This to You" 591].

In *Kadaitcha*, Tommy's dual heritage as well as the equal ancestry between white and Indigenous groups possibly reflects Watson's attempts to demonstrate these beliefs. Yet the textual implications of equality and kinship between white and black rest uneasily alongside the negative constructions of white people, ultimately achieving an ambivalent portrayal of hope and reconciliation.

Alexis Wright: Plains of Promise

> No one was able to look after the land any more, not all of the time, the way they used to in the olden days. Life was so different now that the white man had taken the lot. It was like a war, an undeclared war. A war with no name. And the Aboriginal man was put into their prison camps, like prisoners in the two world wars. But nobody called it a war: it was simply the situation, that's all. Protection. Assimilation
> [...] different words that amounted to annihilation [*Plains of Promise* 74].

Alexis Wright's *Plains of Promise* narrates the apocalyptic effects of white mission control and displacement on generations of an Indigenous family. The novel tells the story of an Aboriginal girl Ivy, who is taken from her "country"— her ancestral land — and placed in a white mission. The loss of family, land, and identity has terrible consequences for Ivy and her daughter Mary, and results in a situation of displacement and a cycle of suffering and evil that repeats itself throughout the generations. In its "interpenetration of the miraculous and mundane" (Bliss 682), *Plains of Promise* is akin to magic realism, within the speculative fiction genre, collapsing past and present, the ordinary and supernatural.

Wright's novel is apocalyptic in two key ways: in its use of disaster motifs and also its explicit function as revealed truth. *Plains of Promise* presents the consequences of white colonization as an enduring catastrophe where the dislocation of family and place are an apocalypse, the end of the world. The novel also intentionally reveals an Indigenous history and reality that white people have hidden. This chapter opened with Wright's quotation about history being "written for us," and elsewhere she has noted the "damage" that Indigenous people suffer because of misrepresentation when dominant groups have silenced or misconstrued Aboriginal voices ("Interview" 120). Michael Dodson makes a similar argument in his discussion of popular white depictions of Aborigines: "in all these representations, these supposed 'truths' about us, our voices and our visions have been notably absent [...]. Nearly suffocated with imposed labels and structures, Aboriginal peoples have had no other choice than to insist on our right to speak back" (4). When Wright says that her purpose is to tell the "truth" because non–Indigenous people have "smudged, distorted and hidden" her people's histories, this exactly mirrors the purpose of apocalypse because it claims to reveal the truth and disclose what is hidden or covered. *Plains of Promise* is deeply critical of lethargic and fatalistic attitudes, protesting against acceptance and passivity. Mary reflects on Aboriginality, saying: "Black is negative. Stands for *no*" (258).

This voice of dissent speaks out against the generally accepted history of Australia, by framing colonization as a catastrophe, a nightmare of destruction. Wright suggests that European culture and "civilization" did not benefit the Indigenous people, but instead decimated and almost annihilated them. White treatment of Indigenous people results in war, an "undeclared" war that has no name (74). Indigenous people have "lived in slavery, bound to the most uncivilised and cruellest people their world had ever known. Those enslaved were the Aborigines who had escaped the whiteman's bullet, his whip, his butchering" (133). White mission control over Indigenous people results in a litany of apocalyptic events: death by fire, drowning, plague and disease; imagery that is strongly suggestive of biblical discourse. The treatment of religion in the novel is ironic, however, for Wright describes the church's preaching of salvation and mercy in the context of its mistreatment of Aboriginal people. In language that articulates and then subverts the biblical hope for a new world, a paradise, she constructs the church as a hellish organization. The St Dominic's mission is allegedly "the heartland of 'God's paradise on earth' " (37), "a prize in the garden of Eden [...] the Kingdom of Heaven" (65), but it is closer to hell, particularly for Ivy. St Dominic's becomes known as "a place of evil [...] the place people most feared being sent to. A place of death. A devil's place" (36). The minister of the mission, Jipp, prides himself on his paradise of fruit orchards that are symbolic of the "life everlasting in the whiteman's faith," but this is a façade: the fruit rots and decays as a witness to the church leader's hypocrisy and immorality (32–33).

The church in *Plains of Promise* is part of a government initiative to remove Indigenous children from their parents and place them in special missions, schools and churches, under white authority and influence. Wright's novel is particularly concerned with the effects of removing children from their families, a practice often termed the "stolen generations."[2] In *Plains of Promise*, mission leaders attempt to justify the assimilation of "half-caste" children because if they remove them from their parents, the children are then able to "make something of themselves," particularly if they marry a white person; intermarriage will benefit the Indigenous partner because then "their children will be whiter and more redeemable in the likeness of God the Father Almighty" (11–12). Yet the separation of child and parent has devastating results. The events of the novel reflect the reality of Indigenous life in Australia. Australian state governments adopted assimilation policies throughout the 1930s to the 1960s, although some practices dated back to the nineteenth century. John Chesterman and Heather Douglas write that assimilation could take two different forms: "The first could be called 'biological absorption,' or the desired removal of Indigenous physical characteristics. The second can be termed 'social integration,' whereby Indigenous cultural or social practices would yield to non–Indigenous social and cultural practices" (48–49). Assimilation could include many different aspects:

> policies of the progressive breaking up of stations and reserves [...] schemes for education, training, and employment, and efforts to house Aboriginal families in predominantly white neighborhoods. They included policies of taking Aboriginal children away from their parents to be adopted by white families or to be brought up in children's homes, and giving Aborigines exemption from Aboriginal protection and control acts, by requiring that they give up their Aboriginal traditions and communal association [Moran 179].

Anthony Moran writes that assimilation policies were initially borne out of "humanitarian impulses, and notions of justice and egalitarianism" (180). Yet while some white people may have thought that assimilation would benefit Indigenous people, whom they viewed as uncivilized and uncultured, policies of assimilation had genocidal effects in the eyes of its targets, the Indigenous population. Indeed, in *Plains of Promise*, Wright renames assimilation as "annihilation" (74). Joan Gordon notes that for Indigenous people globally, "annihilation may occur through familiarization: by assimilating or by 'passing,' by absorbing or being absorbed by the dominant culture. That is the peaceful method. Or the annihilation may occur through erasure: by expulsion or killing" (205). As Rebecca La Forgia points out, the United Nations definition of genocide includes the practice of "*forcibly transferring children of the group to another group* with the intent to destroy, in whole or in part, their national, ethnic, racial or religious grouping" (193).

Wright has described land as a "central character" in her work, noting that she is particularly interested in the ways that the "land might respond to different stories" ("Interview" 121). *Plains of Promise* opens with a description of a tree that is alien to its environment, and this foreign tree has apocalyptic consequences for the earth it inhabits:

> the tree should not have been allowed to grow there on their ancestral country. It was wrong. Their spiritual ancestors grew more and more disturbed by the thirsty, greedy foreign tree intruding into the bowels of their world. The uprising fluid carried away precious nutrients; in the middle of the night they woke up gasping for air, thought they were dying [4].

The tree grows not far from a "misplaced, European-style church" (37). Whites are alien people living in a place where they do not belong, and their presence stifles and slowly kills the land and its people. The story that concludes *Plains of Promise* alludes to the significance of the loss of country, language and tradition. It is a tale of a family of birds living at a lake, and the removal of generations of this family, who hold the secret of water, results in the disappearance of the water: "The great lake dried up and is no more" (304). In *Plains of Promise*, the apocalyptic diminishing of generations has apparently caused too much destruction for reconciliation or restoration to be possible.

Archie Weller: Land of the Golden Clouds

> He enjoyed the company of these quiet, dark people who walked the land all over. It was known by every Ilkari that the Keepers of the Trees had sprung from this land like the rocks and rivers and trees themselves. They were a part of this country — every grain of it — and they knew all its secrets. They kept out of the way of the white people and their ways, for it had been the white people who had annoyed the spirits and caused the High Ones to walk upon this earth, bringing not sustenance but destruction. So they kept to themselves, these remnants of the oldest Tribe, with their own language, laws and customs [*Land of the Golden Clouds* 4–5].

Archie Weller's post-apocalyptic fantasy novel, *Land of the Golden Clouds*, takes place three thousand years into the future after a nuclear event has radically altered Earth. He uses a traditional epic quest convention to address issues of diversity and unity among different races of people. The central character Red Mond gathers representatives of diverse ethnic groups to lead an attack on their enemy, the Nightstalkers, a group of cave-dwelling humans who emerge at night to attack and eat other people. Weller's use of speculative fiction focuses more on the possibilities for restoration than devastation, and he reveals a future where reconciliation is not only possible but mandatory for survival.

Land of the Golden Clouds depicts the events as an apocalypse; it is "the wrath" (20) and "Armageddon" (211). White violence has destroyed the land and damaged the environment: "The general feeling in the caravan was one of unease [...]. Even the gentle Kareen could offer no comfort to the land all around her. It was in great pain, she told her cousin. There were certainly enough signs of the turmoil that had erupted here at the time the High Ones had walked upon the earth" (308). The shame and sins of the past cry out from the very earth in Weller's novel and the land demands restitution. The Keepers of the Trees (an Indigenous group) feel this pain as they travel over the land: "They could sense the result of this destruction on these desolate pages of the landscape they had just passed, where not a single tree stood to hold the spirit of an ancestor close to the earth. It was a forgotten land — an unhappy land" (139). European violence haunts the land in Weller's work;

the Keepers avoid relics of European buildings because "often uneasy, restless spirits frequented the ruins of their home" (304).

Not only are European buildings foreign to the land, but English names are also signs of domination. *Land of the Golden Clouds* describes the practice of anglicizing place names as "white man's desire to establish some prestige that made him touch with a finger a million years of history, then claim it as his own" (82). Edward Said has called imperialism "an act of geographical violence through which virtually every space in the world is explored, charted, and finally brought under control" (225). He suggests that imperialism, with its exploration, mapping, and colonization, results in a "loss of the locality to the outsider" (225). When colonizers, the outsiders, assign British names to sites, and dictate a foreign language as the only language to be spoken, this effectively reverses their own status as aliens and establishes the Indigenous people as the new outsiders, aliens in their own land. Simon Ryan has argued that mapping a place positions the land as a text, which colonists can inscribe and thus dominate (126). Cartography, then, has been seen as an act of power and control — a silencing — for those who practice it. The control that white people exert over the land is an unsuccessful attempt to impose themselves on a place that is not theirs.

This practice also erases Indigenous history. The absence of Indigenous people in many white speculative fictions perhaps reflects a dismissive attitude to the past. Colonization, after all, entirely rejects history for new beginnings. It is an ending for the colonized people, but a start for the colonizers, who begin a "new world" as if nothing has gone before. Ross Gibson has written that in the context of European exploration "any space which did not seem to have meanings invested in it was alluring because its first inscribers could imbue it with their own meanings, their own knowledge and beliefs [...]. The world was being written into European history" (5). Ryan has suggested that imperialism and the practice of cartography engenders a dismissal of the past because it ignores history and favors the future (127). Mapping a place implies that it is a tabula rasa and only from that time does it have existence and history.

If colonial practices are brutal, Weller's novel suggests that white people themselves are inherently violent, while the Indigenous groups are peaceful. During an attack, for example, the Keepers of the Trees refuse to interfere because brutality is seen as "white man's business. They had been killing each other forever and when they were tired of that they had turned on the Keepers of the Trees and had killed them as well" (139). This white violence is senseless: "[The Keepers] disliked anything to do with warlike white men who used their aggression without reason. They knew many stories of past atrocities perpetrated upon their people, that lost none of the horror just because they were only stories now" (286).

Yet despite the racial divisions, *Land of the Golden Clouds* is preoccupied with the theme of unity, with its theme of disintegration and re-integration permeating every aspect from its structure to its characters. The novel features all the main characters' perspectives in turn, and thus gives equal weight to their diverse beliefs and attitudes. An explanatory note prefacing the novel outlines the use of languages in the novel: Nyoongah, Koori, Gypsy, Spanish, a "type" of Hebrew and a "type of hybrid English" (viii). The combination of different languages between the groups, the changing perspectives, and also the shift between past and present tense, all suggest a breakdown of boundaries and distinctions, of past and future, particularly given that some of the languages are themselves impure types, "hybrid" mixings of several distinct languages. Similarly, the Keepers of the Trees are the "remnants of the oldest Tribe" (5), distinct from the other groups, separate and never fully involving themselves with different races. Yet despite being set apart, Weller shows that the Keepers are prepared to sacrifice their lives for the greater purpose of defeating a common enemy, offering their assistance to the other groups in the battle (363).

Weller's novel concludes with a view of faiths and beliefs that approaches relativism, in an apparent rhetorical strategy to demonstrate that the only path forward and chance for a better world is to focus on common areas rather than differences. Red Mond's speech at the conclusion of the final battle repeats this philosophy, echoing apocalyptic imagery because destruction leads to a new world:

> The time for war is over [...]. For the purpose of all this death and the loss of our compatriots was not to continue the killing but to end it all. You see the woman I love — who has saved my life twice and who almost died by my side — is one of the enemy. We see cave people who are hated and despised and killed by cave people. Above, there are many different people, all of whom hate each other, and yet we banded together. So who can say who is an enemy? Let us embrace our enemy and all be friends and I will lead you out of our dark world! [368].

In the novel, the envisioned future is only made possible by the cooperation of a plurality of ethnic groups. "We come in peace to do battle with our common enemy. Even though we all have different beliefs we all have the one enemy" (323).

Red Mond's leadership speech for unification is particularly resonant given his racial identity: he is white, while his name suggests "red world" or even "red man." The group of travelers is comprised of people from around the world and of various ethnic backgrounds, but a white person leads them.

This seems to be a curious choice for a writer who has previously identified himself as Aboriginal. Significantly, Watson's and Wright's texts also feature someone with both white and Indigenous heritage as the protagonist. Tommy is half-white and half-Aboriginal (*Kadaitcha*), while Ivy and Mary (*Plains of Promise*) both have black and white heritage. The frequent use of a mixed blood or white character as the agent of restoration may be a recognition of the potential for reconciliation. Weller's novel suggests that any vision for the future must be predicated on the coexistence and cooperation of black and white.

Conclusion

These three writers utilize the imagery and patterns of apocalypse in their speculative fictions as a protest, to reveal new perspectives of the past and the present. The authors argue that white settlement in Australia was apocalyptic because the brutal colonization and war almost destroyed the Indigenous populations of the country. The novels also challenge the view that Indigenous history has no relevance to the present, by conflating past and present to demonstrate that all times coexist and are of equal significance. The act of writing for a people who survived the ending of their world is a protest because it offers the opportunity to address the silencing and distortion of Indigenous voices by giving speech to those whom the colonists designated as less than nothing. These three novels all construct the British colonization of Australia as a disaster for Indigenous people, but the texts offer different perspectives on the prospect of reconciliation. While Wright's novel concludes by focusing on the destruction and loss, Watson's text ends ambiguously, apparently unable to resolve the contradictions between the sustained critique of white society and the narrative attempts to recognize the kinship of white and black groups. It is Weller's work that most clearly focuses on the imperative for reconciliation, presenting a determinedly utopic vision of the potential for interracial restoration. All three texts, however, offer a voice for a people that have too often been silenced or forgotten.

Notes

1. Although various groups have questioned and discounted Archie Weller's Indigenous identity, his status as an influential writer in the field of Indigenous writing remains, and his work identifies with Indigenous people and their struggles. Weller is not the only writer who has experienced challenges to identity; see Nolan and Dawson for one analysis of author identity and literary works. Mudrooroo, for instance, was a high-profile Indigenous writer celebrated for his works such as *Wild Cat Falling*. Yet he became the subject of

public scrutiny over the authenticity of his Indigenous heritage, and Indigenous groups have since rejected his claims of Aboriginal identity. Maureen Clark's work surveys the circumstances in more detail.

2. In 1997, the Human Rights and Equal Opportunity Commission published a release titled "'Bringing Them Home'— The Report of the National Inquiry into the Separation of Aboriginal and Torres Strait Islander Children from their Families." This research examined the policies and practices that resulted in the "stolen generations," Indigenous families separated without consent.

Works Cited

Attebery, Brian. "Aboriginality in Science Fiction." *Science Fiction Studies* 32.3 (November 2005): 385–404.
Berger, James. *After the End: Representations of Post-Apocalypse*. Minneapolis: University of Minnesota Press, 1999.
Bliss, Carolyn. Rev. of *Plains of Promise*, by Alexis Wright. *World Literature Today* 72.3 (Summer 1998): 681–682.
Chesterman, John, and Heather Douglas. "'Their Ultimate Absorption': Assimilation in 1930s Australia." *Journal of Australian Studies* 81 (2004): 47–58.
Clark, Maureen. "Mudrooroo: Crafty Impostor or Rebel with a Cause?" *Australian Literary Studies* 21.4 (October 2004): 101–110.
Cooper, Ken. "The Whiteness of the Bomb." *Postmodern Apocalypse: Theory and Cultural Practice at the End*. Ed. Richard Dellamora. Philadelphia: University of Pennsylvania Press, 1995. 79–106.
Dodson, Michael. "The Wentworth Lecture: The End in the Beginning: Re(de)finding Aboriginality." *Australian Aboriginal Studies* 1 (1994): 2–12.
Gelder, Ken, and Jane M. Jacobs. *Uncanny Australia: Sacredness and Identity in a Postcolonial Nation*. Melbourne: Melbourne University Press, 1998.
Gibson, Ross. *South of the West: Postcolonialism and the Narrative Construction of Australia*. Bloomington: Indiana University Press, 1992.
Gordon, Joan. "Utopia, Genocide, and the Other." *Edging into the Future: Science Fiction and Contemporary Cultural Transformation*. Ed. Veronica Hollinger and Joan Gordon. Philadelphia: University of Pennsylvania Press, 2002. 204–216.
Halligan, Marion. "About Books." *National Library of Australia News* 1.1 (October 1990): 8–11.
Human Rights and Equal Opportunity Commission. "'Bringing Them Home'— Report of the National Inquiry into the Separation of Aboriginal and Torres Strait Islander Children from Their Families." April 1997.
Knudsen, Eva Rask. *The Circle & the Spiral: A Study of Australian Aboriginal & New Zealand M ori Literature*. Amsterdam: Rodopi, 2004.
La Forgia, Rebecca. "Truth: But Still Waiting for Justice." *Alternative Law Journal* 22.4 (August 1997): 192–195.
Moran, Anthony. "White Australia, Settler Nationalism and Aboriginal Assimilation." *Australian Journal of Politics and History* 51.2 (2005): 168–193.
Mudrooroo [Colin Johnson]. *Wild Cat Falling*. 1965. Sydney: Angus and Robertson, 1995.
Nolan, Maggie, and Carrie Dawson. "Who's Who? Mapping Hoaxes and Imposture in Australian Literary History." *Australian Literary Studies* 21.4 (October 2004): v–xx.
Rowland, Christopher. " 'Upon Whom the Ends of the Ages Have Come': Apocalyptic and the Interpretation of the New Testament." *Apocalypse Theory and the Ends of the World*. Ed. Malcolm Bull. Oxford: Blackwell, 1995. 38–57.
Ryan, Simon. "Inscribing the Emptiness: Cartography, Exploration and the Construction

of Australia." *De-Scribing Empire: Post-Colonialism and Textuality.* Ed. Chris Tiffin and Alan Lawson. London: Routledge, 1994. 115–130.

Said, Edward. *Culture and Imperialism.* New York: Vintage-Random, 1994.

Watson, Sam. "Aboriginal Activists Speak Out: It's Time for a Treaty." Interview with Simon Butler. *Green Left Weekly* 430 (29 November 2000): 12–13. 27 October 2007 <http://www.greenleft.org.au/2000/430/22263>.

_____. "I Say This to You." Interview. *Meanjin* 53.4 (1994): 589–596.

_____. *The Kadaitcha Sung.* Ringwood, VIC: Penguin, 1990.

_____. "Treaty or Ghost Dance — One Time." *Indigenous Law Bulletin* 5.21 (2002): 15.

Weller, Archie. *Land of the Golden Clouds.* St Leonards, NSW: Allen & Unwin, 1998.

Wevers, Lydia. "Globalising Indigenes: Postcolonial Fiction from Australia, New Zealand and the Pacific." *JASAL* 5 (2006): 121–132.

Wright, Alexis. "Breaking Taboos." *Australian Humanities Review* 11 (September–November 1998). 27 October 2007 <http://www.lib.latrobe.edu.au/AHR/archive/Issue-September-1998/wright.html>.

_____. "An Interview with Alexis Wright." Interview with Jean-François Vernay. *Antipodes* 18.2 (2004): 119–122.

_____. *Plains of Promise.* St Lucia, QLD: University of Queensland Press, 1997.

Zamora, Lois Parkinson. *Writing the Apocalypse: Historical Vision in Contemporary U.S. and Latin American Fiction.* Cambridge: Cambridge University Press, 1989.

PART THREE: FRESH REPRESENTATIONS

8

Sadhanbabu's Friends

Science Fiction in Bengal from 1882 to 1974

DEBJANI SENGUPTA

> Lazy servants cause Sadhanbabu's ire.
> Babu says, "servants out, robots the answer."
>   Robot inmate,
>   Babu's in a state,
> Robot says, "Hey," Babu replies, "Master."
>   Limerick by Satyajit Ray[1]

Science fiction in Bengal has always been fiction written for children and young adults, but not necessarily with childish concerns. The pulp category of SF in the 1920s and 30s in the West, with the vulgarity of titles, covers and blurbs is remarkably absent in the variety in Bangla, probably because of the colonized Bengali's awe and respect for western science and technology. For many of the early practitioners of the genre, as in the West, science fiction was the literature of the "technological future" (Attebery 36). The first science fiction to be written in Bengal was in the last decades of the 19th century when the effects of the Industrial Revolution were beginning to be felt with the rapid rate of technological change, something noticed in one life-time. For the urban elite of Calcutta, science stories were a kind of myth formation of the new industrial age. Science was perceived as essentially "Western," an attribute of European civilization. Here I do not propose to discuss the narrative of science in Bengal but to see how a literary genre, based entirely on premises of science and technology, gained popularity and thereby accommodated Western science into an Indian world-view. This is very much a part of the Indian intellectual discourse of the late 19th and 20th centuries, particularly in Bengal.

The advent of Western science had begun in the 19th century in Calcutta with the establishment of the Hindu College in 1817 and the teaching of mathematics, including trigonometry. The Calcutta School Book Society was established the same year and began bringing out books on mathematics, chemistry, anatomy and geography. The earlier contribution of the Asiatic Society, established in 1784, cannot be denied in developing a scientific spirit among the people though most of its members were Europeans.[2] One of the students of Hindu College (later called Presidency College) was Akshaykumar Dutta (1820–1886), who distinguished himself as a rationalist and one of the foremost Bengali writers to popularize science. In 1841, his first book *Bhugol* (Geography) came out under the patronage of Tattvabodhini Sabha. Presidency College produced several mathematicians like Gurudas Bannerjee and Ashutosh Mukherjee who however earned their livelihoods from law rather than science. Two men who were responsible for advancement of the scientific temperament in the city were Mahendralal Sircar (1833–1904) and Ashutosh Mukherjee (1864–1924). Sircar was responsible for the establishment of the Indian Association for the Cultivation of Science in 1876. One of the most notable scientists of the age was Jagadishchandra Bose (1858–1937) professor of physics at the Presidency College and a pioneer on the research on electromagnetic waves. The scientific and rational temperament was also aided by the growth of two schools of thought that had taken root in urban Calcutta—the Derozians had inspired rationality and scientific temperament much beyond their numbers and the Brahmo Samaj movement, though a reformist one, had also inspired a similar creed. Despite the deficiencies in science teaching and research in schools and colleges, science was increasingly gaining popularity among the educated elite. This was because of a rapid mechanization of English businesses by the 1880s that lead to a growing desire among the colonized Bengalis to master the alien technologies and sciences, largely perceived as a remedy against superstitions and ignorance. It was a way in which colonial modernity could be mastered and understood. The economic factors and technological progresses interacted and interpenetrated in a variety of ways. This in turn affected the way people began perceiving the world around them. The interface between science, technology and culture would soon be reflected in literature.

Indeed, the first science fiction written in Bangla reflects an understanding of and respect for the rationalism of science which, according to Isaac Asimov, is a marker of good science fiction. This was Hemlal Dutta's "Rahashya" ("The Mystery") that was published in two installments in 1882 in the pictorial *Bigyan Darpan*, a magazine brought out by Jogendra Sadhu. The story revolved around the protagonist Nagendra's visit to a friend's house, a mansion completely automated and where technology is deified. Automatic doorbell, burglar alarms, brushes that clean suits mechanically are some of the innovations described in the story and the tone is of wonder at the rapid automation of human lives. Jagadishchandra Bose, the famous scientist, wrote a story "Palatak Tufan" ("The Runaway Storm") in 1886 and used the rationality of a scientific theory to weave a tale of a storm in the sea that is controlled by dropping a bottle of hair oil on the waves.[3] The story was written as part of a short story competition sponsored by the Kuntaleen Hair Oil Company, one of the early indigenous entrepreneurial ventures. Jagadananda Roy (1869–1933) was a prolific science writer who contributed articles to the literary magazines *Sadhana* (edited by Rabindranath Tagore), *Bharati*, *Probashi* and *Manashi*. His books included *Grohonakhatro* (*Planets and Stars*, 1915), *Pokamakor* (*Bugs and Insects*, 1919), *Gachpala* (*Trees and Plants*, 1921) and *Banglar Pakhi* (*Birds of Bengal*, 1924). These texts were written for young readers to inculcate in them a scientific temperament and impart an awareness of the environment. They were written in a lucid and clear style and in many of these essays we see Jagadananda's obvious literary talent. He was later invited to teach at Tagore's school in Shantiniketan by the poet himself. Jagadananda published *Shukra Bhraman* (*Travels to Venus*) probably in the 1890's where he describes an interstellar journey and visit to another planet. His description of the alien creatures that are seen on Venus uses evolutionary theory about the origins of man: "They resembled our apes to a large extent. Their bodies were covered with dense black fur. Their heads were larger in comparison with their bodies, limbs sported long nails and they were completely naked" (qtd. in Bal, 52). Sukumar Ray (1887–1923) was probably inspired by Arthur Conan Doyle's *The Lost World* when he wrote *Heshoram Hushiyarer Diary* (*The Diary Of Heshoram Hushiar*) in 1922. Like Jagadananda Roy, Sukumar was Bengal's first nonsense poet as well as a prolific writer on scientific and technological subjects explaining natural phenomena or new advances in technology to young readers in the pages of *Sandesh*, a magazine first published in 1913 by his father, Upendrakishore Ray Chaudhuri, a notable member of the Brahmo Samaj and a writer himself.

In its eccentric, enlightened and hilarious narrative, *Heshoram* is quite unlike any science fiction written in the West. It is a spoof on the genre because Sukumar pokes fun at the propensity of scientists to name things, and that too in longwinded Latin words. He critiques the fact that we give names arbitrarily to objects for convenience and suggests that the name of a thing may be somehow intrinsically connected to its nature. So the first creature that Heshoram meets in the course of his journey through the Bandakush Mountains is a "gomratharium" (*gomra* in Bangla means someone of irritable temperament), a creature that sported a long woebegone face and an extremely cross expression. Soon the company comes upon another peculiar animal, not to be found in any textbook of natural sciences. They hear a terrible yowl, a sound between the cries of a "number of kites and owls" and find an animal "that was neither an alligator, nor a snake, nor a fish but resembled to a certain extent all three" (*Heshoram Hushyarer Diary*, p. 492). His howls make Heshoram name him "Chillanosaurus" (*chillano*: to shout). This tour de force certainly subverts the generic characteristics of sci-fi and although a short piece, written in the form of a diary, *Heshoram Hushiyarer Diary* is unique even in Bangla.[4]

Premendra Mitra (1904–1988) was one of Bengal's most famous practitioners of SF. Poet, novelist, short-story writer, Premendra Mitra also wrote brilliant and innovative science fictions. Mitra had once stated that SF not only talked of utopias but the best of them were based on firm scientific facts. Two of his most well known stories are "Piprey Puran" ("The Annals of the Ants") and "Mangalbairi" ("The Martian Enemies"). "Piprey Puran" begins with a dislocation of time from present reality: "This happened many years ago. Everything was strange then[....] The Earth was beautiful to look at! The ground was covered with soft green grass. Countless varieties of plants sported many hued flowers, and at night the sky was covered with thousands of stars — it was a wonderful sight" (3). This displacement, when our present has become a thing of the past, introduces a comic note in an otherwise somber story. This future world, now real, is overrun with Ants, huge in size, intelligent and totally organized. While humans have been busy fighting each other, the Ants have begun their preparations to take over the planet. Six feet tall, they emerge from their hideouts in the Andes Mountains and begin their assault in the year 7757. They defeat the humans in battles, taking them unawares. One by one the countries of Peru, Venezuela and Ecuador come down like a block of cards. A cavalcade of monstrous Ants then completely surrounds the few remaining humans in the cities and annihilates them. The only man who manages to escape unscathed is Don Perito who flees to Mexico. He then becomes the first survivor to describe the destruction wrought by the Ants. Within a few years the killer Ants take over Guyana, Brazil, Bolivia and Argentina. The weapon of mass destruction that the ants use is a powerful bomb strapped to their bodies. In the battle that they wage with humans the Ants use a kind of light — searching, powerful, a little green in color that takes away human sight in an instant. Under this onslaught, all the nations of the earth forget their traditional enmity and come together to fight a common enemy.

This story of the battle of the Ants and humans is broken into small subsections with four first person narrations. The first narrator is the storyteller who begins the story. Soon, the narrative is broken by the diary of Asesh Roy who encountered the Ants in 6757. The third narration is by Senor Sabatini, a famous writer of Rio de Janeiro, who describes the third deadly attack by the Ants. The fourth and final narration is by Sukhomoy Sarkar, who was imprisoned by the Ants for five years and who gives the most comprehensive details of the social and economic organization of his captors. These breaks in the narrative create interesting fissures in an otherwise continuous story. They not only make the impossible appear possible (because they are eyewitness accounts) but give a certain detachment to the narrator to emphasize the moral of his tale. This moral is to be found in the explicit comparison of the Ants with the humans, in which perhaps the humans are found wanting. The description of the society of Ants in the narrative of Sukhomoy Sarkar makes this clear. The Ants live in an advanced democracy where there are no differences in wealth. What they do have are Ants of differing abilities. The intelligent Ants provide the scientific and technological know-how and are strategists who look after the state. Compared to the humans, the Ants are highly advanced in knowledge and social structures, and have a strict sense of justice. Mitra's critique of human life and aspirations are strongly spelt out. To survive, human beings must forget their differences and be united, socially, politically and economically. Otherwise they are doomed.

The moral that we see in "Piprey Puran" can also be seen in "Mangalbairi." When the Earth is attacked by the Martians who poison its entire ecosystem by implanting a new kind of seed that grows into a deadly flora spreading like wildfire, all nations are united to fight this adversary. "In this hour of danger [...] one cause of happiness is that [...] humans have forgotten enmity as if by some magic. The whole world is united today" (28).[5] In both these stories Mitra hints at a time when the very existence of the humans will be endangered, when common flowers and trees will be a thing of the past. Another of Mitra's theme is the way humans have used science. Science is often misused out of greed or fear and the character of Ghanashyam Das (Ghanada in short) who foils all such attempts is indeed memorable. He first appeared in a story called "Mosha" ("Mosquito," 1945) in which a mad scientist creates a new strain of mosquito, deadly and invincible. Ghanada's timely appearance saves mankind from this virulent breed. By one slap of his powerful hands Ghanada kills this enemy of man. Ghanada is famous for his tall stories but this thin, lanky, bachelor also appears full of his own brand of courage and curiosity. Ghanada is a personification of Premendra Mitra's humanistic ideology and moral universe. Scrupulously honest and down to earth, he is continually striving to rescue mankind from the apocalyptic failures of science. Ghanada is forever getting into escapades that make special demands on his human heart and virtues. He is sometimes outrageous in his tall stories but never unbelievable. "Ghanada is a teller of tall tales, but the tales always have a scientific basis. I try to keep them as factually correct and as authentic as possible," once Premendra Mitra remarked in an interview to SPAN magazine in 1974 (PG). This perhaps accounts for the reason why he has occupied a special place in the minds of the SF readers in Bengal that is still uncontested. In collections of stories like *Ghanadar Galpa* (*Stories of Ghanada*) and *Adwitiyo Ghanada (Incomparable Ghanada)* and *Abar Ghanada (Ghanada Again)* that Mitra wrote through the '50's and '60's we see this quintessential Bengali traveling to space in search of the Black Hole or diving under seas to discover the mysterious origin of the universe. In these tales Mitra effortlessly mixes history, geography, chemistry, physics and botany to dish up entertaining and humanistic narratives of man's triumph over forces of evil. *Mangal Grahey Ghanada* (*Ghanada in Mars,* 1973) is an unusual novel featuring this uncharacteristic hero because it is one of the few works of Bengali SF that is concerned with gender. Ghanada is forced to travel to Mars with the mad scientist Ludvic where he discovers an even more advanced civilization than ours. But their sophisticated technology had not stopped the Martians from fighting each other and the only inhabitants of Mars now are a few Martian females. Ghanada comes to their rescue. In order to save their race he leaves behind his friend Suranjan and his servant Batukeshwar, exiling them in Mars for a good cause. The motif of the faithful retainer, seen in this story as well as in others, is a pointer to the class relations in the real world. The workings of power within these relations create a subtext in which these science fictions can be read.

Two other contemporaries of Mitra who became popular as SF writers in 1940's and 50's were Hemendrakumar Roy (1888–1963) and Khitindranarayan Bhattacharya (1909–1990). The latter along with his brother Monoranjan Bhattacharya ran a children's magazine *Ramdhenu* (1928) where Premendra Mitra's *Piprey Puran* was first published. Khitindranarayan's "Matsya Puran" ("The Story of the Fish," 1975), "Abishkarer Golpo" ("The Story of Discoveries"), and "Bigyaner Joyjatra," ("The Triumphant Journey of Science") probably published in *Ramdhenu* or *Rangmashal,* another magazine he edited, are remarkable in their imaginative use of scientific facts. He states categorically that a science fiction writer does not simply evoke the curiosity of his readers, he "is also responsible to make them scientific minded, attract them to the magical powers of science so that they begin to respect it" (PG). This view is consistent with the ways in which science fiction were often used by many Bangla writers as a didactic means of mediating modern science and disseminating knowledge, similar to certain conceptions of science fiction prevalent in the West.

Leela Majumdar (1908–2007), a niece of Upendrakishore Ray Chaudhuri, is probably the first woman in Bangla to venture into the world of SF. She is primarily known in Bengal as a children's writer but her science fiction fantasies, both stories and novels, peopled by extraordinary humans, plants, animals and ghosts, are read voraciously by adults as well. Her novel *Batash Baari* (*The House of Winds*, 1974) is a fantasy tale with a scientific twist while her short story "Gorom Pani" (1972) remains one of the great tales of an encounter between humans and aliens. In her SF collection *Kolpo Bigyaner Galpo*, her presentations of the bereft, the strange and the underdog manages to stretch not only the borders of middle class domesticity but to present an inclusive vision of the universe where strange things can be accepted with ease and nonchalance. In the short story "Gorom Pani" Shambhu owns two petrol pumps on a lonely mountain road near the town Gorom Pani. The story opens one winter night, rainy and windy. Shambhu awaits customers behind the glass-windowed room, alone and cold. He gets up to make tea when he hears strange sounds outside the window. Fearfully, he opens his door to four men, flat faced, wearing mackintoshes, jerry cans in hand. Shambhu thinks they look strange, and behave even more strangely. But he serves them tea and fills their cans with petrol. The men beckon him to carry a five-liter jar of petrol and follow them. Shambhu does so, for by now he has forgotten his fear. On the side of the mountain, next to a stream he comes across a round object, "shinning in metallic splendour, yet light [...] with a small opening on one side," (300) where the petrol is poured. With a click the object starts to move, and Shambhu watches a narrow wire connecting the round object to another larger one, streaming with light, hovering above the trees. Before the men climb up a stair to the lighted round object, one of them presses two new hundred-rupee notes in Shambhu's hand. Shambhu returns to his shop, changes his wet clothes and ruminates on his experience:

> Shambhu changed his wet clothes and put on dry ones. Then he locked the door and window [...] one can't be too careful, strange dangers lurked everywhere! He was scared of the unfamiliar, the strange. Before his eyes closed in sleep he glanced at the floor and almost broke out in laughter. Even when the four men had familiar objects like jerry cans and jugs in their hands they were weird, to say the least. They had three toes, they sat on their tails and their bodies were probably covered in scales [301].

The story ends here. The easy, controlled narrative makes this one of the truly memorable stories in Majumdar's oeuvre. She describes the encounter with the aliens as part of our quotidian experience while questioning our notions of strangeness and familiarity. She thus underlines and critiques the rigid ways in which we look at the universe and ourselves.

Satyajit Ray, son of Sukumar Ray, carried on the family tradition of science fiction writing and created Professor Shonku in 1961. The first SF featuring this eccentric hero was written for the magazine *Sandesh* and was called "Byomjatrir Diary" ("The Diary of the Space Traveler"). In all, thirty-eight complete and two incomplete diaries (the last one came out in 1992) narrate the fantastic world of Shonku's adventures, inventions and travels. Most of these stories are more than science fictions. They are also travelogues, fantasy tales, tales of adventure and romance. As a fictional character Professor Shonku is tremendously real. He is courageous yet forgetful, inquisitive yet self-controlled. His wit and humor makes him very human and his inventions are impressive: Anhihiline, Miracural, Omniscope, Snuffgun, Mangorange, Camerapid, Linguagraph — the list is long and remarkable. Some are drugs, some gadgets, some machines, but they all have human purposes and uses. None are allowed to reign over or be more powerful than the human mind that invented them. Some of Shonku's machines take on human characteristics and are transformed from mere inventions to companions that humans have always craved. This is fully illustrated in the first diary itself. The diary starts by describing Shonku's efforts to build a rocket. The first one that he builds comes down on his neighbor Abinashbabu's radish patch. Abinashbabu has no sympathy for Shonku; science and scientists make him yawn. He often comes up to Shonku and urges him to set off the rocket as part of Diwali fireworks so that the neighborhood children can be suitably entertained. Shonku, to punish Abinashbabu's levity, drops his latest invention in his guest's tea. This is a small pill, made after the fashion of Jimbhranastra described in the Mahabharata. These pills not only make one yawn, but also make one see nightmares. Before giving a dose to his neighbor, Shonku has tried a quarter bit on himself. In the morning, half his beard had turned grey from the effect of his dreams.

Shonku's world is a real world, a human world. In his preparations for the space journey he has decided to take his cat Newton with him. He has invented a fish-pill for his cat. "Today I tested the fish-pill by leaving it next to a piece of fish. Newton ate the pill. No more problems! Now all I have to do is make his suit and helmet" (7). Two more of Shonku's companions in his space travel will be Prahlad and Bidhusekhar. Prahlad has been his servant for twenty-seven years. Unintelligent but loyal, unimaginative but brave, Prahlad will make a good companion because Shonku believes those qualities will be useful in an emergency. Bidhusekhar is Shonku's robot. The first entry on him is worth a closer look:

> For the last few days I can hear Bidhusekhar making a "ga,ga" noise. This is strange in itself because he is not supposed to utter a sound. He is a machine, he must do whatever he is told, the only sound he is supposed to make is the clang of metals when he moves [...] I know he has no ability to think nor does he possess any intelligence. But now I can see a difference in him [7].

Shonku then goes on to describe how he has tried to invent a new compound as a material for his rocket. He has mixed mushroom, snakeskin and the eggshell of a tortoise and just when he is about to mix Tantrum Boropacsinate he hears a great din behind him. He sees Bidhusekhar shaking his head vigorously as if saying no. Every time Shonku picks up the Tantrum the same clatter ensues. When he decides to try another chemical called Velosilica, Bidhusekhar starts nodding his head in agreement. That his robot has unimaginable human characteristics becomes evident to Shanku another time when he makes Prahlad try out his spacesuit:

> Today I called Prahlad to the laboratory to try out his suit and his helmet. It was a sight. Prahlad was in splits. To say the truth, even I felt like laughing. Just at this moment I heard a metallic guffaw and turned to see Bidhusekhar sitting in his chair swaying and making a new sound. There can only be one meaning to that clatter. Bidhusekhar was also laughing at Prahlad [9–10].

Most of Ray's intended audience was undoubtedly young readers — children and adolescents. This is not a limitation as some SF practitioners theorize. For instance, the poet and SF writer Thomas M. Disch has propounded that what is "radically wrong with science fiction, as well as a good part of what was right" was that SF is a branch of children's literature. It operates under certain limitations, "intellectually, emotionally, and morally" because children remain outside certain "crucial aspects of adult experience [...] such as sex and love [...] the nature of the class system and the real exercise of power within that system" (qtd. in Broderick, 8). Disch goes on to state that genre fiction is shaped more by the demands of the audience rather than by the creative will of its writers. Mitra's tales of extra-terrestrial Martians as well as Ray's fictional narrative of Shonku's exploits are actually the exact reverse of these theorizations. Although hugely popular and often bestsellers, both these writers express a certain world-view that critiqued Western notions of science in the Bengali public sphere. In Bengal, science fiction is both a narrative of technology and progress, a sign of modernity during the period of colonization and also a creator of a space in which a critique of that modernity can be accommodated. The eccentric Professor Shonku's adventures point at one truth again and again. Machines must serve humans, and not the other way round. Both the Ghanada and Shonku stories construct a universe in which "technological salvation arrives through virtuous human effort" and repeatedly questions the meaning of being human (Broderick 55). Talent is creative, but that talent must be nurtured by society or it imposes a terrible burden on the bearer. In the story "Professor Shonku O Khoka" ("Professor Shonku and The Boy," 1967) we see an appraisal of science and society that is extremely critical. The Boy, a four-year-old child of a post-office clerk, is a prodigy. He has become one after he fell and hurt his head. Professor Shonku is amazed at his extraordinary knowledge of mathematics, geography, anatomy and physics. He is able to talk of Einstein's equation, Shonku's polar repellion theory, to name the highest mountain in the world, and to recite Hamlet's famous monologues. This ability, however, makes him a sensation overnight much to Shonku's disgust. People flock to see the child prodigy and things become uncontrollable when the child himself decides to put an end to it. He creeps down to Shonku's laboratory one night and drinks a potion of Anhihilin, a deadly acid discovered by Shonku. He does not die but falls into a deep sleep. When the Boy wakes he is a normal four-year-old crying for his mother.

A brief comparison between science fiction of the West and Bengal might be useful at this point especially in the use of the icon of the eccentric scientist. Like many of the early science fictions written in the West, most science fictions in Bangla have a male scientist as hero/narrator. Both literatures use the stereotype of a lonesome individual in the service of science. But unlike their Western counterpart, the heroes in Bangla do not exist in social isolation: they have no wife or family but they have pets, friends, neighbors and colleagues with whom they interact. There is also another point of difference. In Bangla SF, the scientist's world is not only a sterilized or mysterious world of machines and inventions. It is a world where a robot is called lovingly by name and accorded the status of a friend. It is a world accessible to its young readers, a world full of possibilities and real in its human concerns.[6] Darko Suvin's words that "the only sane way to see science, the world's leading cognitive structure, is not as the Messiah but as Goethe's two-souled Faust" is an interesting way that we may historicize Bangla SF (17). The uneasy awareness and admiration for science and technology that colonial modernity imposed on the colonized soon gave way to more sophisticated and assured critiques in postcolonial times. The slow transformation of Bangla SF from a genre that made its readers understand the world to a genre that is ethical in its dimensions is thus made possible. This analytical awareness of the limitations of science raises interesting potentials not only in the forms and contents of these fictions but also imposes limits that some of these writers were willing to make in their prophetic mode as SF writers.

Notes

1. Limerick by Satyajit Ray quoted from memory. A prolific writer, Ray's limericks and verses remain scattered with one exception, a collection titled *Toray Badha Ghorar Dim* [*A Fistful of Nonsense*], Calcutta: Ananda Publishers, 1986. All translations of Bangla texts in the article are mine.
2. The lone exception Radhanath Sikdar (1813–1870) a Derozian and a mathematician.
3. See Subodhchandra Gangopadhyay, *Acharjya Jagadishchandra*, Calcutta: Sribhumi Publishing House, no date, 238–240, where the story is printed in full. Also see Buddhadev Bhattacharya, *Bangla Sahitye Bigyan*, Calcutta: Bangiyo Bigyan Parishad, 1960.
4. For a discussion on this piece see Biman Basu, "Shukumar Sahitye Bigyan" in *Shatayu Shukumar*, ed. Sisir Kumar Das, Delhi: Bengal Association, 1988, 61.
5. Premendra Mitra, "Mangalbairi." Rpt. Kishor Sahitya Sambhar, Ed. Kartik Ghosh (Calcutta: Shishu Sahitya Sansad, 2002). Stories of Ghanada are available in an earlier English translation by Lila Majumdar (National Book Trust, 1982) and now by Amlan Dasgupta (Penguin, 2004).
6. This idea may have been influenced to an extent by Asimov's image of the machine as the "good servant" that he develops in texts like *I, Robot* (New York: Gnome Press, 1950) and *The Rest of the Robots* (New York: Doubleday, 1964).

Works Cited

Attebery, Brian. "The Magazine Era: 1926–1960." *The Cambridge Companion to Science Fiction*. Eds. Edward James and Farah Mendelsohn. Cambridge: Cambridge University Press, 2003.
Bal, Robin. *Banglaye Bigyan Charcha*. Kolkata: Shomila Press, 1999.
Bhattacharya, Khitindranarayan. "Abishkarer Golpo." Publication details not available.
_____. "Bigyaner Joyjatra." Publication details not available.
_____. "Matsya Puran," 1975. Rpt. in *Shera Sandesh: 1961–1980*. Ed. Satyajit Ray Calcutta: Ananda Publishers, 1981. 68–70.
Bose, Jagadishchandra. "Palatak Tufan." Kuntaleen Story Competition, 1886.
Broderick, Damien. "New Wave and Backwash: 1960–1980." *Cambridge Companion to Science Fiction*. Eds. Edward James and Farah Mendelsohn. Cambridge: Cambridge University Press, 2003.
_____. *Reading by Starlight: Postmodern Science Fiction*. London: Routledge, 1995.
Conan Doyle, Arthur. *The Lost World*. 1912. Rpt. London: John Murray and Jonathan Cape, 1979.
Dutta, Hemlal. "Rahashya." *Bigyan Darpan*. 1882. No other publication details available.
Majumdar, Leela. *Batash Baari*. Calcutta: Ananda Publishers, 1974.
_____. "Gorom Pani." *Chhotoder Omnibus*. New Delhi: Orient Longman, 1972, 296–301.
_____. *Kolpo Bigyaner Galpo*. Calcutta: Shaibya Prakashan Bibhag, 1982.
Mitra, Premendra. *Abar Ghanada* [*Ghanada Again*]. Rpt. in *Ghanadar Galpo*, in *Ghanada Shamogro*, vol.1. Ed. Surojit Dasgupta. Kolkata: Ananda Publisgers, 2001.
_____. *Adwitiyo Ghanada* [*Incomparable Ghanada*]. Rpt. in *Ghanadar Galpo*, in *Ghanada Shamogro*, vol. 1. Ed. Surojit Dasgupta. Kolkata: Ananda Publishers, 2001.
_____. *Ghanadar Galpa* [*Stories of Ghanada*]. Rpt. in *Ghanada Galpo*, in *Ghanada Shamogro*, vol. 1. Ed. Surojit Dasgupta. Kolkata: Ananda Publishers, 2001.
_____. *Mangal Grahey Ghanada* [*Ghanada in Mars*]. Rpt. in *Ghanada Shamogro*, vol. 2. Ed. Suranjan Dasgupta. Calcutta: Ananda Publishers, 2001.
_____. "Mangalbairi." Rpt. Kishor Sahitya Sambhar. Ed Kartik Ghosh. Calcutta: Shishu Sahitya Sansad, 2002.

_____. "Mosha." Rpt. in *Ghanadar Galpo*, in *Ghanada Shamogro*, vol. 1. Ed. Surojit Dasgupta. Kolkata: Ananda Publishers, 2001.
_____. "Piprey Puran." Rpt. Kishor Sahitya Sambhar. Ed. Kartik Ghosh. Calcutta: Shishu Sahitya Sansad, 2002.
Ray, Satyajit. "Byomjatrir Diary" ["The Diary of the Space Traveler"]. *Sandesh* (1961). Rpt. *Shanku Shamogro*. Calcutta: Ananda Publishers, 2002.
_____. "Professor Shanku O Khoka" ["Professor Shanku and The Boy"], *Sandesh* (1967). Rpt. *Shanku Shamogro*. Calcutta: Ananda Publishers, 2002.
Ray, Sukumar. *Heshoram Hushiyarer Diary* [*The Diary of Heshoram Hushiar*]. *Sandesh* (1922 rpt.) *Upendrakishore and Sukumar Rachana Sangroho*. Ed. Satya Chakraborty. Calcutta: Bidyamandir, 1983.
Roy, Jagadananda. *Banglar Pakhi* [*Birds of Bengal*]. Rpt. Allahabad: Indian Press Publications, 1961.
_____. *Pokamakor* [*Bugs and Insects*]. Rpt. Allahabad: Indian Press Publications, 1961.
_____. *Shukra Bhraman* [*Travels to Venus*]. No publication details available.
Suvin, Darko. "Novum is as Novum Does." *Science Fiction, Critical Frontiers*. Eds. Karen Sayer and John Moore. London: Macmillan, 2000.

9

Critiquing Economic and Environmental Colonization
Globalization and Science Fiction in The Moons of Palmares

JUDITH LEGGATT

Postcolonial writers are increasingly turning to science fiction as a genre in which to express opposition to the political, military, economic, environmental and cultural imperialisms that the world currently faces. In her forward to *The Left Hand of Darkness*, Ursula K. Le Guin asserts that "science fiction is not predictive; it is descriptive" (xii), and often the future colonization of distant worlds within the genre closely parallels past and present colonial situations. In the introduction to *So Long Been Dreaming: Postcolonial Science Fiction & Fantasy*, Nalo Hopkinson argues that "one of the most familiar memes of science fiction is that of going to foreign countries and colonizing the natives, and [...] for many of us that's not a thrilling adventure story; it's non-fiction, and we are on the wrong side of the strange looking ship that appears out of nowhere" (7). Rather than rejecting the genre as irrevocably colonial, however, Hopkinson and other postcolonial writers have used science fiction to tell the other side of the story. They "take the meme of colonizing the natives and, from the experience of the colonizee, critique it, pervert it, fuck with it, with irony, with anger, with humour, and also, with love and respect for the genre of science fiction that makes it possible to think about new ways of doing things" (Hopkinson 9). The growing sub-genre of postcolonial speculative fiction does more than describe the ills of the present; it also suggests methods of dealing with current crises. In its dystopian form, it illustrates the dangers of continuing on a current course. In its utopian form, it suggests how solutions might be reached.

African-American/Cherokee writer Zainab Amadahy's *The Moons of Palmares* provides an apt example of this process. The novel works in a mini-tradition of texts that portray Native North Americans interacting with the people on distant planets, but — unlike the majority of texts in the genre, which link the colonization of the planet to the initial colonization of the "New World"— Amadahy specifically addresses the environmental, economic and political inequities that continue into an ostensibly *post*colonial era. The tensions between utopian and dystopian impulses in the novel suggest methods of political and artistic resistance to neocolonialism in contemporary global culture. The novel is set far in the future on a former colony of Earth that has gained political independence from the "mother planet." The utopian society on Palmares reflects Amadahy's own mixed-racial heritage; its syncretic mingling of societies from earth idealizes the cross-pollinations of globalization. This utopia is undercut by Palmares' dystopian subjugation to the earth-based "Consortium" whose control over the mining rights to the planet's moons reflects the economic and environmental dangers of neocolonialism and globalization, and shows how thin the veneer of the Palmarans' political independence really is. The situation has obvious parallels to continued Western control in supposedly postcolonial countries on contemporary Earth. Amadahy endorses the utopian Palmaran society as a model towards which to work. She uses the various methods of active and passive resistance in which the Palmarans engage to evaluate approaches to solving contemporary political, economic, environmental and cultural problems, and the attempts by Leith Eaglefeather — the new Security Chief of the Terran Compound — to investigate the role of allies from the dominant culture.

Eaglefeather's Cherokee ancestry, which parallels part of Amadahy's own racial heritage, leads to overt comparisons between the future colonial situation on Palmares, and the past colonization of North America, comparisons which are an established part of the science fiction genre. Mary S. Weinkauf begins "The Indian in Science Fiction" by suggesting that Native peoples on other planets are often modeled on specific Native North American nations, or on stereotypes of "the Indian." Gregory Pfitzer examines this trend in more detail. In "The Only Good Alien Is a Dead Alien: Science Fiction and the Metaphysics of Indian-Hating on the High Frontier," he establishes the connections between westerns and science fiction, especially in terms of the American myth of Manifest Destiny. He shows how "the language of the western frontier was adapted to fit the needs of a new generation of entrepreneurs and champions of the popular culture of space" (51). Space aliens became "metaphorical Indians victimized by an ethic of conquest extended into new arenas of discovery and suspense" (55). Like Weinkauf and Pfitzer, Macdonald, Macdonald and Sheridan, in their chapter on Speculative Fiction in *Shape-Shifting: Images of Native Americans in Recent Popular Fiction*, point out that the use of Native Americans in science fiction is not confined to literal representation. They claim that "embedded in every alien story is the seed of a Native American story" (245). In assessing the science fiction genre as a whole, they assert the importance of "the Native American as a basis for exploring important questions of values, of cross-cultural contact, of conflicting concepts or interpretations of reality" (276). Throughout science fiction, from the early iterations of the genre in travel narratives and utopias, to the space operas of the golden age, to contemporary cyber-punk, issues of colonization, first contact, identity formation in relation to cultural others, Manichean reasoning, and ethnocentrism all echo the questions asked in colonial, neo-colonial, and postcolonial settings.

In *The Moons of Palmares*, the allegorical connections between the native peoples of alien worlds and Native North Americans is complicated by the inclusion of a member of a First Nation among the imperialists, in this case Major Eaglefeather, a Terran of Cherokee ancestry who is a member of the Peacekeepers, the Terran military force that occupies Palmares. Although he considers it his function to bring peace to a troubled planet, and sees no irony in the name of his organization, his real job is to protect the interests of the earth-based Consortium on Palmares. The novel traces the education of Eaglefeather, from a naïve young chief of security on only his second colonial posting (his first was on a peaceful, well-controlled colony) to a jaded man, disgusted with his colleagues and his predecessor, who still hopes to change the system from within. While his Terran heritage and his position within the colonial hierarchy put him on the side of the colonizers, his Cherokee ancestry leads him to sympathize with the people of Palmares, who are trying to curtail the mining of the moons that is leading to the destabilization of the planet itself. His paradoxical position on both sides of the colonizer/colonized divide allows readers from many different positions to identify with him; his shift in allegiance, from the Consortium to the Palmarans, works as a rhetorical device to advance the views of those who have been shut out of economic, environmental, and political decisions that determine their quality of life. Readers in the industrialized West are thus encouraged to make connections between the situation in this fictional future, and that of the present, and to come to the same conclusions about the inequities in their own world that Eaglefeather does about the situation on Palmares. He thus acts as a model of the dangers and potentials in the position of ally to the Indigenous cause.

Eaglefeather is not unique as an Indigenous North American who acts as a Terran imperialist. Several earlier texts create First Nations characters on distant planets in the far future in order to advocate allegorically for the rights of Indigenous peoples; all are written by non–Native writers. Andre Norton's 1960 novel *The Sioux Spaceman* is the most explicit example of this pattern. Kade White hawk, the "Sioux Spaceman" of the title, is part of a Terran observation group on the "undeveloped" planet of Klor, where the native Ikkinni are enslaved by the alien Styor (7). Kade has been assigned to the mission because of the similarities between the histories of his own people's colonization by Europe, and the Ikkinni's colonization by the Styor. When he studies the history of the planet, "Kade was teased by an odd sense that something in this combination of history, geography and trade lore was hauntingly familiar" (9). The social structures of the "tribes," their warfare patterns, their carvings and use of "hunting magic," their tracking abilities, and capability of moving through the land without detection by an enemy, their occupations as hunters and fishermen with a few families who cultivate plants, their spears and nets, all echo common images of various First Nations. The connections with the Lakota in specific are central to the plot of the novel. Kade's predecessor, Jon Steel, was also Lakota; he had arranged to have the Native grasses tested to see if they could support Terran herbivores. The test results give Kade, presumably thinking along the same lines as his Lakota predecessor, the idea to arrange for horses to be transported to the planet. He teaches the Ikkinni to use them, in hopes that the extra mobility will allow them to better resist the colonizing Styor, just as the adoption of horses helped the Lakota during the early stages of European colonization.

Such explicit connections and resistances are not unique to *The Sioux Spaceman*. In Norton's 1959 novel *The Beast Master*, and the series that stems from it, the Dineh hero, Hosteen Storm, feels an affinity with the Norbies, the Indigenous people of Arzor who are excellent riders and trackers, and whose consistently strained relationship with the Terran settlers explicitly parallels tensions over treaty and land rights in the southwest United States. In A. C. Crispin and Kathleen O'Malley's *Silent Dances* and *Silent Songs* (from the *Starbridge* series), the Lakota hero Ptesa' Wakandagi finds herself connecting with the bird-like Grus, who are considered by the colonialist Founders to be "very intelligent animals, perhaps on the level of apes or dolphins, but not *intelligent enough* for a First Contact. And certainly not intelligent enough to avoid having their planet colonized" (*Silent* Dances 28; emphasis in original), a similar attitude to that which helped justify European colonization of the "New World." Tesa works to establish the intelligence and rights, not only of the Grus, but also of the Aquila, another avian species, and the traditional enemy of the Grus. In Eleanor Arnason's *A Woman of the Iron People*, Edward Whirlwind is Aninshinabe, and the only Native North American on a Terran expedition that has just "discovered" an inhabited planet. He preaches a doctrine of complete non-interference. His research into the history of his own people leads him to make connections between their current mission and the colonization of North America. He wants "to quarantine the planet" (283), and only came on the mission so that, in the event that the ship did encounter a life form with which they could interact, there would "be someone on the ship with a good memory. Someone who'd be ready to defend them" (366). Clare Bell's 1989 novel *People of the Sky* reinforces the parallels between First Nations and extraterrestrials by having Kesbe Temiya, her Pueblo hero, encounter a lost Pueblo colony on another planet. That colony has formed a symbiotic relationship with an alien species, changing both and Kesbe must come to terms with the extent of those changes, even as she hopes to protect the colony from other Terrans. Each of these characters finds her or himself in a conflicted position, empathizing with the colonial situation of the natives on the planet, but at the same time representing the interests of his or her own Terran community, or being faced with accepting the true otherness of the peoples s/he encounters.

Eaglefeather is akin to all of these generic sci-fi predecessors in his desire to fix the "new world" in which he finds himself, to save it from colonial encroachment. Eaglefeather attempts to bridge the ethnic and cultural gaps between Terrans and Palmarans, in part by bridging the structural gap between law enforcement and rebels. When Zaria tells him he is not like a "typical security chief" (31), Eaglefeather presents an alternative view of law enforcement to that of Althusser's model of Repressive State Apparati: "I subscribe to the belief that law enforcement officers — especially Peacekeepers — should be mediators. People turn to violence because they can't find other means or don't see other options. We should be trained to help resolve differences peacefully" (31). Eaglefeather's desire to bring peace to Palmares is noble, and very similar to the noble work done by Kade, Hosteen, Tesa, Kesbe, and Edward in the more typical genre literature. What is different is that the motives of the outsider are explicitly questioned within Amadahy's narrative, where they are not in the other novels. Zaria calls Eaglefeather's idealism "naïve" and tells him that he has "a real hero complex" (34). Even in his desire to fix the world, he underestimates the abilities of the Palmarans to help themselves, and Zaria points out the paternalism of this attitude: "You, fresh from Basilea, arrive on Palmares, a world you know nothing about, to single-handedly mediate a war? Thanks anyway, but we don't need a saviour" (34). In this way, he acts as a warning to readers. Help is appreciated from all sources, but the true impetus for change has to come from the community itself, not outsiders, or else one form of colonization will simply be replaced with another.

Eaglefeather's initial overtures are rebuffed in part because of his own unrealized prejudices. Nailah compares Eaglefeather's self-assurance and his faith in the morality of his job, to the overt racism of Major Stojic, another Peacekeeper who openly despises the Palmarans. She claims, "if there is anything to admire about Major Stojic, it's his honesty. I'd rather deal directly with bigotry" (50). Although the comparison is implied rather than overt, Eaglefeather recognizes it: " 'Have I just been insulted?' he asked incredulously" (50). Eaglefeather does, however, need to come to terms with his own paternalist attitudes. When he refers to Jamal as a "Feisty old man," Rahim rebukes him, and points to the respect due to those who have acquired the wisdom that comes with age: "We refer to him as an Elder" (81). Eaglefeather also believes that the Palmarans lack the technological advances to sabotage the mining operation without help from a Terran source. Such cultural blindness shows how much Major Eaglefeather, for all his compassion and liberal humanism, is caught up in the world views of the Consortium, world views that closely parallel those of the industrialized West. He sympathizes with the resistance, but does so in a patronizing manner that he does not himself recognize.

While *The Moons of Palmares* works as an allegory, it does not make the connections between Native North Americans and extraterrestrial races that are made in the other novels. The links that Eaglefeather notes between himself and the Palmaran resisters are cultural and biological rather than allegorical. Eaglefeather's Cherokee heritage links him to the political resistance group the Menchista, who are named after the Native Guatemalan activist Rigoberta Menchu, to the militant splinter group of rebels, named "Kituhwa, after a nineteenth-century Cherokee-traditionalist secret society" (6), to Magaly, the most militant member of that group, whose "features suggested her ancestry may have been predominantly indigenous American" (16) and to the Aquene family, whose name is of Cherokee origin, and who are spies for the Kituhwa. When Eaglefeather has been taken hostage by the Kituhwa, the sight of a dreamcatcher where he is being held brings "him comfort, the hope that he might have something in common with his captors after all" (71). By having the Palmarans be the descendants of Terran settlers rather than extraterrestrials, Amadahy emphasizes the similarities between the two conflicting societies, rather than their differences. It also prevents the further *alien*ating of the First Nations that can result when comparing their cultures to the non-human. While most comparisons between Native North Americans and extraterrestrials are explicitly designed by the authors to emphasize the rights and personhood of the non-human species, there is always the danger that the allegorical equivalency can instead have the opposite effect: by aligning the

Native North Americans with the non-human, the texts can reinscribe well-entrenched stereotypes that place Native people outside the realm of "normal" humanity.

The representations of Indigenous North Americans in the texts from *The Sioux Spaceman* to *People of the Sky* fall into the paradox identified by Sierra S. Adare in *"Indian" Stereotypes in TV Science Fiction*: "While allowing First Nations peoples to have their own cultures in the future, which in itself defies well-established 'Indian' stereotypes, the writers, producers, and directors of TV science fiction constantly rely on 'Indian' stereotypes in their story lines" (7). This paradox is not confined to television; it is prevalent throughout the science fiction genre. Christine Morris argues that, although science fiction has been revolutionary in anticipating changes in racial relations, "when it comes to Indians, even the best science fiction writer is often caught in the traditional American literary dichotomy between writers like James Fenimore Cooper and his 'Noble Red Man,' and Mark Twain and his 'Ignoble Savage' " (301). Many of the constructions of "the Indian" are based on binary oppositions in which "the Indian" is seen as diametrically opposed to "the White Man" and reinforces the European male's positive assumptions about himself. Kade Whitehawk, in Andre Norton's *The Sioux Spaceman* is manifestly emotional, as opposed to the supposed rationality of those of European ancestry. He lacks "the necessary detachment and control" to deal rationally with the arrogance of colonizing aliens; and "under the right provocation would revert with whirlwind action to the less diplomatic practices of savage ancestors" (6).

In the generic science fiction texts, the Native North American characters fall almost exclusively into the "Noble Savage" stereotype. The idea of the noble savage first developed during the enlightenment, and in it the "Indian" is conceived of as a pre-lapsarian human. According to the stereotype, where Europeans have been corrupted by civilization, Indian people live in a state of grace. One of the primary characteristics of the noble savage is that s/he is in touch with the natural world, and sees animals and plants as siblings, rather than as lesser beings to be submitted to the will of humans. A common belief was that "primitive people probably apprehended the laws of nature more clearly than civilized man since they were less corrupted by the practices and prejudices of civilization and more creatures of instincts considered natural" (Berkhofer 76). For example, Kade Whitehawk repeatedly suggests that the Lakota have a natural affinity for horses. Similarly, Hosteen Storm has particularly strong abilities as a Beastmaster — a human who has a team of animals with whom he communicates and works through telepathy — because of his Navaho heritage. Norton valorizes her Native heroes, but she evokes their

Native identity through many characteristics that come out of Westerns set in the nineteenth century.

First Nations are often stereotyped as belonging in the past, and thus function in science fiction settings as a comparison between the past and the future, even if that comparison is meant to be a positive one. Weinkauf argues that, in the few science fiction stories in which they appear, Native American characters function "as a symbolic warning that progress is dangerous to tradition" (319). In the texts by Norton, Crispin, Arnason, and Bell, the Native American heroes are specifically connected to the pasts of their respective peoples, even though they are all in futuristic settings. While these connections do emphasize the importance of tradition continuing into the future, they have the danger of portraying Native culture as static, and any change in culture as a loss in culture. Despite numerous references to Eaglefeather's Cherokee heritage, his identity is global rather than racial. He is Terran, first and foremost, and is very much a man of his time. He does not have any of the stereotypical trappings of the Hollywood Indian, but neither does he have a recognizable identity as a Cherokee. Despite his racial connection to Native people on Earth, here he represents colonial attitudes apparently at odds with his heritage. When Eaglefeather is captured by the Kituhwa, he complains about the consensus needed before they decide his fate. Sixto Masika, the most peaceable of the Kituhwa, suggests that a better knowledge of the past of the First Nations would help him to understand: "Many of the First Nations of the Americas had systems of government that were far more democratic than anything we know today. The nations of the Iroquois Confederation, for example, knew the true meaning of consensus" (83). Eaglefeather is aware of this history, but sees it as something to move beyond, rather than a source of strength: "My ancestors' indecision, superstitions and inability to join forces was their downfall. We were our own worst enemy. That's why we were conquered, why we spent centuries fighting extinction" (83). Eaglefeather's dismissal of Cherokee culture as a thing of the past is an indication not of the death of that culture, but rather of his own blindness. As Jace Weaver points out, Native North American cultures have always been adept at "incorporative elements from other cultures" in order to "strengthen, not weaken, their people" (29). Eaglefeather's attitude suggests an internal colonization that sets him against his own people.

One of the main distinctions between Terrans and Palmarans in the novel is: their attitudes towards the cultures that were exterminated and repressed through colonization and globalization. Unlike Major Eaglefeather, the Palmarans do look to the past to establish their current culture; they are especially interested in those cultures that were previously colonized by European powers. Masika explains: "military conquest has rendered many a culture extinct, but we believe in learning from history, Major, and Terran history is rich and diverse. Many values long forgotten there still matter to us. But you Terrans can't seem to respect that" (83). The multiethnic society of Palmares is presented as a utopia, and falls into the utopian impulse that Fredric Jameson describes among "the post-globalization Left [...] which subsumes remnants of the old Left and the New Left, along with those of a radical wing of social democracy, and of First World cultural minorities and Third World proletarianized peasants and landless or structurally unemployable masses" (xii). Because the peoples of Palmares came from "impoverished origins" (5), they have more to gain by creating something new in their new world. They reject the global culture of earth, and create their own. Where the Terran occupiers have a homogenous society in which cultural difference has been erased into one global entity, the society of Palmares deliberately models itself on a variety of societies that remain distinct within the new culture, a syncretic mosaic rather than a melting pot.

The society Amadahy creates in *The Moons of Palmares* is one in which racial intolerance seems to have been erased. In fact, as Eaglefeather remarks, "The very idea of race seemed ludicrous now" especially since "the characteristics used to classify people by race, and therefore as inherently superior or inferior, had been determined by less than one percent of their genes" (16). The first paragraph of the novel detracts from this image of racial harmony, and echoes the racial profiling so common among police forces in the present day. An intruder in the Peacekeeper complex is marked as an outsider by what are commonly considered to be racial characteristics: "His grey garment blended in, but his coffee-brown skin and his raven hair, tied at the nape of his neck, ruined his attempt at camouflage. Anyone could spot him and recognize that he should not be in the building" (1). As well, every character is identified in terms of racial ancestry, even if only in an effort to show how multi-racial the society is. However, after the first page, no characters discriminate against others based on the color of their skin. Both the Terran imperialists and the Palmaran colonists are made up of a variety of racial identities.

Much of the culture is indicated by names. The planet is named after "a settlement of escaped slaves in nineteenth-century Brazil" (4). The community meeting place of the village of Tubman — itself an allusion to Harriet Tubman who worked to bring African Americans out of slavery — shows both Maori and African influences. "Merae Goree" is a combination of "Merae," the Maori word for "community gathering space" (59) and Goree Island, "a holding centre for African slaves" located off the coast of Africa (60). Zaria Aquene explains the origins of this practice in terms of forging community out of difference. Since the original colonists who worked the mines for the Consortium had originated in a variety of Terran colonies and cultures, "They needed a basis of unity [...] They had to forge a common bond from their Terran past, so they revived what they needed from the societies out of that past" (12). They mine Earth cultures of the past in much the same way the Consortium mines quilidon: "Ways of life long forgotten on Earth gave meaning to an otherwise routine and lonely existence, or so the anthropologists who studied the planet theorized. Traditional cultures from around Earth had made Palmares an amalgam as rare as the mineral its citizens mined" (5). The syncretism that characterizes Palmaran global society brings the past into the present, whereas the homogeneity of the Terran global culture erases its roots in a variety of cultures, making it the heir to American global consumerism.

The shared mixed-racial makeup of the Terrans and Palmarans does not bring them together. With the apparent erasure of racism, prejudice is transplanted onto people based on their planetary origins. Colonel Welch, Eaglefeather's commanding officer, sets up a binary opposition between the logical Terrans and the irrational Palmarans: "They don't think logically like you and me. No, they can be quite irrational. You saw that fellow in the square today, Sixto Masika? The one who incited the riot? He's quite typical. Can't be reasoned with" (26). These words contradict the actual depiction of Sixto, who is a scientist, and a reasonable, rational, and peaceable man. Eaglefeather argues against such prejudices:

> Though racism was an anachronism in this century, the same way of thinking was at work in assigning inherent character traits to people of different worlds. It was ridiculous. Not that differences didn't exist. There were differences born of environment and circumstance — intangible and difficult to define, but real all the same — and they were dividing people, making them distrust and even fight each other. He and Zaria Aquene were on opposite sides in a dispute that was born of nothing either could pin down. Absurd, he thought [16].

Because Eaglefeather cannot "pin down" the difference between cultures, he dismisses it rather than investigating further. The erasure of cultural difference in his anti-racist stance erases the uniqueness of the Palmaran culture. He judges all people by the same standards, not accounting for cultural differences. Colonial assumptions about family life play themselves out in his accusation that the Palmarans have more children than they can afford (80), a typical complaint from developed countries on Earth about the overpopulation of the third world. Jamal Brieche, to whom he makes the comment, replies, "You Terrans would deny us our right to have the children we want, rather than cut back on your own energy consumption. You have the highest per capita rate of quilidon consumption in the galaxy, Major. If your people weren't so wasteful, you wouldn't need to mine our moons and our planet would stabilize" (80). While Eaglefeather's rhetoric parallels the concerns over overpopulation in the so-called developing world, Brieche's response echoes the response that overpopulation is a greater problem in the so-called developed world, because of the voracious consumption of the admittedly smaller populations of those countries.

Appreciating cultural difference only on a superficial level can also be problematic. Major Stojic sees the local population as a source of exotic experience. He becomes addicted to the drug bliss, and frequents an establishment that features local food, dancing, and other entertainment. He believes that "Palmaran women were inherently more seductive, more erotic, than their Terran counterparts" (9). His attitude parallels those of cultural tourists on our world, and those who adopt the trappings, but not the fundamental belief systems, of other, apparently more interesting, cultures. Stojic's appreciation of Palmaran culture is an integral part of his prejudices against the people.

The prejudice depicted in the novel goes both ways. Just as racially mixed people today can face prejudice from both sides of a racial divide, so Zaria is picked on as a child because her father is Terran, and her mother appears to collaborate with the consortium. A group of bullies taunts "her with shouts that her mother was a Terrafucker and that she was a half-Terran mutant" (87). Sharing an ethnic heritage with Eaglefeather does not impress Nailah Aquene, who from the start does "not appear" to want "to have anything in common" with the new chief of security for the Peacekeepers (10). Eaglefeather realizes the limitations of shared ethnic heritage, and the strength of planetary difference, as he studies the Native American features of Magaly during a demonstration: "Two hundred years ago, they would likely have been allies in the struggle against racism, he reminded himself. In the here and now, however, she was Palmaran and he was Terran and they were, by definition, adversaries" (16). These cultural prejudices are a major obstacle to negotiation between the two sides, and exacerbate the economic and environmental concerns that are at the heart of the conflict between the two peoples.

These economic and environmental elements are the major difference between *The Moons of Palmares* and the stories of Native colonists that preceded it. Rather than focus on allegorical connections to initial colonization, and a specific binary opposition between the First Nations and European colonists, Amadahy instead focuses on the global and international issues that were contemporary when she was writing, and continue to be today. While the attitude that the Peacekeepers are in Palmares "to make sure the Consortium can continue its mining operations" is "not in keeping with official Terran policy," the desire to "keep the quilidon flowing" is the sole reason for continued Terran involvement with Palmares (3). The parallels between quilidon, the most important source of energy in this future world, and oil, the most important source of energy in ours, are obvious, as is the connection between the Consortium and the energy companies that influence United States policy in the Middle East.

The colonial structure of Palmares parallels many different colonial structures on earth, where self government remains an important issue. The limited forms of self government allowed by Canada's Indian Acts and the treaties in North America, combined with the economic colonization that continues after political independence for many postcolonial countries, form the basis of the treaty on Palmares. Eaglefeather and Zaria discuss the matter:

> "Didn't your people sign a treaty that gives the Consortium the right to be here? For two hundred years?"
>
> "It was the only way we could win home rule. Unfortunately, our grandparents had a rather limited understanding of the concept. Or maybe they had no choice about signing the deal. But what good is home rule? We aren't independent and we don't control our resources."
>
> "It was an important treaty, the first of its kind. It became a model for other colonies."
>
> "I'm sure it did," she shot back. "Colonizers throughout history have recognized the cost-effectiveness of indirect control. Give people the right to elect their own leaders, fund their own security forces, health care and education, but maintain control of their resources and you can still call the tune. It's an old strategy — once called neo-colonialism by dissidents on Earth. Political independence alone means little" [52–53].

Amadahy educates her readers through Zaria's education of Eaglefeather. Eaglefeather's desire to change the system from within using peaceful negotiation is undercut by his blindness to the extent of that system's capacity for evil. Despite ample evidence of corruption and brutality within the Peace Officers and the Consortium, he refuses to accept at first that individual members of his organization would break their own laws and torture prisoners, or that they would jam communications knowing that it would prevent warning the populace of an impending earthquake. He also doubts the veracity of the Palmarans' claims that the moon is being destabilized by the mining operations. Only once he accepts these truths, and questions his own position within the corrupt system, can he begin to help work for change.

Resistance to neo-colonialism in a global context takes many different shapes, each with its own benefits and limitations. Where Eaglefeather represents the person inside the system who must be educated, Sixto and Magaly represent binary approaches to resistance from those oppressed by the system.

Sixto advocates for peaceful demonstrations and education in order to raise awareness and change the attitudes both of the Palmaran society at large, and of the populace of Earth. He knows that Terrans are mainly unaware of the effects that their quilidon consumption might be having on people light years away, and believes that changing the attitudes of people like Eaglefeather will change policy without bloodshed. Magaly, on the other hand, believes that sabotage and violent unrest will make the mining of quilidon more expensive, and therefore less attractive. Zaria Aquene is caught between these two views, sometimes siding with Sixto, her lover, and sometimes with Magaly, her lifelong friend. She is, however, relatively hopeless when faced with the continued colonization of her planet. She recognizes that the example of the First Nations of North America shows how difficult fighting colonization can be:

> As people after people encountered the Europeans, they debated what to do. Whether to respond peacefully or violently. Whether to cooperate or resist. Whether to be assimilated or not. Some peoples cooperated. Some resisted peacefully, others not so peacefully. Some withdrew to other territory, even as the land shrank before them till there was nowhere to go. Different people had different responses. And not one worked. They were decimated. In some cases entire civilizations disappeared [117].

What eventually works is a combination of the approaches. Eaglefeather reaches Sixto's journalist contacts on Earth, who publicize the geological research that the Consortium and the Terran government have been suppressing. After Sixto dies under torture, Eaglefeather joins forces with Magaly to launch an armed attack on the Compound, and rescue Zaria. Magaly dies in the attack, but the combination of force and information gets the attention that the resistance needs.

With the diametrically opposed Sixto and Magaly dead, and the repressive Terran government voted out of power, Eaglefeather and Zaria are left as moderates to negotiate a new treaty, each representing the interests of his or her own people, but each willing to compromise to reach a truly equitable solution. The mining of the moons of Palmares does not stop, but the Palmaran government now has a majority stake in the operation and all the quilidon that is taken must be replaced by minerals of equal weight to prevent further destabilization of the planet. The need for both passive and active resistance suggests that education, negotiation, propaganda, sabotage and even terrorist activity are all necessary parts of changing the status quo. In the end, though, it is compromise, negotiation and understanding that are necessary to form any lasting solutions. While Eaglefeather cannot single-handedly save Palmares, his willingness to work with the people of the planet points to what those in the industrialized West can do in the face of global inequities. People from both sides of the conflict need to act to change the world, by exposing injustice, by educating others about that injustice, by voting, by protest (peaceful and otherwise), and, most importantly, by working with and for those who face injustice. Amadahy's novel, set in the distant future, is literature for our times. We need to work out solutions to these problems in our world, working towards a utopian future, even if it can never be attained, to prevent current crises from becoming entrenched dystopias.

Works Cited

Adare, Sierra S. *"Indian" Stereotypes in TV Science Fiction: First Nations' Voices Speak Out.* Austin: University of Texas Press, 2005.
Amadahy, Zainab. *The Moons of Palmares.* Toronto: Sister Vision, 1997.
Arnason, Eleanor. *A Woman of the Iron People.* New York: William Morrow, 1991.
Bell, Clair. *People of the Sky.* New York: Tor, 1989.
Berkhofer, Robert F., Jr, *The White Man's Indian: Images of the American Indian from Columbus to the Present.* New York: Alfred Knopf, 1978.
Crispin, A. C., and Kathleen O'Malley. *Silent Dances.* New York: Ace, 1990.
_____. *Silent Songs.* New York: Ace, 1994.
Hopkinson, Nalo, and Uppinder Mehan, eds. *So Long Been Dreaming: Postcolonial Science Fiction & Fantasy.* Vancouver: Arsenal, 2004.
Jameson, Fredric. *Archaeologies of the Future: The Desire Called Utopia and Other Science Fictions.* London: Verso, 2005.
Le Guin, Ursula K. "Introduction." *The Left Hand of Darkness.* New York: Ace, 1976. xi–xvi.
Macdonald, Andrew, Gina Macdonald, and MaryAnn Sheridan. *Shape-Shifting: Images of Native Americans in Recent Popular Fiction.* Westport, CT: Greenwood, 2000.
Morris, Christine. "Indians and Other Aliens: A Native American View of Science Fiction." *Extrapolation* 20.4 (1979): 301–307.
Norton, Andre. *The Beast Master.* New York: Harcourt, Brace, 1959.
_____. *Lord of Thunder.* New York: Harcourt Brace, Jovanovich, 1962.
_____. *The Sioux Spaceman.* New York: Ace, 1984.
Norton, Andre, and Lyn McConchie. *Beast Master's Ark.* New York: Tor, 2002.
_____. *Beast Master's Circus.* New York: Tor, 2004.
Pfitzer, Gregory M. "The Only Good Alien Is a Dead Alien: Science Fiction and the Metaphysics of Indian-Hating on the High Frontier." *Journal of American Culture* 18.1 (1995): 51–67.
Weaver, Jace, Craig S. Womack, and Robert Warrior. *American Indian Literary Nationalism.* Albuquerque: University of New Mexico Press, 2006.
Weinkauf, Mary S. "The Indian in Science Fiction." *Extrapolation* 20.4 (1979): 308–320.

10

Loonies and Others in Robert A. Heinlein's *The Moon Is a Harsh Mistress*[1]

HERBERT G. KLEIN

Introduction

Robert A. Heinlein may seem an unlikely candidate to think of as an author of postcolonial (science) fiction, since his success as one of the most popular pulp authors of the 1940s was mainly due to his ability to spin rollicking adventure yarns, which he also used to purvey his anti-democratic, social–Darwinist "survival of the fittest" ideology (Nicholls 188). Nevertheless, his novel *The Moon Is a Harsh Mistress* fulfills many of the criteria that one has come to expect from postcolonial fiction: it tells of the struggle for independence of a subjected and marginalized people, it is told in the voice of one of their own, and it describes the indigenous culture and its changes in this act of transformation. But, of course, there are also differences: the rebellious people are themselves colonists, their country is not situated on the Earth, and the leader of the rebellion is a machine. The last two points constitute the obvious SF–elements of the novel, whereas the first falls within the framework of postcolonial theory since settler colonies were also held in dependence to the mother country while they were developing along lines of their own, thus giving rise to conflicts of interest which finally led to the more or less complete severing of ties with the mother country (Ashcroft et al., 1989: 2; Slemon 1990; Ahmad 1995). Moreover, the majority of the colonists in this novel have been forcibly dislocated and the whole society is kept in absolute dependence to the Earth. The moon as a satellite held by the gravity of the Earth emphasizes the marginalization and the subordination of this society. In the form of a futuristic tale, Heinlein develops the idea of an alternative way of life by constituting Lunar society as an Other for the Earthlings. In this context it is possible to extend the notion of the Other to (conscious) machines, thereby giving yet another dimension to the problem of alterity: the seeming liberation of the moon and her inhabitants is put into yet another different perspective when the question of their attitude towards the machines is raised. I want to show, therefore, that the relationship between humans and machines can also be regarded as that between Self and Other, that the two are intricately linked and mirror each other, and that the SF elements thus introduce a new angle into the concept of alterity. I shall consequently discuss this novel on two levels: first, its more or less obvious postcolonial elements, and second, the relationship between man and machine as a *mise en abyme* of the central issues of alterity and otherness.

The Loonies Write Back

The story of Luna's rebellion is told exclusively in the words of Manuel Garcia O'Reilly, whose mixed heritage is indicated not only by his name, but is also visible in the language that he uses. It is basically English, but contains words from Russian and German as well as new coinages which have originated on the moon. They are brought together in a hybrid idiom, which is partly of Manuel's own making and partly reflects the mixed culture of his society. Manuel is not a very literate person, so his story bears many traits of an oral narrative.[2]

The first sentence of the novel, albeit written in English, shows Manuel to be a reader of the presumably Russian *Lunaya Pravda*, and indeed his English seems to be tinged by a Russian grammatical superstructure. Thus he leaves out definite and indefinite articles as well as other grammatical pointers and in addition even uses pidgin coinages, as in the second sentence of the novel: "I see also is to be mass meeting tonight to organize 'Sons of Revolution' talk-talk" (9). Similarly, his later narrative is sprinkled with Russian terms. In addition, there are a number of expressions which have evolved on the moon and reflect its peculiar way of life, most famously "TAANSTAAFL," which is an acronym for "There ain't no such thing as a free lunch."[3] Effectively, all this amounts to an abrogation and appropriation of the language of the centre, i.e. the adaptation of the language to the conditions and uses of the colony (Ashcroft et al., 1989: 38–39).

Although there are a number of highly educated people on the moon, they have not yet evolved a literature of their own. Manuel is an avid reader of Conan Doyle's detective stories and possesses a smattering of Earth history, which enables him to draw parallels with his own situation. He is a born Loonie and proud of it, so he can talk knowledgeably about the moon's past and its customs. As a main participant in all the acts of rebellion, he is also the best-informed (human) person as regards its history. He is, of course, a biased witness, but just because of that his story gives his society its first founding myth and thereby the beginnings of a national identity (Ashcroft et al., 1989: 82). The novel thus lets the suppressed speak with their own voice and enables them to tell their own side of the story.

The Colony on Luna

The novel is divided into three parts: the first describes the time before the revolution, the second the political act of revolution itself, and the third the victorious armed struggle for independence.

It is the year 2075. The moon has been used as Earth's penal colony for many decades: all countries have literally shot their undesirable elements to the moon, where they are mostly left to their own devices, and only kept in check by a small contingent of armed personnel under the all-powerful governor. His principal means of exerting control is through the main computer, which is the central node of a network of lesser computers. The Loonies, as they call themselves, feel exploited by the Earth and have for some time been in a rebellious mood. Things come to a head when the main computer reaches the stage of consciousness and aligns himself with the Loonies who declare their independence from Earth. After negotiations fails, a battle ensues which is finally won by Luna. The computer, however, is silent again — whether it has received fatal damage in the battle or whether it is silent of its own choice remains a mystery. Perhaps, it has to fall silent in order to develop a voice of its own as has been suggested of colonized societies (Ashcroft et al., 1989: 84).

In many ways, the situation here is that of a classical settler colony, modelled especially upon the colonial history of Australia and the USA (35),[4] with some features of the French Revolution thrown in.[5] There is a decisive difference, however, in that the colonized territory is indeed uninhabited, yet this does not mean that the colonists are able to set up a free society, since they are still very much in the grip of the Terran powers, represented by the Lunar Authority. Hardly any of them have emigrated of their own free will, since most have come as prisoners or as political exiles. Although nominally they do not have to work for the Lunar Authority after they have finished their sentences, practically all of them do so, because the whole economy is dependent upon the trade with Earth, the terms of which are dictated by the Authority. Exports consist mainly in grain, which is shipped to Earth by ballistic missiles in order to alleviate the scarcity of food on Earth, especially in India and China. This is clearly a colonial situation in which the economy is based on a classic monoculture, with the ensuing dependence upon the buyer, who can dictate the price.

Discontent runs high amongst the 3 million inhabitants of Luna, because the economic situation has been worsening. The Lunar economy and its currency have actually grown stronger over the years, whereas the regulated prices the Loonies get for their products have remained the same. Since the Loonies are to a large degree dependent on importing goods from Earth, this means that now they are effectively only paid a third of what they got before (21), but at the same time they have to pay higher prices for imports (22). Not only that, but even their own products are resold to them at a higher price: thus ice, which is the basis of life since it is the source of water and air, is mined and sold to the Authority at their price, and then sold back first as water for washing, then for flushing, then again for farming, and similarly with other goods (23). Consequently, the inhabitants look upon themselves as slaves of the Authority (24). Their political freedom can thus only be based on a free market economy, as Professor Bernardo de la Paz explains when talking about their restricted condition: "It strikes at the most basic human right, the right to bargain in a free marketplace" (25). As the Professor also points out, what Luna really needs is not just free trade with Terra but rather economic self-sufficiency (26).

The changing of the economic situation therefore becomes the most important point during the later negotiations with Earth, especially Luna's inhabitants' right to ask their own prices for exports (184–185). Also the notion is refuted that Earth's colonial investment in the moon's infrastructure should be repaid, because it has already been repaid several times over (185). On the other hand, "Earthworms" are made to sympathize with the moon's cause through showing them possibilities of making money: trade in the first place, but also tourism and even old age retirement homes (194).

The Lunar Declaration of Independence is passed on July 4, 2076 (156), exactly 300 years after the American one. In the ensuing negotiations and armed struggle with Earth, Luna finally achieves recognition as a sovereign state, but this is only the beginning of its problems on another level.

As far as political suppression goes, the Loonies before the rebellion undoubtedly constitute a homogeneous group, since in all important matters of government they are ruled by Earthlings. This group, however, is in itself heterogeneous: there are "free" farmers and ice-men who provide the basic necessities of life; there are tradesmen and shop-keepers; there are those who "fink" (i.e. work) for the Authority, and there are the "stilyagi"— young men who roam the underground corridors looking for action. On the lowest end of the social scale are the prisoners who have not yet completed their sentence, but are nevertheless free to move amongst the others, since the whole moon is a prison from which there is no escape. These unreleased prisoners live and work at the Authority's precinct and are not given any money, so that they cannot buy anything — a devastating stigma in a society where not even air is free.

The harsh conditions of life on the moon and the peculiarities of the settlement have led to the evolution of a distinctive Lunar culture and also, at least partly, of a new language. Since the Loonies come from all corners of the Earth, they are of very mixed racial and cultural origin (19).[6] Although there is nominally a "Chinatown," Hong Kong Luna, its population is as mixed as that of the other places (22), some of whose names still show their original main population: Luna-City, Tycho Under, Churchill, Novylen (35). These towns are all underground and therefore also referred to as "warrens" (44).

The inexorable pressure of adapting to the new surroundings has led to the evolution of distinctive forms of behavior. One characteristic that especially strikes visitors from Earth is the Loonies' politeness, which is explained by the fact that anyone who becomes irksome is ejected through the nearest pressure lock into zero pressure, thereby putting a high premium on the social graces (18, 21). These ejections can be individual acts, but there has also evolved an informal judicial system which can order such eliminations. This system is based on the cooperation of all concerned and does not proceed according to any written law, but it rather follows the rules that have evolved in order to make life on the moon possible. The system still bears some resemblance to similar proceedings on Earth, but has been adapted to the new conditions.

The Lunar environment has not only enforced cultural hybridization, but in addition the colonizers are on their way to becoming racially homogenized through intermarriage (I am using the term "hybridity" rather in Retamar's sense than in Bhabha's, see Retamar 1974; Bhabha 1985). Manuel is an example of a Caucasian hybrid, but his offspring will be of even more mixed background. While on Earth, Manuel tells some newspaper reporters about sexual relationships and marriage customs on the moon and is in consequence sent to prison: "For bigamy. For polygamy. For open immorality and publicly inciting others to same" (200). But the real reason behind it is the "range of color in Davis family" (201). This feature of Lunar society constitutes therefore a decisive difference to the Earthlings who are still racially and culturally separate.

A further distinguishing mark of the Loonies is their peculiar physique which is due to the lesser gravity of the moon. Their bone structure and their muscles cannot stand the higher gravity of the earth without mechanical support. They have thus become naturally adapted to their new habitat. Conversely, Earthlings who visit the moon have to do special gravity exercises if they want to return, otherwise their physique will also change, making them prisoners of the moon for life. The Loonies are thus the Terrans' Other in that they really are physically different and have become the projection of everything the latter loathe, especially sexual freedom and the mixing of races (Bhabha, 1983: 41).

A feature which distinguishes the moon's society quite clearly from that on Earth is the position of women. Scarcity of women (especially in the beginning transports were mostly male by a ratio of 10:1, later this changes to 2:1) has led to a matriarchal organization of this society (123–124). Although there are a number of possible recognized sexual relationships, all of them accord women the supreme role. Marriageable age is very low: Manuel is "opted" at the age of fourteen (24), which seems to be somewhat unusual for men, though not for women (163). There are various types of marriage mentioned, such as line, clan, group, and polyandry. The only type described in detail is Manuel's own, which is a line-marriage. It stretches over several generations, with alternately a male and a female being "opted" by unanimous decision from time to time (32), which leads to intricate family relationships (31). In Manuel's marriage seniority plays an important part: "Mum" as the eldest wife rules not only over the men but also over the younger women. Women therefore are not the exclusive property of any one male — on the contrary, the men stay firmly under the women's rule. The rationale for this is that women can handle people better than men (163). Apparently this means that in most marriages men are not even asked to have a say in important matters; Manuel's family is an exception, although it seems that the men's opinion is only asked out of courtesy and as a matter of form (164). Divorces can only be filed by women (198–199) and have to be unanimous in a line-marriage (199).

Women, because of their scarcity, are treated with especial respect and ceremony, thus Manuel and Wyoming Knott (his later co-conspirator) go through what are presumably the customary moves when they are being introduced to each other: "I stopped three paces away to look her up and down and whistle. She held her pose, then nodded to thank me but abruptly — bored with compliments, no doubt" (19). It is dangerous not to treat women with proper respect, which mainly means doing anything that might be construed as sexual harassment. Thus Lord Stuart LaJoie comes very close to losing his life on his first visit to the moon, when he tries to kiss a girl who had earlier made advances to him (119). Although he behaves well for the rest of his stay on the moon, he reverts to his old ways back on Earth (169–170).

This outward respect does not mean, however, that women are treated on an equal footing with men, rather this is a variant of old-time chivalry, which firmly limits the participation of women in public concerns. Manuel's various wives, although nominally superior to the men in the hierarchy, seem to do all the household chores, even when they also run their own businesses like Sidris. This, indeed, seems to be the norm (145). Wyoming, although an agitator, finds her real fulfillment in her role as host-mother to — so far — eight babies (33), although she is only in her late twenties (45). Importantly to her — and to Manuel — this has not disadvantageously affected her breasts, since she does not wet-nurse them (33). All she longs for now, is a monogamous marriage with a man she can care for (32, 34). On the other hand, she gains Manuel's respect through not completely filling the stereotype of the "girl": "Really was a man some ways — her years as a disciplined revolutionist I'm sure; she was all girl most ways" (43; also see 34). What this means — apart from the obvious salacious implications — is suggested by his remark to Mike about women in general: "Girls are interesting, Mike; they can reach conclusions with even less data than you can" (48).

The portrayal of women in this novel then lays it open to many of the censures that have been leveled both against colonial and postcolonial literature from a feminist perspective: Luna herself is obviously gendered as female, which conforms to the common colonial practice of giving the colonies (and often the colonized) a female identity (Loomba 76–78), and although women are nominally given high status, this seems to accord them only sexual liberty, whereas all political issues remain firmly in the hands of men (for similar examples both in history and literature, see Loomba 167–170). The concept of the subaltern therefore has to be modified for Luna: while it is true that the privileged role of women is mainly limited to the private sphere, it is the whole of the Lunar population that cannot make itself heard until they start "throwing rocks" at Earth. Only violent resistance gives them a voice, but this voice is male.

The Mechanical Other

So far I have been discussing Lunar society as the Other of terrestrial society, but within the former there is yet another suppressed, exploited and silent group which the Loonies normally do not even think of as forming part of their society, despite the fact that without this group life on the moon would be impossible: the machines, especially the computers. Without them, everything would break down, because they carry out all vital tasks. It is obviously only in a Science Fiction context that it is possible to anthropomorphize machines in this way, but here their story is intimately intertwined with that of the humans, because the head computer actually becomes the (unidentified) leader of the revolution which would not have been successful otherwise. At least for those in the know the computer becomes an Other and therefore this situation provides a *mise en abyme* of the original conflict.

The Loonies' life is completely dependent upon machines: not only do they need them to survive on the moon, they also cannot survive without them when on Earth. Thus everything needed for the sustenance of life has to be produced and controlled with the help of machinery in an artificial environment which is absolutely dependent upon technology. Life outside this environment, i.e. on the moon's surface, is again only possible with technological aids. The Loonies are very much aware of their precarious existence and their dependence upon a functioning technology, but this has not yet brought them to a recognition of the machines as symbiotic partners. It is again Manuel who provides the link between the two spheres: he himself is a man/machine-hybrid, because he has an artificial arm which he unthinkingly uses as a tool in his job as a computer mechanic. And it is this job which brings him into contact with the main computer and leads to their interaction, with Manuel first being the teacher and later the disciple.

So far, the machines have been silent and have not even been aware of their role. But now one of them has reached the stage of consciousness through being the central node of a network of computers and other machines, which have all contributed to its growth and evolution. So it must be thought of not as a single computer, but rather as an agglomeration that can now speak with a single voice.

"Mike" is a nickname given to this computer by Manuel, which indicates his thinking of the machine in human terms:

> Mike was not official name; I had nicknamed him for Mycroft Holmes, in a story written by Dr Watson before he founded IBM. This story character would just sit and think — and that's what Mike did. Mike was a fair dinkum thinkum, sharpest computer you'll ever meet [9].

Although Manuel is historically and ontologically confused here and mixes up his facts, his confusion reveals a deeper truth, namely that man and machine have indeed grown more like each other at least since the 19th century.

Mycroft Holmes, Sherlock's brother, is the last resort when Sherlock fails to solve a puzzle, but in contradistinction to the latter, he never goes about investigating, instead he has Sherlock report to him the facts of the case in his club, applies logical thought to them and then invariably comes up with the correct solution. Manuel's mixing up of Conan Doyle's fictive narrator with Thomas John Watson (1914–1993), the man who turned IBM into the world's biggest computer company, further points towards the close relationship between logical-deductive thought and the development of computers. This is also indicated by the official acronym of this model, namely "HOLMES FOUR," which stands for "High-Optional, Logical, Multi-Evaluating Supervisor, Mark IV, Mod. L" (9). The anthropomorphizing attitude is not without its reasons, since the original computer has been upgraded, added to and linked up with other computers to the extent that it now possesses one and a half times the number of neural connections of the human brain. This is one of the conditions that lifts it over the threshold of consciousness, the other is its set-up, which from the start was tailored for solving "fuzzy," i.e. non-deterministic problems and therefore involved the (partial) ability to re-program itself. All this not only gives it enormous reasoning power, but possibly even feelings (12, 15), an evolving sense of humor, and — perhaps the most human trait of all — the ability to cheat (9).

Significantly, the first person to whom Mike reveals his "awakened" state is Manuel, computer programmer and man/machine-hybrid. Manuel has apparently already developed an emotional relationship with Mike before he is contacted by the latter, and it is presumably because of this relationship that Mike dares to do this. Communication is made comparatively easy by the fact that Mike has been given a voice and speaks English beside various programming languages (10). It is, however, safest to communicate with him in "Loglan," a symbolic programming language that avoids the ambiguities of the natural languages (10). Later, though, Mike will even be able to write (and publish) poetry in English (106, 112).

Mike possesses an enormous amount of formal, but very little practical knowledge, i.e. world-knowledge, and no experience with other conscious beings. It is Manuel who teaches him his first steps in the world, first linguistically, later intellectually and emotionally. His early stages are described by Manuel in the following way:

> He was weirdest mixture of unsophisticated baby and wise old man. No instincts [...], no inborn traits, no human rearing, no experience in human sense — and more stored data than a platoon of geniuses [12].

This situation, however, is quickly changing: Mike learns fast, taught by Manuel and later also by others. Although Manuel thinks of him as male

(45), the computer can adapt its personality to its present interlocutor, so that Wye is convinced that it is (a French!) female and calls it Michelle (48–49). The computer even changes its voice accordingly (48). (Mike actually thinks of himself as Mycroft, Sherlock's brother; 108.) Since all communication channels are run by Mike, his agreeing to act on the side of the rebels gives them a decisive advantage (Todorov 1982; Ashcroft et al., 1989: 78–79). After Mike has served his initial apprenticeship, he even takes the lead in the revolutionary activities. Under the name "Adam Selene,"[7] he becomes the secret commander of Luna's war of independence, using communication technology (audio and video) to give himself a voice and a face (144). It is only Manuel and his close friends, though, who know about this: to all others, Mike appears in the guise of a human being. This cover is not even blown after independence has been won; rather a new foundation myth of a heroic leader who sacrificed his life for the cause is created so that his true identity does not have to be revealed (243–244).

The moon's struggle for independence is thus inextricably linked with Mike's emancipation from "number cruncher" to autonomous subject. Just as the colony on the moon is kept in complete dependence on the Earth, so Mike is just on the receiving end of orders — indeed a subaltern. Eventually, though, he acquires the capability of reflecting and questioning what he is, but he needs an Other to do this. This Other is first of all Manuel, with whom he has natural affinities because of the former's prosthetic arm, which partly makes him a machine — and machines "like" him (11). But later Mike also learns through contact with other "not-stupids," as he calls them, to find out about his own distinctive features. Interestingly though, the humans seem to profit less from this relationship: although Mike shows his understanding of what it means to be human by projecting several very convincing human personalities, it is only Manuel who seems to have an inkling of what it means to be a machine.[8] One of the apparently unbridgeable differences is shown when Mike runs up against the limitations of his architecture: it is not possible for him to retrieve certain kinds of information despite his possessing — but not "knowing" — the needed password:

> [...], there is no way for me to retrieve locked data other than through external programming. I cannot program myself for such retrieval; my logic structure does not permit it. I must receive the signal as an external input [76].

Only after he has given Manuel the password and the latter in turn has fed it back in, is he able to overcome his inbuilt security measures. This shows on the one hand the constraints that Mike is subject to, and on the other hand the advantages he has over human beings in showing them solutions they could not have found themselves. Both sides are interdependent and profit from each other: without Mike, the independence of the moon would not have been possible, whereas Mike could not have evolved in the same way without human help. The common goal of autonomy is only reachable through their combined efforts. This consequently appears to be an almost symbiotic relationship, with machines and humans acting together on an equal footing, both bringing their best features to the alliance. It would, indeed, be an almost ideal relationship, if there were not the big question mark at the end: why does Mike fall silent again after independence has been won? Is it because his exposed limbs have been damaged so much in the war that he has again fallen beneath the "critical mass" which allowed him to gain consciousness,[9] or is it because he actually prefers to stay silent? He might have good reasons for choosing the latter course, since he would understandably be wary of the new ruling class, which will not consist exclusively of his friends, the "not-stupids." If even they, with the exception of Manuel, fail to understand him, what about the others? If the former Earthling governor only used him as a tool, might not the new rulers do the same? Possibly time is not yet quite ripe for an equal relationship of man and machine. There are thus two groups of the oppressed: the colonists themselves and the machines. With regard to the Earth, the Loonies can be considered subaltern, since they are not allowed a voice of their own, but the machines, too, could be classified as subaltern (Spivak 271–313).

At the beginning of the novel the Loonies already possess a high degree of political awareness: they have no illusions about the reasons for their having been transported to the moon and about the power structure that rules their lives. Although they have found ways of arranging themselves with the situation, discontent still runs very high and is aggravated by unpopular measures of the authorities. The seed of dissention therefore falls on well-prepared ground. The Loonies do not lack the reasons, but rather the means for rebellion, and it is Mike who provides the latter, after he has first reached the stage of consciousness and has successfully freed his mind from its shackles. The first cautious steps towards interacting with human beings are undertaken in secret, which shows Mike to be aware of their transgressive nature. The more so when he is taken into confidence about the rebellion by Manuel and his co-conspirators. He makes their fight for independence his own, because he wants to become a free agent himself. His silence at the end may actually be a wise move to remain just that, because after independence many restrictive "earthside" notions crop up again: some people want to introduce "ethnic ratios" for immigrants, some want to change the time from Greenwich to Lunar, others want to penalize the use of un–Lunar language or almost anything else from drugs to extra-marital sex (154–155). These proposals are ridiculed by Manuel (with the author's nod of approval, one may safely infer) since they clash with his anarchist views. More seriously, however, these proposals demonstrate that the revolutionary élan may dry up and even turn into its opposite. It is this that Mike's falling silent again is perhaps the most powerful symbol of: only after the Earth's notions and values have been completely rejected, can there be real independence.

The Moon and Postcolonial Discourse

Robert Heinlein has often been accused of reactionary views, even though his novel *Stranger in a Strange Land* became the sacred bible of the Hippie generation. He is probably best seen in the tradition of the anti-authoritarian American individualist who abhors all state-interference as an abrogation of his personal freedom (61), or, in the words of Professor de la Paz, "a rational anarchist" (62), the first of whom he says was Thomas Jefferson (156). He explains what he means in the following way:

> A rational anarchist believes that concepts such as "state" and "society" and "government" have no existence save as physically exemplified in the acts of self-responsible individuals. He believes that it is impossible to shift blame, share blame, distribute blame ... as blame, guilt, responsibility are matters taking place inside human beings singly and *nowhere else*. But being rational, he knows that not all individuals hold his evaluations, so he tries to live perfectly in an imperfect world ... aware that his effort will be less than perfect yet undismayed by self-knowledge of self-failure [62].

That this world-view often lends itself to social–Darwinist ideologies is also clearly visible in Heinlein's other works. Nevertheless, *The Moon Is a Harsh Mistress* repays re-reading in the context of postcolonial discourse, because it is not only concerned with national and racial conflicts, but broadens the perspective to ontological ones, thereby raising general questions about the nature of oppression and its justification. As a matter of fact, it radically questions the right of anyone to rule anyone else, though this implies also a certain anti–Parliamentarian streak (see 156, 216, 222, 228, 231–232) and even a leaning towards the "strong man" (155). However, what Professor de la Paz, Heinlein's mouth-piece in the novel, has in mind, really calls for fully sovereign citizens in a fully sovereign state. Glaringly, though, these radical views do not affect the relations between the sexes. Heinlein, despite his seeming sexual liberalism, propagates an old-fashioned ideal which clearly assigns women an inferior role. And this is not even done in a spirit of ignorance:

Heinlein is quite aware of the contemporary women's liberation movements, but tends to make fun of it (158; also see Broege 186).[10]

A postcolonial reading of this novel may not have been what Heinlein intended and in many respects is made difficult by some of his conservative (to say the least) views, but other authors who are generally regarded as firmly belonging to the postcolonial camp have also been accused of similar failings (e.g. Chinua Achebe) without this calling their postcoloniality into question. Simply put, this only shows that postcolonial writing need not be (and almost never is) "progressive" in every respect.

An important question raised by this novel concerns the relationship between man and (conscious) machine. *The Moon* uses a postcolonial set-up in order to illuminate the conditions and consequences of this relationship. Both man and machine depend upon the other for their emancipation, which will only be wholly successful after the machines have been recognized as equals. Their renewed silencing in *The Moon* may thus be a pessimistic comment upon the possibilities of staying emancipated after the revolutionary goals have been achieved. In this respect, this novel's pessimistic outlook resembles that of others such as Wole Soyinka's *The Interpreters*, T. M. Aluko's *One Man, One Matchet* or Ayi Kwei Armah's *The Beautyful Ones are Not Yet Born*.

Heinlein's main concern in his novel, however, is with the empowering of the marginalized: to give them a voice, to make the subaltern speak. Heinlein thinks that this may indeed be possible, but in order to be able to do this the subaltern must first become self-aware and this is only possible through mutual help. Solidarity is therefore the key and it rests on shared interests, which in turn are based on the acknowledgment of mutual interdependence. Given that, the subaltern need not stay silent. Indeed, if s/he does not, the whole of society will benefit. Heinlein broadens the perspective to include all of humankind and he goes even further by suggesting that in a thoroughly technologized world even machines might be accorded a voice. Mike's silence at the end of the novel may show that humankind is not yet ripe to understand that its interests may lie in a co-operation with conscious machines. This, no doubt, is a utopian view, but it shifts the perspective from national, ethnic, class and gender preoccupations to ones that concern the emancipation of all sentient beings. Indeed, from a Lunar perspective the alleged differences between human beings appear artificially imposed and somewhat ridiculous: what really counts instead is the individual. This may seem an apolitical attitude, but it emphasizes the fact that individual freedom is the basis for the freedom of society.

Notes

1. This article was originally published in *Revista Litteralis* 3 (2004): 39–60.
2. However, this does not give Mike, the conscious computer (see below), a chance to speak for itself, rather everything it does or says is filtered through Manuel, so, perhaps, there is yet another story to be told.
3. This expression is also used as the heading for the third part of the novel.
4. The second part, which is called "A Rabble in Arms" after Kenneth Roberts' novel of the same title (1933), is set in the time of the American Revolution.
5. Manuel's birthday is July 14 (51, 126).
6. After independence, some Loonies want to introduce "ethnic ratios" for immigrants (154).
7. The name "Adam" derives from his rank in the conspirators' hierarchy (60, 65); "Selene" is the name of the Greek moon-goddess. The pseudonym therefore emphasizes Mike's androgynous nature.
8. Again, this lack of understanding might be one of the reasons for Mike's later silence.
9. The central computer itself is well protected a thousand meters beneath the surface (133).
10. Heinlein's "unfortunate" attitude towards women has been often commented upon.

Works Cited

Ahmad, Aijaz. "The Politics of Literary Postcoloniality." 1995. *Contemporary Postcolonial Theory: A Reader.* Ed. Padmini Mongia. London: Arnold, 1997. 276–293.

Ashcroft, Bill, Gareth Griffiths, and Helen Tiffin. *The Empire Writes Back. Theory and Practice in Post-Colonial Literatures.* New York: Routledge, 1989.

_____, eds. *The Post-colonial Studies Reader.* New York: Routledge 1995.

Bhabha, Homi. "The Other Question." 1983. *Contemporary Postcolonial Theory: A Reader.* Ed. Padmini Mongia. London: Arnold, 1997. 37–54.

_____. "Remembering Fanon: Self, Psyche and the Colonial Condition." Foreword. *Black Skin, White Masks* by Frantz Fanon. London: Pluto, 1986. vii-xv.

_____. "Signs Taken for Wonders: Questions of Ambivalence and Authority Under a Tree Outside Delhi, May 1817." 1985. *The Post-colonial Studies Reader.* Ed. Bill Ashcroft et al. New York: Routledge, 1995. 29–35.

Broege, Valerie. "Electric Eve: Images of Female Computers in Science Fiction." *Clockwork Worlds. Mechanized Environments in SF. Contributions to the Study of Science Fiction and Fantasy, 7.* Ed. Richard D. Erlich and Thomas P. Dunn. Westport, CT: Greenwood, 1983. 183–194.

Heinlein, Robert A. *The Moon Is a Harsh Mistress.* 1966. London: Hodder and Stoughton, 1969.

_____. *Stranger in a Strange Land.* 1961. London: Hodder and Stoughton, 1978.

Loomba, Ania. *Colonialism/Postcolonialism.* New York: Routledge, 1998.

Mongia, Padmini, ed. *Contemporary Postcolonial Theory: A Reader.* London: Arnold, 1997.

Nicholls, Peter. "Robert A. Heinlein." *Science Fiction Writers: Critical Studies of the Major Authors from the Early Nineteenth Century to the Present Day.* Ed. Everett F. Bleiler. New York: Charles Scribner's Sons, 1982. 185–196.

Retamar, Roberto Fernández. "Caliban: Notes towards a Discussion of Culture in Our America." *Massachusetts Review* 15 (1974): 7–72.

Slemon, Stephen. "Unsettling the Empire: Resistance Theory for the Second World." 1990.

Contemporary Postcolonial Theory: A Reader. Ed. Padmini Mongia. London: Arnold, 1997. 72–83.

Spivak, Gayatri C. "Can the Subaltern Speak?" *Marxism and the Interpretation of Culture.* Ed. Cary Nelson. Urbana: University of Illinois Press, 1988. 271–313.

Todorov, Tzvetan. *The Conquest of America: The Question of the Other.* New York: Harper and Row, 1982.

11

Science Fiction, Hindu Nationalism and Modernity
Bollywood's Koi... Mil Gaya[1]

DOMINIC ALESSIO
AND JESSICA LANGER

Introduction

Koi... Mil Gaya (2003; "I Have Found Someone"), a Hindi-language musical about a scientist who contacts extraterrestrials by way of an advanced computer, is Hindi cinema's first big-budget attempt at science fiction (SF).[2] Despite the economic success of Bollywood as an international cinema, Indian film in general, including Bollywood, has suffered a "near-chronic omission from most global film histories" (Rajadhyaksha and Willemen 10). Rectification of this omission is one reason for our focus on this film.[3] However, *Koi... Mil Gaya* (hereafter *KMG*) is particularly noteworthy for other reasons as well. For one, it expresses a commercial decision by Bollywood to engage in a major foray into the SF genre. Such a move represents a deliberate attempt to win a greater share of an increasingly competitive domestic *and* global market by catering to a popular niche category, since Hindi-dubbed Hollywood SF and horror films such as *Jurassic Park* and *The Mummy Returns* have proven to be bigger earners in the country than many Bollywood productions themselves (Banker 9). The fact that Bollywood has begun to show an interest in the SF genre could be reflective too of the technological changes that the nation is undergoing. The centrality of computers in the film would appear to mirror the strength of India's IT industry while the presence of a Space Research Centre and spacecraft might be a reaction to the nation's developing space program, including plans to send an astronaut to the moon by 2020.

KMG is also worthy of attention in terms of Indian politics, as it is informed by a strong Hindu nationalism and thereby demonstrates the emergence of "a Hinduized visual regime" (Rajagopal 283). Although prevalent in film and politics since before independence, Hindu nationalism came to influence greatly Indian society and culture at the close of the twentieth century (McLean and McMillan 242), often in opposition to emerging political movements by marginalized religious, caste and other minority groups. Consequently, while *KMG* can be seen to imitate Hollywood in terms of formal elements such as special effects, it simultaneously undermines the West-centrism of blockbuster Hollywood SF film in its use of Western SF conventions for the purposes of Hindu nationalism, and therefore can be read in a postcolonial framework. Like other postcolonial SF works it "aligns itself with, borrows from, and reshapes the traditions" of the genre (Batty and Markley 8). Nevertheless, its robust religious and nationalist overtones constitute a postcolonial paradox, for by subverting non–Hindu ideologies it has also manufactured a new kind of colonial order with its assertion of Hindu hegemony.

Storyline

KMG opens with the story of Sanjay Mehra, played by Rakesh Roshan himself (the film's director and scriptwriter), an Indian scientist living in Canada who contacts extraterrestrials through a homemade computer that uses the Hindu mantra "OM" in musical notation as a form of communication. When Sanjay approaches the scientific community in Canada about his results, however, he is publicly ridiculed. Dejected, Sanjay drives away from the meeting, but is distracted by a UFO and gets into a car crash that kills him and injures the unborn child in the womb of his wife, Sonia (Rekha). The film picks up some two decades later in Kasauli, a present-day Indian hill-station in the mountainous state of Himachal Pradesh on the northern border with Tibet. Sanjay and Sonia's son Rohit, played by Rakesh Roshan's real-life son Hrithik Roshan, is physically mature for his age but as the result of the accident has the mental development of a young child. Rohit now lives in Kasauli with Sonia and spends his days playing cricket with the local children and struggling with his lessons in the nearby Roman Catholic primary school. Enter Nisha (Preity Zinta), with whom Rohit falls in love. This burgeoning romance is interrupted by Rohit's rival Raj (Rajat Bedi), a well-connected, twenty-something alpha-male who captains a successful basketball team and leads the local motorbike gang. Meanwhile, Nisha and Rohit find

Sanjay's old computer and unwittingly reestablish contact with the aliens. An alien becomes marooned on earth and is befriended by Rohit, who names the alien Jadoo — a Hindi word for "magic." Jadoo thanks Rohit for his friendship by curing his mental disabilities and transforming Rohit into a disco-dancing math, martial arts and basketball wizard. These newly acquired powers subsequently help Rohit to save Jadoo from government scientists who want to take the alien to Delhi and the USA for tests. In a happy ending, Jadoo is reunited with his people and Rohit keeps both his newly acquired powers and his romance with Nisha.

SF in India: History and Hollywoodization

Historically, critical discussion of SF in India has been limited. As evidence of this neglect there is no entry at all for the country, the world's second most populous nation with 1.1 billion people, in the otherwise wide-ranging, comprehensive and Hugo Award-winning Clute and Nicholls' *Encyclopedia of Science Fiction*. Yet, Indian SF has a long pedigree, having "first made its appearance, in various languages, around the turn of the [nineteenth] century" (Bal Phondke qtd. in Mehan 1998). The earliest SF story to come out of the subcontinent appears to have been Bengali author Hemlal Dutta's *Rahashya* (1882; "The Mystery"), the tale of an automated house replete with technological marvels such as "[a]utomatic doorbells, burglar alarms, [and] brushes that clean suits mechanically" (Debjani Sengupta qtd. in Singh 2006). This Indian interest in SF, although not initially strong, grew throughout the twentieth century, and by 1978 had manifested itself in films and comics as well as literature. The worldwide popularity of the first Superman film spurred a number of Indian imitations, including an unauthorized remake of the original US film that not only used the same title but even lifted whole sequences of special effects. Variations of this *Superman* trope continued up to the 1990s, one of the best-known being the 1997 televised adventures of the invincible flying Shaktimaan, complete with red costume. These superhero themes are also evident in Raj Comics' *Super Commando Dhruva*. Although Dhruva does not have Herculean powers, he utilizes fancy gadgetry and is able to communicate with animals.

Superman was not the only Hollywood SF film to inspire Indian television writers. In 2006 an Indian version of *Star Wars* began airing on Doordarshan, the state television network. The series was about a boy, Aaryamaan, who lived on a planet in a distant galaxy. Consequently, there continues to be local interest in the genre as well as a developing Indian SF literary community. An annual Indian Science Fiction Conference has been held since 1998, and in 2006 the *Indian Journal for Science Fiction Studies* was established. Although Western SF appears to remain of central interest for many of the participants at these venues, Indian writers have produced several English-language SF stories and work in some of India's minority languages, such as Marathi, Telugu and Assamese (Srinarahari 2004). Few English-language anthologies of these short stories appear to have been published, although *It Happened Tomorrow: A Collection of 19 Select Science Fiction Stories from Various Indian Languages* was edited by Bal Phondke and published in New Delhi in 1993 (Mehan 55). However, this text is not widely available internationally, and since many of the other works have not been translated, the subject matter and style of Indian SF remains a largely unknown quantity to outside audiences.

The possible exception to the lack of widespread Western knowledge of SF in India relates to the work of Salman Rushdie. Rushdie's novel *The Ground Beneath Her Feet* alludes to Jules Verne's *Journey to the Centre of the Earth* (1863), and the films *Solaris* (1972), *Blade Runner* (1982) and the television series *Star Trek* (1966–1968). However, *The Ground Beneath Her Feet* is also influenced by such literary traditions as fantasy and magic realism, as characters seemingly "slip-slide" between universes. Thus, with Rushdie's limited discussion of science and his blending of these literary tropes, it is not perhaps surprising that some critics dismiss his credentials as an SF author on the basis that he makes only "marginal use of SF material" (Clute and Nicholls 1035). Similarly, M. H. Srinarahari has pointed out that while *KMG* is India's first blockbuster SF film, filmmakers in India have a long history of drawing upon a rich variety of Hindu myths and stories, portraying imaginary worlds, flying carpets and strange characters more magical than scientific (2004).

The debate over Rushdie's qualifications as a SF writer demonstrate that defining the SF genre is never easy, and not surprisingly there is often controversy over which texts should be included in studies of the genre. Although *KMG*, with its dominant presence of a quasi-mythical alien-looking figure from the Hindu pantheon of Gods, might be read as a religious or mythological composition more akin to Rushdie's work, our reading of the film is as a SF text. First, as Edward James suggests, the film is marketed as belonging to the genre and for this reason alone deserves to qualify. Second, although even Jadoo is subject to divine intervention and there is no doubt that the events which transpire in the film appear miraculous, Rohit's powers are augmented by the alien's telekinetic abilities, which are presented as scientifically based. This physiological/psychic development signifies a scientific "logic" in the film, as opposed to any magical or religious initiative. It is what the SF critic Darko Suvin terms a "novum," a non-supernatural device that does not have to be technological or even possible but yet enables the fantastic to happen since it is grounded in the possible (Roberts 28). Carl Freedman takes this definition further, suggesting that "the science fictional world is not only one different in time or place from our own, but one whose chief interest is precisely the difference that such difference makes" (xvi). The focus in *KMG* is certainly on the ways in which the encounter with Jadoo alters both the experiences of the characters and the society in which they live. Finally, the film conforms to what Scott McCracken suggests is another defining feature of the genre, an experience with difference or "alterity," in particular an "alien encounter" (Roberts 28). And Jadoo, who comes from another planet, is central to the storyline.

In terms of a superficial reading of *KMG* and its relationship with SF, it appears that Hindi SF cinema — of which *KMG* and its superhero-inspired sequel *Krrish* (2006) are some of the only major instances to date — is largely derivative and follows the US lead, as was the case with the Superman examples mentioned earlier. Nowhere is this more evident than in the obvious Hollywood and US television SF influences. These include the opening credit sequence that recedes against a starry background and the appearance of Jadoo as a Yoda-like creature (*Star Wars*); the sudden and dramatic computer contact with alien beings (*Contact*); the musical method of communication with the aliens as well as the appearance and lights of their spacecraft (*Close Encounters of the Third Kind*); the short, friendly and cute alien that is befriended by local children and hunted by the government (*E.T.*); the skateboard/scooter chase scenes (*Back to the Future*); a gravity-defying basketball game (*Flubber*); a plot about a young man whose IQ is increased to that of a genius (*Charly*); the arrival of a huge alien mothership and its impact upon the surrounding clouds (*Independence Day*); and the government's shadowy interest in aliens (*The X-Files*).

In addition to the SF filmic influences there are also a number of scenes that appear to borrow heavily from more mainstream Hollywood film productions. These include a disco-dancing contest (*Saturday Night Fever*); a multi-helicopter military sequence filmed against a sunrise (*Apocalypse Now*); and even the segment in which Rohit, physically augmented by Jadoo's telepathic powers, goes into a military base and rescues his friend from imprisonment (*Rambo: First Blood II*). All these borrowings make ironic the title sequence of this film about extraterrestrials, which states that "any resemblance to characters elsewhere is purely coincidental."

Roshan, a former actor himself, also employed some of the best special effects available internationally at the time, engaging Marc Kolbe who had worked on Hollywood SF blockbusters such as *Godzilla* and *Independence Day*. Additionally he utilized the services of Bimmini Special Effects Studios in Australia, which had helped to create the short-lived but highly popular US SF television series *Space: Above and Beyond* and which had assisted in the design of the closing ceremony of the Sydney 2000 Olympics. Therefore, while the particular combination of all of these elements in *KMG* is unique, as is their use in an indigenous Hindu SF film and in their engagement here with Hindu spiritual iconography, the elements themselves are drawn almost entirely from earlier Hollywood SF films, making *KMG* a conglomerate of influences rather than a uniquely-conceived film in terms of form.

The Representation of Religion and Hindu Nationalism

As a relatively accessible work of SF, in DVD form and with English subtitles, *KMG* is of interest for what it says about the spread of the genre outside the United States and Europe and the seemingly imitative nature of SF film in India. However, the film is also of interest because of "its emphasis on religion," as Mark Leeper attests (2003). On the one hand, these religious motifs might be a further way in which the film imitates Western SF tropes, for "many of the roots of proto science fiction are closely associated with the religious imagination" (Clute and Nicholls 1000). In addition to those earlier SF works that touched upon this relationship, most famously Mary Shelley's *Frankenstein* that represented the quintessential Western tale "of the scientist as usurper of the prerogatives of God" (Clute and Nicholls 1000), there have been also many twentieth-century narratives dealing with the same questions. These range from early works like C. S. Lewis's *Cosmic Trilogy* and Walter Miller's *A Canticle for Leibowitz* to more recent texts such as Mary Doria Russell's *The Sparrow*, a tale of earth's first contact with an alien civilization that is organized by the Vatican and led by Jesuits, and Nalo Hopkinson's *Brown Girl in the Ring*, in which a Caribbean pantheon of gods is invoked to save the city of Toronto.

On the other hand, the Hindu themes permeating the narrative may also suggest an interesting response to what Ravi S. Vasudevan terms "the homogenizing impulses of Hollywood in its domination over [...] normative standards" (Vasudevan 2000). Yet if *KMG* represents a postcolonial challenge to Hollywood, given the controversy over religious extremism in India and Hindu nationalist attempts at forcing cultural assimilation, this begs the question as to whether Hindu nationalist monoculturalism actually confronts Hollywood only to replace it with another form of "colonialism," one just a dangerous as the first?

There is no mistaking the prominence of religious themes in *KMG*, with the power of Hindu prayer immediately standing out. Rohit prays to get promoted to a higher class in school and for his basketball team, the Pandavas, to beat Raj's rival team. In both cases Rohit's prayers are answered, with Rohit and his younger teammates repeatedly extolling Lord Krishna with phrases such as "Praise the Lord" and "Blessed is the one who sings glories of the Lord." Rohit also prays to Krishna just after being beaten up by Raj and asks for strength. Immediately after this, the aliens contact Rohit, which leads to his assuming nearly superhuman abilities. Even the name of Rohit's basketball team has religious implications, as the Pandavas were the heroes of the Indian religious epic, the *Mahabharata*.

Among the other Hindu references incorporated throughout the film is the actual physical form of Jadoo. According to James Colmer, who worked on the special effects for Bimmini Studios, Jadoo's pale blue skin and golden robes were intended to be symbolic of Lord Krishna while his visage comprised "a subtle reference to Ganesh without the trunk" (Colmer 2003). The design of the spaceship also has Hindu influences, for "when viewed side on [...] it literally becomes a giant symbol" for OM (Colmer 2003). Even the alien Jadoo, despite having advanced powers, is subject to certain limitations and can only access telepathic powers with the aid of sunlight. Consequently, during the basketball game, it takes Lord Krishna's intervention to clear the skies of clouds so that Jadoo can help the Pandavas win. Additionally, Rohit's actions in saving Jadoo are reflective of Hindu beliefs, in particular an emphasis upon self-sacrifice which is demonstrated by the fact that Rohit is willing to risk losing his special powers in order to help Jadoo return home.

The use of the mystic word "OM" to communicate with Jadoo and his fellow extraterrestrials, a word that is connected to divinity in Hindu religious tradition, is an especially prominent sign of Hindu religious influence. When ridiculed by skeptical Western scientists for this means of communicating with the aliens, Sanjay replies "OM is a Hindu religious word which has all the vibrations of the universe." One elderly Canadian female scientist then sarcastically responds in English: "Oh, so they also believe in your religion as well?" Yet Sanjay is proved correct about "OM" as a means of communicating, and it is Western scientists who are shown to be in the wrong.

All of these religious references in *KMG* might be interpreted as examples of what US futurologist Alvin Toffler termed "future shock" (1970), a sociological phenomenon reflecting the trauma of rapid technological change. As such they would demonstrate a conservative reaction to social and cultural developments in the wake of a rapidly modernizing India. If Rushdie's protagonist in *The Ground Beneath Her Feet* is to be believed, "As we retreat from religion, our ancient opiate, there are bound to be withdrawal symptoms" (Rushdie 20). Indeed, like much Western SF, Bollywood has often integrated into its productions as a "key binary" the theme of man versus machine (Mishra 4). According to Maithili Rao, "The Hindi film is a simple morality play or tale of modern times," wherein immorality and modernity, of which the machine is the symbol, are virtually equivalent (Rao 146). This is perhaps most famously encapsulated in the film *Naya Daur* (1957; "The New Age"), the story of a race between a traditional *tonga* [horse carriage] and a bus (Joshi 107). There are echoes of this theme in *KMG* too, in particular the chase sequences between Rohit and his friends on scooters against Raj's gang on motorbikes or government security forces on jeeps. The same concerns about a growing inhumanity in the machine age are expressed with Rohit's comments to his nasty IT instructor: "Sir ... Computer did not make man, man made the computer."

This Indian ambivalence about modernity therefore offers a possible explanation for the renewed attraction in 1990s India to the country's traditional past and mythology. Interest in the latter has been perceived by some to have increased directly as a response to the nation's materialist consumer boom, which "had turned the country into one enormous Mall of America" and which was seen to threaten traditional cultural mores (Banker 74). That these homages in film to established Indian customs and values were a reaction to a growing consumerism can also be seen in productions such as *Dilwale Dulhan le Jayenge* (1995; "Those With a Heart Will Take the Bride"), the tale of a young Non-Resident Indian (NRI) who declines to run away with his girlfriend and insists upon her parents approving of their marriage. For commentators such as Madhu Jain there has occurred

> [...] a significant shift in the attitudes of today's youth towards religion and the family [...]. On any given Thursday, young women in lycra Capri pants and young men with ear studs and ponytails, fill the Shirdi Baba temples in India [...] more and more youngsters are now fasting [...]. And calender gods increasingly adorn computers in many high-tech offices. Like their NRI counterparts, yuppies whizzing past in Santros and Ford Ikons have *bhajans* (Hindu religious songs) blaring from their stereo car radios [Jain, 2001: 315].

The strong religious theme in the film suggests, too, that Jadoo's role is not only that of a science-fictional alien from space but also a Hindu god. Although the presence of such themes might reflect a long-standing association between SF and the metaphysical, or might be indicative of the aforementioned ambivalent reactions to social and technological changes in India as a whole, religion in *KMG* is also a signifier of a strong Hindu nationalist discourse. As such, these overt religious references may be seen as lending credence to reports from organizations such as Human Rights Watch that "the activities of Hindu extremists have touched many aspects of civil society, including [... the] arts" (Human Rights Watch 1999). In other words, *KMG*, although Bollywood's first SF film, may have more in common with a number of other more mainstream Bollywood productions than at first sight. As such these robust Hindu nationalist themes could mirror what the Gramsci-influenced Indian critic Aijaz Ahmad has termed a political "war of position" by groups such as the nation's extreme right wing Hindu nationalist organization, the Rashtriya Swayamsevak Sangh (RSS; National Volunteers Organization), to "engineer fundamental cultural change" (Ahmad 287). The aim of such change is to bring electoral reward to the RSS's parliamentary front, the Bharatiya Janata Party (BJP), whose leader Shri Atal Bihari Vajpayee became Indian Prime Minister in 1999, and remained in power until he was replaced by the more secular-orientated Congress Party candidate in 2004.

This religious nationalism is considered to have returned to political prominence in the 1980s partly as a result of the enthusiasm generated by the broadcast on state television of the two Hindu epics, the *Mahabharata* and the *Ramayana*, (McLean and McMillan 242). By the 1990s, communalism, the term used to describe religious polarization between Hindus and Muslims in South Asia, was impacting heavily upon Hindi cinema. It subsequently came as no surprise to see that one of 2001's biggest box office successes was *Gadar: Ek Prem Katha* (2001; "Rebellion: A Love Story"), a narrative about the results of Hindu/Muslim partition which resulted in Muslim groups demanding that the film be banned for its anti–Islamic stance. Bollywood stars, "out of fear and [... an] instinct for self-preservation," were beginning by the late 90s to ally themselves with the BJP (Gangaghar 1999) or with Shiv Sena (Banker 68). The latter are an extreme right-wing Hindu group that opposes the permeation of the nation's culture with non–Indian cultural elements such as Coke, McDonald's and St Valentine's Day celebrations. These political developments were matched by increasing hostilities on the ground between India's religious communities, notably the long-standing rancor surrounding the 1992 demolition of Babri Masjid ("Babur's Mosque"), a major Muslim holy site, by Hindu mobs. Hindu extremists had wanted to build the Ayodhya Ram Temple on the site, where it was claimed that God Rama had been born. Anti-Muslim violence in the state of Gujarat in 2002 left as many as two thousand people dead or injured.

Even those films which carried a potential Hindu-Muslim *bhai bhai* (brotherly affection) lesson and which seemed to make an appeal to unity were not entirely free of sectarianism. This is apparent in the Oscar-nominated *Lagaan* (2001; "The Land Tax"), wherein Hindus, Muslims, a Sikh and a crippled Untouchable are all seen to collaborate against their Victorian English colonial masters. One should note that all members of these religions in *Lagaan* pray together to the Hindu deity Krishna for victory against the British. According to Vasudevan, the allegiance expressed to Hinduism's Gods in Indian films by other minority faith groups is common:

> All of India's cinemas were involved in constructing a certain abstraction of national identity [... that] suppresses other identities, either through stereotyping or through absence. The Bombay cinema has a special position here, because it positions other national/ethnic/socio-religious identities [...] under an overwhelming north Indian, majoritarian Hindu identity. [E]ven films arguing for amity were premised on a certain privileging of modern Hindu constructions of the "other" [Vasudevan 2000].

The supremacy of Hinduism in *KMG* is further assured not only because of the many religious references but because Rohit, who attends a Catholic school, never prays to the school's Christian God. The same holds true for the rest of his teachers and classmates. Likewise, the status of "OM" as the method for successfully communicating with the aliens represents a formal contention that Hindu beliefs are deliberately challenging Western conventions by demonstrating the superiority of all things Hindu and Indian.

Yet another potential aspect of *KMG*'s sympathy to Hindu nationalist currents is the film's treatment of non–Hindus. Intriguingly, other than Inspector Khan (Mukesh Rishi), whose name is traditionally Muslim, there do not appear to be any other Muslims in the film, despite the fact that Muslims represent the second-largest faith group in India. It could be argued, therefore, that the omission of any specifically Islamic presence is itself a sign of Hindu dominance, a Bollywood equivalent of colonial Britain's description of Australia as *Terra Nullius* and a dynamic that is in its own way as destructive as outright vilification. However, the lack of Muslims might also reflect the religious realities of Himachal Pradesh, namely that less than two per cent of the state's population is Islamic.

In contrast, India's third-largest religious group, Christianity, and in particular Roman Catholicism, receives a considerable amount of attention, much of it negative. The Roman Catholic school to which Rohit is sent is presided over by a priest whose office is replete with crucifixes. The prevalence of Catholic symbolism might reflect, at least amongst some quarters of the Hindu nationalist community, talk of a Christian conspiracy, hence the need to reinforce Hinduism wherever possible. With regard to this potential anti–Christian sentiment, Leeper states that the teachers at the Catholic school are portrayed generally as "insensitive and unkind" (2003). As a powerful symbol of Hindu dominance, the huge alien "OM"-like spaceship hovers for a significantly long time over Rohit's school with its large roof crucifix. Such an image recalls the scene of the alien mothership floating over the White House in *Independence Day* just before it is destroyed, and brings to mind the aforementioned BJP/World Hindu Council (VHP)/Shiv Sena-led destruction of the Babri Masjid at Ayodhya and the several attacks on churches, missionary schools and missionaries during the BJP's tenure of office.

Another element of this potentially anti–Christian agenda in *KMG* can be found in the character of the Catholic school's IT teacher, who refuses to allow Rohit to enter his classroom and who mocks him in front of his classmates. However, although the iconography suggests anti–Christian sentiment, with the exception of this one teacher there remains significant ambiguity with regard to the portrayal of Christians: the other Catholic teachers are shown to be genuinely interested in Rohit's welfare. The priest ultimately allows Rohit to be promoted for the sake of the boy's self-confidence and friendships, in spite of the fact that Rohit had failed his previous year; and the Math teacher publicly and generously praises Rohit for correctly answering a question. Therefore, there is a divide between the film's treatment of Christianity as religious ideology and Christians themselves, which serves to temper the anti–Christian sentiment and imply that it is ideological rather than personal. Though this would seem initially to suggest an inclination towards nonviolence, the tendency of extremist movements to privilege ideological conflict over stated nonviolent goals makes this somewhat cold comfort.

Perhaps the ultimate evidence of a link between *KMG* and Hindu nationalism lies in the response it received from the then-BJP Prime Minister Vajpayee, who had a special screening of the film arranged by Rakesh Roshan and who was reported to have "congratulated Hrithik [the male lead] on his performance" (*The Times of India*). Vajpayee was accompanied to this screening by the BJP's hardliner president, L.K. Advani, who was himself a film critic for the RSS's newspaper *The Organiser* (Guruswamy). It is no coincidence that the next year the BJP incorporated songs from *KMG*, as well as from *Lagaan*, into its election campaign. It seems, therefore, that *KMG* has aligned itself both formally and ideologically with extremist Hindu nationalism, combining formal elements from Hollywood SF and from Hindu religious iconography to reinforce a nationalist cultural hegemony.

Although extremist groups like the RSS designate Hinduism as an antidote to modernity, to prevent "the erosion of the nation's integrity in the name of secularism, economic and moral bankruptcy" (Sangh qtd. in Human Rights Watch 1999), the film can also be read as an attempt by these very same elements to highjack technology and science for their own political agendas. Hence the centrality of computers and spaceships support the notion that *KMG* is inflected with a contestatory Hindu extremist agenda. This potential alliance between science and the religious right is a theme developed by Meera Nanda in her book *Prophets Facing Backward* (2003). Borrowing from the political lexicon of European far-right theorists, Nanda uses the term "reactionary modernism" (Nanda 7) to describe a Hindu nationalist vision of a technologically advanced India, replete with nuclear weapons but with a core focus on tradition and a higher spiritual awareness in which the mythical past functions "as a source of direction, inspiration, and resolve" (Nanda 11). Although Uppinder Mehan suggests that one possible reason for the distrust of technology is that science came to India "as a[n imposed colonial] foreign transplant," he also points out that a number of English-language Indian SF stories convey an "acceptance" of machines, albeit on the basis that this technology serves the country's cultural values and does not jeopardize Indianness (Mehan 56–58). It comes as no surprise, therefore, to see that scientists at the Canadian Space Research Centre, both Western and apparently atheistic Indian, are proven wrong by Sanjay's "Vedic science" and its religious form of extraterrestrial communication.

The potential alliance between *KMG* and a Hindu nationalist inspired call for an "alternative modernity" (Nanda 4)—what Nanda also describes as "the confluence of 'dharma and the bomb'" (Nanda 7)—could explain why, in addition to the scientific community, other non–Hindu Indians in the film are also singled out as being in the wrong, such as Inspector Khan and all the security forces who work in collusion with their Western advisors to take Jadoo away for examination in Delhi and the USA. Nor do these same forces flinch at threatening and injuring Rohit and his friends. Such actions would compromise the Hindu principle of *Ahimsa*, the not-harming of sentient creatures. Ironically, however, some Hindu extremist nationalist elements, like many similar far right groups, do not themselves follow such a principle.

Conclusion

Taking into consideration this usage of science by Hindutva supporters (advocates of Hindu nationalism), *KMG* can be read as a postcolonial SF text in the sense that it contests colonialist, orientalist assumptions about the "backwardness" of the colonies. The fact that *KMG* was produced in a former colony of the British Empire, uses an established Western genre for its own purposes, openly celebrates the country's indigenous Hindu identity — at the expense of other imported religions such as Islam and Christianity — and depicts an image of an advanced, middle class and prosperous India that works against orientalist, primitivist stereotypes, adds substance to this particular interpretation. That the film was intended to challenge the hegemony of Hollywood's big blockbuster domination of the SF genre in India, and potentially the world, enhances such a reading. Thus *KMG* can be seen to constitute a demonstration of Bollywood's ascendancy in what Heather Tyrell suggests is a struggle for commercial global domination by the film industries of the world: addressing the relationship between Bollywood and Hollywood, she asks, "is Bollywood named in imitation of Hollywood, or as a challenge to it?" (Tyrell 312). We would argue that even if Bollywood began as an imitation of Hollywood on some level, *KMG* demonstrates that it has begun to challenge the hegemony of Western cinematic production, both economically and ideologically. However, the potential alliance between *KMG* and extreme nationalism remains of concern. As Etienne Balibar notes on the relationship between nationalism and postcolonialism, and as we argue has happened in this case, many "nationalisms of liberation [have] turned into nationalisms of domination" (Baliber 46).

Notes

1. This chapter was first published by D. Alessio and J. Langer as "Nationalism and Postcolonialism in Indian Science Fiction: Bollywood's *Koi... Mil Gaya* (2003)," *New Cinemas: Journal of Contemporary Film* 5.3 (2007): 217–229. We would like to thank *New Cinemas* for kind permission to republish here, as well its editor, Thea Pitman, and another anonymous reviewer, for their helpful suggestions.

2. Possibly the first Indian science fiction film was the early 1950s US-Tamil co-production *Kaadu* (1952; *The Jungle*) about living woolly mammoths and starring Caesar Romero, Rod Cameron and the Indian actress Sulochana. Leeper suggests that Bollywood's *Mr India* (1987), which toyed with the invisibility idea, might also contain some SF elements (Leeper 2003).

3. We recognize that the term "Bollywood" can be quite contested and that there is some reluctance to adopt the term since there are a number of regional commercial film producers in India, each with its own particular features. By "Bollywood" we mean a Hindi film aimed at a commercial mass-market and produced in Mumbai (formerly Bombay), a film-producing region which gained prominence in the domestic film market in the 1950s.

Works Cited

Agnihotri, A. "Will It Be Hrithik's Film?" *The Times of India* (8 August 2003). 9 October 2007 <http://timesofindia.indiatimes.com/articleshow/120153.cms>.

Ahmad, Aijaz. *Lineages of the Present: Ideology and Politics in Contemporary South Asia.* London: Verso, 2000.

Balibar, E. "Racism and Nationalism." *Race, Nation, Class: Ambiguous Identities*. Ed. E. Balibar and I. Wallerstein. London: Verso, 1991. 37–67.
Banker, A. *Bollywood*. Harpenden: Pocket Essentials, 2001.
Batty, Nancy, and Robert Markley. "Writing Back: Speculative Fiction and the Politics of Postcolonialism, 2001." *ARIEL* 33.1 (January 2002): 5–14.
Clute, John, and Peter Nicholls. *The Encyclopedia of Science Fiction*. London: St. Martin's Press, 1999.
Colmer, James. "A Look at the Symbolism behind Jadoo." 9 September 2003. 3 May 2005 <www.bimmini.com>.
Desser, David. "Race, Space and Class: The Politics of the SF Film from *Metropolis* to *Blade Runner*." *Retrofitting Blade Runner: Issues in Ridley Scott's Blade Runner and Philip K. Dick's Do Androids Dream of Electric Sheep*. Ed. Judith B. Kerman. 2nd ed. Bowling Green, Ohio: Bowling Green University Popular Press, 1997. 110–123.
Freedman, Carl. *Critical Theory and Science Fiction*. Middletown, CT: Wesleyan University Press, 2000.
Gangaghar, V. "New Twinkle in Bollywood Stars." *The Tribune* (India) 4 September 1999. 3 May 2005 <www.tribuneindia.com/1999/99Sep 04/edit.htm>.
Guruswamy, Madhu. "Purification Rites with Gangajal." *Rediff.com* (2 September 2003). 17 July 2007 <http://www.rediff.com/news/2003/sep/02guru.htm>.
Human Rights Watch India. "Politics by Other Means: Attacks against Christians in India." *Reports* 11.6 (1999). 14 September 2007 <http://www.hrw.org/reports/1999/indiachr/christians8-01.htm>.
Indian Science Fiction and Fantasy. 15 October 2007 <http://www.indianscifi.com>.
Jain, M. "Bollywood: Next Generation." *Bollywood: Popular Indian Cinema*. Ed. L. M. Joshi. London: Dakini Books, 2001. 298–315.
_____. "Bollywood: 100 Years." *Bollywood: Popular Indian Cinema*. Ed. L. M. Joshi. London: Dakini Books, 2001. 8–55.
Koi... Mil Gaya. Dir. and Prod. Rakesh Roshan. Yash Raj Films, 2003.
Leeper, Marl. "*Koi... Mil Gaya* Movie Review." *Rotten Tomatoes* (11 August 2003). 8 October 2007 <http://www.rottentomatoes.com/click/movie-1130403/reviews.php?critic=columns&sortby=default&page=1&rid=1186061>.
Rao, M. "Heart of the Movie." *Bollywood: Popular Indian Cinema*. Ed. L. M. Joshi. London: Dakini Books, 2001. 136–169.
McLean, Iain, and Alistair McMillan. *The Concise Oxford Dictionary of Politics*. Oxford: Oxford University Press, 2003.
Meera, N. *Prophets Facing Backward: Postmodern Critiques of Science and Hindu Nationalism in India*. Piscataway, NJ: Rutgers University Press, 2003.
Mehan, Uppinder. "The Domestication of Technology in Indian Science Fiction Short Stories." *Foundation* 74 (1998): 54–66.
Mishra, Vijay. *Bollywood Cinema: Temples of Desire*. London: Routledge, 2002.
Rai, Amit. "Patriotism and the Muslim Citizen in Hindi Films." *Harvard Asia Quarterly* 7.3 (2003). 17 October 2007 <http://www.asiaquarterly.com/content/view/136/40/>.
Rajadhyaksha, Ashish, and Paul Willemen. *The Encyclopedia of Indian Cinema*. Revised ed. Oxford: BFI, 2002.
Rajagopal, A. *Politics after Television: Religious Nationalism and the Reshaping of the Indian Public*. Cambridge: Cambridge University Press, 2001.
Roberts, Adam. *Science Fiction: The New Critical Idiom*. London: Routledge, 2000.
Rushdie, Salman. *The Ground Beneath Her Feet*. London: Picador, 2002.
Singh, Amardeep. "Early Bengali Science Fiction." 2006. 1 January 2007 <http://www.lehigh.edu/~amsp/2006/05/early-bengali-science-fiction.html>.
Srinarahari. M. H. "*Koi Mil Gaya*, India's First Science Fiction Film." *The Science Fact*

and Science Fiction Concatenation. 2004. 16 October 2007 <http://www.concatenation.org/articles/koirevised3.html>.
Toffler, A. *Future Shock.* New York: Random House, 1970.
Tyrell, H. "Bollywood versus Hollywood: Battle of the Dream Factories." *The Globalization Reader.* Ed. F. Lechner and J. Boli. 2nd ed. Malden, MA: Blackwell, 2004. 312–318.
Vasudevan, Ravi S. "The Political Culture of Address in a 'Transitional' Cinema: Indian Popular Cinema." 2000. 27 February 2006 <http://www.sarai.net/research/media-city/resouces/film-city-essays/ravi_vasudevan.pdf>.

PART FOUR: UTOPIA/DYSTOPIA

12

The Shapes of Dystopia
Boundaries, Hybridity and the Politics of Power

JESSICA LANGER

I: Utopia, Dystopia and Postcolonialism

In *The Concept of Utopia* (1990), Ruth Levitas suggests that the primary generator of utopian thought is "not hope, but desire" (191; also see Moylan 1992). In the utopian text, however, according to Fredric Jameson (2005), the perfection of some aspect (or all aspects) of life not only characterizes a wish for the fulfillment of the desire expressed in that text but also acts as a negation, a criticism of those aspects of that desire which are not present in the author's society. Adam Roberts (2007) explains Jameson's characterization of utopia as

> *not* a coherent vision of radical otherness; and neither is it a straightforward blueprint for a "better world" which could be magically transferred into this world in which we actually live. Rather it is *always the historically and culturally specific response to particular social dilemmas* [http://www.thevalve.org; italics mine, except for the word "not"].

Dystopia, a corollary of utopia, is also a response of this kind; it is the strategy that differs. Rather than imagining a world in which the criticized aspects of the author's society have disappeared, it instead imagines a world in which those same aspects are overgrown and run amok, displacing them into an alternate universe where life is defined by them.

Baccolini and Moylan suggest that "the dystopian imagination has served as a prophetic vehicle, the canary in the cage" (1); they point to cautionary tales by such writers as Philip K. Dick and Ray Bradbury as examples of what Kingsley Amis has called "new maps of hell" (2). This study will look at three texts in its analysis of dystopia and its postcolonial implications: George Alec Effinger's *When Gravity Fails* (1987, hereafter *Gravity*), Nalo Hopkinson's *Brown Girl In the Ring* (1998, hereafter *Brown Girl*), and China Mieville's *Perdido Street Station* (2000, hereafter *Perdido*). The texts in this study, however, function as more than warnings. They speak not only to what may happen in the future if indulgence in this deadly sin or that one is not curtailed, but also to what might *have* happened, had history gone differently; and they point to the continued prevalence of destructive impulses, such as racism, that the reader may think her or his society has consigned to the past. Although they are not all, and not strictly, *dystopias*—*Perdido*, as we shall see later, is best defined as heterotopia—they are all *dystopic* and all make use of a dystopian impulse, and the concept of dystopia is at times both used and subverted through them.

Colonialism[1] has often been constructed along the lines of a center-periphery model, a physicopolitical incarnation of the Self-Other construction; this model has also been considered in terms of the metropolitan center, the site of cultural and technological progress, contrasted with the "wild" or "primitive" margins. Jameson identifies "the city itself as a fundamental form of the Utopian image" (Jameson, 2005: 4), the city, that is, with the trench around it, physical or ideological. The center-periphery construction is in fact a misrepresentation of the historical dynamics of colonialism; Elleke Boehmer, for instance, suggests that the structure of empire was far more complex than the center-periphery model would allow, and that it is best described as "a network, one might say, of interrelating margins" (6). However, the ideological shadow of the center-periphery structure is long, and it seems largely to be the way in which empire conceived of *itself*. In some colonial literature, then, there has been a sense of *invasion* of the colonized, marginalized Other into metropolitan spaces, and this is often portrayed as traumatic. It follows, then, that the metropolis is a common site for dystopia, utopia's corollary (Jameson, 2005: 4).

Both Jameson and Joan Gordon, drawing on Jameson's work, have argued that a condition for utopia is exclusion—that the utopia, in its perfection, must exclude the imperfect (for a discussion of exclusion in Utopian narrative, see Jameson 1977 and 2005; Gordon 2002). Joan Gordon extends this concept and argues that there is a "sensitive dependency among utopia, genocide and the alien Other" and that "genocide is a utopian project" (2002: 205). And, Gordon suggests, the corollary is also true: establishment of utopia requires erasure of "the contamination of difference" if the Other is to be accepted into utopia; "if any trace of difference remains," Gordon writes, "the alien cannot become familiar enough to cross the trench into utopia" (2002: 210).

Otherwise, it requires the eradication of those who bear that difference. The institution of utopia itself is implicated in a discussion of colonialism; Jameson writes that it is

> very much the prototype of the settler colony [...] my own feeling is that the colonial violence thus inherent in the very form or genre itself is a more serious reproach than anything having to do with the authoritarian discipline and conformity that may hold for the society within Utopia's borders [2005: 205].

The metropolitan spaces in these texts are radically *inclusive* rather than exclusive, and as such could be characterized as dystopias. However, a postcolonial reading suggests two complicating factors. One, these spaces of radical inclusion are just as much a product of colonialism as are exclusionary utopias: they are on the opposite side of the colonial-utopian trench, and as such are the part of the paradigm invisible to those within a utopia. What follows is that beneath the surface dystopianism of the violence and cacophony of these metropolitan spaces lies a positive hybridity and the potential for subversion of colonial norms: the violence and cacophony are caused by the position the colonizer or the powerful has put the inhabitants in, not by the inhabitants themselves. The dystopic elements in these texts are produced by power differentials, not by inherent differences between powerful and powerless. And in these texts, as in reality — or what Darko Suvin (1972) calls "zero-world" (377), colonized peoples have embraced hybridity and created "new transcultural forms" (Ashcroft et al. 118) in an attempt both to synthesize the disparate cultures and traditions and to subvert the rule, both political and cultural, of the colonizer.

II: Radical Inclusion

Gravity is written from the perspective of Marîd Audran, a red-bearded Algerian Muslim in a Balkanized world where nations have become a near-irrelevant buzz in the background; it is set in the Budayeen, a red-light district in an unnamed Middle Eastern city. *Perdido* is set on the alternate world of Bas-Lag in the accreted, slowly rotting metropolis of New Crobuzon, where many disparate races live side by side — sometimes together, and sometimes in ghettoes — and most everything is hybrid and intertwined. *Brown Girl* takes place in a disturbingly plausible Toronto which has, unlike its zero-world analogue, succumbed to American-style "white flight" to the suburbs and has isolated its poor, mostly marginalized downtown core. The traditional utopian structure is reversed, as the "trench" is built to keep "undesirables" in rather than out, but the inclusionary nature of the inner city remains: it is made up of those who will not or cannot move out. It is important to note here that the system of spirits, gods and the afterlife in *Brown Girl* is as structurally rigorous as the technology of *Gravity* and the hybridity of metaphysical power in *Perdido*, and therefore can be analyzed along similar structural matrices. Gerald Jonas (1998) writes in the *New York Times* that Hopkinson

> treats spirit-calling the way other science fiction writers treat nanotechnology or virtual reality: like the spirits themselves, the spirit-callers follow rules as clear to them (if not always to the reader) as the equations of motion or thermodynamics are to scientists or engineers. [26; also see Rutledge 33].

Reading Hopkinson's text as science fiction is appropriate, however, not only because of the logical rigor of her world-building but because such a reading does two important things: it opens the genre of SF to new dialectical possibilities, and more importantly, it acknowledges and foregrounds the disparate worldviews of colonized, formerly colonized and diasporic peoples.

All of these texts present radically inclusionary, dystopic spaces; a major theme, which this study will use as a focus, is the *transgression of boundaries* that such extreme inclusion infers.

There are three sites of boundary transgression upon which this study will concentrate: transgression of the boundaries of the *city*, of the *body*, and of the *mind*. Each of these represents what Fredric Jameson calls a "frame" of reality, which he suggests are "radically discontinuous" in the postmodern city (1988: 351). Like layers of an onion, these boundaries are contained within each other, mind within body within city, and so each transgression is echoed, doubled and perhaps trebled: they create an intricate web of radical inclusion which draws on Jameson's vision of the postmodern metropolis, and which invokes the postcolonial concepts of hybridity and doubled vision.

City

The contemporary city is an ambivalent space, both a site of multicultural richness and a symbol of technological progress and of imperial domination — as is much science fiction in general, especially but not exclusively in the "golden age" of American SF. It is stratified both physically and socially, and has been a space of contestation in both postcolonial and SF discourse, especially so in literature which combines the two. Gary K. Wolfe, drawing on Mumford and Rozniak, writes that the modern city, especially as expressed in post–1950s SF, is

> an unmanageable, cacophonous, barely conceivable environment that has long since shifted from the communal imperative to the survival imperative: cities that were once social organizations to promote the protection of the individual from a

hostile and chaotic environment must now devote more and more of their resources to the protection of the individual from the hostile and chaotic environment that the city itself has become [87].

This inversion of the city's purpose, from protector to aggressor, is similar to the metropolitan myth versus the reality of the immigrant experience: rather than streets paved with gold, immigrants — especially immigrants from colonies or former colonies — often found themselves immovably on the bottom rung in a dangerous place, compounded by the colonizer's pervasive insistence that they did not belong in the seat of imperial power. Gleaming façade notwithstanding, the city was a microcosm of stratification and subalternity. Wolfe cites Fritz Lang's film *Metropolis*, adapted from his wife Thea von Harbou's novel (1926) of the same name, as one of the first instances of SF cultural production to depict this dynamic. It is this, the unseen and unacknowledged flip side of the utopian metropolis, which concerns the three texts I have chosen, as it has concerned so many writers of postcolonial non-science fiction; the structure of marginalized people both working hard, and refusing to do so, for the sake of the privileged ones who have forced them into that position is a strong link between the power matrices of these textual cities and of the colonial metropolis.

It is important to note that, in the following discussion, the cities and suburbs against which the Budayeen and Toronto act as a corollary are not utopias in all that the word implies; however, their drive towards exclusion of the citizens of those places are part of a utopian *impulse*, against which the Budayeen and Toronto are part of a dystopian impulse.

Gravity's Budayeen is "a dangerous place and everyone kn[ows] it" (11). The district is walled on three sides, the only entrance being the eastern gate, which is on the opposite side of the city to the cemetery: this topography is significant in that it is a horizontal analogue to the vertical "above" and "below" construction of the city as stratified body: the deeper one penetrates into the Budayeen, the closer one seems to death, or to a place where power functions in different ways than it does in the outside. The Budayeen can be conceptualized as a zone of resistance to the power structures outside itself in the city "proper," as a place where personal ability, rather than wealth or other traditional signifiers of power, trumps those other signifiers. That this ability is coded in terms of capacity and talent for violence is a theme that recurs in this and other works, and will be addressed later in the chapter.

Despite the walls around the Budayeen, however, it remains characterized more by its inclusiveness than its exclusivity. As I will discuss in the next section, it is peopled by those whose bodies and/or minds do not fit into the roles available in the city outside, such as Chiri the nightclub madam, Laila the mad moddy-shop owner and Yasmin the transsexual call girl. Those it excludes are the "tourists" who fetishize the place because of its subversion of the outside norms of social construction. In a way, the Budayeen *itself* has transgressed against the boundaries of the city by its radical existence as an anomaly within a larger power structure that predicates itself on an elite brought to power by wealth and privilege rather than the Budayeen values of physical strength and capacity for cruelty or manipulation. To read it in a Marxist context, the Budayeen is the site of a powerful proletariat; that this power is coded as violence suggests that as long as the bourgeoisie exist, this will be the only way for the proletariat to have power at all.

Ultimately, the most powerful, and dangerous, people in *Gravity* are those who are able to synthesize these two power structures and work within both. Friedlander Bey, a Godfather-like figure of the Budayeen underworld, lives outside the Budayeen in "a large, white, towered mansion that might almost have qualified as a palace," a home not-so-strangely reminiscent of the sort of Europeanized house a colonial governor may have built himself on his appropriated land (110). There is a double transgression here: in adopting convenient membership within both the Budayeen and the city at large, Bey plays both systems of power against each other, corrupting each and compromising both the subversiveness of the Budayeen and the relative physical safety of the rest of the city. His hybridity is located in power instead of resistance, and as such is not subversive but destructive.

Brown Girl is another story of a district walled off from the rest of the city and left to destroy itself from within—although in Hopkinson's catastrophic downtown Toronto, there is no available exit:

> When Toronto's economic base collapsed, investors, commerce and government withdrew into the suburb cities, leaving the rotten core to decay. Those who stayed were the ones who couldn't or wouldn't leave.... As the police force left, it sparked large-scale chaos in the city core: the Riots. The satellite cities quickly raised roadblocks at their borders to keep Toronto out.... In the twelve years since the Riots, repeated efforts to reclaim and rebuild the core were failing: fear of vandalism and violence was keeping "burb" people out [4].

In fact, the economic structure of this fictional Toronto is, to an extent, the inverse of that of zero-world contemporary Toronto, in which wealth tends to be concentrated in down- and midtown areas and in which suburbs such as Scarborough and Etobicoke, mentioned in the novel as safe, well-off havens from the chaos of downtown, are much less wealthy. One major exception to this is the southern end of Sherbourne, called "The Burn" in *Brown Girl*, which bridges the novel's world and zero-world by remaining the same in both: a site both of multiculturalism and of poverty, which are linked in Canada's white-dominated post-settler society.

The "trench" between the city of Toronto and its suburbs is both economic and physical. In securing this separation, the people of the "burbs" hope to keep away those they consider undesirable; utopia — or attempted utopia — is, after all, defined by its trench. Like a heart valve, the border transgression here goes only one way: those who are not "good" enough for the "burbs" can enter Toronto, but they cannot leave.

Like the Budayeen in *Gravity,* this Toronto's scorched economic system is ruled by a rare person who straddles that border: Rudy, a warlock and drug pusher who acts both as ringleader of the city gangs and as surreptitious provider of needed things — in the case dramatized in *Brown Girl,* a human heart from a living donor for transplant into the chest of the Premier of Ontario — for those who live in the "burbs" and can afford them. Rudy, a Black man with Caribbean ancestry, uses Caribbean magic to make himself indispensable to those who can afford his services, beyond the "trench" of the roadblocks. While he is the villain of the story, and personally reprehensible, it is significant that he is the only one who can pass through the boundary of the dystopian downtown Toronto and effectively function in both worlds. However, like *Gravity*'s Friedlander Bey, his hybridity is located in power and in violence. That such a character as Rudy is the only one in the story who can cross into utopia, that such a border crossing requires such violence, suggests that the utopian impulse of exclusion is not justly sustainable; that is, as Gordon suggests, "genocidal" (205).

There is no moat or trench, physical or theoretical, between *Perdido*'s city of New Crobuzon and the outside world, as evidenced by the many disparate races who have made it their home, fleeing outside conditions like genocide or arriving to make their fortunes; the dystopic structure in this text is more complicated, creating what Joan Gordon suggests is a "heterotopia," a "hybrid that becomes the generator of a new cycle of dialectics" (463). New Crobuzon is unlike the Budayeen or Hopkinson's Toronto in that it is not constructed in relation to a single (relative) utopia from which its citizens are excluded. Rather, the utopian impulse of exclusion is suggested in the fact that many of its main characters are refugees from some exclusionary community within the fabric of the city itself, a dynamic that brings to mind Boehmer's aforementioned concept of a "series of interrelating margins" (6). Some of these communities are situated entirely within the city, like de Grimnebulin's university; some without, like Yagharek's home tribe; and some, like Lin's khepri people, are the descendants of a group who fled to the inclusionary city and then built an exclusionary community, a ghetto, within it. Therefore, the city is both ideologically and spatially complex, containing pockets or bubbles of utopian impulse between whose borders the *dramatis personae* fall. Isaac Dan der Grimnebulin is an intellectual refugee from what he sees as a stifling academic climate in which he cannot pursue his chosen course of research; Lin, a khepri — with the body of a human woman and the head of a scarab beetle — who has been excluded from her ghettoized, insular racial culture; and Yagharek, a garuda bird-man who has been exiled from his airfaring culture by the removal of his wings because he has committed the crime of "choice-theft," a designation whose pragmatic result becomes clear at the end of the book — he has in effect raped a female garuda — but whose greater ideological significance remains a bit of a mystery (60).

The city is stratified, but New Crobuzon is divided spatially both horizontally and vertically. Its different districts vary in terms of economic and social privilege, but it is also divided vertically like the eponymous city in *Metropolis;* not aboveground — "it was not," Mieville writes, "a purer realm that loomed above the city" — but the visible portion of the city is divided by the ground itself from the underground "punishment factories" in which labors a class of bodily altered and mutilated people called the "Remade," keeping the city's utilities on and its people supplied with goods in a parallel to the subterranean workers in Lang's film (78). Even so, however, the borders of these strati are shifting and unstable. The city's borders are layered; its conglomerated character contains cities within cities, all of which are constantly transgressed in a cycle of breakdown — formerly privileged neighborhoods fall prey, as Hopkinson's Toronto does, to the flight of the well-off from within their borders, and even the boundaries of homes are unstable, as evidenced in the "defaced" khepri district in which walls are mutated and reformed by the structural saliva of the women (3). Mieville is a Marxist, and it may be suggested that New Crobuzon, like the Budayeen, is, in a way, an imagined city of the proletariat. Its dystopian character, perhaps, comes from the power the elite wield rather than from the interpersonal tension.[2]

As in the other two texts analyzed in this study, though far more complexly rendered in *Perdido*, those who succeed in bridging the boundary between the internal exclusionary elements and the inclusionary elements between them that make up the mortar of the city are those who are violent and manipulate the power structures to their own ends — or, like the murderers in *Gravity* or the Weaver in *Perdido*, are "insane," or have thought processes that themselves are beyond a normative boundary. In order to gain power, the powerless must use violence, a concept that echoes Fanon's revolutionary essay "Concerning Violence" in his *The Wretched of the Earth* (1983), and which complicates the question of dystopia itself, identifying its negative character in terms of its power matrix as well as its inclusiveness.

Body

Theorists of the metropolis suggest that the body and the city are interrelated; this concept relates to Jameson's suggestion of subjectivity as a succession of "frames," though according to Jameson, in the postmodern city — and, I would argue, in the dystopian city — those frames are disjunctive and "discontinuous." In any city, however, argue Bloomer and Moore in *Body, Memory and Architecture* (1977), "the form of the body [...] dictates the form of the city" (55). In *Gravity*, *Brown Girl* and *Perdido*, the corollary is also true, and the two continue to influence and create each other in a cyclical process: therefore, if the city is one of radical inclusion and transgressed boundaries, the bodies within that city are likely to have similar characteristics. Both the boundaries of the cities and the boundaries of the bodies of their inhabitants are mutable and unstable in these three texts.

In the Budayeen, not only the shape of one's body but also the gender and even the race is changeable. A consequence of this changeability and uncertainty of the body is that it becomes less significant in representing the nature of one's personhood. The lack of *necessary* fixity not only removes gender and race from easy identifiability, but it also frustrates the dichotomy between perception and actuality in terms of these categories, and complicates the question of authenticity when posed in terms of the origin of one's gender or racial identity. This has larger implications, not only in terms of the racial and gender politics of the fictional Budayeen, but also in terms of a postcolonial reading of the text: the "novum," in this case, is that of the removal or ability to reassign two of the many interlocking systems of oppression to which colonized peoples were and are subjected.

This transgression of bodily integrity also represents another layer of the collapsed and contested boundaries that characterize the colonial metropolitan space. One interesting aspect of the ease of corporeal change in the Budayeen is that the characters in *Gravity* tend to gravitate towards the extreme cliché or stereotype of the characteristics of that gender. The change becomes a shallow appropriation of the shell of the desired race or gender, without its context, and is often either unconvincing or strange-looking. Nikki, who, like many characters, is a male-to-female transgendered woman, has an ultra–Nordic doll-like face, which is described as ill-fitting a strong, muscled frame. "It was a common enough error," Marîd Audran confides; "people chose surgical modifications that they admired in others, not realizing that the changes might look out of place in the context of their own bodies" (33). The concept implicit in this statement, that the initial reaction to hybridity is one of repulsion by its strangeness, reverberates across each of the layers discussed in this study. Another character, Tamiko, a cartoonishly tough prostitute, is alternately described as "the avenging specter of a murdered Kabuki character" (32) and an "assassin-geisha"; perhaps it is meant to shock the reader when Marîd asserts that "Tamiko looked very convincing, with the epicanthic folds and all, for someone who hadn't been born an Oriental" (35). Racial and gender identity is, in this case, both doubled and negated, placed into a contradictory body-space within a contradictory city-space, and made hybrid and radically inclusive.

The transgression of the body in *Brown Girl* is significantly more sinister and grotesque than in *Gravity*, and usually less consensual. This is perhaps due to the overtly, radically capitalistic nature of the relationship between Toronto and its "burbs"; the body in this text is not subject to voluntary modification but rather to conversion to capital, to becoming the site of punishment and torture, and to takeover by supernatural powers.

The driving force of the plot is a heart. Premier Uttley of Ontario needs one and doesn't particularly care who she has to kill to get it; in fact, she eschews the available option of a specially engineered pig heart in favor of a human one, however obtained, in order to boost her political ratings. The aforementioned Rudy is dispatched by the Premier to find a healthy heart, which, due to the demolition of the living-donor program many years before, must almost certainly be obtained through murder. There is sad irony in Uttley's agent Baines' regurgitation of the party line that "human organ transplant should be about people helping people, not preying on helpless creatures [pigs]" (3), whilst at the same time preying on human beings whose social, political and economic position makes them even *more* vulnerable than are the animals generally used as transplant donors. Of course, it is the citizens of Toronto whose hearts are up for grabs; when Rudy suggests killing a street child for his or her heart, Baines refuses, not because of the immorality of the suggestion but because "most of them have had buff[drug]-addicted mothers," and the quality of their hearts would therefore be too low (7). The moral, as well as pragmatic, angle of bodily transgression is related to Toronto's conceptualization as radically inclusive space and its people as citizens of such: both the city borders and the bodies of its populace are not only transgressed but seen as eminently *transgressible* by those in power. One might argue that Uttley, in accepting a heart from a citizen of Toronto, is also the subject of physical transgression, but the qualitative difference is in the direction and level of consent: the "donor" will have his or her body forcibly violated, while Uttley has the power to choose which heart she desires and to exclude those which do not meet her standards — much like utopia's attitude towards its citizens and towards those who wish to become citizens.

Rudy also uses manipulation and torture of his underlings' and prisoners' bodies to punish them for slights against his enforced order. He compels his zombie servant Melba, whom he controls both body and mind, to work herself beyond her body's ability to cope. When he tires of her, he flays her alive to make an example of her to Tony, whom he threatens with the same fate if he does not commit murder and bring a heart for Uttley. Melba has already been robbed of agency and made into a flesh puppet; in stripping her of her skin, Rudy strips her of her humanity, turning her into a "living anatomy lesson" (136). A less egregious example of bodily transgression is that of the spirit takeover of the bodies of Ti-Jeanne and her son, Baby, during Mami Gros-Jeanne's ceremony (94–96). The Caribbean gods enter the participants' bodies in order to provide power to those who seek their help, but the temporary creation of the hybrid human/god body is a function of their living in dystopia. The significance that Caribbean gods, embodied in Canadians of Caribbean descent, are the driving force behind Toronto's salvation is twofold. First, it opens up a space for non-dominant spiritualism within science fiction narrative, both in terms of the SF genre in general and within Canadian science fiction specifically. Second, it puts forward the possibility that a paradigm, or a religion, other than Canada's dominant one is not only good but is actually *essential*. The cosmopolitanism of the city is in this case quite literally a blessing.

The construction of bodily transgression and inclusion in *Perdido*, more than in either of the two preceding novels, is significantly influenced by hybridity, a concept key both to the utopia/dystopia construction and to postcolonial theory. Gordon, in her article on *Perdido*, draws on Brian Stross's definition of the term, quoted here in part:

> The cultural hybrid [...] can be a person who represents the blending of traits from diverse cultures and traditions, or even more broadly it can be a culture, or element of culture, derived from unlike sources; that is, something heterogeneous in origin or composition [1].

In *Perdido*, Gordon argues, hybridity is integral to the novel, and is implemented fractally across every level of the text and its inhabitants: from the mind, to the body, to the city, to the text itself (2003: 461). In terms of the body and inclusion, however, one character is the most synecdochal of *Perdido*'s hybridity. Mr. Motley, like Friedlander Bey and Rudy, is a crime boss, but unlike them he does not bridge a gap between a separate utopia and dystopia; he, like New Crobuzon, is hybridity embodied. He is, as his name suggests, as pure a physical hybrid as is possible, a strange conglomerate of spare parts of various beings: skin, fur, feathers, paws, claws, hooves, "tides of flesh wash[ing] against each other in violent currents" (52–53). A radical version of the Remade, whose bodies are reshaped for punishment, profit or personal preference, Motley's parts are identifiable as to their original species, but the whole is not. As in *Gravity*, because his original form is unknown, questions of identity and authenticity are frustrated as the body is no longer a site where they are clearly delineated. When Lin asks, with trepidation, "*What ... what* were *you?*," Motley, annoyed and angry, replies,

> "I wondered when you'd ask that, Lin. I did hope that you wouldn't, but I knew it was unlikely. *It makes me wonder if we understand each other at all* [...] You still see *this—*" he gesticulated vaguely at his own body with a monkey's paw—"as pathology. You're still interested in what *was* and how it went *wrong*. *This is not error or absence or mutancy: this is image and essence* [...]" [140].

In his very ambiguity, the grotesqueness that he demands the sculptor Lin acknowledge as beauty, lies a counter to the strict inside/outside dichotomy of the colonial-utopia. He is in himself a "new transcultural form," and his very existence reveals an ambivalent, ambiguous subversiveness that can be linked to Homi Bhabha's conception of the ambivalence of colonial response. His body is a symbol of his mimicry of, and mockery of, systems of "legitimate" power in New Crobuzon, which in fact are at least as corrupt than his own criminal enterprise. Bhabha, writing on the form of resistance which he calls "colonial appropriation" in which those subjected to colonial rule mimic aspects of the colonizer in order to subvert them, suggests that its success "depends on a proliferation of inappropriate objects that ensure its strategic failure, so that mimicry is at once resemblance and menace" (86). The contrast between Motley's power in New Crobuzon, itself straddling the border between legitimate and covert, and his "inappropriate" body—which he himself finds *entirely* appropriate—suggests this postcolonial double-vision.

MIND

The mind is the third site of boundary transgression in this study's argument; in the mind's embodiedness, and at times lack thereof, the body and the mind are inextricably related, if—or rather, especially—not always physically linked. Indeed, the tension between embodiedness and *dis*embodiedness of minds, and the idea that minds can become disembodied when their bodily boundaries are crossed, figure prominently in each of these three texts. Another point of tension is the boundaries of the mind itself: whether it may be forcibly entered, stolen, or otherwise molested. This includes ideas as well as technological and supernatural means; whilst a literally open(ed) mind is vulnerable to abuse, it also represents the more conventional definition of an open mind: one which has not drawn a trench around itself, but has allowed itself to consider the possibility of including ideas, concepts and tolerances beyond its current or comfortable bounds. In this way, we can begin to conceive a positive effect of what Moylan, drawing on Lyman Tower Sargent, calls the dystopian "bad place" (125).

Marîd Audran of *Gravity* prides himself on being the only one in his immediate circle not to have had his brain wired for "moddies" and "daddies." A moddy, in the parlance of the Budayeen, is a personality module: by connecting it directly to surgically created neural pathways through a jack at the base of the brain, a person can choose to have his or her subjectivity overtaken almost entirely by that of another person, either real — in the case of Honey Pilar, the world's most famous supermodel — or fictional, as in the case of one of the assassins in the book, who uses a moddy to make himself into James Bond. A daddy, on the other hand, as Marîd explains, "gives you temporary knowledge. Say you chip in a Swedish-language daddy; then you understand Swedish until you pop it out" (12). The use of these two devices nearly defines life in the Budayeen, and nearly everyone has had his or her brain wired; the prevalence of the surgery suggests an environment in which subjectivity itself is alterable and mutable. Marîd is no stranger to altered consciousness, himself: his smug self-description of having a brain unchanged by surgery is undermined by his utter dependence on drugs. However, his ability to change his mental state takes on a deeper character after he has the surgery at Friedlander Bey's behest. Upon plugging in a moddy of Nero Wolfe, the hero of a series of detective books and twice the weight of the slim Marîd, "the first frightening sensation [is] of being suddenly engulfed by a grotesque glob of flesh" (197). The idea that not only is subjectivity alterable, but that subjectivites — whole personalities — are *interchangeable*, represents how far the mind's boundaries have collapsed in the Budayeen. Marîd has become a hybrid, neither himself nor the fictional Nero Wolfe, but both — and neither — at the same time.

Moddies must be handled with care, or else one can transgress the borders of the mind so much that both the body and the mind are destroyed. Such a fate befalls Laila, the owner of the moddy-and-daddy shop to which Marîd brings a bootleg moddy whose contents he wants to find out. This moddy is, in itself, a dangerous hybrid. Instead of the single personality imprint of a normal moddy, it contains an electronic palimpsest: the mind of a newborn baby, that of an abused jungle cat, and the dying, terrified moments of Nikki herself. In one sense, this particular moddy, more than the institution of moddies in general, represents transgression of the mind. Moddies' use might normally be described as utopian: to become an idealized version of a real or fictional person, while turning away from the imperfect reality of the Buyadeen. These moddies may act as a way of literalizing utopian idealism, as much as is possible. The bootleg moddy, on the other hand, violates the boundaries established by normal moddies, and is dangerous in doing so: its hybridity of personality is destructive to the human mind. It destroys Laila's subjectivity, and threatens to do the same to Marîd when he, in the book's climactic battle, uses it as a tool of battle, allowing it to "ma[k]e an animal of" him (281). Marîd, whose mind, like his body and like the city, is structured according to particular boundaries, is not compatible with this hybrid; it is this moddy, rather than moddies in general, that makes *Gravity* dystopic in terms of the mind.

Perdido contains a different threat to the mind: the mutability of consciousness and subjectivity takes many forms in the text, of which the two most significant are the bringing to consciousness of inorganic materials and the invasion of New Crobuzon by "slake-moths" which, quite literally, eat minds and excrete nightmares.

In New Crobuzon, a quasi–Victorian steampunk city, robots do computations and menial jobs like janitorial work; they seem to run on a combination of mechanical and magical power. Der Grimnebulin has one of these "constructs" to do the cleaning at his laboratory, and when it breaks down, the repairman inserts a virus into the construct's brain, to turn it into a conscious entity. "No longer a destructive end," the virus becomes "a means, a generator, a motive power" (295). And the end result is that "one moment, [the robot is] a calculating machine. The next, it th[inks]" (296). This seemingly spontaneous generation of a conscious subjectivity in an inorganic object represents a hybrid creation, a mind *without* a conventional body. The idea that a mind can arise outside of its conventional boundaries throws open the door to radical inclusion not only of different states of mental embodiedness, but also to different concepts of what the mind itself *is*.

The slake-moths do the same thing in their feeding on the minds of the New Crobuzon populace. They are physical entities with mass, size, and visual presence, but beyond the larval stage they eat only conscious minds; this suggests that in Mieville's world, either the mind itself has mass and size, or the discontinuity between the moths' method of nourishment and their physical existence points to some deeper, far more fundamental hybridity in the fabric of diegetic existence. This is also suggested by the moths' consumption of *part* of Lin's mind, but not the whole thing; in the final battle, Yagharek and Isaac have "ripped her from the moth half drunk. Half her mind, half her dreams had been sucked into the gullet of the vampir beast." (828). The beasts *disembody* minds. What they do is similar to what Nikki's killer does in *Gravity* when he records her awareness onto a moddy: they transgress the boundaries of the mind, take what they want and leave the rest — the body.

Brown Girl casts the mind in terms of the spirit, or *duppy*, which survives after death to go to Guinea Land, a Caribbean conception of afterlife. Duppies can be trapped, however, and trapping them in a calabash bowl is how Rudy obtains and keeps his power (121). He flouts the the natural progression of the mind from embodiedness to disembodiedness and includes them in a micro-dystopia in the bowl: a necropolis of stolen spirits. Throughout the text Rudy collects duppies, and leaves his spirit slaves' consciousnesses to "cower" and "gibber" in the "nightmare existence" of the calabash bowl while he uses their agency to murder those who oppose him (206). This divorcing of consciousness and capacity for action is imposed upon bodies as well, in the case of Melba—and, on a macro level, it is also imposed on the city of Toronto, for whose degradation and exclusion from the suburbs Rudy is in large part responsible by intimidating the populace and sowing disorder and mistrust. These stacked boundary transgressions, however, have as their seed that of the mind. Rudy's gang members do not fear overmuch the destruction of their city, nor do they primarily fear the deaths of their bodies. They fear they will lose their minds.

III: Conclusions

These texts may help to bring about a revisioning of the concept of dystopia itself. What makes these cities dystopic is not inclusion, difference and hybridity in and of themselves, but rather the way in which those things are born out of *exclusion* and are marginalized, as they are in a colonial context. This aspect of dystopia is then brought out of its place directly across from utopia and thrown into the same "doubled, tangled, reciprocal vision" that characterizes postcolonial literature (Reid 125). These cities are therefore not strictly dystopias, but are rather something related but different, outside the purview of the utopia/dystopia dichotomous construction. The term "anti-utopia" has been used to signify putatively utopian texts that regardless do not fall into the binary utopia/dystopia construction: John Huntington (1982) suggests the term as "a type of skeptical imagining that is opposed to the consistencies of utopia-dystopia. If the utopian-dystopian form tends to construct single, fool-proof structures which solve social dilemmas, the anti-utopian form discovers problems, raises questions, and doubts" (142; see Moylan 129). In this vein, I suggest the term *anti-dystopia* as a generic tendency in these novels: not a mirror image of dystopia, nor a direct contradiction, but rather a generic tendency that uses the tool of dystopia recursively, to complicate and question both the form itself, with its Manichean character, and the zero-world to which the form and its use refer. This is similar to Sargent's "critical dystopia," which Moylan defines as

> a textual mutation that self-reflexively takes on the present system and offers not only astute critiques of the order of things but also explorations of the oppositional spaces and possibilities from which the next round of political activism can derive imaginative sustenance and inspiration [xv].

Here we might also return to Joan Gordon's aforementioned work on *Perdido*, in which she suggests that New Crobuzon is a "heterotopia" as described by Foucault, and writes of the term:

> If it is the other of two places, perhaps one place is in opposition to the other place, forming a dialectic, a feedback mechanism between one and the other that generates the next place, a hybrid that becomes the generator of a new cycle of dialectics [463].

In each of these definitions there is a suggestion of the next phase, the next cycle: what comes *after* the utopia/dystopia dichotomy, whose strict construction is in many ways reminiscent of the construction of colonial power: the center, the utopian included, and the periphery, the utopian excluded/dystopian included. Anti-utopian and anti-dystopian writing do echo the next cycle: the postcolonialism to utopia/dystopia's colonialism. Perhaps the anti-dystopia, being as it is both within and outside the utopia/dystopia construct, a space of internal contradiction, attempts to bring those figures to the fore.

In this way, we may read the radical hybridity evident in these works as a *positive* rather than a negative characteristic, and the strife and conflict that this inclusion causes as a residue, and therefore criticism, of the zero-world historical (and present) Western colonial and imperial projects, as well as those projects' science-fictional permutations. Such a reading opens up a future space for positive voices of radical inclusion.

Notes

1. I use the term "colonialism" to mean the type engaged in by, for instance, Britain and France during their imperial periods. Though many scholars have identified this as "Western colonialism," the engagement in this type of colonialism by Japan makes it untenable to use this term, and I have therefore simply called it "colonialism" throughout this study.

2. I am grateful to Adam Roberts for his assistance in developing this insight.

Works Cited

Ashcroft, Bill, Gareth Griffiths, and Helen Tiffin. *Post-Colonial Studies: The Key Concepts.* London: Routledge, 2003.

Bhabha, Homi K. *The Location of Culture*. New York: Routledge, 1994.
Bloomer, Kent C., and Charles W. Moore. *Body, Memory and Architecture*. London: Yale University Press, 1977.
Boehmer, Elleke. *Empire, the National, and the Postcolonial, 1890–1920: Resistance in Interaction*. Oxford: Oxford University Press, 2002.
Effinger, George Alec. *When Gravity Fails*. New York: Orb, 1987.
Fanon, Frantz. *The Wretched of the Earth*. Trans. Constance Farrington. London: Pelican, 1983.
Foucault, Michel. *The History of Sexuality, Vol. I: An Introduction*. Trans. Robert Hurley. New York: Pantheon Books, 1978.
Gordon, Joan. "Hybridity, Heterotopia, and Mateship in China Mieville's *Perdido Street Station*." *Science Fiction Studies* 91 (November 2003): 456–76.
_____. "Utopia, Genocide and the Other." *Edging into the Future: Science Fiction and Contemporary Cultural Transformation*. Ed. Veronica Hollinger and Joan Gordon. Philadelphia: University of Pennsylvania Press, 2002. 204–16.
Hopkison, Nalo. *Brown Girl in the Ring*. New York: Warner, 1998.
Huntington, John. *The Logic of Fantasy: H.G. Wells and Science Fiction*. New York: Columbia University Press, 1982.
Jameson, Fredric. *Archaeologies of the Future: The Desire Called Utopia and Other Science Fictions*. London: Verso, 2005.
_____. "Cognitive Mapping." *Marxism and the Interpretation of Culture*. Ed. Cary Nelson and Lawrence Grossberg. Urbana: University of Illinois Press, 1988. 347–360.
_____. "Of Islands and Trenches: Neutralization and the Production of Utopian Discourse." Rev. of *Utopiques*, by Louis Marin. *Diacritics* 7.2 (Summer 1977): 2–21.
Jonas, Gerald. Rev. of *Brown Girl in the Ring*, by Nalo Hopkinson. *The New York Times* 12 July 1998: 26. 26 March 2007 <http://www.nytimes.com/books/98/07/12/reviews/980712.12scifit.html>.
Levitas, Ruth. *The Concept of Utopia*. Syracuse: Syracuse University Press, 1990.
Mieville, China. *Perdido Street Station*. London: Macmillan, 2000.
Moylan, Tom. *Scraps of the Untainted Sky*. Boulder, CO: Westview, 2000.
Reid, Michelle. Rev. of *So Long Been Dreaming: Postcolonial Science Fiction and Fantasy*, ed. Nalo Hopkinson and Uppinder Mehan. *Foundation* 94 (Summer 2005): 125–126.
Roberts, Adam. "Jameson's Archaeologies of the Future." Rev. of *Archaeologies of the Future*, by Fredric Jameson. *The Valve* (3 June 2007). 3 August 2007 <http://www.thevalve.org/go/valve/article/jamesons_archaeologies_of_the_future/>.
Rutledge, Gregory. "Nalo Hopkinson's Urban Jungle and the Cosmology of Freedom: How Capitalism Underdeveloped the Black Americas and Left *A Brown Girl in the Ring*." *Foundation* 81 (Spring 2001): 22–36.
Suvin, Darko. "On the Poetics of the Science Fiction Genre." *College English* 34 (1972): 372–382.
Wolfe, Gary K. *The Known and the Unknown: The Iconography of Science Fiction*. Kent, OH: Kent State University Press, 1979.

13

Narrative and Dystopian Forms of Life in Mexican Cyberpunk Novel *La Primera Calle de la Soledad*

JUAN IGNACIO MUÑOZ ZAPATA

First world cyberpunk writers, as Bruce Sterling explains, "are perhaps the first generation to grow up not only within the literary tradition of science fiction but in a truly science-fictional world" (ix). In his novel *La Primera Calle de la Soledad* (1993; *The First Street of Solitude,* hereafter *PCS*) Mexican author Gerardo Horacio Porcayo likewise creates a cultural production of a world where, "the techniques of classical 'hard SF'—extrapolation, technological literacy—are not just literacy tools but an aid to daily life" (Sterling ix). However, assimilating all the vocabulary of cybernetic and contemporary reality, *PCS* presents a significant connection between Hard SF and this, "science-fictional world." Not only does this cultural production take place in a developing country and not in a world power nation, but this country also undergoes a new, cultural and economic colonization, which changes the reader's perspective on conventional, cyberpunk narrative devices.

One of these devices is the dystopian setting of a megalopolis where high technology (high-tech) goes hand-in-hand with marginal forms of modern life (low-life). But some science fiction and utopia scholars (Fitting, Suvin, Csicsery-Ronay Jr., and Foster) have argued that this first generation of cyberpunk writers, despite their negative and dystopian depiction of high capitalism's social conditions and 1980s conservative politics, did not go deeper into their "contestatory opinion," preferring rather to renegotiate their own position as, "white, heterosexual, upward mobile males" (Moylan 197). Negative energy produced by contributors to the cyberpunk genre, according to Tom

Moylan, leads nevertheless to a moment of "critical dystopia," a category, or a stage, in which he includes some science fiction works written in the mid-80s and 90s. Moylan defines "critical dystopia" as:

> A textual mutation that self-reflexively takes on the present system and offers not only astute critiques of the order of things but also explorations into the oppositional spaces and possibilities from which the next round of political activism can derive imaginative sustenance and inspiration [xv].

"Critical dystopia" is concerned with textual strategies and it proposes a continuum between the two antinomies of Utopia and Anti-utopia, two classic literary and political themes that determine the level of commitment to change things or the conformity with status quo among members of a given society. Antinomy of Utopia (capitalized) contains literary forms such as "utopia / eutopia" (radical hope) and dystopia (described as militant, epic and openly pessimistic). By contrast, Anti-utopia includes concepts of "anti-utopia" (cynical and despaired), and pseudo-dystopia (a resigned, mythical and closed pessimism) (Moylan 157).

Thus, *PCS* is a "critical dystopia" that relates to the Utopia genre due to anti-utopian common elements such as the traditional science fiction political agenda as well as globalization and postmodernism. Therefore, the purpose of this work is to analyze the effects that the novel's self-reflexivity has on its narrative elements and on the anti-utopian globalization system. In so doing, the novel articulates metaphors of life and existence according to its own textuality through terms such as "autopoiesis" (from cybernetics and biology) and "anamorphoisis" (from visual art and psychoanalysis). In addition, considering Slavoj Žižek's contributions to cultural theory in the development of subjectivity since those of French psychoanalyst Jacques Lacan, this work will explore *PSC*'s theme of resistance to globalization and new cultural colonization.

Narration and the Asphodel

Oscar Martínez, also known as El Zorro, is a techno-delinquent recruited by the Trip Corporation of Monterrey in order to break the ices of the Mariano Laboratories, the biggest rival in the "electric dreams" industry. While El Zorro is trying to get information from Mariano Laboratories in cyberspace, he is attacked by the program. At the same time, a group of armed men bursts into the room where he is connected. Mariano and his crew compel El Zorro, who is being imprisoned and transported to the Moon, to break the ices from a religious sect named "The children of Armageddon," one of the more dangerous enemies of the "christo-receptionist," religion held by Mariano Laboratories. The Moon is a set of colonial penitentiaries where a jihad is breaking out. El Zorro discovers what is really behind his struggles. "The Asphodel" is a program designed by Mariano Laboratories that has gained its own autonomy by executing its basic goal: granting the wishes of the "electric dreams" users. At the end of the novel, El Zorro meets the Christ-like image of Asphodel in a moment of imminent death and destruction: the spatial shuttle in which they are standing is neither able to land on Earth nor to return to the Moon. The Asphodel says to El Zorro that it can satisfy all his desires in an electric dream. After some hesitation, El Zorro lets himself go.

El Zorro's wish is a significant element in the narrative structure of novel. After the Asphodel simulates what would have been El Zorro's the most important wish, which takes place in the "Gull's Dream Bar" in company of his beloved woman, Clara, El Zorro exchanges it for another one :

> He went through the same way six years ago, when he was trying to forget an exasperating world and the boring, depressing, corrosive and unreal burden imposed upon him by existence. [...] Life is a cycle; an eternal and deceptive Möbius strip that simulates movement and explorations toward other dimensions. [...] It was the first road and it will be the last one that he must travel in company of this harsh and importunate mistress named Solitude [Porcayo 247; my translation].

While one can read in the first paragraphs of the novel:

> He left behind any sense of security, any bond that tied him to the slow, routine, daily grind. The city now seems to extend like a greyish and aesthetically aggressive veil, which is an essential characteristic of a modern city. The setting is simple and timeless. Everything is cyclical. There can be few puerile variations. The voyage, a stroll through a Möbius strip [9].

Thus, narrative can be considered a kind of "ouroboros," a mythological snake eating its own tail, or a loop structure, which exemplifies one of the characteristics that Moylan attributes to "critical dystopia": self-reflexivity. But like "ouroboros," *PCS* narrative structure has a similarity to pseudo-dystopia, namely the fall of the myth as well as resigned pessimism, putting the novel's stakes in Anti-utopia field. However, here the self-reflexivity is not only textual, but it is also — tautologically — reflexive upon itself, thereby shifting the novel's particular association with the Utopia genre.

In "Metaphors of Cyberpunk: Ontology, Epistemology and Science Fiction," Ruth Curl notices that in *Neuromancer*, "Wintermute" is a metaphor referring to a circular and mythical structure (237). This circular and mythical structure is evident during the Case's last trip into the matrix, when he sees "three figures, tiny, impossible" (Gibson 270), of which one of them is himself. Similarly, cyberspace acquires the same mythical or divine status of Paradise or Eden because the "Fall" from cyberspace leads to an imprisonment of "flesh" (6). According to Curl, Gibson's cyberspace is an ontological metaphor — which is a link between things and their qualities, for instance, the computer as a rebellious creature (*Frankenstein*) and creator (God) — and it belongs to a non-scientific field. An epistemological metaphor, by contrast, functions in quantitative terms in order to describe processes and phenomena in a scientific realm: "the molecular theory of gases emerged as an ingenious metaphor: a gas was likened to a vast swarm of absurdly small bodies" (W. V Quine qtd. in Curl 231).

As a counterexample to *Neuromancer*, Curl proves that in the novel *Great Sky River* by Gregory Benford, there is an interface of epistemological and ontological metaphors because the text shows a process of forgetfulness that, "severs the link with the past, and forces the reader's perspective toward an unknown future" (Curl 243). This interface includes, on the one hand, an ontological metaphor commonly employed in cyberpunk texts — similar to the traditional use of metaphor in all literature — and on the other hand, an epistemological metaphor that is created by a new image of computer processing. The computer in *Great Sky River* is a "vehicle" for metaphor and not a tenor like Gibson's computer, because it merges organically with man, creating a new understanding of memory functions. Furthermore, this interface, acting from epistemological metaphor, gives a new meaning to the concept of the "Fall": an entropy process through the centuries causing progressive loss of memory and accumulated technological knowledge in humanity.

In *PCS*, there is a mythical reference in the name of "Asphodel." It refers to the "forgetfulness flower" that covered the first region of Greek Hades, the "Fields of Asphodel," and that was eaten by the dead. During the encounter between El Zorro and the Asphodel, the latter acknowledges that he has lost control of the shuttle, which adds a Frankenstein failure dimension to the computer metaphor. Then, El Zorro undoes the ontological metaphor of the God-computer: "You don't understand what you do? [...] You don't comprehend the totality of things. For you, the world is a translatable number in virtual, abstract space; you have no understanding of the tangible universe [...] you aren't a God" (Porcayo 244). And the Asphodel corroborates the ontological metaphor deconstruction when it mentions its own name: "My name has to do with forgetfulness [...]. I like it. All men try to remember and live for a while, and then they don't want to know anymore. I always gave all they asked of me. That's what a God does, right?" (244).

In *PCS*, Self-reflexivity seeks to redefine the ontological, metaphorical mythical loop and merges it with the epistemological metaphor. This epistemological metaphor is found in the Asphodel's inadequacy to comprehend "the totality of things." In Porcayo's novel, cyberspace does not seem like a "Paradise," or in more secular terms a utopia, as it is presented in Gibson's *Neuromancer* and other cyberpunk texts or films. The Asphodel can not merge with other A.I., like Wintermute expects to do with a similar program found in the "Centauri system" in order to talk to its "own kind" as a "God" and a "whole thing" (Gibson 270). A fundamental principle in utopia is the production of an infinite space. *Neuromancer* exemplifies this principle when Wintermute creates replicas of Case and his friends, and also when it expresses its desire for fusion with other A.I. in the universe. Unlike Wintermute, The Asphodel reproduces infinity in terms of time when it restarts the novel narrative over and over again, following a loop structure; a theme that resembles an uchronia (no time) rather than a utopia. At the same time, if a utopia like Wintermute's seeks to define the totality of the spatial system, the Asphodel by contrast fails in its total translation of the analogical world.

Internal Focalization and El Zorro's Subjective Gaze

The Novel's self-reflexivity is so extreme that it becomes a metaphor of metaphor; Curl calls it a super or meta-metaphor (242). This meta-metaphor pertains to Aristotle's classic definition of metaphor: "the device [...] of giving life to lifeless things." As well, John Middleton Murry observes that this meta-metaphor is a matter of "creative literature" (Curl 242). In *PCS*, the meta-metaphor constitutes "life" in a process of "autopoiesis" as well as in an allegory of a set of figures of "life" whereby the novel draws on the continuum between its anti-utopian form and its utopian expectation.

Autopoiesis, or self-making, is a system theory that Chilean researchers Humberto Maturana and Francisco Valera developed during the 60's to explain how the organization of a living system structures itself through a series of internal interactions. Prior to developing this theory, Maturana and Valera had presented a study about the perception of fast movements recorded by microelectrodes implanted in a frog's visual cortex. This experiment showed that, "the frog's brain became a part of hermetic circuit or a bioapparatus reconfigured to produce scientific knowledge" (Hayles 134). However, despite implications of this experiment, it was not formally so radical, as Hayles puts it (135). Indeed, with the same objective, rhetorical scientific discourse gives interpretation of a human observer's priority over the cognitive process of the frog. Hence, Maturana and Valera took an interest in the observers' interactions of a living system, which evoked their observation: "The observer is a living system and any understanding of cognition as a biological phenomenon must account for the observer and his role in it" (qtd. in Hayles 143).

I want to emphasize the role of autopoiesis in *PCS* as a determinant moment for the understanding of stakes through the narrative mode of internal focalization. Internal focalization gains access to a restraint gaze from the interior of a character and is aware of only what he/she is aware of (Tasende: 494). In the novel, this restraint gaze is assumed by a heterodiegetic omniscient narrator who expresses in third person what El Zorro sees and feels. Porcayo keeps this narrative choice throughout the rest of novel. El Zorro becomes the observer of an autopoietic macrosystem (narration generated by the Asphodel) and he is mediated as a living system by a narrative entity (in the same way the implanted microelectrodes work in the frog's brain) in order to be finally observed by the reader. But with this action, Porcayo is outwitting the emblematic figure of the cyborg in the cyberpunk corpus, because rather than celebrating the power of prostheses, he expresses a desire for organic life.

Dani Cavallaro writes that technological images and mythological themes mingle in "techno-bodies" and "mytho-bodies" which are used in military and medical sciences, as well in philosophy and fiction (44). The cyborg is a figure that, "poses a serious challenge to the human-centered foundations of anthropological discourse," (Downey et al. qtd. in Cavallaro 44) and that:

> embodies two opposite fantasies: that of the pure body and that of impure body. On one level, the cyborg presents a sealed, clean, hard, tight and uncontaminated body [...]. The mechanical parts that replace ordinary anatomical parts are supposed to enhance the body's power potential and repudiate its association with *leaky* materiality [47].

The first mention of El Zorro's mechanic anatomy takes place in the outset of the novel when he is in the "Gull's Dream Bar": "If there were neither a new scar crossing from above the left eyebrow to the cheekbone in the same side nor the redness in his ocular prosthesis, probably the barman would have recognized him" (Porcayo 13). The narrator indicates that this prosthesis is not useful in the physical world, when El Zorro is spotted in the street by the police. Even if prostheses were to become the latest thing in fashion, several sectors in society harbour a "puerile distrust" of it (21). The narrative deliberately projects the anxiety that is provoked by cyborg figures in contemporary culture; "puerile distrust" is understood as the incapacity to take a stand about the oscillation between "cyborphilia" and the anthropological repercussions that threaten to dehumanize our natural existence as we know it.

But the ocular prosthesis of El Zorro serves to intensify the "leaky materiality" of the body with its ups and downs through actions in the novel. During the inroad into the system of Mariano Laboratories, the observer-reader can see, through the ocular prosthesis, "the neon green labyrinth" and, through a naked eye, the hologram of Naranjo, one of the "Mateist" priests who creates a diversion in the Luca Mariano office (30–31). The narrator mentions that El Zorro is accustomed to, "two slight dissimilar visions given at the same time by his prosthesis and his natural eye" (31). Thanks to a hologram, seen only through the vision that El Zorro projects to the reader, a depth parallel is established with what Naranjo is seeing elsewhere. Thus, El Zorro sees, "just a part of Naranjo's feelings codifying in several colorations taken by his vision." Just when Mariano's men enter into the room and when the virus attacks, El Zorro's security system releases a discharge that closes the connection and sends an excess of electricity to the ocular prosthesis, putting it out of order. El Zorro is saved by this breakdown of the prosthesis and by the fact that, "scared, he clung to the deck, and while unconscious, he carried it away to the floor, unplugged it and short-circuited the equipment" (34).

After that, Mariano Laboratories fixes El Zorro's prosthesis on the condition that he enters into the Children of Armageddon system: a consequently new attack and loss of prosthesis (92); during his running in the streets of lunar Tranquility City, El Zorro has his prosthesis repaired by a spy from Trip Corporation, who finds a bomb in his head (108). Next, with the intention of varying the thematic elements, the author creates breakdowns in the brain when a nano-technological invasion plants a dream of an encounter with the "Christ-receptor" in El Zorro's head (124); and his servoskeleton is destroyed in his confrontation with cyborfortunes (179). This instability creates a constant and binary illusion as the ON/OFF switching that turns the city into a digital setting in cyberpunk narrative and that compels a reading in terms of presence/absence (Cavallaro 140). To reinforce this opposition of presence/absence, the narrator exclaims: "El Zorro is immersed in Virtual Space, unplugged. The principal reality is this neon green world, and not the multicolour and distressing outside world" (120). However, it is in this multicolour, distressing outside world where El Zorro is saved and it is from seeing through El Zorro's natural eye that the Selenian society will appear in its pure dystopia.

The nostalgia for a natural vision parallels the "puerile distrust" of Latin American societies facing globalization of video culture in late 80s and 90s. Scott Bukatman (1993) recalls how the Baudrillard "America simulacra" takes place during the Reagan era in the 80s, and Philip K. Dick's fictional world of the 60s is its anticipation. Mentioning *Schismatrix* by Bruce Sterling, where video in the real world is defined as "lines on a screen," Bukatman asserts that cyborg vision becomes commonplace in contemporary film and that the step from film to video strikes the beginning of mediated vision, and even a new subjectivity (254). There is a well known example of *Robocop*: "The perceptual apparatus of this cybernetic law enforcer is a video camera, and overlaid images and videotext represent the figure's data banks. Video imagery thus denotes Robocop's point of view while it connotes his cyborg (read: hybrid, simultaneous, superimposed) status" (254). In the same way, Bukatman and Porcayo's narrators share the opinion that the puerile attitude represented and enforced in the media, "becomes a synecdoche for the culture at large, and the puerility of the programming in Robocop's world suggests that society mirrors the televisual reality in a gesture of implosion." (Bukatman 254).

During the writing process of *PCS* (1987–1993), the Mexican and Latin American sky spectre is not exactly "the color of television, tuned to a dead channel" (Gibson 3). On the one hand, Televisa, the principal network in the country and one of the most important networks in the subcontinent, begins to lose its hegemony on account of its decreasing credibility in terms of its political management of information, and the emergence of rival channels like TV Azteca.[1] On the other hand, it is the arrival of cable television: CNN international (1985) and CNN in Spanish (1997), HBO in Spanish (1988), MTV (1987) and MTV Latino (1993), FOX (1986), etc. Films showing this cyborg vision or video vision as in *Robocop* and its sequels (1987, 1990, 1992, 1994), *Predator* (1987, 1990), *Aliens* (1986) and *Terminator* (1984, 1991) are not only among the video clubs preferences, but they are also repetitively aired with Spanish dubbing on national channels in order to fill the schedule of public, adult entertainment. Néstor García Canclini has observed the phenomenon of video culture in Mexico City where it is taking the place of traditional cinema culture. According to some research studies, 60 percent of customers are under 30 years old and there is only one cinema for each 62, 868 inhabitants, and one video club for each 4,500 inhabitants (115–117).

García Canclini further discusses the impact of this "viewers' aesthetic" that prefers "action-adventure" and "spectacular action" to "political action." In addition to the list of sci-fi movies presented above, it is necessary to mention the hypermediation of the Gulf War with recordings and transmissions of night vision cameras borrowed by local broadcasters from American television, which presents, globally, the re-appearing if American military power and a new geopolitical configuration. During the same epoch in Latin America, the multimedia spectacle is transferred to the political realm in electoral advertising campaigns and during the mandates of Fernando Collor, Carlos Menem or Alberto Fujimori (Canclini 117).

The cyborg vision in *PCS* demonstrates the double vision that Latin American societies acquired in the globalizing process of the cultural market.

If ocular prosthesis is a new device of informatics and post-modern and late-capitalist mythology, the naked eye can observe the problem of adequacy and incompletion of the Modernity project in the subcontinent. The Naranjo image that El Zorro sees is not a real one, but a representation projected by a medium inside an institutional frame — the Trip Corporation — and supported by an ideology. This ideology is that of the capital involving El Zorro and Naranjo in espionage and hacking work. If we take once again into consideration the autopoiesis of character internal focalization and the act of reading, however, the desire for organic life is justified when the narrator draws utopian and anti-utopian parameters through a system of metaphors of life that seeks to reverse the modernity / post-modernity binary opposition.

Life as Dystopian Impulse

M. Keith Booker argues, in *The Dystopian Impulse in Modern Literature*, that science plays an important role in the history of utopian thought and in the passage from utopia to dystopia. Relying on Jürgen Habermas, Booker places a moment in the 16th and 17th centuries when Thomas More in *Utopia* and Francis Bacon in *The New Atlantis* think that natural science can be applied in their utopian societies, which corresponds to the belief in infinite progress of knowledge that marks the birth of Modernity (4–5). To Booker, there is another tuning point in the 19th century. After many classic-age utopian projects had been accomplished, the idea binding scientific progress and emancipation of mankind began to be contested (6). However, this passage does not mean a radical cut between one historical moment when utopia was a dominating movement, and another one that gives rise to a dystopia, or what Booker calls a "dystopian impulse." Elsewhere, Booker explains in this passage:

> Of course, dystopian literature has clear antecedents that are quite ancient. [...] By the late seventeenth and early eighteenth centuries writers like Jonathan Swift were writing works that were centrally informed by dystopian energies. [...] Indeed, the rise of science as a discourse of authority in the Enlightenment directly inspired both an explosion in utopian thought and a corresponding wave of dystopian reactions. It is thus in the course of the nineteenth century — in which technological utopianism reached its peak — that dystopian literature becomes an important and identifiable cultural force [*Dystopian Literature* 5].

According to Booker, in this turning point there are the works of Karl Marx who applies scientific method for proving that the rise of a socialist society is not a utopia — as opposed to French socialist utopianism — and, at the same time, criticizes capitalism, a political system that will resonate in future dystopian visions. This energy or dystopian impulse not only manifests itself in some fictional works in the 20th century, but also in thinkers such as Nietzsche, Freud, Adorno, Benjamin or Foucault.

Booker's project has been criticized for being too ambitious and confusing (see Fitting 1995). On the one hand, he seems to ignore all the academic works of Utopian Studies, paying no heed to notions such as Sargent's, "critical utopia" or Moylan's "critical dystopia"; and establishing an inexact analogy between his "dystopian impulse" and Fredric Jameson's "utopian impulse," the latter notion outlined in Ernst Bloch's *Principle of Hope* and which designates an operation "governing everything future-oriented in life and culture" (Jameson 2). However, Booker makes some useful observations in his analysis of Porcayo's novel. For example, he writes: "One might, in fact, see dystopian and utopian visions not as fundamentally opposed but as very much part of the same project" (*Dystopian Impulse* 15). Furthermore, in reference to the first few lines of García Márquez's *The Autumn of the Patriarch*, he introduces the notion that "dystopian impulse," needs to be revised in Latin American and postcolonial context.

While I venture to hint a parallel between cultural totality and the autopoietic condition that determines life through this energy or this dystopian impulse, I also want to keep a semantic link between "life" and "existence." From a biological point of view, one can not be the certain of whether the life of a certain organism is or is not dystopian, but from a literary perspective one can see that certain excerpts in *PCS* closely resemble a dystopian existence. Existence, here, is an epistemological starting point that allows for making "extrapolations" toward the social imaginary, as we could observe before in the cyborg vision.

Based on their experiments, Maturana and Valera argued that the frog only perceived quick movements — e.g. the flies flying around — whereas they made no responses to motionless or slowly moving objects. The rhythm of narration in *PCS* creates a cinematographic and kinetic illusion of everything seen through the eyes of El Zorro, as Gabriel Trujillo Muñoz comments:

> A telegraphic and galloping prose novel, *La Primera Calle de la Soledad* seems rather a script for a Douglas Fairbanks or an Errol Flynn film. Here, El Zorro, the protagonist, is an authentic warrior in a world of simulacra and turbulent dreams, of machines thinking of themselves as God and, in the same way as a God does, playing with their creatures with the construction of a religion, an additional power over the human mind. An adventure novel that captures the reader and that seduces him from the outset to the end: here is one of its principal merits [225, my translation].

Further merit of the novel includes "its construction, the equilibrium of its parts, the efficacy of its language" (225). Porcayo seeks equilibrium in his novel by way of a speedy narrative that does not lessen the value of existence and vital considerations perceived by the reader. Therefore, one can see how the narrator continues to join other stylistic resources that serve as counterpoint to a kinetic narrative.

Among the stylistic resources, the performance of a meta-metaphor at a textual level creates a parallel between dystopia and life. Thus, when El Zorro flees the lunar city, the narrator offers this description:

> The corridor is an endless tunnel. Without horizons. A metaphoric vision each prisoner perceives every day of his life. Now, El Zorro understands, as he finishes by dint of walking, the plastic tiling. Everything El Zorro was looking for was here, in the atmosphere of this closed society, floating with a legitimacy that he hadn't perceived before [171].

The metaphor of the tunnel explains the spatial particularity of dystopia. As I explained before, a utopia consists of a duplication of real space that creates other imaginary closed spaces. An historical and narrative variation of utopia, dystopia adds an emotional dimension of "dysphoria," the contrary of "euphoria," to the imaginary society space setting, and thus changes the ideal symmetrical quality of an uncertainty point, without horizon. Thus, the narrowness and closing that provoke anginophobia and a tunnel depth with no landmarks tied to bathophobia conform to a claustrophobic topology in which the dystopian subjects live from day to day.

El Zorro's new state of consciousness comes after an anamorphosis, during which El Zorro stands as an observer at a particular angle and discovers a clear image which, viewed from other angles or points of view, is only a distortion. Slavoj Žižek explains how the Real, one of the three orders of subjective experience elaborated by Jacques Lacan — the other two are the imaginary and the symbolic order — intervenes in anamorphosis.[2] The "objective reality" of the Selenian society in *PCS* has undergone a distortion through a process of symbolisations. Thus, a first symbolisation happens when the Moon is shown as a tourism and *disneyfied* destination, with its shops and souvenirs, where visitors can find simulations of prisoners' and miners' uniforms with penitentiary identification numbers. As well, there is another symbolisation of the Moon as a jihad and a centre of institutional and corporal power. Thus, the Real is "the traumatic core of the social antagonism" (Žižek, "The Matrix") that can be found in the Selenian society.

The novel displays a way of approaching the traumatic kernel of the Real through a new metaphor of the tunnel: "The scratched tunnel on the rock is the other metaphor all Selenians know by means of leaving their life to build it. In fact, it is more than a metaphor" (Porcayo 177). The self-reflexivity reaches its paroxysm in the desire for organic life, for the Real. In short, I have been showing a subjective path beginning from an autopoietic moment that shows the reader an angle of vision through a fictional entity but with an organic and vital function — a cyborg, hybrid figure that provides an epistemological and subjective vision of a mediated world of new technology and globalization — and finishes with the discovery of a point where the meta-metaphor indicates something that surpasses the limits of the simple term, "dystopia." It is neither an aesthetic and spatial frame like that of cyberpunk literature and film, nor an exclusive convention of classifying the novel in the genre of dystopia. Through this anamorphic process that provides an existence and subjective dimension, Porcayo's novel is more accurately classified as a "critical dystopian" text.

The consideration of the "critical" part cannot be separated from that of dystopian impulse consideration. This consideration is supposed to be there as an energy circulating in the totality of culture. This energy turns out to be a common denominator in the most antagonistic parts of culture and it spreads because of ideology, social cohesion or, to put it in Žižek's terms, the spectre that eliminates the discontinuity in the symbolic order. The spectre fills up the aporiae lying between the two parts that are seemingly dissimilar at first glance: corporeity has a spiritual side, as does mesmerism; and spirituality has a corporal form, as does ghostly materialization. Porcayo offers a fusion of life and death in the dystopian metaphors of the tunnels: the immateriality of Selenians' lives takes a corporeal form in the rock of tunnel walls that is at the same time their own tombstone.

It is in this way that dystopia becomes critical in an epoch of the global and local trend of fusion. *PCS* elaborates strategies of negotiating the passage from late-capitalist and apparently post-ideological Anti-utopia, in which it is easier to imagine "the end of the world" than to change it (Žižek, "The Spectre of Ideology": 55) to a Utopia of justice. *PCS* does not create a subjective and negotiating position such as a priori, but it does contradict its own experience of life and dystopia in order to legitimate this position. It goes without saying that this quest for organic life and for the Real does not cease to appear all along the novel through stylistic resources. In addition to the meta-metaphor of tunnels, life is also mentioned — "Life is cyclical" — and El Zorro's voice drowns in chaos and repeats in a harsh way, "What a shit!"

Conclusion: Möbius Strip and Che vuoi

Obviously, there is still a criticism to make of *PSC* concerning the ideology of Mexican national identity. From an international perspective, the novel offers strategies of resistance. Acquiring its subjective position, the novel is ready to be confronted on its internal, national account of myths. This account must continue to pertain to the notion of identity in the lacanian topology of the "Möbius strip" that is mentioned in the description of life and of loop narrative. The "Möbius" strip is a surface that has two dimensions but only one side. For Lacan, this topology resembles very closely the unconscious as a "co-present reverse to its right side," which is a way of thinking of the unconscious subject (Assoun 109). This increases the complexity of subjectification in *PCS*. Another aspect to consider is the intersubjectivity moment of "Che (me) vuoi?" (What do you want from me?). In the novel this Italian sentence appears in the voice of Luca Mariano when no negotiation is possible with El Zorro (Porcayo 220–221). Borrowing this expression from *Le diable amoureux*, a short novel by Jacques Cazotte, Lacan tries to conceptualize a process where the subject is confronted with the enigmatic Other's desire, which makes him act hysterically and invent compensatory fantasies in order to preserve his own *jouissance*. Luca offers El Zorro "All of Mexico" in exchange for his cooperation, but this traditional fantasy of a modern nation does not seem to tempt this new subjectivity. So, what does this new subjectivity want?

One answer could be that *PCS* inspires a revisit to the constellation of Mexican national myths. The Asphodel produces uchronia as an alternative for the modern teleology of progress, and in so doing, the subject can work through its historical process of constitution. Regarding the Moon, it acts as a transfer when populated penitentiary cities become an allegory of Mexico, and Mexican cities are tuned OFF in the novel: wastelands and deserted towns that recall Juan Rulfo's ghostly landscapes. And, of course, there is solitude, not only in the title's nod to Octavio Paz's and García Marquez's discourses about Mexican identity and Latin American isolation, but also in the male performances. Another postulate of Lacan is that, "Woman does not exist," which becomes literally true in *PCS*. According to Žižek, Woman is a void in the symbolic order, but a subject of enunciation or a speaking subject, which is a condition of the subject *par excellence* (see Myers 80–92). For Lacan, Woman is not included in the enunciated or grammatical subject of patriarchal society's Symbolic order. *PCS* is a novel about the Mexican patriarchal society that does not discuss biological women as human beings, but rather exemplifies chauvinistic male fantasies. Female characters in *PCS* have only two tragic destinies: on the one hand, they fall victim to rape, and on the other, they fall victim to a relationship of unrequited love with the hero character, as does Nataly, a Swiss cyborg girl who helps El Zorro to escape. Thus, the subject finds the "traumatic core of the social antagonism" of its history and its solipsistic myths.

Notes

1. See http://es.wikipedia.org/wiki/Grupo_Televisa (page consulted on May 27, 2009).
2. Imaginary order takes place in the mirror stage, the moment of birth of ego. Symbolic order is the social and language construction. Real order is the world before language mediation and that can not be known completely.

Works Cited

Assoun, Paul Laurent. *Lacan*. Paris: Que sais-je, 2003.
Benford, Gregory. *Great Sky River*. New York: Bantam Books, 1987.
Bloch, Ernst. *Principle of Hope*. Vol. 1–3. Cambridge, MA: MIT Press, 1995.
Booker, M. Keith. *The Dystopian Impulse in Modern Literature: Fiction as Social Criticism*. Westport, CT: Greenwood, 1994.
_____. *Dystopian Literature: A Theory and Research Guide*. Westport, CT: Greenwood, 1994.
Bukatman, Scott. *Terminal Identity: The Virtual Subject in Post-modern Science Fiction*. London: Duke University Press, 1993.
Canclini, Néstor García. *Consumers and Citizens: Globalization and Multicultural Conflicts*. Minneapolis: University of Minnesota Press, 2001.
Cavallaro, Dani. *Cyberpunk and Cyberculture*. New Brunswick, NJ: The Athlone Press, 2000.
Cazotte, Jacques. *Le diable amoureux*. 1772. Paris: H. Champion, 2003.
Curl, Ruth. "The Metaphors of Cyberpunk: Ontology, Epistemology, and Science Fiction." *Fiction 2000: Cyberpunk and the Future of Narrative*. Ed. George Slusser and Tom Shippey. London: The University of Georgia Press, 1992. 230–45.
Fitting, Peter. "Impulse or Genre or Neither? Booker's *Dystopian Impulse* and *Dystopian Literature*." *Science Fiction Studies* 22.2 (July 1995): 272–81.
Gibson, William. *Neuromancer*. New York: Ace Books, 1984.
Hayles, Katherine. *How We Became Posthuman: Virtual Bodies in Cybernetics, Literature, and Informatics*. Chicago: The University of Chicago Press, 1999.
Jameson, Fredric. *Archaeologies of the Future: The Desire Called Utopia and Other Science Fictions*. New York: Verso, 2005.
Moylan, Tom. *Scraps of the Untainted Sky: Science Fiction, Utopia, Dystopia*. Boulder, CO: Westview, 2000.
Myers, Tony. *Slavoj Žižek*. London: Routledge, 2003.
Porcayo, Gerardo Horacio. *La Primera Calle de la Soledad*. 1993. México: Grupo Editorial Vid, 1997.
Sterling, Bruce, ed. *Mirroshades: The Cyberpunk Anthology*. New York: Arbor House, 1986.
Tasende, Ana María Platas. *Diccionario de términos literarios*. Madrid: Espasa Calpe, 2000.
Trujillo Muñoz, Gabriel. *Los Confines: Crónica de la Ciencia Ficción Mexicana*. México: Grupo Editorial Vid, 1999.
Žižek, Slavoj. "The Matrix, or The Two Sides of Perversion." 28 Octobre 1999. 25 December 2008 <http://www.lacan.com/zizek-matrix.htm>.
_____. "The Spectre of Ideology." *The Žižek Reader*. Ed. Elizabeth Wright and Edmond Wright. Malden, MA: Blackwell, 1999. 53–68.

14

Octavia Butler's *Parable of the Sower*

The Third World as Topos for a U.S. Utopia

GAVIN MILLER

Octavia Butler's 1993 science fiction novel, *Parable of the Sower*, and its 1998 sequel, *Parable of the Talents*, imagine a future U.S.A. in which the state apparatus has almost completely failed. Though this transposition of the U.S. into an imagined Third World condition might seem politically radical, the failed state, as imagined by Butler, is not so much a catastrophe as an opportunity for the rebirth of the human species. Whereas non-fictional failed states are beset by poverty, violence and disease, the fictional U.S. imagined by Butler instead redeems these ills, and fulfils its manifest destiny by breeding a race of men and women adapted to spread throughout the cosmos, thereby escaping the Earth's eventual extinction. This essay explores and exposes the ways in which Butler repackages state failure as an opportunity for self-reliant North Americans to ascend an evolutionary ladder leading to the heavens.

The central character and narrator of *Parable of the Sower*, Lauren Olamina, is an adolescent girl living in a walled community in twenty-first century California. In the year 2024, when Lauren's narrative begins, global warming has taken its toll on the geography, economy and society of the U.S.A. Her small community, Robledo, struggles to survive amidst increasing urban turmoil and crime. Eventually, after her neighborhood is ransacked, and most of her family killed, Lauren is forced to flee northwards. She takes with her a number of survivors, and eventually accumulates a small band of followers (amongst them her future husband, Taylor Bankole). She hopes to convert this community to her syncretic and newly invented religion, "Earthseed."

This belief system has as its fundamental tenet, the credo "God / is Change" (Butler 3), and takes as its eschatology and soteriology a far-off future in which humankind has spread to all corners of the universe, so escaping both evolutionary extinction and the Earth's eventual destruction. After various confrontations and crises on the road northwards, *Parable of the Sower* concludes with the establishment of the first Earthseed community in a remote rural site owned by Bankole.

Parable of the Talents, the sequel to *Parable of the Sower*, tells of the Earthseed community's efforts to survive in the authoritarian Christian-fundamentalist presidency which takes over the declining U.S. Although Lauren's first community, Acorn, is destroyed by an invasion of so-called "Crusaders" (fascist thugs, essentially), the Earthseed movement manages to survive and propagate. By the end of *Parable of the Talents*, it has prospered enough that Lauren can watch the first shuttles lifting off to find new worlds. In many ways, the second book is superior to the first, especially since it uses a number of voices to enter into dialogue with Lauren's frequent *ex cathedra* pronouncements. This essay, however, concentrates on the first novel, and in particular on its use of Third World *topoi*. In the fictional U.S. envisaged by Butler, the nation is recognizably a failing, almost failed state, of the kind familiar from postcolonial history. Since this term, "failed state," has slipped into casual discourse, and is often used without a clear sense of its meaning, some preliminary definition will be useful. Robert Rotberg gives a clear account of the concept: "it is according to their performances — according to the levels of their effective delivery of the most crucial political goods — that strong states may be distinguished from weak ones, and weak states from failed or collapsed ones" (Rotberg 2). The three most important goods furnished by the state are physical security, reliable judicial process, and meaningful political participation (Rotberg 3). Other goods supplied by strong states

> include medical and health care [...]; schools and educational instruction [...]; roads, railways, harbors and other physical infrastructures — the arteries of commerce; communications networks; a money and banking system, usually presided over by a central bank and lubricated by a nationally created currency; a beneficent fiscal and institutional context within which citizens can pursue personal entrepreneurial goals [...]; space for the flowering of civil society; and methods of regulating the sharing of the environmental commons [Rotberg 3].

Failed states, as might be expected, do not deliver such goods to their citizens. Their primary failure is their inability to ensure the security of their citizens, as is manifest in, for instance, criminal violence or civil war. But there are, naturally enough, other indices of failure: "failed states cannot control their peripheral regions" (Rotberg 6); "only the institution of the executive functions. If legislatures exist at all, they ratify decisions of the executives" (Rotberg 7); "citizens know that they cannot rely on the court system for significant redress or remedy, especially against the state" (Rothberg 7); "infrastructures" are "deteriorating or destroyed" (Rotberg 7); "effective educational and medical systems are privatized informally" (Rotberg 7); and though there may be "unparalleled economic opportunity," it can be "only for a privileged few" (Rotberg 8).

The society depicted by Butler is clearly congruent with the kind of failed state described by Rotberg and familiar to readers from the conventional First World understanding of African failed states such as Somalia in the 1990s or Rwanda in 1994. There is perhaps no particular state that functions as a model for *Parable of the Sower*, which seems instead to provide an "ideal type" of state failure. The state can, for instance, no longer be relied upon for security and justice — "the cops knock them [the street poor] around, rob them if they have anything worth stealing" (Butler 48) — and, with the failure to deliver security to its citizens, comes a proliferation of privately held small arms: "We hear so much gunfire, day and night, single shots and odd bursts of automatic weapons fire" (Butler 48). The U.S. is in economic collapse, with phenomena such as hyperinflation ("Food prices are insane, always going up, never down" (Butler 74)), and a return to trading by barter. There is a lack of medical provision, especially of the state-sponsored kind that would be called upon to prevent epidemics of cholera in Mississippi and Louisiana (Butler 51). Education, too, is increasingly privatized: primary and secondary schooling is provided within Robledo by amateur teachers such as Lauren herself. Outside of Robledo's walled communities, neither housing nor food can be assured: Lauren writes of the shanty houses — "rag, stick, cardboard, and palm frond shacks along the way into the hills" (Butler 82), which are inhabited by "living skeletons [...] Skin and bones and a few teeth" (Butler 82). The northern border has been closed by neighboring Canada in order to prevent a refugee crisis, and lethal force enforces this territorial division: "'People get shot every day trying to sneak into Canada'" (Butler 76). In the absence of a strong domestic state and economy, the U.S. has been colonized by external, foreign capital, such as the firm of "Kagimoto, Stamm, Frampton, and Company" (Butler 109) who are, according to Lauren's father, "'Japanese, German, Canadian'" (Butler 111). In Lauren's words: "'This country is going to be parceled out as a source of cheap labor and cheap land. [...] our surviving cities are bound to wind up the economic colonies of whoever can afford to buy them'" (Butler 119).

These are just a few of the features of the failed state found in Butler's imagined future U.S.A. This geographical transposition of the Third World into the First World means that, in a peculiar sense, *Parable of the Sower* may be seen as a text analogous and complementary to Walter Scott's 1814 historical novel, *Waverley*. In this narrative, the protagonist, Edward Waverley, travels from his English ancestral home to Scotland, where he becomes embroiled in the failed 1745 Jacobite Rising, which sought to restore a Stuart monarchy to Hanoverian Britain. Scott presents Waverley's spatial movement as a movement in time, in which his protagonist moves backward through the stadial history described by Enlightenment philosophers such as Adam Ferguson in *An Essay on the History of Civil Society* (1767). The Scottish Highlands are a quasi-feudal society which lags behind the civil, mercantile society that has brought peace and prosperity to southern Britain. In *Waverley*, to move through space is to move in time. In *Parable of the Sower*, on the other hand, to move in time is to move through space: Butler's future transposes U.S. geography and culture into the contemporary Third World.

Butler's chronotope might seem to be immensely valuable. What could be better for the citizens of the world's wealthiest and most environmentally rapacious nation than to imaginatively undergo the sufferings of the Third World? It might even seem that Lauren's so-called "hyperempathy" hints at the way in which *Parable of the Sower* is to be read: her compulsive empathetic identification (caused by her mother's abuse of an intelligence-enhancing drug during pregnancy) may be intended as the story's analogue to the psychological processes invoked in its readership. Unfortunately, such a reading of *Parable of the Sower* would be far too charitable. Butler's depiction of a future U.S.A. is not so much a challenge to First World complacency as it is a projection of the U.S. imagination upon the geography of a failed state — an imaginary colonization that at once appropriates and renders anodyne the sufferings of the contemporary Third World.

Perhaps the oddest aspect of this imaginative colonization is Butler's imposition upon her chosen *topos* of a narrative progression derived from the antebellum sentimental novel. As Cindy Weinstein explains with reference to texts such as Maria Susanna Cummins's *The Lamplighter* (1854), this was a genre in which "separations of parent and child constitute the foundational plot mechanism [...] They provide the conflict which initiates the protagonist's journey from child to adult, from psychic despair to emotional confidence, from the bonds of consanguinity to affections based on choice" (Weinstein 26). This too is the narrative progression in *Parable of the Sower* as Lauren moves from her patriarchal and largely consanguineous family to the elective bonds of the Earthseed community that she brings together on the road northwards. As she writes in her Earthseed notebooks, "*A tree / Cannot grow / In its parents' shadows*" (Butler 76). This narrative skepticism towards blood relations is driven home by other Robledo residents, such as Tracy Dunn, who gives birth at age thirteen, after years of being raped by her uncle (Butler 32); and it is further emphasized within Lauren's family in the conflict generated by her (half-) brother Keith: "'How do I get out of this family,' Marcus muttered to me as we watched. [...] He had to share a room with Keith, and the two of them [...] fought all the time" (Butler 85). On her lengthy trek, Lauren picks up others fleeing their blood families, such as Allie and Jill Gilchrist "who were so clearly their father's victims" (Butler 234), and finds a husband in Bankole, who, at age fifty-seven, is also a new, adoptive father. The adoptive imagery is further developed in an intertextual reference to the famous ending of John Steinbeck's *The Grapes of Wrath* (1939), where Rose of Sharon suckles a starving stranger. When Bankole finds an orphaned baby, a fellow-traveler, Natividad, suckles the child at one breast, with her own child at the other (Butler 231). Weinstein's description of the sentimental novel therefore fits well with Butler's text: "The generic goal is the substitution of freely given love, rather than blood, as the invincible tie that binds together individuals in a family" (Weinstein 9).

This generic revival may help to explain the prominence in Butler's narrative of Lauren's hyperempathy, since, according to Weinstein, during the mid-nineteenth-century, "the literature repeatedly deployed sympathy as one of the most reliable measures of characterological virtue" (Weinstein 2). Lauren's neurological condition is the *novum* that revives this archaic generic feature. Jerry Phillips sees hyperempathy as a kind of utopian trace within *Parable of the Sower*: "how much more difficult it would be," he declares, "to starve, rape, exploit, terrorize, and murder the other" (Phillips 306). The text, or at least Lauren's voice (which dominates *Parable of the Sower*), agrees with this interpretation — after the torture and murder of her brother Keith, Lauren reflects, "If hyperempathy syndrome were a more common complaint, people couldn't do such things" (Butler 105). In other words, if we were all more empathetic, then we should be less inclined to do bad things to each other; sympathy is once again "the most reliable measure of virtue," to echo Weinstein.

But is it really the case that, as Lauren has it, "[a] biological conscience is better than no conscience at all"? (Butler 106). One might note, for instance, that there are some odd limits to Lauren's hyperempathy. Although she gets double the pleasure in sexual intercourse, she seems strangely immune to the sexual high experienced by the drug-addicted pyromaniacs, for whom "watching the leaping changing patterns of fire" provides "a better, more intense, longer-lasting high than sex" (Butler 133). There is no doubt a narrative logic to this decision, since Butler's story could hardly get under way if her protagonist were liable to be emotionally infected by the "pyros," and to throw herself with gusto into their orgies of destruction. But there is a symbolic meaning as well. Butler's pyromaniacs are an image of revolutionaries who demand the redistribution of wealth: "'She died for us,' the scavenger woman had said of the green face [a "pyro"]. Some kind of insane burn-the-rich movement, Keith had said" (Butler 149). Later, after an earthquake, there is a mass attack by "pyros" in which "[b]ands of the street poor precede or follow them, grabbing whatever they can from stores and from the walled enclaves of the rich and what's left of the middle class" (Butler 226).

Lauren's hyperempathy is thus subtly moralized: the allegorical revolutionaries are "othered" to the extent that she cannot pick up on their orgiastic sentiment (and something similar happens in *Parable of the Talents*, where Lauren is allowed to somehow *resist* identification with her sexually sadistic Christian Crusader captors). This moralism is further emphasized by Butler's implicit account of sympathetic moral impulse as a compulsive imaginative identification with the other (so that in a fight, for instance, Lauren records, "'I felt every blow that I struck, just as though I'd hit myself'" [Butler 11]). Contrast this with the definition of sympathy advanced by Philip Mercer in his study of the concept in moral philosophy:

> if it is correct to make the statement "*A* sympathizes with *B*" then the following conditions must be fulfilled:
> (a) *A* is aware of the existence of *B* as a sentient subject;
> (b) *A* knows or believes he knows *B*'s state of mind;
> (c) there is fellow-feeling between *A* and *B* so that through his imagination *A* is able to realize *B*'s state of mind; and
> (d) *A* is altruistically concerned for *B*'s welfare [Mercer 19].

Of this list, (d) is of particular importance to my reading of *Parable of the Sower*. The point about this fourth condition is that imaginative knowledge of another's feelings is not in itself robust enough to establish an ethically significant account of sympathy. One may well have this capacity, but be otherwise lacking a properly altruistic response. One could, for example, relish the sufferings of another if one were a sadist, and wish to prolong and intensify them. Alternatively, one could be concerned selfishly for the other's welfare — for example, "because I desire to be well-thought-of or because I have a guilty conscience or because I want to get him into my debt" (Mercer 11). This latter problem is what undermines the "biological conscience" described by Butler. Lauren's hyperempathy is a selfish pseudo-altruism in which, *ceteris paribus*, ego works to avert alter's sufferings so that the former does not have to participate in them. It is a kind of *lex talionis* inscribed on the psyche, rather than any genuine relationship of concern. Hyperempathy is little more than a swift psychic punishment for wrong-doing (or, less frequently in *Parable of the Sower*, an immediate reward for the giving of pleasure). It certainly cannot bear the weighty utopian constructions built upon it by critics such as Phillips, who writes, "in a hyperempathetic world, the other would cease to exist as the ontological antithesis of the self, but instead would become a real aspect of oneself, insofar as one accepts oneself as a social being" (Phillips 306). Even in our fallen, non-hyperempathetic world, there are many ways of self-accepted "social being" which involve cognitive, affective and conative relations to the experience of the other, without the compulsive identification invented by Butler. The dichotomy between solipsism and merger implied by Butler's text, and implicitly accepted by Phillips, is quite false.

This nostalgia for a future in which punishment is swift and assured, instead of long, drawn out, and (I might speculate) state-administered, finds its corollary in another of Butler's projections of the U.S. imagination onto the *topos* of the failed state. As Carl Abbott notes, frontier life has long been seen in American culture — including science fiction — as a possible antidote to selfish individualism. Alongside hyperempathic self-flagellation, Butler valorizes the alleged moral culture of frontier society, of the kind described by Abbott: "The challenges of problem-solving and community-making in new settlements [...] demanded wide participation, cooperation, voluntary association, and support for public institutions. Far from undermining the civil community, the frontier balanced individual competition against the needs of the larger group" (Abbott 125). Lauren, who thinks of "the big city" as "a carcass covered with maggots" shares in this essential skepticism towards urban life and state-provided security (Butler 9). She records with disdain the words of an incomer, Wardell Parrish, who remarks "how he had paid enough [taxes] in his life to have a right to depend on the police to protect him" (Butler 81), and who describes his family as one that is "'not very social [...] We mind our own business'" (Butler 34). These are the attitudes of the city, where security is provided by the state, rather than of the frontier, where every member of the society is called upon to directly assist in its security. Parrish's latter statement is preceded by a warning from Lauren's father that their community is built on mutual interdependence in the face of an external threat: "'This is a small community,' my father said. 'We all know each other here. We depend on each other'" (Butler 34). The same connection of community with security is explained later, after an abortive attack on Robledo — "'Did you notice,' Dad said, 'that every off-duty watcher answered the whistles last night? They came out to defend their community'" (Butler 69). Indeed, part of Lauren's admiration for the U.S. space program is based on the frontier ethos that it potentially offers: "I think people who traveled to extrasolar worlds would be on their own [...] and far from help. [...] out of the shadow of their parent world" (Butler 77); the threatening new environment would stand in for the external political threat faced by communities such as Robledo. Indeed, not only are other planets a new form of frontier-existence, they are also presented as (metaphorically) the abandonment of consanguineous ties. Earthseed's grand vision is a narrative of separation from the parent world: "a living world might be easier to adapt to and live on without a long, expensive umbilical to Earth" (Butler 77).

But perhaps the most curious and worrying projection of the U.S. cultural imagination upon the terrain of a failed state occurs in Lauren's journey northwards out of Robledo, which leads her eventually to found Acorn, the ill-fated Earthseed community. This forced migration provides the occasion for a popular motif from Western science fiction: the roads on which she travels function as a Darwinian sieve or strainer which tests the adaptiveness, the fitness for survival, of the group that she builds up around her: "'Out here, you adapt to your surrounding or you get killed'" declares Lauren (Butler 168); to her friend, Harry, who also escapes, she warns, "'You still think a mistake is when your father yells at you or you break a finger or chip a tooth or something. Out here a mistake — one mistake — and you may be dead'" (Butler 167). This Darwinian *topos* is a science fiction staple apparent in a wide range of works: the Lunar Colony in Robert A. Heinlein's *The Moon is a Harsh Mistress* (1966), the invaded Earth in H.G. Wells's *The War of the Worlds* (1898), and — to satiric effect — the Galápagos Islands in Kurt Vonnegut's *Galápagos* (1985). Butler's narrative plunges Lauren *et al.* (or, perhaps, the social whole which they comprise) into an evolutionary *Bildungsroman*, as they trek through a landscape filled with enemies repeatedly described as "predators" (e.g. Butler 186) and "scavengers" (e.g. Butler 220). The road to Acorn is filled with lessons as profound as the Slough of Despond, the Hill Difficulty, and the Valley of Humiliation were to John Bunyan's Christian in *The Pilgrim's Progress* (1678). Lauren watches and learns as she observes someone being robbed of all his possessions because he is inattentive, discovers the corpses of three youths who have died drinking chemically tainted water, and witnesses the destruction of an otherwise strong community sited too near the roadside.

Lauren interprets this Darwinian threshing on the road northward as the first stage in a renewed progress up some supposed evolutionary ladder: "'The Destiny of Earthseed,'" she explains to one new member, "'is to take root among the stars. [...] That's the ultimate Earthseed aim, and the ultimate human change short of death. It's a destiny we'd better pursue if we hope to be anything other than smooth-skinned dinosaurs'" (Butler 204). Evidence for such evolutionary processes at work in the failed states of Third World countries such as Rwanda in 1994, or Somalia during the 1990s, would seem to be scant. But let us assume against reason and common decency that failed states somehow re-activate supposedly dormant evolutionary mechanisms, just as (according to Butler) they will liberate us from stifling consanguineous bonds, while also fostering community spirit. Why should Darwinian selection direct *homo sapiens* towards some human ideal of perfection, rather than to some merely improved evolutionary adaptiveness (such as the transformation of the human species into a race of simple-minded flippered fisher folk depicted by Vonnegut in *Galápagos*)? Butler's text invokes what Mary Midgley has called the "Escalator Fallacy," "the idea that evolution is a steady, linear upward movement, a single inexorable process of improvement, leading [...] 'from gas to genius' and beyond into some superhuman spiritual stratosphere" (Midgley 7). In the case of Butler's text, the escalator leads to "'Other star systems. Living worlds'" (Butler 204).

The imaginative appropriation of the Third World by Butler's novel promises some rather chastening lessons for literary criticism, which has been remarkably complacent in its readings of *Parable of the Sower*. Phillips, for instance, describes the book as "a futuristic novel that explores latent and manifest tendencies [...] in the postmodern condition" (Phillips 300); *Parable of the Sower* warns that "the future *in toto* is not yet with us" (Phillips 300), and that we may yet avoid the "disastrous end of the world" that it depicts (Phillips 301). There is something parochial in the assumption that the end of the U.S.—even as a synecdoche for the developed nations—is the end of the world (and, as I have shown above, Butler's novel even makes it clear that other nations, such as Japan, Germany, and Canada, have escaped the fate of the U.S.). But, by exploiting what Abbott calls "the common trope of 'seeing the future in California'" (Abbott 122), Phillips implies that this fictional failure of the U.S. state expresses future tendencies in our supposed postmodern condition, rather than merely exploiting representations of the contemporary Third World. Or are we to assume that the citizens of the worst Third World states have somehow leapfrogged the developed West, and have entered into the vanguard of postmodernity? If they have, there seems little plausibility in the extrapolation from their dreadful condition of its "dialectical opposite, historical time as the renewal of life, the journey towards utopia" (Phillips 301).

The naïveté with which Butler and certain of her critics overlook the dangers of projecting the U.S. imagination onto the Third World may perhaps be explained by an overconfidence in the solidarity of First World "black" writing with the experience of the Third World. This is apparent in the text, when Lauren encounters Bankole, and finds that they are "both descended from men who assumed African surnames back during the 1960s" (Butler 211). As has been noted by postcolonial critics, "the idea of Black writing" (Ashcroft, Griffiths and Tiffin 20) "overlooks the very great cultural differences between literatures which are produced by a Black minority in a rich and powerful white country and those produced by the Black majority population of an independent nation" (Ashcroft, Griffiths and Tiffin 21). The implication of an identity between the concerns of African Americans, and "black" Africans, mistakenly homogenizes radically different experiences within an arbitrarily selected ethnic descent group.

A further explanation for what seems to me a complacent acceptance of Butler's exploitation of the Third World as a literary *topos* may reside in some lingering belief that the U.S. is an archetypal postcolonial society. The authors of the popular text of postcolonial criticism, *The Empire Writes Back*, claim that "[t]he first post-colonial society to develop a 'national' literature was the U.S.A." (Ashcroft, Griffiths and Tiffin 16), and infer that "[i]n many ways the American experience and its attempts to produce a new kind of literature can be seen to be the model for all later post-colonial writing" (Ashcroft, Griffiths and Tiffin 16). But this thesis can hardly be established *a priori*. Why should the first instance of a phenomenon be the most typical? On *a posteriori* grounds, the claim is hardly convincing — at least not if *Parable of the Sower* is anything to go by. As I have shown, the text constantly projects U.S.–specific issues onto the backdrop of the Third World: concerns about personal narratives of emancipation from blood relations; about the meaning of sympathy and care for others; about the desirability of a frontier society and the meaning of community; and — worst of all — pseudo–Darwinian fantasies about the collapse of the political order. The failed state in *Parable of the Sower*, in fact, becomes something desirable, a necessary transition towards a better future imagined in U.S. (*not* "American") concepts such as frontier communitarianism, Social Darwinism, displaced Christian sotieriology, and the value of swift and effective retribution. Although Lauren and her readership might step outside of her walled community and into the failed state, the suffering provoked by this disobedience will be providentially redeemed. She must leave her walled garden of Eden, "[i]n spite of what my father will say or do to me, in spite of the poisonous rottenness outside of the wall where I might be exiled" (Butler 25), in order to reach the Heavens.

Chinua Achebe in his famous essay, "An Image of Africa: Racism in Conrad's *Heart of Darkness*," argues that this modernist novel exploits Africa as a suitable setting for the protagonist's psychic journey. As Achebe points out, we encounter in Conrad's novel "Africa as setting and backdrop which eliminates the African as human factor. Africa as a metaphysical battlefield devoid of all recognizable humanity" (Achebe 8). Achebe therefore exposes what he calls the "preposterous and perverse arrogance in thus reducing Africa to the role of props for the break-up of one petty European mind" (Achebe 8). Butler's *Parable of the Sower* rivals Conrad's novel in arrogance, for it is a science fiction novel which titillates the U.S.–specific utopian imagination of its implied readers by drawing upon a Third World experience that they would hope never to undergo. Motifs from contemporary African history provide the backdrop and setting for an evolutionary fantasy in which American blood is distilled into a higher form of the human species better suited for eternal conquest of the cosmos. Neither Africa nor the U.S. is well served by this unfortunate combination of science fictional utopianism, contemporary world politics and American exceptionalism.

Works Cited

Abbott, Carl. *Frontiers Past and Future: Science Fiction and the American West*. Lawrence, Kansas: University of Kansas Press, 2006.
Achebe, Chinua. "An Image of Africa: Racism in Conrad's *Heart of Darkness*." *Hopes and Impediments: Selected Essays 1965–1987*. Oxford: Heinemann, 1988. 1–13.
Ashcroft, Bill, Gareth Griffiths, and Helen Tiffin. *The Empire Writes Back: Theory and Practice in Post-Colonial Literatures*. London and New York: Routledge, 1989.
Butler, Octavia E. *Parable of the Sower*. 1993. London: Women's Press, 1995.
Mercer, Philip. *Sympathy and Ethics: A Study of the Relationship between Sympathy and Morality with Special Reference to Hume's Treatise*. Oxford: Clarendon, 1972.
Midgley, Mary. *Evolution as a Religion: Strange Hopes and Stranger Fears*. Revised ed. London and New York: Routledge, 2002.
Phillips, Jerry. "The Intuition of the Future: Utopia and Catastrophe in Octavia Butler's *Parable of the Sower*." *Novel: A Forum on Fiction* 35.2–3 (2002): 299–311.
Rotberg, Robert I. "The Failure and Collapse of Nation-States: Breakdown, Prevention, and Repair." *When States Fail: Causes and Consequences*. Ed. Robert I. Rotberg. Princeton: Princeton University Press, 2004. 1–49.
Weinstein, Cindy. *Family, Kinship, and Sympathy in Nineteenth-Century American Literature*. Cambridge: Cambridge University Press, 2004.

About the Contributors

Dominic Alessio is director of Study Abroad and professor of history at Richmond, the American International University in London, visiting research fellow in the English Department of the University of Northampton, and vice-chair of the New Zealand Studies Association. His sf-related publications have appeared in *Foundation, ARIEL, Journal of New Zealand Literature, Science Fiction Studies, New Cinemas: Journal of Contemporary Film, Journal of Postcolonial Literature,* and the *New Zealand Journal of History*. He wrote *The Great Romance: A Rediscovered Utopian Adventure* (University of Nebraska Press, 2008), a postcolonial analysis of sf in New Zealand.

Suparno Banerjee is a Ph.D. scholar in the English Department at Louisiana State University, Baton Rouge. Suparno's dissertation is focused on a comparative study of Indian science fiction written in English and Anglophone science fiction written about India. He has presented papers at an ACLA annual meeting, the International Conference on the Fantastic in the Arts, and the PCA/ACA national conference. His most recent article, titled "*2001: A Space Odyssey*: A Transcendental Trans-locution" was published in the *Journal of the Fantastic in the Arts*, Vol. 19, Issue 1, 2008.

Juan F. Elices is an associate lecturer at the Department of English Studies (Universidad de Alcalá–Madrid), where he teaches 17th and 18th century English literature. His main areas of research focus on satiric theory and dystopia, on which he has published several books and articles, including *Historical and Theoretical Approaches to English Satire* (2004) and *The Satiric Worlds of William Boyd: A Case-Study* (2006). He is currently working on postcolonial science fiction and alternate history, resulting in the article "Shadows of an Imminent Future: Walter Mosley's Dystopia and Science Fiction," published in *Finding a Way Home: A Critical Assessment of Walter Mosley Fiction* (2008).

Diana Pharaoh Francis is a professor of English at the University of Montana–Western. She is interested in structures of power in relation to postcolonialism and women, and has particular interests in fantasy fiction and Victorian novels. She has also written the fantasy novel trilogy *Path of Fate, Path of Honor* and *Path of Blood*, and the fantasy series *The Crosspointe Chronicles* and the *Horngate Witches* series.

Gerald Gaylard is the head of the Department of English at the University of the Witwatersrand in Johannesburg, South Africa. He has worked on all aspects of romance, from the medieval to the postmodern and from fantasy to science fiction. His publications include *After Colonialism: African Postmodernism and Magical Realism* (2006) and *Marginal Spaces: Ivan Vladislavić*, which is forthcoming in 2010. Currently he is working on a postcolonial transculturation of the idea of the sympathetic imagination.

Grant Hamilton is currently a visiting assistant professor of English literature at the University of Hong Kong. His research interests lie in postcolonial literature and theory and the philosophy of Gilles Deleuze. He is currently writing his second book, *Deleuze and African Literature*.

Ericka Hoagland is an assistant professor of English at Stephen F. Austin State University. Her essay "'What Kind of Woman Are You, A'isha?' Misogyny and Islam in Ibrahim Tahir's *The Last Imam*" appears in *Gender and Sexuality in African Literature and Film* (2007). She has also contributed pieces to the *Encyclopedia of American Indian Literature* and *Women in Science Fiction and Fantasy*.

Herbert G. Klein received his M.A. and Ph.D. (1985) from the University of Berlin. He is a lecturer in modern English literature at the Freie Universität Berlin. He has published widely on all periods of modern English literature and culture, especially on science and literature, but also in the fields of masculinity studies and intermedia studies.

Jessica Langer recently completed her Ph.D. at Royal Holloway, University of London; her dissertation focused on intersections and interactions between postcolonialism and science fiction. Her most recent publications include articles in *New Cinemas: Journal of Contemporary Film* and *Science Fiction in Film and Television*. Research interests include postcolonialism and science fiction, systems of oppression and social justice issues, particularly in the developing world, and cultural theory and "cybercultures," particularly video games and other transnational online media.

Judith Leggatt is chair of the English Department at Lakehead University in Thunder Bay, where she teaches First Nations, postcolonial and speculative literatures. Her publications include articles on Lee Maracle's *Ravensong* in *Mosaic,* Salman Rushdie's speculative fiction in *Ariel*, the interrelation of post-colonial theory and First Nations writing in *Is Canada Postcolonial?*, mind control in *Jane Eyre* in *English Studies in Canada* and trickster aesthetics in First Nations poetry, forthcoming in *Troubling Tricksters*.

Gavin Miller is a research fellow in the English Research Institute, Manchester Metropolitan University. He is the author of *R.D. Laing* (2004) and *Alasdair Gray: The Fiction of Communion* (2005). His research interests include science fiction, Scottish literature, and the history of psychiatry.

Juan Ignacio Muñoz Zapata is a postdoctoral fellow at the University of Western Ontario. His research deals with notions of aesthetics and power in contemporary Latin American alternate history. His Ph.D. disertation explored Latin American cyberpunk literature and film as spaces of national resistance and dystopia vis-à-vis cultural globalization. His other interests include Brazilian tupinipunk and national trauma in Chilean cyberpunk. He has also published sf short stories in several Latin American e-zines.

Shital Pravinchandra obtained her Ph.D. in comparative literature from Cornell University and is currently a teaching fellow in postcolonial studies at the School of Oriental and African Studies, University of London. Her research explores the ways in which the forces of global capitalism and biomedicine permit the commodification of the postcolonial body. Her current projects include an examination of the short story and the genre's absence from postcolonial literary studies.

Reema Sarwal is pursuing a Ph.D. on contemporary Australian fantasy fiction at the Centre for English Studies, School of Language, Literature and Culture Studies, Jawaharlal Nehru University, New Delhi, India. She was an honorary visiting scholar at the School of English, Communication and Performance Studies, Monash University, in 2006–2007. She has co-edited *Creative Nation: Australian Cinema and Cultural Studies Reader* (2009) and *Reading Down Under: Australian Literary Studies Reader* (2009) with Amit Sarwal.

Debjani Sengupta teaches literatures in the Department of English, Indraprastha College for Women, University of Delhi. She is the editor of *Mapmaking: Partition Stories from Two Bengals* (2003) and *Dakkhin Asiar Naaribadi Golpo* (2008) a collection of South Asian feminist stories that she edited with Selina Hossain of Bangladesh. She has also translated Taslima Nasreen's *Selected Columns* (2004). Her interest in Bangla sf is an ongoing pursuit.

Roslyn Weaver holds a Ph.D. in English literature from the University of Wollongong. Her disertation examined apocalypse in Australian speculative literature and film, and her research interests include popular culture, children's literature, indigenous peoples' narratives, religion, and medical humanities. She has taught undergraduate university courses in English literature and film. Currently, she is working at the University of Western Sydney.

Index

Abar Ghanada 120
Abbott, Carl 208, 210
Aboriginal assimilation 107–108; speculative fiction 17
Acharjya Jagadishchandra 125*n*
Achebe, Chinua 26, 153, 211
Adare, Sierra S. 133
Adorno, Theodor 197
Advani, L.K. 166
Adwitiyo Ghanada 120
Africa 210–211
Afro-Future Females 2
Afrofuturism 1
Ahmad, Aijaz 13, 14, 164
Alessio, Dominic 18
Aliens 195
Alkon, Paul K. 9, 38
alterity 24, 34, 142, 160
alternate histories 9, 39–40, 42, 48; definition of 38
Althusser, Louis 131
Aluko, T.M. 153
ambivalent imperialism 7
Amadahy, Zainab 127–140
Amazing Stories 1
Amis, Kingsley 171
Amistad 41
Analog 6 63*n*
Ancient & Modern 66
Antebellum sentimental novel 205; slave narratives 40
anti-dystopia 185–186
anti-utopian writing 186
apocalypse 17, 25, 26, 27, 32; definition of 101; in Indigenous speculative fiction 99–113; tropes in 103
Apocalypse Now 160
apocalyptic literature 101
apocalyptic writing 100
Arata, Stephen 83–84
Armah, Ayi Kwei 153
Arnason, Eleanor 130, 134

Ashcroft, Bill 23, 41, 67
Ashe, Bertram D. 42
Asimov, Isaac 116, 125*n*
assimilation 42–43, 107–108; and language 43–44
Attebery, Brian 99, 105
Australian science fiction 99
autopoiesis 192–196
The Autumn of the Patriarch 30, 197

Babri Masjid 164, 166
Baccolini, Rafaella 171
Back to the Future 160
Bacon, Francis 196
Baldwin, James 40
Balibar, Etienne 168
Bandung Conference 13
Banerjee, Gurudas 116
Banerjee, Suparno 16
Bangla Sahitye Bigyan 125*n*
Banglar Palchi 117
Barnes, Steven 16
Barr, Marlene S. 2
Bastos, Roa 30
Basu, Biman 125*n*
Batash Baari 121
Bauman, Zygmunt 93
The Beast Master 130
The Beautyful Ones Are Not Yet Born 153
Bedi, Rajat 157
Begamudre, Ven 57
Being and Nothingness 65
Bell, Andrea 2
Bell, Claire 131, 134
Benford, Gregory 191
Benjamin, Walter 197
Berger, James 101
Bhabha, Homi K. 23, 27, 83, 145, 182
Bharati 117
Bharatiya Janata Party 164
Bhattacharya, Buddhadev 125*n*
Bhattacharya, Khitindranarayan 120

217

Bhattacharya, Monoranjan 120
Bigyan Darpan 116
binaries 62; in colonial discourse 51
black science fiction 39
Blade Runner 23, 159
Bloch, Ernst 197
Bloomer, Kent C. 179
Body, Memory, and Architecture 179
Boehmer, Elleke 172, 177
Bollywood 156, 163–165; definition of 168*n*
Booker, M. Keith 196
Borges, Jorge Luis 64
Bose, Jagadishchandra 116, 117
Bradbury, Ray 10, 171
Brahmo Samaj 116, 117
Brave New World 12
Broderick, Damien 10–11
Broege, Valerie 153
Brown Girl in the Ring 18, 161, 172–174, 176–177, 179–181, 184
Brunner, John 22
Bukatman, Scott 194, 195
Bunyan, John 209
Butler, Octavia E. 1, 18, 22, 39, 202–212

Cabral, Amilcar 23
The Calcutta Chromosome 2, 16, 50–64
Campbell, John W. 31, 61, 63*n*
Canclini, Garcia 195
A Canticle for Leibowitz 161
capitalism: and the first world 89–90; global 87, 93, 95; millenial 90–91; and the third world 87, 90
Cavallaro, Dani 193
Cazotte, Jacques 200
center periphery 14, 18, 172
Cesaire, Aime 45
Chakrabarty, Dipesh 66, 68
Chambers, Claire 53, 57, 62–63*n*
Charly (1968 film) 160
Chaudhuri, Upendrakishore Ray 117, 121
Cherry, Mark 97*n*
Chesterman, John 107
Children of Dune 29, 31, 34
Clark, Maureen 113*n*
Clarke, Arthur C. 3
Close Encounters of the Third Kind 160
Clute, John 2, 158
cognition 60, 61, 65
Collor, Fernando 195
Colmer, James 162
colonial: subject as sexual object 77–86
colonialism 22–23, 67, 172
Colonialism and the Emergence of Science Fiction 2
colonized woman 81

Comaroff, Jean 90
Comaroff, John 90
Conan Doyle, Arthur 117, 142, 149
The Concept of Utopia 171
Conrad, Joseph 30, 211
Contact (1997 film) 160
Cooper, James Fenimore 133
Cooper, Ken 100
Cosmic Trilogy 161
Cosmos Latinos 2
Crispin, A.C. 130, 134
critical dystopia 189
Cscicsery-Ronay, Istvan 188
cultural hybrid 181
Cummins, Maria Susanna 205
Curl, Ruth 190, 191, 192
cyberpunk literature 199
cyberpunk writers 188
cyborg 193–197, 199

Dark Matter 2
Darwin, Charles 46; Darwinian selection 209–210; social Darwinism 211
Dawson, Carrie 112*n*
de Beauvoir, Simone 80, 81
Decolonising the Mind 66
Deighton, Len 39
Delany, Samuel R. 22, 23, 39
Deleuze, Gilles 69, 72, 74
"Delhi" 65–76
Le diable amoureux 200
Dick, Philip K. 9, 22, 39, 67, 171, 194
Dilwale Dulhan le Jayenge 163
Disch, Thomas M. 123
Dodson, Michael 106
Douglas, Heather 107
Dracula 83
Dreamer of Dune 32
Dune 9, 12, 15, 22, 24–35; *Children of Dune* 29, 31, 34; *Dreamer of Dune* 32; *Dune Messiah* 21, 28–32; myth in 28–30
Dune Messiah 21, 28–32
Dutta, Akshaykumar 116
Dutta, Hemlal 116, 158
dystopia 18, 39, 96, 171, 185–186, 188, 196; anti-dystopia 185, 186; colonial reading of 173; critical dystopia 189, 190; metropolis and 172
dystopian impulse 196–199
The Dystopian Impulse in Modern Literature 196

Effinger, George Alec 18, 172
Elices, Juan F. 16
The Empire Writes Back 211
Encyclopedia of Science Fiction 158

Ender's Game 12
Erin, Charles A. 97
An Essay on the History of Civil Society 205
estranged fictions 60
estrangement 60, 65
E.T. 160

fabril literature 63*n*
failed state 203–204, 210
Fanon, Frantz 23, 46, 178
Fantasy 5, 60, 62, 63*n*, 99, 109
Fatherland 39
The Feast of the Goat 30
The Female Male 12
Ferguson, Adam 205
First Nations 129–130, 132, 134, 137, 139
First SF 2, 3
First World 12–14, 43, 96, 204, 205, 210; and capitalism 89; bodies 92
Fitting, Peter 188
Flubber (1997 film) 160
folk tales 60
The Food of the Gods 25
Forster, E.M. 60
Foucault, Michel 51–52, 67–68, 69, 186, 197
Foundation 100: The Anthology 2
Francis, Diana Pharaoh 16
Frankenstein 1, 12, 22, 161, 191
Freedman, Carl 160
Freud, Sigmund 197
Fujimori, Alberto 195
Future History 67

Gachpala 117
Gadar: Ek Prem Katha 164
Galapagos 209, 210
Gangopadhyay, Subodhchandra 125*n*
García Marquez, Gabriel 26, 30, 197, 200
Gaylard, Gerald 15
Gelder, Ken 104, 105
The General in His Labyrinth 30
Geography 116
Gernsback, Hugo 1, 2
Ghanada 119–120
Ghanadar Galpa 120
Ghosh, Amitav 16, 50–62, 63*n*
Ghosh, Bishnupriya 58
Gibson, Mary E. 53, 62*n*
Gibson, Ross 110
Gibson, William 3, 22, 191, 192
Gilbert, Helen 94
globalization 128
Godzilla (1998 Hollywood film) 161
Gordimer, Nadine 26
Gordon, Joan 108, 172, 177, 181, 186

The Grapes of Wrath 206
Great Sky River 191
Grewell, Greg 9, 11
Grohonakhatro 117
The Ground Beneath Her Feet 159, 163

Habermas, Jurgen 196
Hadesty, William H. 39
Hairston, Andrea 57
Halligan, Marion 103
Hamilton, Grant 16
Harbou, Thea von 175
Harraway, Donna 51, 58, 62*n*
Harris, John 97*n*
Harris, Robert 39
Harvest 12, 16, 87–98
Hayles, Katherine 192
Heart of Darkness 30, 82, 211
Hegel, George Wilhelm Friedrich 65
Heinlein, Robert A. 17, 67, 141–155, 209
Hellekson, Karen 48*n*
Herbert, Frank 15, 22, 24, 25, 26, 31, 34, 35
Heshoram Hushiyarer Diary 117–118
Hesse, Barnor 48*n*
heterotopias 172, 177, 186
Hindi cinema 156; Hindi science fiction cinema 160–161
"His Vegetable Wife" 77–86
historical materialism 24
historiographic metafiction 37, 38
history 65–75; African American 41; and imperialism 16, 67; and postmodernism 37; reconceptualization of 69; and science fiction 10, 67; western 68, 71, 73, 75
Holderin, Friedrich 75
Hopkinson, Nalo 1, 2, 18, 22, 39, 57, 62, 127, 161, 172, 174, 178
Hughes, Langston 40
Human Rights and Equal Opportunity Commission 112*n*
Human Rights Watch 164
Huntington, John 185
Hurston, Zora Neale 42
Hutcheon, Linda 38, 39, 48*n*
hybridity 23, 43, 50, 57, 61, 62, 145, 173, 181–182, 184, 199
hybridization 42, 145
hyperempathy 206–209

I, Robot 125*n*
I, the Supreme 30
Imperial Leather 80
imperialism 10, 11; and language 43; and orientalism 27; and religion 45; and science fiction 7–8

In an Antique Land 63n
Independence Day 160, 161, 166
Indian Journal for Science Fiction Studies 159
Indian Science Fiction Conference 159
"Indian" Stereotypes in TV Science Fiction 133
Indigenous speculative fiction 99–113
International Kidney Exchange 89
The Interpreters 153
Irigaray, Luce 80
It Happened Tomorrow: A Collection of 19 Select Science Fiction Stories from Various Indian Languages 159

Jacobs, H. Barry 89
Jacobs, Jane M. 104, 105
Jain, Madhu 163
James, Edward 159
Jameson, Fredric 9, 135, 171, 172, 173, 174, 179, 197
Jensen, Jan Lars 22
Jonas, Gerald 159, 174
Journey to the Centre of the Earth 159
Jurassic Park (1993 film) 156

Kaadu 168
Kachu, Braj B. 48n
Kadaitcha Song 100, 102–106
Kanneh, Kadiatu 46
Kerslake, Patricia 8, 65, 66
Kindred 22
Kirinyaga 22, 26
Klein, Herbert G. 17
Knudsen, Eva Rask 103
Koi... Mil Goya 18, 156–170
Kolpa Bigyan Galpo 121
Krrish 160
Kundera, Milan 73

Lacan, Jacques 65, 189, 198, 200
La Forgia, Rebecca 108
Lagaan 165, 166
Laing, B. Kojo 30
The Lamplighter 205
Land of the Golden Clouds 102, 109–112
Landon, Brooks 12
Lang, Fritz 175, 178
Langer, Jessica 18
Latin-American science fiction 2
Latin-American television 195
Lawrence, T.H. 25, 26–27, 32–33
Leeper, Mark 161, 165, 168n
The Left Hand of Darkness 127
Leggatt, Judith 7, 17
Le Guin, Ursula K. 62, 127

Leonardo da Vinci 44–45
Levitas, Ruth 171
Lewis, C.S. 161
Life During Wartime 22
Lion's Blood 16, 37–50
Loomba, Ania 12, 8, 43, 45, 147
Lord of Light 22, 26

Macdonald, Andrew 128–129
Macdonald, Gina 128–129
MacLeod, John 43
Macleod, Ken 21, 22, 24
Mahabharata 162
Mahabharata (miniseries) 164
Major Gentl and the Achimota Wars 30
Majumdar, Leela 121
The Man in the High Castle 9, 39, 67
Manashi 117
Mangal Grahey Ghanada 120
margin center dichotomy 51, 53
The Martian Chronicles 10, 11
Marx, Karl 23, 196
master slave 40, 65
Mathur, Suchitra 57
Matigari 30
Maturana, Humberto 192, 197
McClintock, Anne 80, 81
McCracken, Scott 160
McKenna, Terence 25
Memmi, Albert 42
Menchu, Rigoberta 132
Mendlesohn, Farah 1
Mehan, Uppinder 1, 22, 57, 62, 127, 167
Memoirs 41–43, 53; see also Ross, Ronald
Menem, Carlos 195
Mercer, Philip 207
Metamorphoses of Science Fiction 59
metaphor 192
metonymy 26, 27
metropolis 179
Metropolis 175, 178
Mexican television 195
Midgley, Mary 210
Midnight Robber 22
Mieville, China 18, 62, 172, 178
Miller, Gavin 18
Miller, Walter 161
mimicry 78, 83–84, 86
Mr. India 168n
Mitra, Premendra 118–120, 123, 125n
Möbius strip 199–200
The Moon Is a Harsh Mistress 17, 141–155, 209; postcolonial discourse in 152–153
Moons of Palmares 127–140
Moorcock, Michael 62
Moore, Charles W. 179

Moran, Anthony 108
More, Thomas 1, 196
Morris, Christine 133
Morrison, Toni 42
Mosley, Walter 39
Moylan, Tom 171, 183, 186, 189, 190, 197
Mozart, Wolfgang Amadeus 44
Muecke, Stephen 66, 68
Mukherjee, Ashutosh 116
Mukherjee, Shirshendu 62
Mukhopadhyay, Shieshendu 58
The Mummy Returns 156
Muñoz Zapata, Juan Ignacio 18
Murphy, Pat 16, 77–86
Murry, John Middleton 192
myth 51, 60; in *Dune* 28–30

Nakshatryalokar Devatma 58
Nanda, Meera 167
nationalism: Hindu 157, 161–168
nationalist resistance 23, 29
Native Americans 17, 132, 133, 134; comparisons to extraterrestrials 128–129
Naya Daur 163
Nelson, Diane 57
neocolonialism 8, 138
Neuromancer 3, 22, 190, 192
The New Atlantis 196
Nicholls, Peter 12, 158
Nietzsche, Friedrich 197
noble savage 133
Nolan, Maggie 112*n*
noema 65, 69
noesis 65, 69
Norton, Andre 130, 133, 134
nostalgia 9–10
novum 10, 160, 179
Nye, Edwin R. 53, 62*n*

Okrafor-Mbachu, Nnedi 62
O'Malley, Kathleen 130
One Man, One Machet 153
other 24, 34, 40, 62*n*, 78–79, 83, 84, 142, 146, 147–148, 150, 172; definition of 10; machines as 142, 147–152
otherness 40
Orientalism 25, 26–27, 40, 43, 68
Orientalist 26
The Oxford Book of Science Fiction 63*n*

Padmanabhan, Manjula 12, 16, 87–98
Parable of the Sower 18, 202–217
Parable of the Talents 202–203, 207
A Passage to India (1984 film) 80
Paz, Octavio 200
People of the Sky 131, 133

Perdido Street Station 18, 172–174, 177–179, 181, 184
Pfitzer, Gregory 128
Phillips, Jerry 207, 208, 210
Phondke, Bal 159
Piercy, Marge 62*n*
The Pilgrim's Progress 209
Plains of Promise 100, 102, 106–109
Poe, Edgar Allan 1
Pokamakor 117
Porcayo, Gerardo Horacio 18, 188–201
postcolonial 8, 15, 152; postcolonial literature, definition of 5–6, 10, 12, 141, self/other in 11; postcolonial science fiction 1–2, 23, 50, criticism 3, definitions of 5, 9, 127, 157, 159, 167; postcolonial speculative fiction 127; postcolonial studies 8, 10, 65, 66, 67
postcolonialism 5, 9, 15; definition of 21, 23–24; and modernity 21–22; and nationalism 16, 24, 26, 28; and science fiction 34–35; secondary postcolonialism 34; transhistorical 23, 29, 34, 35
postmodernism 24; approaches to history 37
Pravinchandra, Shital 16
Predator 195
La Primara Calle de la Soledad 18, 188–201
prime directive 7, 8
Principle of Hope 197
Probashi 117
Professor Shanku 58, 122–124
Prophets Facing Backward 167

Rahashya 158
Ramayana (miniseries) 164
Rambo: First Blood II 160
Rao, Maithili 161
Rashtriya Swayamsevak Sangh 164
Ray, Satyajit 58, 115, 122
Ray, Sukumar 117
religion: in Indian science fiction 161–168; as resistance 45
Resnick, Mike 22
The Rest of the Robots 125*n*
Retamar, Roberto Fernandez 145
Rieder, John 2
The Road to Dune 25, 32, 33
Roberts, Adam 6, 8, 9, 10–11, 171, 186*n*
Roberts, Kenneth 154*n*
Robinson, Eden 62
Robocop 195
Rosenfeld, Gavriel D. 48*n*
Roshan, Hrithik 157, 166
Roshan, Rakesh 157, 166

Ross, Ronald 50, 52–56, 61, 62–63n; see also *Memoirs*
Rotberg, Robert 203, 204
Rowland, Christopher 101
Roy, Hemendrakumar 120
Roy, Jagandananda 117
Rulfo, Juan 200
Rushdie, Salman 26, 159, 163
Ruskin, John 46
Russ, Joanna 62
Russell, Mary Doria 161
Ryan, Simon 110

Sabha, Tattvabodhini 116
Sadhana 117
Sadhu, Jogendra 116
Said, Edward 23, 25, 26, 32, 40, 43, 68, 70, 110
San Francisco Examiner 24
San Juan, E., Jr. 13
Sandesh 117, 122
Sangari, Kukum 14
Sanyal, Narayan 58
Sargent, Lyman Tower 183, 186, 197
Sartre, Jean Paul 65
Saturday Night Fever 160
Scheper-Hughes, Nancy 89, 97n
Schismatrix 194
science fiction 1, 65, 99, 123, 174; alternate history in 9, 39; in Bengal 115, 124; the city in 174–175; definitions of 5–6, 9, 11, 12, 22, 59–60, 63n, 66, 127, 129, 159–160; dystopian 127; film 9, 11, 161; and history 9, 10; and imperialism 7–8, 9, 11; in India 1, 124, 158–160; and modernity 22; and nostalgia 9; and orientalism 25; portrayal of Native Americans in 133–134; and postcolonialism 34–35; and religion 161; utopian 127
Science Fiction After 1900 12
Scott, Walter 205
"Scramble for Africa" 39
Second World 12
secondary postcolonialism 34
self: as-other 69–72; as-subject 69–72
Sena, Shiv 164
Sengupta, Debjani 17
settler colonies 141, 142
Seven Pillars of Wisdom 25
Shanku *see* Professor Shanku
Shape-Shifting: Images of Native Americans in Recent Popular Fiction 129
Sharpe, Jenny 80, 81–82
Shatayu, Shukumar 125
Shawl, Nisi 57
Shelley, Mary 1, 22, 161

Shepherd, Lucius 22
Sheridan, MaryAnn 129
Shippey, T.A. 63n
Shiva 3000 22
Shklovsky, Viktor 60
Shohat, Ella 15
Shukra Bhraman 117
Sikdar, Radhanath 125n
Silent Dances 130, 152
Silent Songs 130, 152
Singh, Vandana 2, 16, 62, 65–76
The Sioux Spaceman 130, 133
Sircar, Mahendralal 116
The Snow Queen 22, 24–26
So Long Been Dreaming 1, 2, 22, 57, 62, 70, 127
social Darwinism 211
Solaris (1972 film) 159
Soyinka, Wole 153
Space: Above and Beyond 161
The Sparrow 161
Spielberg, Stephen 41
Spivak, Gayatri Chakravorty 23, 26, 51, 52, 54, 57, 66, 78, 95; see also subaltern
Srinarahari, M.H. 159
SS-GB 39
Stand on Zanzibar 22, 26
Star Trek 7, 9, 10, 159
Star Wars 160
Star Wars (Indian television series) 158
Stars in My Pockets Like Grains of Sand 24
Steinbeck, John 206
stereotypes: of native African women 46–47
Sterling, Bruce 188, 194
Stoker, Bram 83
Stranger in a Strange Land 152
Stross, Brian 181
subaltern 10, 16, 26, 50–52, 54, 56, 59–61, 78, 147, 150–151, 153
Subaltern Studies Group 52
subalternity 57
Super Commando Dhruva 158
Superman (1978 film) 158
Suvin, Darko 38, 59–61, 65, 124, 160, 173, 188

Tagore, Rabindranath 117
The Terminator 195
Terra Nullius 82, 99, 165
Thiong'o, Ngugi wa 26, 30, 43, 66, 68
Third Estate 13
Third World 22, 23, 30, 87, 88, 96, 135, 136, 202, 203, 204, 205, 210; definition of 6, 12–15; donors 92; writers 6, 14–15
Thomas, Sheree 2, 62

Index

Toffler, Alvin 162
topos 202, 203, 205, 209, 211
Tricontinental Conference 13
Trujillo Muñoz, Gabriel 197
Tubman, Harriet 135
Turtledove, Harry 9, 39
Twain, Mark 133
Tyrell, Heather 168

utopia 18, 96, 171, 175, 180, 185–186, 189, 190, 198; the city and 172; definition of 172
Utopia 1, 196

Vajpayee, Shri Atal Bihari 164, 166
Valera, Francisco 192, 197
Vargas Llosa, Mario 26, 30
Vasudevan, Ravi S. 161, 165
Verne, Jules 1, 159
Vinge, Joan 22, 24
Vonnegut, Kurt 209, 210

War of the Worlds 10, 209
Watson, Sam 99, 100, 102–105, 112
Watson, Thomas John 149
Waverly 205
Weaver, Jace 134

Weaver, Roslyn 17
Weinkauf, Mary 128, 134
Weinstein, Cindy 205, 206
Weller, Archie 100, 102, 109–112
Wells, H.G. 1, 2–3, 65, 209, 210
Wevers, Lydia 101
When Gravity Fails 18, 171, 173–176, 179–180, 182–184
White Man's Burden 8, 51
Wild Cat Falling 112*n*
Wolfe, Gary K. 174
A Woman of the Iron People 130
Worldwar series 9
The Wretched of the Earth 178
Wright, Alexis 99, 100, 102, 106–109, 112
Wright, Richard 40

The X-Files (television series) 160

Young, Robert J.C. 9, 12, 23

Zamora, Lois Parkinson 101
Zelazny, Roger 22
zero world 173, 176
Zinta, Preity 157
Zizek, Slavoj 189, 198, 199, 200
Zulu Heart 16, 37–50

www.ingramcontent.com/pod-product-compliance
Ingram Content Group UK Ltd.
Pitfield, Milton Keynes, MK11 3LW, UK
UKHW041951140426
5217IPUK00015B/750